THE EDGE OF HELL

The Edge of Hell

A Novel of the Civil War

By
S.K. Keogh

The Edge of Hell
S.K. Keogh

Copyright 2020 S.K. Keogh
Leighlin House Publishing

ISBN: 978-1-7350506-1-4 (Paperback)
ISBN: 978-1-7350506-0-7 (e-book)

Connect with S.K. Keogh at

www.skkeogh.com
www.facebook.com/S.K.Keogh
www.twitter.com/JackMallory

This book is also available in ebook at most online retailers.

Cover design by Jennifer Quinlan, Historical Fiction Book
Covers
11th Michigan Infantry battle flag image courtesty of
Michigan's Save the Flags project.

To the silent voices that remain with us.
May we always listen.

PART I

BURR OAK

"Michigan has done nobly thus far, and
the 11th is considered as good if not better
than any regiment yet sent to the war from that State."

-- Louisville Journal

CHAPTER 1

Gettysburg. The name echoed in the mind of eighteen-year-old Nate Calhoun as he drove the two-horse team along the road leading to Burr Oak. Tree frogs shrilled from the old oaks and maples that grew in the yards of the farms he passed. The overhanging limbs of the trees closest to the road offered welcomed shade. Sweat trickled down his face from beneath his worn hat as he watched the play of the horses' shadows traveling in and out of the July sunlight. But he paid little attention to the rest of the world around him, to the rich summer fields planted to either side, to the dust that clung to his clothes. His thoughts remained far away, in Pennsylvania, in Mississippi, in Tennessee. If only he could be taking part in fighting the war as his four brothers were, if only he were not the last one left, the last one tied by responsibility to his parents, to the farm. If only…

Nate had never heard of Gettysburg, so when news of the great battle had reached their small southwest Michigan community, he had gone to the school to use a map of the United States to locate the hamlet in Pennsylvania. After that, his village of Burr Oak, indeed all of St. Joseph County, waited in tortured suspense for casualty reports.

Just yesterday, Nate's family had received the blessed news that his eldest brother, Matthew, had escaped harm during the battle, though his regiment—the First Michigan Infantry—had indeed suffered. Twenty-four agonizing hours passed before Nate learned of his second brother's fate. Joseph, a corporal in the Seventh Michigan Infantry, had survived the storm on Cemetery Ridge, unscathed. Nate's other two brothers were not at Gettysburg; Ryan's regiment, the Eleventh Michigan Infantry, was in Tennessee, as was Brian's Nineteenth Michigan Infantry.

Off to the southeast the shriek of the Michigan Southern & Northern Indiana Railroad engine announced its departure from Burr Oak. Perhaps it had brought more mail and news. Maybe one of his brothers had written. He clucked the horses into a brisk trot.

3

When he reached the edge of the village, he smelled the ashy scent left behind by the train as it headed for Sturgis to the southwest. He swung the team eastward on Front Street. To either side of him arose the majestic oaks from which the town derived its name. He eased the team down to a walk. Sunlight spilled over the simple homes, over the faces of children who waved at him and called his name from the yards. At the beginning of the war, nigh unto seven hundred souls called Burr Oak home, but the population had been drained by the departure of so many of the young men off to fight the war. So many...but not him. Nate dreaded coming into town when news of the fighting was so fresh because he felt ashamed and cowardly, though no one had ever accused him of being a shirker. Perhaps it was only his imagination that made him think his neighbors held a low opinion of him. After all, just last week Elias Cooper's wife had said how she thought it wonderful of him to stay and help his folks.

Nate's mood darkened as he drove past the train depot. He tugged his hat lower over his eyes and hunched his shoulders, said nothing to those who were there, some talking, some looking lost and deflated, perhaps from a lack of fresh news. Nate turned the team left onto Third Street, then halted near a young buckeye tree to give the animals shade. He hopped to the wooden walkway that ran along the shop fronts and entered Keenan's Mercantile.

The store stifled in the July heat, ventilated only by the propped-open doors, front and back. One other villager, George Bordner, meandered among the organized wares while James Keenan, the proprietor's son, busily rearranged stock behind the counter. At the age of twenty-five, James was of prime age to join the army but he, like Nate, had family responsibilities, which consisted of running the store for his frequently inebriated father. Similarities between the two young men ended there.

When Bordner approached the counter to settle for the items in his arms, he asked, "Are you coming to the street dance Saturday night, James?"

"Well, sir, I haven't given it much thought, really."

"The whole village will be there, of course. The ladies will be having a benefit bake sale for the regiments and their families, you know." He hesitated, and his voice lowered. "I was very sorry to hear about your uncle's death. Lieutenant Keenan was a good man."

"Thank you, sir," James said, betraying no emotions.

Bordner sadly shook his head as he paid for his merchandise. "Well, perhaps we'll see you Saturday."

"Yes, sir. Thank you."

Nate waited until the man's footfalls faded outside before he approached the counter. He set a small sack of flour and a bolt of calico on the counter and leaned a pitchfork next to him, saying, "I need to put these things on our account."

When James reached for a ledger under the counter, his dark blond hair flopped across his low forehead and draped down near his gray eyes. He opened the book and considered the figures. A frown twitched his small mustache. Nate did not like James, never had. Maybe that was because of his good looks—he was tall and slim whereas Nate was some six inches shorter with features prone to natural softness—and all the girls gushed over James, though the Keenan family history made some hesitant to be closely associated. Maybe his dislike stemmed from James's higher education and abundance of money…at least what seemed like an abundance to Nate. Or maybe it was because James seemed so indifferent and aloof, as if he were better than the rest of the community.

Nate told himself that he should think more charitably about James because of the loss of his uncle, yet he found himself unable to do so. Considering how James and his father had never closed the mercantile even to grieve, Nate figured the loss had meant little to them. And to think that James would forego the town dance, no matter the nobility of the charity behind it, seemed almost callous to Nate.

At last James looked up. "Can't do it, Calhoun. You've reached your credit limit. I told your father last time—"

"What limit?"

"Everyone's got a limit, otherwise we wouldn't have a store left."

"We always pay up. What's the idea?"

"It's been a long time. I'm sorry."

Nate heard no contrition. "I'll put back the cloth."

James shook his head. "It won't be enough."

"The devil you say."

James slapped the book shut, reddening. "If I say yes to you, I'll have to say yes to the rest of the town. Then what? We offer credit, not charity."

"I'm not askin' for charity," Nate snapped. "Things is tight till harvest, then you'll get your money. We're not farmin' as much land as before the war; can't do it with just me and Da'. In case you ain't noticed, all of me brothers are fightin' this war."

"So, because of that you expect a handout?"

"Handout? The Calhouns don't live on handouts, James Keenan.

We work harder than you, sure, and a sight more hours. In fact, I don't see why you run this store instead of your father. If you ask me, I say 'tis just so you don't have to go and fight."

James bristled. "I don't see you marching off to the 'Battle Hymn of the Republic.'"

"You just might be surprised about that."

"I fancy I would. You can't leave your mother's skirts."

Nate swung a lightning fist, but James jumped back.

"Hey, now!" Seamus Keenan's voice kept Nate from lunging over the counter. "What's this, lads?"

Nate turned to see the large man in the front doorway, a puzzled scowl upon his ruddy, stubbled face, ashine with sweat. His wide shoulders strained the seams of his light blue shirt, and a heavy paunch sagged over the waistband of his brown trousers.

Nate waited, both embarrassed and uneasy, for he had seen the damage Seamus's temper could reap. But that was usually when he was drunk, and he did not appear so now. Instead, he seemed oddly soft.

"What's this about, son?"

"Nothing," James muttered.

"Certainly something." Seamus put a hand on Nate's shoulder, and the boy looked up into his uncharacteristic, blunt-toothed smile. "Unhappy with our prices, Nate?"

"No, sir," he mumbled.

"Well then, let's ring you up, and you can be on your way before that storm hits. I can see it in the southwest and feel it in my bones."

Nate cast James a dark look. "I won't be buyin' these goods, Mr. Keenan."

"And why not?"

Nate jerked his chin toward James. "Your son says our credit's no good 'round here."

Seamus frowned. "That can't be."

"They've reached their limit," James said.

"Let me see." Seamus opened the ledger on the counter and studied the figures.

Nate slowly relaxed. He wondered if the man even knew what he was looking at, for everyone in Burr Oak acknowledged James as the one who ran the mercantile, top to bottom. Still, Nate felt confidence return; in fact, a touch of smugness, for he had James over a barrel in front of a father who would never admit he was unfamiliar with the Calhoun account. James knew it as well. Nate could plainly see the discomfort on his face.

"Well, now. I don't see a problem. James must be mistaken."

"I'm *not* mistaken, Pa."

"These are just trifling things," Seamus said. "We'll simply add them to the account."

"Pa, we can't make exceptions."

Seamus picked up a pencil and scribbled down the items. "If we can't make *exceptions* for patriotic families like the Calhouns—with four brave boys gone to fight—then who can we make exceptions for? And who are we to deny them, what with my poor brother dead, fighting for the same cause? Now, James, let's not be blinded by a few dollars."

James seethed, his narrow jaw tight.

"Come now," Seamus continued. "Put this book back where it belongs."

Moving stiffly as he obeyed, James's eyes remained hard on Nate.

Nate gathered the items in triumph. "Much obliged, Mr. Keenan."

"Have a good day, lad," Seamus called as Nate headed out into the street.

Before leaving town, Nate stopped at the post office but was told that one of his neighbors had picked up not only his mail but the Calhouns' as well and had promised to drop it off at their farm on his way home.

As Nate drove out of town, some of the earlier gloom left him, thanks to getting the upper hand on James. After all, just last week James had insulted him by asking Katie Moylan to supper, knowing full well, like everyone in Burr Oak, that Katie was his girl. She had declined the offer, of course, but all the same, Nate had feared she would accept it.

When Nate had blustered over the affront, Katie assured him of her loyalty but conceded, "Wouldn't it have been fun to see all the girls go green with envy?"

"Your father won't have you gettin' mixed up with the likes of James Keenan, even if you wasn't my girl. You know all the stories 'bout him and his father. What decent man—"

"They're stories only, Nate. Do you believe everything folks say?"

Nearly home now, Nate slapped the reins on the team's rumps and sent the horses into a trot. Seamus Keenan had been right about the weather. Above the knee-high corn on one side of the road, clouds rose like angry mountains, and a freshening breeze stirred the green acres of potatoes on the other side. Products of his own hard work. How proud his father was of their farm, a dream realized after leaving

Ireland as a pauper devastated by the Great Famine ten years ago. After five years of slave labor in Boston's sweatshops, the family pooled their savings and journeyed westward to buy an uncultivated plot of twenty fertile acres outside of Burr Oak. Over the following five years, Daniel Calhoun had purchased another sixty acres, and the farm prospered.

On the top porch step of the white, two-story house, Nate's father sat alone, an incongruous sight this time of day, for he usually took no leisure until well after supper, after the animals had been tended to for the night. Even stranger than his father's presence was his demeanor. He remained with head bowed, hat hiding his tanned face, even when Nate drove into the yard. His leathery hands hung down over the threadbare knees of his trousers, a single sheet of paper in one hand. Instead of heading for the barn, Nate pulled up short, dismounted, and sprinted across the yard. Only when he stopped at the foot of the steps did his father lift his graying head. Rare tears trembled in his blue eyes, eyes so much like Nate's, his grimy, usually jovial face distorted. From inside the house drifted the faint sounds of Nate's mother crying.

Knees weakening, Nate whispered, "What is it, Da'?"

His father croaked out, "Ryan."

Nate stared at the limp paper.

"'Tis from Captain Bennet. There was a fight...in Tennessee...Elk River." He lowered his head again. "Ryan was taken prisoner."

***

James turned on his thin mattress, his nightshirt sticking to him. The moist heat of early morning joined forces with the dead air of the previous night to make him eager to go downstairs. Last night's storm had not succeeded in cooling the air for more than the time it took to blow through town. From the other bedroom, he heard a loud rumble of snores. Whiskey kept the heat from suspending his father's sleep. Since Uncle Pat's death, the drinking had gotten worse. James knew it was grief-driven even though his father refused to show or claim such emotion.

James left his bed to prepare breakfast. Besides the two bedrooms, the only other room in their living quarters was a central kitchen with a small table and two chairs. They never entertained, so there was no need for more chairs or a parlor. Whenever he contemplated his drab surroundings, he could not help but think wistfully of the house over on Main Street where they used to live with his mother. That one-story clapboard house had been a home to him. This space above the store would never be more than a place where two men slept and ate. After the death of his mother five years ago, his father had sold the house to James's uncle. Since Uncle Pat had left at the start of the war, it sat lonely and empty regardless of multiple invitations from his uncle for them to live there. Each time his father refused the offer, he gave no reason; he did not have to. Now what would become of the house? Since news of Uncle Pat's death at Gettysburg, James could not bring himself to ask.

As usual, the only things that could awaken his father were the scents of coffee and frying bacon. He grunted and groaned his way out of bed and shuffled into the dining room where he dropped into one of the chairs. He wore a clean shirt, yesterday's rumpled brown trousers, and suspenders, which hung down around his thighs. His sandy hair stuck out in wild clumps until he absently attempted to tame it with his fingers.

James set the food on the table and sat across from him. Although he had something important to discuss, he balked, still smarting from his father's intrusion yesterday during his confrontation with Nate Calhoun. It had been a strange occurrence, for usually his father showed little interest in what happened in the store or in any other aspect of their lives anymore. Over time, he had withdrawn more and more from life, spending his days drinking in town or gone somewhere unknown. Often his father sat beside the Prairie River near where James's mother had died, a bottle near at hand, staring vacantly at the water.

Before Uncle Pat's death, his father had spoken little about the war, as if it did not exist. But since that day, when he did discuss something other than the store, it was a rambling lament about this latest blow to the family. Those words had stirred James's old guilt, a guilt felt every day since the start of the war and made nearly unbearable whenever casualty reports arrived in Burr Oak. He knew what others in town thought of him, especially those who had lost loved ones. Sure, they never openly expressed their disdain to him, but he knew those underlying thoughts existed. They looked at him and wondered why their son or brother had been killed while here he stood, able-bodied and in the flower of his youth, as if he had no care in the world. How wrong they were. Many times, he had been tempted to enlist, to get away from the silent accusations, but always he stayed to run the store for his father. The business succeeded only because James had nothing else and thus threw himself into its running, for his father had lost the desire to manage it since the day James's mother had died. He had hoped that his parent's interest would return to the store instead of stagnating in black memories. But when he had watched the life drain from his father's face upon hearing about Uncle Pat's death, he had despaired of ever winning back his father's spirit. This was why, after his father's platitudes toward Nate Calhoun and his family's wartime sacrifices, James had decided to take drastic measures.

Having little appetite, unnerved by what he was about to say, James left the table and moved to the window overlooking Third Street. Near the water pump below, the solitary buckeye tree stood in shadow, its saw-toothed leaves motionless. A robin fluttered down from its branches and landed on the trough in front of the store, its nacarat breast round and beautiful. It was an odd place for a tree to be, here among the busiest section of Burr Oak, but William Betts must not have thought so when he brought the tree from Detroit and planted it there in 1852. That had been four years before the Keenans had moved from Pennsylvania to join Uncle Pat in the mercantile business. The tree had since established itself as a central part of the community. Villagers gathered under it to read mail, gossip, and discuss business. Often, when the store became too close and stuffy, James would wander outside to sit beneath the tree, regularly eating his lunch there.

This damned town. I won't miss it. If only Pa had moved us away like I wanted after Ma died.

"Gossip won't run me out of town," his father had declared. "We have a business here."

But James knew staying had more to do with his mother being buried here than it did with the store.

He turned back to the table and sat down, his palms suddenly sweating. He wiped them on his trousers and stared at the meager food. Memories of his mother's skillful cooking killed the rest of his appetite. He could still see her with her apron on in the kitchen, busy over her pots and pans. Before every meal, she had always led them in prayer. He had not prayed since her death. Then, there had indeed been things for which to give thanks. They had been part of the community, participated in social events, went to the Methodist Episcopal Church. Preacher Langdon. Oh, how well he recalled Langdon, the man who had destroyed his family.

His father busily downed the last of the bacon, attention only on his plate, never complimenting the meal. The old anger and regret crowded James's thoughts, and he tried to fight it off. Although he never liked to admit it, he blamed his father as much as his father blamed himself for the death of his mother. Only once, during an argument about his father's drinking, had James ever voiced his feelings. A backhand blow that sent him reeling made it quite certain he would never do so again.

Licking his lips, James harnessed that bitterness into strength and resolve. He swallowed in a dry throat before saying, "Pa, there's something I need to tell you."

His father grunted, kept his bloodshot eyes on his eggs.

"I—I'm going to be leaving."

Apathetic, his father responded, "Leaving for where?"

"For the army."

His father stopped eating and considered him from beneath his unhappy, lowered eyebrows. Was there alarm or concern buried somewhere in him? Then he scraped the last of the eggs together on his plate and consumed them. "You're talking nonsense, boy."

"No, I'm not. This is a long time overdue."

His father scowled. "I'll hear none of this. I need you in the store."

The remark wounded him. True enough their relationship was not what it had been five years ago, but he liked to think he was more than a store clerk to his father. After all, he had done his best to please his parent and to try, though fruitlessly, to regain some of the warmth both had lost to the Prairie River.

James did his best to sound confident. "You used to run the store."

"I still run the store," his father blustered. "Don't you forget it."

"Then what does it matter if I go?"

"It matters because I say so."

"You can run the store without me. You *should* run it."

His scowl deepened. "Don't get impertinent with me, boy."

Some of James's courage wavered beneath his father's dark look. "What I meant was I think it would do you good to run the store without me. It would…it would…"

"Keep me sober?" he growled.

James forced himself to hold his parent's stare. "Maybe."

"What I do with my time is none of your affair, boy." He shoved his chair back and stood. "Now, I'll hear no more of this nonsense. I expect you downstairs, opening, in the next fifteen minutes."

"Pa…" He stood, reached out a staying hand, but his father wheeled away and headed down the stairs.

CHAPTER 2

Mosquitoes cruised in the deepening twilight but could not keep up with the Calhoun wagon. Birdsong drifting from tree to tree provided conversation where none existed among the wagon's passengers. The humidity from earlier in the week had been replaced by a comfortable summer warmth. Riding in the wagon bed, Nate turned his face to the dying rays and closed his eyes. He thought of Ryan, as he knew his parents did. Could his brother see the sun? Or was he locked away somewhere dark and alone?

His father clucked the team into a trot along the eastbound road into Burr Oak. Nate's mother, sitting next to his father, appeared distracted, her attention far down the lane, beyond the village, the county, the state. Though normally rather plain in looks, tonight she was far from that, adorned in her Sunday finest, the muted pink and blue of her dress lending a soft tone to her skin. The green of her eyes often carried Nate's thoughts to the hills of Ireland.

She had almost remained home tonight, but her husband's gentle urging had finally moved her and Nate as well, shaking him from his sadness. "You're acting as if Ryan is dead—dead and buried—but he's not," his father had said. "A prisoner of war, he is. And that's a sight better than dead, to be sure."

When the wagon rolled into town and turned onto Third Street, pride managed to resurrect Nate's characteristic smile. So many people had already gathered, chatting and laughing, while more rode and drove in from all directions, from farms near and far, drawn together by Burr Oak's strong sense of community. He admired their resilience and vowed that he would enjoy the party tonight and not think about the decision he had recently made. Instead, he would see to it that his mother did not dwell upon Ryan's predicament and that Katie Moylan's concern for her brother's wounding at Gettysburg would not grow.

Lanterns, dancing in the breeze, hung from awnings along Third

Street and from lines stretched across the street. A bonfire crackled and sparked at the north end. Not far from it, a bandstand had been constructed, commanding a view of the "dance floor" and the tables beyond, laden with food contributed by those who attended. The musicians—mainly older men from the community, dressed in their finest—tuned their instruments in serious anticipation. At intervals along the street, barrels decorated with red, white, and blue bunting silently solicited cash donations to assist the families of those who had fallen at Gettysburg.

The Moylans arrived at the same time as the Calhouns and pulled their team abreast. John Moylan had come alone with his two daughters. Nate frowned at the thought of Katie's mother at home, too concerned for her distant son's health to attend. He had hoped she would join her family for a few hours of distraction.

But his melancholy was short-lived when Katie smiled at him, and he rushed to help her from the wagon. She smelled temptingly of rose water. Her long brown hair had been pulled back and up beneath a short-brimmed, lacy pink and white hat, her eyes shining like polished emeralds. Her long dress flowed down in a crisp, rustling wave to cover a modest hoop. Tiny pale roses covered the whey-colored cotton, her skin a creamy alabaster below the short, puffy sleeves and above the dip of a collar that revealed the rise and fall of small breasts, all pleasing to Nate's admiring gaze.

The two families exchanged pleasantries before joining the crowd of partygoers around the tables. Soon varied conversations enveloped them. No one lingered long upon the war except to heartily wish for its swift end. They filled their plates with chicken sandwiches, fruits, and vegetables from Burr Oak Township farms, then the Calhouns and Moylans sat under the young buckeye tree with other neighbors to talk and laugh. The band provided sometimes-strained background music.

As he ate, Nate spotted Seamus and James Keenan on the fringes of the crowd near the tables. They stood with the Dorns, and the conversation did not appear light. James, not taking part in the exchange, shifted his weight from foot to foot, appearing preoccupied and uneasy as he drank his punch, often gazing down the street toward the railway.

Setting aside his plate, Nate's father stood with a mischievous grin and offered a hand to his wife, bowing. "Come now, me darlin'. They'll be startin' any minute now, and I should be dancin' off all this fine food, otherwise you'll be rollin' me out of bed in the morn." He laughed. "Are you comin', John Moylan?"

"Aye." The ruddy-faced man got to his feet and swept his youngest daughter into his arms, twirling her and causing her to laugh. "If you're lucky, Daniel, Iris will allow you a dance. But only if I can free your wife from your iron embrace long enough to dance a jig with me."

Although Nate's mother still looked drawn, the men's banter stirred color to her cheeks and a smile to her lips. She was the finest dancer in the county, her talents displayed many a Saturday evening either at the Moylan farm or at home. The two families had been a tight-knit clan since the Moylans bought land a short distance from the Calhouns, each helping the other to work the land and harvest the crops. Many a summer night they spent on each other's porch, exchanging stories of their native land, easing away the homesickness that still lingered after all these years.

The sun set with an orange flash reflected upon the gay expressions of the dancers and the colorful dresses of the women. Nate, nearly as gifted as his mother, danced exclusively with Katie, not wanting to let her go for fear of the night ending and of what he must reveal to her. He drank in the sights, sounds, and smells, knowing he would need these memories to sustain him in the coming months.

While resting at one of the tables, sharing lemonade with Katie, he watched James among the crush of dancers out on the trampled ground. The band played a waltz, and he moved fluidly with his partner, Heather Cabot. Nate scowled at the way he held her without appearing awkward. Heather was a year older than James, dressed in a muted gray, unadorned dress. A pretty girl with blonde curls and a shy smile, she had married before the war but had lost her husband in the first battle of Bull Run. Since then, she had become withdrawn and rarely laughed. In fact, to see her waltzing surprised him, for it was only two years this month since her husband's death.

Nate's mother had once said, "That James Keenan boy; now there's a fine-looking lad who needs a good woman like Heather to get him out from behind that store counter."

The waltz ended. James bowed to his partner and escorted her to her family where they sat only a rod away from Nate.

"Poor Heather," Katie said. "Since Sam was killed, this is the most fun I've seen her have."

"I know; I was just thinkin' that. Ma's invited her over for supper with her folks, but her parents always come alone."

A shadow fell across Nate when someone stopped next to him, blocking the light of an overhead lantern.

14

"Excuse me, Miss Moylan." James's voice gained Nate's attention.

Struck speechless, Katie stared a little wide-eyed at the young storekeeper. The band started a lively tune, the fiddle busy sawing out cheery notes.

"Would you like to dance?"

Nate stood and took Katie's hand. "This dance is taken."

"Nate," she protested, ignoring his attempt to tug her away.

"It's all right, Miss Moylan," James grinned, irritating Nate further. "Perhaps later." With a bow and a dismissive glance at Nate, he withdrew.

Katie shot Nate a sharp look. "How could you be so rude?"

"He was just tryin' to get back at me for what happened in the store."

"So, you're saying he didn't really want to dance with me?" Her fine sable eyebrows lowered.

"Of course he did. Any man would."

"So what if I'd danced with him? That doesn't mean I care for you less."

"You don't understand, Katie."

"What don't I understand? Your jealousy?"

He faltered, glanced around in search of his parents, found them some distance away. He whispered, "Come with me."

At first hesitant, she slowly complied, and he led her down the street toward the depot.

"You embarrassed me, Nate. Leaping up and grabbing hold of me." Moonlight shone upon her, the small hat casting her face in darkness now that they were away from the lanterns. "People were staring."

"I'm sorry."

He squeezed her hand tighter as they left the party far behind and drew near the depot. The railroad tracks glistened like two silver ribbons stretching away from them. He gazed down their mysterious length.

The anger left Katie's voice. "What is it, Nate?"

"I acted the way I did because…because I don't want fellas like James gettin' any ideas…while I'm gone."

She pulled him to a halt. "While you're gone?"

He took her hands in his, caressed her petal-soft skin with his thumbs. "I'm gonna join up."

Her eyes widened, and she choked out, "What?"

"The Eleventh Infantry. I wrote Captain Bennet yesterday and told him I'm leavin' to join 'em this week."

"Nate, you can't…"

"I can't stay. I can't keep sittin' here, waitin' for it to end. You should understand. Think of your brother; you didn't see him stayin' behind."

She shook her head. "But what about your folks? Your father can't run the farm alone. Please, Nate—"

"He'll have to. Your father will help."

"Have you told them? Surely they wouldn't give you permission—"

"No." He frowned. "I'll tell 'em tomorrow. I wanted 'em to enjoy the dance. Ma needed this."

Her grip grew painful. "But you can't go. You can't leave." With desperation she whispered, "I can't lose you."

He kissed her cheek. "You won't lose me. The Rebs already got one Calhoun; that's all they're gettin'."

"Don't make light of this. You don't know what you're getting yourself into."

"Well," he teased, "I recollect two years ago when Katie Moylan was nigh unto burstin' with pride when our brothers marched off to war. In fact, there was a look in her eyes that said she wisht her beau was a part of the brave legions. But, alas, he hung back to plant corn. More's the pity!"

"Nate, stop. You know how it was when the war started—no one knew how long and terrible it would be. Now…I won't be able to bear worrying about another person. This whole town—"

"Katie. 'Twill be all right. I promise." He felt stronger just saying the words. "There'll be no need to fret."

Hope lightened her voice. "What if your father says no?"

"It don't matter what he says. I'm leavin' Monday."

"Monday? Why so soon?"

"The sooner the better. Me mind just ain't here no more. But, leavin' you…" He took her hands again, did not want to hear any more disturbing words. "You'll write me every day, won't you?"

Tears spilled down her cheeks, shining in the moonlight. "I won't let you go."

He drew her into his embrace, held her close, murmured, "I'll be back before you know it."

***

James awoke with a start. He stared at his closed bedroom door, wondered what had awakened him. He heard nothing but the crickets' creaking night song through his nearby open window. He tried to relax and drift off, but images returned to nag him, to chew away at his courage and resolve while music from the dance still echoed in his head. With a frustrated sigh, he rolled onto his side to keep the moonlight from his eyes.

He had enjoyed the dance, though he had not expected to, not with the prospect of enlisting weighing heavily upon him, especially since his father had forbade it. He had drunk too much punch and eaten too much food, but when he reflected upon his uncle's description of army rations, he could excuse his gluttony; home cooking might be years away once he stepped aboard that train the day after tomorrow. After a weary week of taking inventory at the store—done surreptitiously, lest his father grow suspicious—the dance had provided a physical and emotional release that he needed more than he had known. For those few hours, he had not thought about his uncle's death.

With pleasure, James remembered Nate Calhoun's irritation when he had asked Katie to dance. He had done it as much for that reaction as for a desire to dance with the pretty girl. There had been other times when he purposefully goaded Nate, and, truth be told, his motivation had been jealousy; not jealousy of Nate's relationship with Katie but of the family life the boy had, something lost forever to him. Perhaps he should have been sympathetic to the boy because of the news of Ryan's capture, but he found himself unmoved, especially because Ryan had always treated him with barely veiled contempt.

Footsteps sounded on the stairs. He held his breath, listened for the telltale loss of rhythm in his father's stride but heard none of that, though his parent had imbibed at the dance. Curious, James waited to find error in his perception. When his father reached the upper floor, he paused, then crossed over to just outside James's room. James stared at the doorknob, and when, after a long pause, it began to turn, he quickly closed his eyes. Once inside, his father hesitated, causing further anxiety, for why on earth had he come into this room? Was he so drunk that he could not find his own bedroom? No, his father's steps had been too assured, and if he were indeed tight again, James would have smelled alcohol by now.

The steps shuffled closer. James fought to keep from opening his eyes. His father stopped near the rolltop desk beside the bed. James detected a slight scent of whiskey but nothing akin to the usual rankness. There was a rustle of cloth, like that of a hand dipped into a pocket, fishing about and causing a slight chink of metal against metal and a crinkling of paper. Then the rustle stopped, and an object quietly settled atop the desk. A pause, the silence broken only by his father's breathing. Then he turned and left the room, shutting the door.

James waited until his father's steps retreated to the other bedroom and the door closed before he propped himself up on one elbow. On the desk, moonlight illuminated a golden orb atop a scrap of paper. Gingerly he drew them to his mattress. His breath caught as his fingers traveled over his uncle's pocket watch, a heavy, engraved timepiece. Opening it, he raised it into the moon's glow. The men of Uncle Pat's company had presented the watch to him when he was promoted to captain. James still remembered the letter in which his uncle had described the occasion. The watch, along with a few other personal items, had accompanied the news of his death to Burr Oak. James had not been allowed to admire the timepiece long, for his father had taken it and the contents of the small box into his bedroom and hid them.

With the watch in one hand, James held the slip of paper closer to the window where he strained his eyes to read: *I know you are leaving. Take Uncle Pat's watch. He would want you to have it. Keep it safe.*

James read the note twice, a lump rising unexpectedly in his throat. Abruptly he folded the paper and stared at the watch, studied the chain snaked atop his blanket. Shame touched the edge of his thoughts, for no doubt his father assumed that his son was bound for the Army of the Potomac and Uncle Pat's regiment, but this was not the case. James had no desire to be among men who might compare him to his much-respected, fighting uncle.

He marveled at his father's intuitiveness as well as his gesture. Whatever had possessed him to do such a thing, especially after their exchange earlier in the week? Had the dance, drink, and grief combined to make him nostalgic? Would he rescind his kindnesses come morning?

James crawled back to his pillow and returned the note to the desk. But the watch he kept close, turning it over and over, hoping it would somehow give him courage.

***

Color drained from Nate's mother as her fork clattered to her plate. His father stood deliberately from his chair at the breakfast table, turned away from his sweating son, and paced to a window with leaden feet. Morning sunlight whitened his hair in a disturbing way. He remained at the window as oppressive silence stretched through the large house, a house that had once echoed and shook with the voices and tread of five young men.

Nate's mother rose unsteadily, hand braced on the table in a familiar stance of defiance, but this time the picture lacked strength. Her voice was quiet, solid. "You can't go, Nathan. I'll not have it."

"Ma, I'm goin'."

"No. You're needed here. Your father can't run this farm by himself. It'll be the death of him."

"Mr. Moylan will help."

"He has his own place to run." Anger trembled her words. "What are you thinking, young man?"

"I think it's time I do somethin' instead of lettin' the rest of St. Joe County fight for me."

"Do what? Run off and get yourself killed or…or captured? This family's done its share."

"I'll send you me pay. I'll get a bounty, too. You can hire someone to help."

"Hire someone, he says!" Her hands fluttered in a display of futility. "And who will we be hiring? How many able young men are left?"

Nate stood. Why did his father say nothing? Why could his mother not understand?

"I'm leavin' on the train tomorrow morn. Cap'n Bennet's expectin' me."

His mother's voice grew stronger. "No, Nathan. Haven't you been listening to me?"

"Aye, but you haven't been listenin' to *me*. I aim to be a soldier. 'Tis all fixed. I'm meetin' up with the Eleventh, with Ryan's company."

His mother advanced toward him. "I'll lock you in your room if I have to, Nathan Timothy Calhoun, so help me." She spun toward her husband. "Daniel, talk sense into your son."

Finally, his father drifted to her side. The sadness in his blue eyes made him appear much older than his sixty years. Touching his wife's arm, he spoke calmly. "Even a locked door and bars wouldn't be stoppin' the lad. He's got his Irish up, and he's just as stubborn as the both of us."

She stared. "Daniel, you're not going to let him go. Not him, too."

His father studied him so long and hard that Nate felt inexplicably ashamed, and he had to look away. "You're breakin' our hearts, don't you see, lad?"

"Da'—"

"Sure, and you do see. But you can't help yourself. I saw it in your brothers' eyes. I see it now in yours. I could just as soon bottle up the wind and expect it not to blow." He drew closer. "I can't give you me blessing, but I can give you me prayers."

Nate's mother let out a sob of disbelief.

Nate smiled wanly. "Thank you, Da'. Thank you for seein'."

"Aye, I do see, better than you, I'm afraid." His gaze grew even more melancholy. "For the thing is this—you don't understand what you're about to become a part of."

***

A steady rain fell all Monday afternoon to blanket the small Burr Oak depot in gloom. The chuffing train sat dull and morose on the tracks, awaiting its passengers. From beneath the platform overhang, Nate stared down the tracks for as far as he could see to the southwest. Uncertainty and excitement jumbled his insides as he remembered his father's words from yesterday. He had never travelled farther than White Pigeon or Three Rivers since moving to Burr Oak, seemingly a lifetime ago. He had been cocooned here in the safe bosom of the flat farmlands. What lurked beyond that curtain of rain?

He set his small valise down and turned to Katie and his father. They looked miserable, as gray as the world around them. His mother had said her tearful goodbye at home, the bitterness of the previous day gone and replaced by earnest blessings for his safe return. She had given him a New Testament, a book small enough to be easily carried on his person and one in which he had placed Katie's picture and a lock of her hair. Then his mother had retreated to her bedroom and closed the door. Although Nate wished she were here, he was relieved to no longer witness her tears.

Blinking hard, his father reached to shake hands, his familiar grip calloused and chilled. "Mind yourself, lad. Soldiers are a rough lot. Remember your upbringin'."

"I will, Da'."

"If you run into your brothers, give 'em our love. And if you find out anything about Ryan, let us know straight away."

Nate nodded and blinked away tears, fearing Katie would see them.

"Well…" His father wavered, then pulled him into a strong

embrace. "Goodbye, lad. Don't forget how much we love you." Abruptly he forced himself back, hesitated there but an instant, unable to look up. "Katie dear, I'll wait for you at the wagon." With that, he spun on the heels of his worn work boots and strode from the platform. Watching him go, Nate frowned. Long hours lay before his father this day, tasks that he would now toil upon alone.

A sudden burst of rain drove Katie and Nate even farther under cover, closer to one another. Katie's eyes were steady and wet beneath her small green bonnet, her hands clasped in front of her matching dress. His heart ached to see her this way—so small and alone. He almost wished the train would leave without him. His arms enfolded her as he whispered soothingly to her, a fruitless effort.

She softly lamented, "What if I never see you again?"

"Don't be sayin' that. I'll be back. Me and all me brothers. And your brothers, too. You'll see. That's why I'm a-goin'—to get this war over with as fast as possible."

She attempted to collect herself, to wipe away the tears. "You'd best not be running off with one of those Southern belles."

He grinned and kissed her. "Now, why would I do a daft thing like that?" He ran the back of his hand along her cool, damp cheek, allowed the lightheartedness to pass. "When I *do* come back, I want you to be me wife, Katie."

Her lips parted in a shocked reaction that Nate thoroughly relished. Her fingers kneaded his shoulders until she finally managed, "Wife?"

Surely she could see his heart pounding through his shirt. "Marry me, Katie Moylan, and there won't be a happier man alive."

"Oh, Nate," she gasped and threw her arms around his neck.

He held her tightly, then took her face in his hands and kissed her. He did not want to let her go; he wanted to marry her now, war or no war. But the train's whistle shrilled. They looked longingly, frantically at each other, then he kissed her one last time as the train began to chug forward. She clung to him, but he pried himself away and hurried to jump on board. Katie's farewell carried above the laboring engine. He waved and called to her until they could no longer hear one another, and she was but a small figure blurred by the cinereous rain.

∗

"That was quite a scene out there," a familiar voice mocked Nate as he settled into a seat halfway down the car, a car which carried only a few

21

passengers, most seated to the rear.

The sight of James Keenan sitting across the aisle took Nate by surprise, for James rarely left Burr Oak. The young shopkeeper wore a sarcastic grin beneath his tawny mustache. With his feet propped upon the facing seat and hands clasped in his lap, his appearance of casualness failed to ring true.

Nate shot him a quick glare. "What of it?"

"Looked like you were professing your undying love, Calhoun." He raised an eyebrow. "But did she profess the same?"

"The devil take you, James Keenan. For your information, Katie and me are engaged. Hear? She's goin' to be me wife, so find yourself someone else to dance with from here on out. Understand?"

James momentarily looked taken aback, but the smirk returned. "Engaged, is it? Why would she agree to that, farm boy?"

"Because she loves me; somethin' you know nothin' about. And I may be a farm boy, but at least me father ain't a drunk."

James's brows lowered over stormy eyes. "Shut up about my father."

"Don't like it, huh? Well, that's all he is. Everyone in Burr Oak knows he's a drunk, and that he's a murderer as well—"

James's hand flashed out in an attempt to grab Nate, but Nate pulled out of reach, startled by the young man's instant fury. His feet now on the floor, James leaned across the aisle and hissed, "Keep your lies to yourself, Calhoun. If I ever hear you say that again, I'll—"

"You won't be hearin' me say nothin' for a good long spell, I reckon." Nate hid his unease with a dismissive wave, squared his shoulders, and regained his confidence. "I'm on me way to join the army."

"What?"

"You heard me. I'm goin' to be fightin' Rebs within the week, I fancy. Fightin' Rebs while you count pennies at your store."

Nate had not expected the odd expression on James's face, his sudden silence equally remarkable.

"I'm joinin' Ryan's old outfit. Company D, Eleventh Michigan Infantry."

Slowly James turned to stare toward the head of the car, his expression melting into a scowl. He quietly cursed and settled deep into his seat

"What's the matter?" Nate asked. "Feelin' a wee bit guilty, are you?"

"I've nothing to feel guilty about."

"Then why do you look so sickly?"

James glanced at him with irritation. "Maybe you'll figure it out by the time we get to Tennessee."

For a long moment Nate could say nothing. Surely James was not enlisting, too. But what else would take him not only from Burr Oak but to Tennessee? Maybe James was simply making game of him. Yet when he studied his expression, it was plain that James was dead serious.

"You ain't enlistin'."

James said nothing, crossed his arms.

"Not in the Eleventh anyways. If you was enlistin', you'd be joinin' your uncle's regiment. That is, if you *was* enlistin'."

"Goes to show how much you know." James got to his feet. "I can see if I keep sitting by you, my ears will fall off before we even leave the state." With that, he stalked to the front of the car. Nate stared after him, still in disbelief.

PART II

CHICKAMAUGA

"A dense cloud of smoke enveloped our lines,
and in some places the position of the foe could only
be known by the flash of his guns."

-- Colonel William L. Stoughton

CHAPTER 3

The bustle of military activity at the train depot in Decherd, Tennessee, made Nate feel small and insignificant in his worn homespun clothing. Soldiers passed by him without a glance. The sight of them with their rakishly angled hats and shining brass buttons quickened his pulse. Civilians were rare pale vessels moving in this sea of blue uniforms. Shouts and calls echoed as he gathered his valise, the impatient breathing of the Nashville and Chattanooga Railroad engine adding to the harried atmosphere, soot settling upon his shoulders. Everyone moved with such purpose, and with good reason, considering what a soldier on the train coming from Murfreesboro had said—the Confederates were less than forty miles away in Chattanooga, just the other side of the Cumberland Mountains. Nate had seen the mountains' deep-green bulk to the east through the train windows, had marveled at their size and seemingly impenetrable wall they created.

Wagons waited for supplies to be unloaded from the train. These were mainly manned by black men, a sight that gave Nate pause. The only blacks he had seen before now were glimpsed during his travel south, the occasional servant at the various depots along the way, standing dutifully near their master or mistress. Nate had tried not to stare at them. He had read about the Abolitionists in the East who considered ending slavery as important as preserving the Union, perhaps more so, a concept beyond Nate and his rural village. He and his family and friends spoke little about the plight of the South's slaves, for it had no impact on their daily lives. Even now, studying those nearby, he found that his only true interest was curiosity and perhaps a little discomfort over the concept of slavery.

James stepped next to him on the platform. They had spoken little during the three-day journey, but now Nate was glad to have someone beside him whose similarity in dress made him appear less odd among those around him.

"Well, here we are," James said with an air of confidence.

"Pilgrims in an unholy land."

Before Nate could respond, a resonant male voice gained their attention. "Nate Calhoun?"

They turned to see a tall first sergeant regarding them with sharp blue eyes. He looked to be about James's age.

"I'm Nate Calhoun. How'd you know?"

"First Sergeant Benjamin Hart, Company D, Eleventh Michigan. I heard you were on your way to join us. You have some of Ryan's look about you."

Nate smiled with instant pride. "You heard tell right, Sergeant. And I know your name from me brother's letters. From Bronson, ain't you? Ryan always spoke highly of you."

Hart's smile came easily. "Well, we miss your brother, sure enough. The whole regiment does."

James interrupted. "I've come to enlist in the Eleventh as well, Sergeant."

Hart critically sized him up as he removed his slouch hat and ran his fingers through his sweaty dark hair. "And who are you?"

"James Keenan from Burr Oak, same as Calhoun."

When Hart glanced between the pair, Nate took a step away from James, and judging from the sergeant's skeptical perusal of James, he had understood the gesture.

Nate asked, "Have you gotten any news about Ryan?"

"'Fraid not. Hope to God he gets exchanged soon."

"Was you at Elk River? Can you tell me what happened?"

Regret shadowed Hart's expression. "Let's talk on the way to camp. Have to get back. Follow me, gentlemen."

Hart led the way off the platform and down the rail line, his gait uneven. According to Ryan's letters, Hart had severely injured his right hip falling onto a tent stake last summer. Nate hoped that if he came out of this war with a limp, he would acquire it in a more glorious way.

They reached a wagon loaded with boxes of ammunition. A young private sat holding the mules' reins, a piece of hay dangling from his mouth. His attention lingered upon Nate.

Hart gestured to the boxes. "Climb aboard, gentlemen." He struggled up next to the soldier. "Let's go, Evans."

Decherd was small, its main buildings just north of the railroad tracks. As they headed south out of town, the civilians they passed paid them no heed. Thinking of Burr Oak left far behind, Nate imagined how humiliating it would be to have the enemy occupy his village. Yet perhaps not all the citizens resented them. He had read that some of the folks in Tennessee were still loyal to the Union.

A multitude of ruts lined the road and made the wagon constantly jar and bump, causing Nate and James to cling to the boxes lest they get flung over the side. Hart grumbled about how much rain had fallen in recent weeks. Nate could smell the dampness still clinging to the earth.

Wagons and horses choked the road, all branches of the service represented—the red piping on the uniforms of artillerymen, the more prevalent blue trim of infantry, the occasional yellow of cavalry. An atmosphere of purpose enveloped Nate, invigorated him, drew a smile to his wondering face. This was where life really mattered these days, where a man could be a part of something historic, something for the greater good.

"So, tell me how Ryan got captured, Sarge," Nate urged. "Cap'n Bennet didn't give us no details in his letter."

Hart's attention remained on the muscled hindquarters of the near mule, his expression grave. "Our regiment was ordered to the support of some of our boys that had run into two brigades of Wheeler's Reb cavalry. A couple of regiments from John Beatty's brigade went forward with us. Our Colonel Stoughton ordered a heavy skirmish line forward, and the boys drove the Johnnies half a mile, but then the Rebs got up two divisions of reinforcements. We held our own till dark." He exchanged a troubled glance with the driver before continuing. "Orders came to pull back. Lieutenant Platt was serving as aide-de-camp that day. The Johnnies got hold of him somehow, and Ryan tried to get to him, but the Rebs gobbled him up, too."

Nate waited for more, but it became clear Hart would offer nothing else. Touched by the distress his brother's loss caused these men, he did not press for more information. Perhaps others in Company D could tell him more. He glanced at James for his reaction, but the young man's wide gaze was focused far beyond Hart, and Nate turned to see what had caught James's attention.

They had just topped a small rise in the road and now had a breathtaking view of the green splendor of the Cumberland Mountains rising to the south and east. For as far as he could see between here and the green giants, military camps dotted the sparsely farmed land, the white tents covering the ground like dull snow, smoke curling up from hundreds of cook fires. On either side of the road, tents stretched in straight lines to form company streets. Among them, men moved about, others lounged on the ground, talking, laughing, playing music on harmonica or banjo, singing. A startling spread of humanity seemingly

29

so out of place here in the wild valley below the mountains. In an open field, a company drilled under the bark of an officer. Flags stirred lazily on staffs, flags of all sizes and shapes, regimental flags, brigade flags, national flags. One set of regimental colors caught Nate's attention, and his excitement grew as he drew nearer.

The breeze displayed the two flags in languid, flowing waves from their nine-foot staffs set before a spacious wall tent. A defiant eagle stretched its wings upon the dark blue field of the regimental colors while beyond it the Stars and Stripes provided a magnificent background. The sight of the national colors returned Nate to the beginning of the war when the Eleventh had rendezvoused in White Pigeon, and he had ridden the train to visit Ryan. That day had been a special one for the regiment. Not only were the men issued weapons, but they received their first national flag in a grand ceremony filled with stirring speeches from officers and civilians alike. Among the speakers was then-Lieutenant Colonel William L. Stoughton, whose words that November day still rang in Nate's ears: "It may be exposed to the winter blast and the battle's storm but those who bear it hence will never return with it dishonored. Henceforth, we shall cherish it as our own, and as we defend it and the sacred cause it represents, so may our memory live in the hearts of our countrymen."

Now, as if on cue, Colonel Stoughton himself stepped from the wall tent, accompanied by another familiar figure—Captain Benjamin Bennet from Burr Oak. Bennet had raised Company D, then known as the Bronson Guard, for it had been formed in the town of Bronson in Branch County, east of St. Joseph County. Before that, Bennet had fought with the First Michigan at Bull Run, his early service having earned Nate's undying admiration. Ryan's letters had never had a single disparaging word about his company commander.

"Captain, sir!" Hart called with a grin, causing Evans to haul on the lines and drag the mules to a stop before the officers. "Brought your new recruit from the train station."

When Bennet saw Nate, a smile broke through his dense, dark beard. In a quick bound, Nate dismounted and stood as tall as possible before his new commanding officers.

"Well, lad. I see you made it at last."

Proudly Nate squared his shoulders, forgetting James, who stepped from the wagon with more dignity than he. "Yes, sir. You know I would've come sooner if I could've."

"I was honored by your request to take your brother's place." Bennet clapped a hand upon Nate's shoulder and stepped to the side.

"Colonel Stoughton, sir, allow me to introduce Nate Calhoun from Burr Oak, younger brother to our Ryan captured at Elk River."

Stoughton, not a tall man but appearing every inch a soldier in his fine uniform, offered a smile and a handshake. "I believe we met long ago, young man, in White Pigeon when your brother joined the regiment."

"That's kind of you to remember, sir."

Stoughton's gaze was warm and intelligent, his clear voice reminding Nate that he had been a lawyer before the war. "Your brother served gallantly with the regiment. We miss him."

"Thank you, sir." Nate tossed a haughty glance over his shoulder at James, who had drawn closer.

Bennet's attention shifted, and his eyes narrowed slightly. "Is it James Keenan I see there?"

"Yes, sir," James replied. Nate found his tone a bit disrespectful and remembered that Seamus Keenan and Benjamin Bennet had had their differences back home.

The captain pushed his hat back from his high forehead. "You came to enlist?"

"Yes, sir."

Bennet glanced at Stoughton, who watched closely but hid any curiosity that might have stirred him. Bennet turned to Hart, the sergeant having dismounted from the wagon and sent it on its way. "I'll entrust these men to you, Sergeant." He gave Nate a quick wink. "Make sure Nate's mustered into my company."

When the officers had continued across the company street, Hart sized James up. "The Captain didn't seem particularly glad to see you, Keenan."

"I'm not here to be popular," James retorted. "I'm here to fight Rebs."

Hart grunted. "Well, step lively then, gentlemen; the adjutant won't wait all day."

***

James felt more at ease and less conspicuous once he had his new uniform. At the quartermaster's, he and Nate were each issued a forage cap, dress hat, overcoat, dress coat, pants, two pairs of drawers, two shirts, socks, and brogans. Then they were loaded down with haversack, cartridge box, cap box, bayonet and scabbard, rubber and woolen blankets, canteen, knapsack, mending kit, mess kit, and tent half. Last of all, they received ammunition and Springfield muskets. James thrilled at the heft of the nine-pound rifle and itched to fire it.

Hart asked, "Ever shoot a gun before?"

Scowling, James hesitated.

"Well?"

"I have," Nate piped up. "Huntin' with me brothers and Da'."

"What about you, Keenan?"

"Once or twice," he lied.

"That's all? What have you been doing all your life?"

"My family owns a store. I ran it."

"Is that a fact? Well, maybe we ought to give you to the quartermaster."

"No, thanks. I'm here to shoot some Rebs."

"From the sounds of it, you'll be lucky to shoot a barn."

"I'm a fast learner."

"You'd better be, or else you're gonna be a fast dier."

By the time Hart led them to their company street, it was noon, and fifes and drums shouted out the Dinner Call. The rattle of the snares and the shrill notes of the fifes sent a strange wave of excitement through James. Something about the martial sound solidified his realization that he really was a soldier now, and the pride that swelled his chest held at bay the hint of homesickness that had been dogging him.

Voices raised from a small group settled around a cook fire.

"By gaw, is that Nate Calhoun?"

"Hey, Sarge, over here!" a second voice called.

Several of the young men left their meals to hurry over, eyes bright, grins welcoming.

"If it ain't the Dell boys!" Nate cried, soon surrounded by faces familiar from Burr Oak. Familiar yet some not pleasantly so to James.

Tall, reedy Abner Dell and his younger brother Jeremy earnestly returned Nate's greetings. The Dells, whose family farm was just the other side of the Prairie River from Burr Oak, had always appeared underweight to James when dressed in dirty trousers and grimy shirts, but somehow their uniforms made them look as if they had gained not only bulk but muscle as well.

When Abner caught sight of James lingering beyond Nate, his grin faded, and James stiffened. "Well, if it ain't ol' James Keenan. How the blue blazes he end up down here, Nate? He get drafted?"

James bristled. "The hell you say."

With practiced agility, Jeremy stepped between them. "Now,

c'mon, you two. We're not back home. We've got a war to fight, not each other."

"I came on my own accord," James growled. "Reckoned they could use some good soldiers, seeing how they have you."

"Still full of yourself, huh, Keenan?" Abner laughed harshly. "Well, mebbe I'll stop by your tent later and read you the latest letter from my wife. You remember Mattie, sure."

Anger rushed color to James's face. He dropped all that he carried and reached to push Jeremy aside, but a black-haired corporal clamped a hand down upon his shoulder and cautioned, "Stand fast, soldier. This ain't Burr Oak." When James gave him a subdued glare, the noncom's brown eyes narrowed as if bothered by the sun. "Recollect your place."

"Well, Corporal May," Hart grinned, "since you seem to handle Keenan so well and since you're short a couple of men in your squad, I reckon he's yours to have. Both of 'em. I'm sure Nate will fit in just fine."

May protested, "I don't need Keenan; Hank will be back."

"Only through a medical miracle," Hart flatly responded. He pinned the recruits with a pointed look. "Dysentery. It's in your future, boys."

James said, "I'm sure I'm needed in some other squad, Sergeant."

"I say you're needed in this one, soldier."

"Sure," Abner said with a glint in his eye, "leave him with us, Sarge. Preacher Langdon—I mean, Sergeant Langdon—will have a lark with him. I'm sure you recollect Robert Langdon from Burr Oak, don't you, Keenan?"

James stared. Surely Dell was lying. "Langdon's not in the Eleventh."

"Is now." Abner laughed sardonically. "The bastard got transferred in."

Jeremy scoffed. "More like booted out of the Thirteenth."

"That's enough gossip, you parcel of women," Hart scolded. "Langdon's a part of Company D now. We'll not be talking behind his back."

"Best not be." Grinning, Jeremy flicked the red hair from his eyes. "The Preacher hears of it, he'll be obliged to break your head open like a melon. Reckon the army's made him an ornery cuss. Or mebbe 'twas Keenan who made him thataway."

James barely heard them, barely saw them. Instead, he saw Langdon five years ago, covered with blood from a head wound inflicted by a board, a board swung in a fit of black rage by Seamus

Keenan. Langdon—selfish, shrewd, and calculating—had used his title of pastor to fool all in Burr Oak. It was James who had revealed his true character and made life there so uncomfortable that he moved to Three Rivers.

Abner gave James one last look of disdain, then said, "Go on, Nate. Pitch your tent and come back here. We wanna hear all the news from home. What Mattie writes me probably ain't the half of it, truth be told."

A disgruntled David May led the two recruits to the end of the company street. There he showed them how to button together the tent halves that each of them carried and how to fashion a forked branch vertically at either end, then secure a horizontal branch to connect the two to form a crude A-frame tent. Stakes secured all. When finished, Nate looked proudly at their new home, but James felt dismayed; he knew dog tents were small, but he had not imagined them *this* small. And to have to share it…with Calhoun…

May left them, and Nate rushed back to his friends.

Glad to be alone in the privacy of the tent, James dug out a small looking glass and used it to admire his new appearance. He grinned. How much better he looked than that damned, scrawny Abner Dell. If Mattie Carter saw the two of them next to one another now, he knew she would find him the most dashing. The jealous thought made him frown. Where the hell had that come from? He had managed to put Mattie out of his thoughts after Abner had gone to fight in '61 and Mattie had moved to Sturgis to live with her folks. Something about seeing Abner and knowing their history would be retold for the benefit of the regiment made James furious. He had not come here to be surrounded by unpleasant memories.

Putting the looking glass away, he pulled out his uncle's pocket watch. His thumb ran over the engraved cover as he thought of his father. The morning after discovering the watch in his room, James had thanked his father, but the sentiment had been waved away, his gaze avoided, and nothing offered except a mumbled acknowledgement.

A guttural voice spoke from just outside the tent, startling him. "So, you finally grew a backbone and enlisted."

James stared up at the squinted, murky brown eyes of Robert Langdon, who stood with feet braced apart, fists on his hips, cigar clamped in his mouth. For some reason, his chevrons seemed a particularly bright blue in the July sunshine. When last seen, he had sported only a mustache, but now a sparse beard, peppered with gray, bristled on his hard jaw. Lines on his forehead were more plentiful than

James remembered. His trim body looked thinner and sinewy. He was not the handsome preacher of old. The war had aged his face and body beyond their forty years, and his Bible had been forsaken the day Seamus Keenan had gone looking for him.

"The army must be getting mighty desperate," Langdon said, "when they take the likes of you, boy."

"That's something, coming from you." James crawled outside to stand in front of Langdon, glad to be a couple of inches taller. "Who did you pay to get those stripes?"

Langdon's upper lip curled, revealing tobacco-stained teeth. "I paid for 'em, all right, with hard work. Shiloh, Corinth, Stones River."

"Hard work, eh? I'd like to hear others' opinions on that. But no one from the Thirteenth is around here to talk. How convenient."

Langdon crossed his arms. Thin, wispy brown hair spilled from beneath his slouch hat; the gray around his temples James did not recall from three years ago when he had last seen Langdon in Three Rivers. "You can ask anyone about my fighting, Keenan." He took the cigar out of his mouth and blew smoke in James's face. "Hear tell you're in my squad. Well, I'll show you the meaning of hard work. You'll rue the day you signed up with this outfit." He wheeled and strode down the tent row.

CHAPTER 4

The campfire felt good to Nate's aching body. He removed the stiff brogans from his throbbing feet and found several blisters beneath his wool socks. Around him, the murmurs of tired soldiers and the song of night insects lulled him. Hundreds of campfires dotted the velvet canvas of the warm night, filling Nate's nose with their soothing smoky scent. Music and singing floated from the next company street, drawing a smile from his lips. The star-filled carpet of black sky stretched to nothingness in the west and to the even blacker shoulders of the mountains to the east.

Around him, the men of Company D lounged, some old friends, some new. He had been pleased by how readily he had been accepted, though he knew much of that ease had to do with Ryan. Some days he felt the burden of having to uphold his family's reputation among these men, veterans of Stones River, men who had seen things he could only imagine, men who were not as eager as he had expected to cross the Cumberlands and clash again with those same men they had so recently fought. Their reluctance puzzled him because he knew from Ryan's letters, as well as from simple observation and keen listening, that they were brave fellows. Well, if the rumors were true, any reluctance would soon be irrelevant, for they would have new orders to follow.

Corporal May whistled at the sight of Nate's battered feet. "Langdon's been pushing you boys right hard. Have to say you're holding up well, Nate."

Abner blew a few stray notes on his harmonica, then said, "He's had you a-goin' almost nonstop for a whole week. If'n it wa'nt for Cap'n Bennet, I fancy the Preacher would've kilt you by now."

Jeremy grinned from next to his brother, the sheen of coffee glinting upon his lips.

"He's tryin'," Nate muttered with a grimace. "Truth be told, lads, I'm done in. But what vexes me is I'm made to suffer just 'cause of Keenan."

36

"What is it anyway," May asked, "that makes Langdon hate the lad so?"

Abner took the harmonica from his lips. "You ain't heard that story yet?"

"No. Recollect I ain't from Burr Oak like you fellas." May stretched his hands toward the fire. "Is the story a good one?"

Abner grinned. "It is."

Nate shifted closer to the fire, attention on Abner. He had heard the story about Langdon and the Keenans many times and several versions, so varied that by now he believed nothing and everything.

"Well," Abner said, "you've heard Langdon was a preacher in Burr Oak several years ago. From what I understand, Grace Keenan—James's mother—went to Langdon several times to talk about a problem, rumored to be about her husband, ol' Seamus. Well, it seems Langdon got a little more involved with that member of his flock than a preacher should, if you take my meanin', boys. When Seamus Keenan found out, he nigh went crazy. And who wouldn't? His wife was the most beautiful woman in Burr Oak."

"In the county," Jeremy interrupted with enthusiasm.

Elias Cooper, silently puffing on his pipe next to Nate, nodded sagely. Elias was the oldest among them, a quiet, gentle man whom Nate had known since first coming to Burr Oak. Elias's enlistment had taken Nate by surprise, for the older man was devoted to his wife and children, but obviously his kind wife understood his patriotism.

"Well," Abner warmed to his storytelling, tucking away his harmonica in a pocket, then rubbing his hands together, "Seamus went after the Preacher, nigh kilt him."

Nate rubbed his feet and grumbled, "Wish he had, then the black-hearted devil wouldn't be tormentin' us now."

"They say Seamus was tighter than a drum when he went after the Preacher. We all know how he likes to pull a cork. Afterwards, James and his ma tried to talk sense into him, but Seamus wouldn't listen, wouldn't listen to no one. He went crazy, and then," Abner paused to look at the ring of expectant faces, "he kilt his wife."

May's eyes widened.

"Nah," Elias drawled through his sandy-red beard. "That ain't the truth. I hear tell it was an accident."

"Aye," Nate agreed. "That's what me mother told me."

"Of course," Abner said. "What else would any mother tell her little boy?" He tousled Nate's hair, and Nate swiped at him. "Seamus and James made it look like an accident; otherwise, Seamus woulda been hanged."

Thoughtfulness reflected from the fire-licked faces.

"But," said Nate, "if Langdon did all that, why does he hate James? I can understand James hatin' him but—"

Abner leaned forward, drawing his brother with him. "It was James what got Burr Oak against Langdon. He tolt everyone the Preacher raped his mother—"

"No, no," Elias interrupted, looking uncomfortable with this new line of talk. "Not raped. He just said Langdon made advances."

"Did he tell you that? 'Cause that's not what I heard," Abner insisted. "Look at Langdon if you want proof. He's capable of a lot worse'n rape. You know what he did when he was with the Thirteenth."

"What?" Nate asked, keen to know more about his tormentor.

Jeremy jumped back into the conversation. "Why, he done raped a white girl and her darky in Corinth, then he kilt the nigger."

The other veterans nodded, some murmuring their belief. Nate gaped at them. If everything said was true, how could Sergeant Langdon and Preacher Langdon be the same man? He had thought Robert Langdon a man of God, regardless of the conflicting stories about him and the Keenans; after all, they were only stories, and he would not put it past James Keenan or his inebriated father to mar a good man's reputation and run him out of town if Langdon had owed money to the store. *God knows James loves a penny.* Yet if a former man of the cloth turned into a rapist and murderer in war time, perhaps he had had those propensities to begin with.

Abner slapped Nate's leg to draw him back. "And where's Keenan right now? Off by hisself in his tent. Why? 'Cause he knows we all know about him. And he always did think he was better'n us. He won't make much of a soldier; you'll see."

"Now, Nate here," May said with a warm smile, "none of us has any doubts about him. Ryan was the best this regiment had to offer. Captain Bennet says all the Calhouns are alike, and he would know, now wouldn't he?"

A shadow crossed Elias's face behind the curling smoke of his pipe. "God damned shame about Ryan."

The familiar pangs of homesickness and sorrow over his brother's loss dragged Nate into silence, and his gaze wandered deep among the golden fingers of the fire. He forgot about James; he forgot about Langdon; he forgot about his body's aches and bruises. An arm encompassed his shoulders, and he looked up into the warm brown eyes of Elias Cooper. He could not recall ever hearing Elias curse before tonight. So, if this war drove a good man like Elias to blasphemy and a former preacher to rape and murder, what would become of him?

***

After the morning's long march, James welcomed an oak tree's support for his sore back. Just as inviting was the shade its branches offered, like an umbrella against the boiling midday August sun. Around him, the men of Company D guzzled from canteens and grabbed a bite of hardtack from their haversacks, faces coated with thick dust, runnels of sweat leaving trails. He tried to hide his fatigue from the relaxed veterans, especially from Langdon, who sat against an adjacent tree. These men had been at this work nearly two years, had endured dozens of such patrols. How he longed to take off his blistering brogans, pour water over his burning feet. The straps of his knapsack had rubbed raw spots on his shoulders, but he did not dare take off his sack coat and shirt to examine the damage lest Langdon use such a weakness to his advantage.

Nate sat a rod to his right with the Dell brothers. He looked a little pale and pinched, which made James feel better. If he had to suffer, at least Nate shared his discomfort.

Regardless of his physical trials, James was glad to be out of camp, even if it was for just a day or two on a detail to help protect the railroad between Bridgeport, Alabama, and Cowan, Tennessee, where the Eleventh now camped. Anything was better than constant drill at the hands of his merciless sergeant, though James admitted to only himself that he had learned much from Langdon, including marksmanship. True, he lacked Calhoun's natural dead aim, but at least he did not embarrass himself.

He fingered his musket now, uneasy being away from the protective bulk of the regiment and the brigade. Guerrillas were common, and now and then Confederate cavalry pushed out from Chattanooga to harass and keep track of General William Rosecrans's troops. Around him, the men talked eagerly of seeing action again now that the repaired railroad would allow supplies to flow forward to support any planned offensive. And surely there would be an offensive. After all, Chattanooga was the gateway to the South, a place where General Braxton Bragg's Army of Tennessee now squatted in wait, denying the Federal army access.

"It won't be long, boys." Langdon's gravelly voice rang confidently. "Soon the Army of the Cumberland will be moving across the Tennessee River. Then we'll find us a fight. Rested up and ready to go."

"Trouble is Bragg's boys will be just as rested as us," First Sergeant Hart said. "We should have pushed right on after Tullahoma."

"Had to repair the railroad," said David May.

James's gaze drifted to their company commander, twenty-two-year-old Frank Lane, who stood across the road in a grove of pines, talking with a shabby-looking civilian. Captain Lane listened intently to the man, one hand upon his smooth chin. Lane, a Bronson boy, had been promoted from second lieutenant to command Company D at the beginning of the month after Bennet was promoted to major. James had a feeling Lane did not necessarily want the post, but all the same their new captain seemed determined to do his best. Lane followed the civilian's pointing hand to the east, nodding. Something stirred in James's gut as he observed the officer's intent expression. The unsettling sensation traveled up his spine, made him shudder but a moment before it settled into his stomach again with a dull ache.

His attention drifted beyond the civilian to a black man mounted on a worn, scrawny mule. The middle-aged slave held the reins of his master's equally scrawny horse. What struck James was a characteristic he had noticed among all the blacks seen since he had come south—a marked apathy on their faces. No expression, no words unless spoken to, eyes almost vacant, though James had a feeling the vacuity was manufactured, for whenever he observed slaves working together, their gazes contained as much life as James saw among his comrades. The Eleventh's officers had a few black servants, but they had livelier expressions and spoke more openly. They obviously viewed their futures with hope, while those belonging to the local populace, if they had any hope of freedom, were careful not to show it while with their masters. James tried to imagine free blacks in Burr Oak, but he shook his head at such an absurd concept. He and Burr Oak were for the Union, not abolition. How could it be otherwise?

Lane called across the road, "Sergeant Langdon!"

Langdon took his time getting to his feet. "Yes, sir."

"Reb cavalry's rumored to be nearby. I want you to take five men and scout ahead. There's a narrowing of the road not far from here. When you reach it, wait for us there. If you spot anything, send back word."

"Yes, sir." When Langdon's gaze fell upon James, a queer grin raised one corner of his slash of a mouth. "Keenan, Cooper, Calhoun, Jeremy and Abner. Fall in!"

Scrambling for his musket, James joined the others in the road. Excitement brightened Nate's eyes. James, however, could offer no such response to their orders, though he wished he could appear as eager as his messmate.

They left the company behind, everyone wary of the trees on either side, the rising green foothills of the Cumberlands pressing in upon them with smothering force. Thus isolated, all banter and conversation ceased, and they followed Langdon with muskets at the ready. James kept to the rear of the group, the sweat on his skin now chilling him. He knew better than to question why Langdon would pick men as green as he and Nate for this detail. The knot in his stomach tightened.

A mile onward the road narrowed, the tree-covered slopes squeezing closer. Langdon halted, cautious eyes on the road ahead, an unlit cigar clenched in his teeth. James had yet to learn where Langdon acquired his seemingly endless supply of tobacco.

Langdon ordered, "Calhoun and Keenan will come with me. We'll take the right. The rest of you deploy to the left of the road and move forward. Don't get ahead of us. When you reach the high point of that rise, halt and keep your eyes on the road. If we see any Rebs, you wait till I open fire before you start shooting, hear?"

"The Captain said to send back word if we see anything," James quickly reminded him.

"They hear shooting, that's all the word they'll need." Langdon scowled at him. "Don't turn yellow on us, Keenan."

James's face colored, and he started to protest, but Langdon turned his back on him and trotted forward. James's heart pounded in his ears as they climbed up the right-hand slope into the timber. They deployed in a crouched line and moved over the uneven ground as quietly as possible amidst the sparse underbrush. James was certain his heartbeat echoed up the mountainsides. To his right, Nate stared ahead, licking his lips, sweat pouring from beneath his slouch hat. James hoped he was as scared as he looked.

Suddenly Langdon dropped to his belly, motioning the others down. James took cover behind an ancient, moss-draped log and strained to see through the shadows. From the road, faint sounds drifted to him. The jangle of accoutrements, the shuffle of shod hooves, voices. Over the slight rise in the road came a detachment of cavalry…or at least that was what James guessed them to be. The dozen riders had little military bearing, dressed in a ragtag assortment of colors, moving loosely with the rhythm of their muscled mounts. The sight of them mesmerized James—his first glimpse of the enemy, of men whose cause had killed his uncle. When the leader of the small band raised his hand, the detachment halted. The man's attention drilled down the road where it opened beyond this rise, offering no cover. James glanced at Langdon for orders, but the sergeant said nothing, studying the cavalry.

With a quick order, the Confederate detachment split in two; six swung to the far side of the road, the others rode up the slight rise of ground toward the hidden trio. James's hand shook as he ran it over his musket to make sure the percussion cap was in place, then he slid the long barrel gradually forward along the top of the log, aimed at one of the troopers. The Confederates halted not far from their position and dismounted. One man remained with the horses while the others continued to advance, guns at the ready. James's guts cramped, his sweaty hands slipped on the polished metal, perspiration trailed into his eyes and stung him, but he dared not move or breathe. What the hell was Langdon waiting for?

"Fire!" Langdon roared, and at once the Union muskets went off.

Two of the six in front of James went down. A volley from Elias and the Dells exploded off to the left. Shouts went up from the Confederates on both sides of the road. Off to the left, a horse bolted, riderless. The four remaining Rebels on James's front dropped behind trees and returned fire. James sank lower behind his breastwork, wishing he could melt into the forest floor. Surely Captain Lane would hear the crash of gunfire echoing down the narrow valley. As James reloaded, he glanced at the prone men out there on the forest floor…dead men. Had he killed one of them? He half expected them to rise, but they did not.

Through the drifting blue-gray smoke, Langdon hissed, "Fall back! Fall back!"

Ears ringing, James pushed backward, the acuity of his senses strengthening the scent of black powder. A hand roughly grabbed his shoulder and halted him. Frightened, he turned to see Langdon next to him, the cigar now gone, eyes hard and gleaming in the sunlight filtering through the trees.

"Stay here, Keenan."

"What?"

"Cover us, you damned fool."

"What?"

"Not afraid, are you?" With that, Langdon darted after Nate, moving from tree to tree.

James stared after him, dazed until a shot ricocheted off the wood near his head and whined away. He finished ramming the ball home in his musket barrel, his fingers trembling.

"Damn you, Langdon," he muttered. His shot missed its mark, and he cursed himself, frantically reloading, near panic as the enemy inched closer. How long would it take before they realized he was alone? Had Elias and the Dells also fallen back? There was no time to look to his left. From behind a tree, a Rebel charged his position, and James fired. The ball struck the bearded man in the arm, spun him to one side, slammed him back into the tree. Blood spurted between his clutching fingers, his features contorted.

Fear urged James's muscles to carry him away from this place. But to succumb to the impulse would mean disobeying a direct order. What if the Rebs overran his retreating companions? He would be to blame.

Another trooper darted forward, eyes searching the woods. Three survivors from across the road regained their mounts and urged the animals down the slope toward the road, coming to reinforce their comrades.

Orders or no orders, he had to get the hell out of there.

James finished loading, then climbed to a crouch and fell back. The Rebels fired after him, the bullets striking trunks or leaves or whirring past his head. Why was it so hard to breathe? To bolt headlong would mean exposing himself. Terrified but determined, he pulled up behind another tree and fired at the Rebels. Although he did not hit anything, the shot checked their pursuit. His lungs wheezed in the heated air as he tore open another cartridge and reloaded.

A high-pitched cry froze James—the hair-raising Rebel yell that his uncle had written about in his letters. Two of the mounted Rebels charged through the trees, the horses ducking and diving through the branches and undergrowth. Sunlight glinted on raised sabers. With his stare glued upon their approach, somehow James managed to cap his musket. A sound welled from his own throat—a deep, primal, frightened yell. He fired at one of the troopers not a rod away. The ball ripped the Rebel's chest and flipped him from his wild-eyed horse.

There was no time to reload; the second rider was upon him, wielding the saber. James deflected the blow with his musket, the vibration of metal striking metal jarring his whole body. Instinctively he blocked the saber again. The next blow glanced off his shoulder, ripped his uniform and seared his flesh. The horse shied away, giving James time to grab his musket by the barrel and swing it like a club. The stock crashed against the Rebel's arm, knocked the saber free. The horse reared and spilled its stunned rider, but with startling speed the cavalryman scrambled up.

A musket fired from directly behind James. The Rebel catapulted backward into a bush, his chest blown open in a bloody explosion. James wheeled. Nate stood braced against a tree, chest heaving as if he had run a long distance, eyes wide as he looked from James to the dead Rebel, smoke curling from his half-raised Springfield. James's knees gave way. He looked for the other Rebels, saw them reclaiming their mounts and spurring them back to the east.

Elias smashed through the brush behind Nate and halted next to him to survey the scene. "Jesus God," he panted.

The rattle and shouts of Company D rushing up the road reached James. He leaned on his musket, near collapse, and fought the urge to vomit. Nate seemed shocked to see him still alive. Then the boy's gaze reached beyond James to the man he had killed, and the color drained from his face.

CHAPTER 5

"What're we waitin' for, Sarge?" Nate asked Hart as the sergeant rejoined the squad hunkered in the warm September darkness.

"Waiting for the moon to rise," Hart answered stolidly, "so we can see where the hell we're going. Patience, lad. Once we're across that river, we'll have enough Johnnies to last us till Christmas."

The banks of the Tennessee River, where Major General James Negley's division lay, were heavily wooded. From this dense cover, Nate's wide eyes tried to make sense of the landscape before the regiment. To their front flowed the placid river, maybe seventy rods across, a dark ribbon that stretched to north and south, blending with the night. Far distant to either side of Negley's division, other elements of the Army of the Cumberland were to cross the river, all in an effort to flank the Confederate army out of Chattanooga to the northeast. On the other side of the river rose a daunting black wall known as Sand Mountain—Nate guessed it to be close to a thousand feet high—one of many obstacles said to be awaiting the Federal army here at the start of the campaign. Rosecrans's forces had already struggled across the Cumberland Mountains after which the Eleventh, numbering barely over four hundred men, had rested near Cave Spring, Alabama, west of Stevenson.

Although each day's task had tired Nate, his spirits remained high, his very being energized by the rugged beauty surrounding him, the likes of which he had never seen or imagined. The green mountains trapped the heat in the narrow valleys where dust choked the soldiers, the blue sky stretching above like a roof from mountaintop to mountaintop. Every evening, he had written home about the mountains and the few simple folk they encountered, scraping out a living, somehow growing corn and other crops in the valleys.

Late this day, September 1, the Eleventh had broken camp and marched to Caperton's Ferry where they now waited to cross. Two divisions from the Twentieth Corps had preceded them. Colonel

Timothy Stanley's brigade, including the Eleventh Michigan, would make the crossing over a ribbon-like bridge made of pontoons. Besides the Eleventh, Stanley's brigade consisted of the Nineteenth Illinois Infantry and the Eighteenth Ohio Infantry, as well as the First Ohio Light Artillery, Battery M. All good western boys; none of those Pennsylvania fellows or Kentucky troops. Nate felt certain the brigade would show itself well in the fight that was coming. He held doubts only about himself. He wished he were as confident in his ability as the rest of Company D. Since coming to James's aid in that skirmish, he could do little wrong in his comrades' eyes. Sometimes he wondered if they saw him or Ryan.

Nate pointed toward Sand Mountain. "How the devil we goin' to get over that? What about the wagons and such?"

Corporal May answered, "They're going up to Bridgeport. I heard the First Michigan Engineers built a trestle bridge there. Rebs done wrecked the other one."

Nate considered May in the night, figured the corporal, unlike him, welcomed the darkness. Since the battle of Stones River last December, May suffered from some sort of eye disease that caused him to be sensitive to light. Though the former cooper never complained about the ailment, he went about the daylight hours in a constant squint. "Sober, honest, and brave," Lane had once described David May, and Nate had yet to witness otherwise.

To Nate's left, James sat against a poplar, musket across his lap as if expecting the enemy at any moment. *He looks as wide awake as me.* Nate wondered if James's wound from the skirmish with the Rebel cavalry last month still pained him. The shopkeeper had said little about it; in fact, James said little about anything since then…to anyone.

"Our corps is so spread out," Nate said. "What if the Johnnies hit us now?"

Hart stretched out on the ground, rubbed his right hip, then put his slouch hat over his eyes, sighing. "Ol' Rosey's got the Rebs fooled, from what I hear tell. Our cavalry is up north of here, above Chattanooga, scaring the hell outta the Johnnies with a diversion. Them and Crittenden's Twenty-first Corps. Making a show to fool Bragg about where the rest of us are crossing."

With his endless enthusiasm, Jeremy said, "When them Rebs see us a-comin', they'll run like rabbits."

"Don't bet on it," Hart murmured sleepily. "There's a lot of fighting coming, boys. Might make Stones River look like a skirmish."

Nate's eyes widened. "You reckon so, Sarge?"

"I can feel it. Now, you best get some sleep. We'll have hard marching through them mountains once we cross over." His voice trailed away into snores.

Nate could not imagine sleeping right now. No doubt Hart was correct about the fight to come; after all, the Rebs certainly would not let them just walk into Chattanooga.

He looked around at the men of the Eleventh, gathered in dark clumps—no fires—talking low, no music or laughter. He caught sight of Colonel Stoughton near the riverbank with other officers. Stoughton's small, soldierly form there in the night gave him confidence. At least they would be led into battle by a competent commander, for had he not heard only praise for Stoughton in all things, including his conduct at Stones River? Since Nate had joined the regiment, Stoughton had often spoken to him, even praising him for his part in the skirmish last month. Something in Stoughton's dignified bearing always reminded him of his father.

Even when the moon rose, the silver-blue light barely lit the region. Finally, the Eleventh filed out upon the pontoon bridge. Nate paid close attention to his feet, feeling the gentle give and sway beneath him. Next to him, James did the same, but now and then his gaze rose to the ominous bluffs ahead. He wondered if James was afraid, if his confidence had been so shaken by the skirmish last month that he might shirk his duties. But something told Nate that the brush with the Rebs had strengthened James's resolve to prove himself, considering the veil of doubt Langdon had cast afterwards. The sergeant maintained that he had directed James to withdraw at the same time as the others, though James vehemently insisted that Langdon had ordered him to remain behind. Although he had not admitted it to anyone else, Nate—unlike the others in Company D—believed James's version of the events more than Langdon's. And if his messmate's claim was true, then James had been braver than all of them. Nate wondered how he would have behaved in such a situation, especially knowing Langdon's ulterior motives.

To his exasperation, the brigade halted on the east bank. Being on the enemy's side of the river with the wide water at their backs heightened Nate's uneasiness. But he tried to emulate the relaxed demeanor of the veterans around him, listening to their hushed voices, a stray chuckle here or there, the voice of nineteen-year-old Lieutenant Borden Hicks of Company E—Bird, as some called him—cracking wise as usual and drawing muffled laughter from his men.

Nate grinned to himself when he recalled Hicks's tale of when he had been promoted to second lieutenant, how he had donned the largest pair of shoulder straps he could find and then acquired a horse for his lofty station, only to be teased by some cavalrymen when he rode through their camp with his pant legs riding up. "Pull down your pants, Lieutenant!" the troopers had called out. "Pull down your pants!" Hicks had concluded his story by saying, "Since then, whenever I have the occasion to ride a horse, I prefer to remain afoot."

When orders finally came for the brigade to fall in, the regiments struck out upon a small road that seemed to shrink in the darkness. The moonlight struggled to reach through the scrubby cedars and pines. Men who tripped over loose rocks on the crude lane sent up what seemed like a deafening racket, often accompanied by curses and oaths. Nate tried to balance his loaded knapsack and musket as they continually shifted and rubbed during his effort to remain upright and not smash into anyone else.

Mercifully, the order drifted back for the Eleventh to halt, and heavy sighs and moans overrode the chorus of night insects.

"Hey, Sarge," Abner called in a hoarse voice. "How 'bout we boil us some coffee? Might peel back my eyelids some."

Langdon grumbled, "You'll wait for orders."

Quietly, so only James could hear, Nate said, "Can't be Rebs holdin' us up; don't hear no guns."

James shook his head, his breathing labored, and studied the scrubby undergrowth, peered back down the mountain road beyond the dark, snaking column.

Eventually orders sifted through Stanley's brigade, passed from regiment to regiment: "By the right of companies to the rear into column."

Abner muttered, "What now?"

"In place, rest!"

"How 'bout that coffee now, Sarge?" Jeremy said.

"In place, Dell," Langdon echoed Lane's order.

"I reckon someone got us lost," Elias murmured as he found space to gingerly lie down.

The speed with which the men fell asleep amazed Nate, and he envied them for their ability to adapt and take advantage of the halt. He struggled to find a tolerable space on the ground among his comrades. Using his knapsack as a pillow, he lay with his eyes open and tried to occupy his thoughts with Katie but found it difficult to think of anything except the Confederates.

He glanced at James only a couple of feet away and found his eyes just as round as his as he scanned the ghostly trees. When their gazes met, Nate quickly looked away and closed his eyes, pretended to fall asleep, but he figured he did not fool James any more than he fooled himself.

Somehow he slept for a couple of hours, but before first light, the division was on the move. Nate started stiff, sore, and chilled, but soon the rugged march loosened his muscles and stirred perspiration. Their route easily kept him alert, for in some places its width narrowed to a harrowing degree. On the right hand, the rocky bluffs of Sand Mountain rose straight up for hundreds of feet, crowded them toward the bank, which in turn plunged a hundred feet to the Tennessee River. The first hint of daylight reflected upon the waterway that stretched in a silvery ribbon for miles. Morning birdsong echoed up from the valley, portraying a false peacefulness to the world.

Jeremy said, "Don't reckon they coulda found a worst road if'n they tried."

Abner added, "Hain't enough room for a hog."

The day was filled with starts and stops, frustrating the men. Once the sun had cleared Sand Mountain, it increased their misery and baked them in their toil until it finally sank beyond the Cumberlands. Through the twilight, a faint sonata of hammering drifted up from the river, and torchlight flared above the water like fireflies.

"Hey, Sarge," Nate called up the column to Langdon. "Looky yonder. Is that the bridge our corps wagons are to cross?"

"Must be."

"Don't look like nothing's been crossing," said John Coe, a Branch County man in the next file.

True enough, no wagon train or columns of Union troops marched over the bridge, partially constructed with pontoons and the rest by trestle. In fact, part of the trestle appeared to have collapsed, and black dots of distant engineers scurried in a frantic race to repair the damage. The work appeared close to completion, and wagons could be seen on the west bank, in and around the town of Bridgeport, backed up in a snarl of delay along with an entire division of troops.

"That must be Baird's boys," May said through the dust caked on his weary face. "I heard they were supposed to cross at Bridgeport."

"Don't look like our wagons will be gettin' to us anytime soon," Elias added.

The brigade's route changed from northeast to south, and the real work lay before them, for now they faced the rugged ascent of Raccoon Mountain, which lay off the northern tip of Sand Mountain. Nate's whole body ached from the long, hot day. He was blistered and beat, unprepared for a daunting climb. The air chilled with the setting of the sun, but even that relief failed to rekindle his stamina.

When orders sifted down to halt for the night, he whispered a prayer of thanks and trailed off the path with his squad where he collapsed. No amount of farm work had prepared him for this kind of toil. Glancing at James's pinched face, he realized his fellow Burr Oaker was even worse off than he, yet James uttered no complaint.

"Water," came the word of discovery, trickling through the weary ranks, drawing thankful responses. Canteens were handed over to water details that soon returned with the most delicious, satisfying cool spring water Nate had ever tasted.

Cook fires blossomed among Company D and eased away some of the fatigue with the heavenly scent of coffee. Once warm food and drink flowed into the men, murmuring voices filled the scrubby trees, and the day's labor fell away.

Major Bennet wound his way among the men of the Eleventh until he came to his old company where the men warmly greeted him. Nate offered up his cup of coffee as Bennet settled next to him with a grunt.

After Bennet handed the tin cup back, he stroked his beard thoughtfully and listened to the men's questions about the march. "We can't go much farther," Bennet said, "not without our wagons. But once they cross that river, we're going to have a job of work ahead of us, lads, to get them over this mountain. So, try to get some sleep tonight." He smiled at Nate, the firelight turning his blue eyes to a dark bronze. "Don't stay up late writing letters to your sweethearts." He chuckled.

Nate was glad the darkness hid the color that rose to his cheeks. The thought of Katie so far away stirred homesickness, but then he looked around the fire at the relaxed, affable faces of his company and realized that these men were now his family. The shared toil of the past days had bonded him to them the same way working the fields back home had strengthened the connection with his brothers and their father. Bennet and Stoughton were now parent figures, and this thought comforted him. The two officers had proven equal to the reputation Ryan's letters had bestowed upon them. And both their brigade commander and division commander had reputations of similar quality. It did not surprise Nate to hear that they would not advance without their wagon train. After all, James Negley, nicknamed "Commissary General" Negley, always made sure his men did not suffer from want of provisions, a trait that, along with his genial personality, had endeared him to his troops.

Once Bennet left them, Nate took his advice and unrolled his blanket, as did his comrades. Soon conversation faded away and all he heard before drifting off was the gentle language of the dying fire.

***

True to Bennet's prediction, the next day the Eleventh worked until four in the afternoon to assist the division wagon train up the treacherous mountain roads. Even General Negley and his staff took their places among the laboring men. Nate had never heard so much cursing in his life as the men forced the mules upward with shouts and whips and kicks. Often the animals simply planted their feet and refused to move, regardless of the abuse or perhaps in protest of it. At first Nate felt sorry for the creatures, but by the afternoon, even he was tired of their antics. Sweat poured from man and beast, white lather smeared beneath harnesses, perspiration darkening the mules' coats and causing the men to strip off their sack coats. Ahead of them rang the sound of axes and shovels as other regiments worked to make the way passable. Teams were doubled on the division's artillery to haul the great guns upward, the pushing and pulling men living in fear that one of the cannon might break free and tumble downward to smash whatever lay in its path.

By the time the regiment was able to leave the task to others and continue up the steep, rocky slopes, Nate was exhausted. Next to him all the way, James said little, often rubbing his left arm where one of the mules had nipped him. The difficult work had taken an even greater toll on the formerly-sedentary young man—he stumbled often in the thick dust and on the rocks; he limped and coughed. The unrelenting heat affected all of them. Jeremy, as sturdy as anyone, passed out during the climb, as did several others. Some simply sat down, unable to take another step, uncaring as the regiment continued without them.

After six more laborious miles, they reached the summit. The land flattened to a plateau many miles across, populated by scrubby oaks and pines but few humans. Huge limestone boulders hunched in a haphazard pattern, the ground sandy and uninviting. The brigade halted for the night, and the men collapsed without thought to anything but rest and water. However, their hopes of drink went nearly unanswered, for the scant water found proved brackish.

Soon night closed in, the moon rising bright in the star-filled sky. For as far as Nate could see, campfires danced as the men of Negley's division bedded down. Some had gone foraging and now returned with little to show for their efforts. First Sergeant Hart made his way from company to company, passing the word that in the morning the Eleventh would be the vanguard of the whole Fourteenth Corps.

"Good," Abner muttered. "Then them mules will be far behind us."

"You sure you won't miss them, Dell?" Langdon sardonically asked. "I'm sure I could get you on a detail with the train, if you want."

"You do that, Sarge, and you'll find yourself short a man come rollcall," Abner said.

Langdon's grin drifted away into the shadows. "Any man deserts this company, I'll hunt him down myself and shoot him."

Nate exchanged a glance with James and knew Langdon's threat was not an idle one.

***

"Darned Rebs." Elias Cooper took a long, thoughtful pull on his pipe. "They oughta know we're gonna get acrost somehow; might just as well have left the bridge in one piece."

James looked with disgust over the dry gulch that barred the Eleventh's progress. What remained of a bridge—only scraps of wood—lay scattered at the bottom of the formidable gulf. Morning sunlight cast half of the scar-like trench into shadow. Colonel Stoughton stood near the edge, surrounded by the regiment's officers, conferring. The Eleventh had a diverse population, and James had no doubt that Stoughton would soon call for such men whose talents in their former lives lent themselves to bridge building.

The regiment had been marching since first light and had already covered four miles but had yet to traverse even half of the mountain's plateau. James was relieved that the previous day's climb lay behind them and the ground was now relatively flat, but he could just as easily look a short distance to the east, beyond the next valley, and see yet another daunting blue-green mountain, veiled in morning haze. Perhaps that was their next obstacle. But where in all of this lay the Rebel army? Were the Rebs still indeed in Chattanooga? Someone had destroyed this bridge, and he doubted the scarce local populace was responsible. Surely the bridge's absence inconvenienced them as much as it hampered the invading Federal army.

Soon orders came to stack muskets, and as the morning turned into afternoon, the Eleventh labored to resurrect the bridge. They utilized a deserted mill partway down the slope as the center bent. The regiment's makeshift engineers placed heavy stringers from the banks on either side to the building's plates and used the mill's sheeting and roofing to cover the roadway. The men worked with a will, for no one wanted the rest of the division to catch up to them and find that the regiment's lack of ingenuity had stalled the corps's advance. And constructing a bridge was certainly more rewarding than fighting with mules and teamsters. Although James had little more skill than the ability to swing a hammer, he still found satisfaction in his contribution. The men's spirits had recovered from the climb up the mountain, and all worked in concerted union until they finished the task around two in the afternoon, their alacrity stirring James's pride not only in himself but in all those around him. Accustomed to working alone, he discovered surprising pleasure in toiling with so many others on a common goal.

Once finished, the men tramped over the bridge in high spirits and continued the march across the mountain with fresh speed and energy. Upon reaching the eastern slope, the regiment paused to gather its collective breath before the plunge downward. James considered the narrow valley before them as he guzzled the last of his canteen's water. The looming bulk of Lookout Mountain seemed insurmountable, but he figured soon they would be clawing their way across it regardless. The valley below looked more promising—a green trough where trees were thick and protective, occasionally opening where a farmer scraped out an existence between the beauty of the protective ranges.

"I reckon we're officially in Georgia now, boys," Langdon announced. "Other side of that next mountain and we can turn the Rebs' left flank."

Jeremy moaned. "We have to climb *another* mountain? We ain't no goats, Sarge."

"I heard there's supposed to be a gap," May said.

Abner added, "Rebs probably ruined that, too, like the bridge. Then we can *dig* our way through. Hain't done that."

Yet, James thought.

The descent of the eastern slope was far easier than the ascent of the previous, and by four in the afternoon, the Eleventh reached the floor of the valley where orders came to make camp. Nearby flowed a blessedly pure spring whose waters washed away James's fatigue as well as his thirst. Word passed through the ranks that they would remain there until the rest of Negley's division caught up.

Captain Lane had somehow acquired a copy of the Chattanooga *Daily Rebel*, and he in turn passed it along to James. After dinner, James settled outside his tent to read. The sun had already ducked

53

below the summit of Sand Mountain, throwing Lookout Valley into gray darkness, and soon would plunge the encampment into total night, so he stuck the blade of his bayonet into the ground and placed a lit candle in the socket.

Next to him, sharing the light, Nate stretched on the ground, using his pack as a desk on which to scribble a letter, as he did most every day. James could not see the words, did not try hard to do so. Unlike James, who had finished school at his mother's insistence, Nate had enough formal schooling to write only passably and to read with considerable difficulty. James had once teased him about his poor penmanship, and Nate had snapped back that he had more important things to learn when growing up than the alphabet and how to add numbers.

"What good did all that book learnin' do you when we was fightin' them Rebs last month?" Nate had challenged him.

That had been enough to cow James. He had given up trying to convince anyone of the truth of that skirmish and the part he had played. But comments such as Nate's were always wielded like weapons whenever someone felt the need to put him in his place.

Now his gaze left the newspaper and touched upon Nate's letter. His isolation was never so great as when the Eleventh received mail from home. There were always several letters and bundles for Nate, as well as for most of Company D. Always James stood like a forgotten stranger among the happy, eager recipients. He felt even worse when Nate read his letters aloud, except for some from Katie, to their messmates. The others read theirs as well, the news from Burr Oak comforting in its sameness and simplicity.

James had received only one piece of mail since leaving home, and that was from Heather Cabot several weeks ago. The note had been short and stiff; probably just a perfunctory gesture to fulfill her promise to write him. She revealed much when she wrote how corresponding with a soldier reminded her too painfully of her dead husband. Often when he was alone, he reread the letter until the paper frayed, not so much because of his feelings for her—of those he was uncertain—but because he felt linked to his past that way. At least running the mercantile had given him a place of importance among the Burr Oakers. Here, he was less than a soldier in their eyes; here, there was no power of money or position.

Nate looked up from his letter with sudden interest and said, "'Tis a mortal sin to kill someone, but if you kill someone durin' a war, is it still a sin?"

"How should I know? Ask your mother. She's the Catholic, not me."

"She's not here, plain enough, so I'm askin' you."

"How the hell would I know?"

"I'm just askin'. You sure are ornery tonight."

James returned his attention to the newspaper, snapped the page to emphasize his superiority in the reading business. "If killing during a war is a sin, then hell ought to be overflowing by now. There won't be any room for the likes of us."

"I hope not." Nate paused. "You don't go to church, do you, James?"

"Not anymore."

"Don't you have a hankerin' to go...now, I mean? Bein' a soldier and fighting—"

"If I started going just because of fighting, I'd be a hypocrite, wouldn't I? So why bother?"

"Well...what about repentance? You know, the penitent man—"

"Save your Bible-thumping for someone else, Calhoun. Go talk to Langdon."

Nate sat up. "What's wrong with you? Ever since I saved your skin—"

"You didn't *save* anyone. I would've gotten out of that scrap just fine. I took care of the other Rebs that day, didn't I?"

"I don't know. Did you?"

"You would've seen for yourself if you hadn't skedaddled out of there like a rabbit."

"I was obeyin' orders."

"Yeah? Then what about later? Maybe you didn't come back on your own like a big hero. Maybe you were just obeying orders then, too."

"Well, right now I wish I hadn't gone back. Then you would've got what you deserve."

With that, Nate gathered up his pencil and paper and stalked off in the direction of Elias's tent.

CHAPTER 6

The crown of the rising sun touched the crest of Pigeon Mountain and bathed the eight-mile expanse of McLemore's Cove in pink light. The cove—yet another narrow valley for Negley's division to cross—spread before James, wild and little touched by man. The division's current position lay at the foot of Stevens's Gap, a rugged slash that had allowed passage over Lookout Mountain two days ago, a passage made troublesome not only by the trees felled by the Confederates but by their infantry as well.

Late yesterday afternoon, General Negley had ordered Stanley's brigade forward into the cove on a reconnaissance mission that resulted in a brief skirmish with Rebel cavalry and the capture of a couple of prisoners. Then Stanley's regiments had withdrawn to the gap to protect the division trains. Everyone had gone to sleep that night with misgivings, for no one knew the position of the rest of the Federal army, and the truth of the matter could be that Negley's division was entirely isolated. Rumors flowed, perhaps originating with prisoners, rumors of a large force of Rebels just across the cove at Pigeon Mountain, a force that could easily swallow up Negley's men if they were not reinforced.

By eight o'clock, the entire division was on the move, and James hoped this meant support was not far behind them. Colonel William Sirwell's brigade—regiments from Ohio, Pennsylvania, and Indiana—led the way down the narrow, cedar-fringed road that trailed away toward Pigeon Mountain and Dug Gap, where it was rumored more obstacles and Confederate troops awaited. No Rebel cavalry disputed their path. In fact, the entire cove lay in serene repose, the sun a burning orange globe that already cooked the men tramping in their woolen uniforms, uniforms almost gray with days' worth of dust. The spicy scent of cedars and pines drew a smile from James as he marched, listening to birdsong and the voices of his company, by now a familiar, soothing sound. It seemed a lifetime ago that they had left Tennessee.

A shout went up from the rear of column and traveled toward the Eleventh.

Captain Lane peered behind them for a long moment before a smile broke across his face. "General Negley's coming, boys. Step smartly now."

James turned at the clatter of hooves to see Negley, a handsome bear of a man, cantering up the column with his staff. The dark blue Second Division flag, with its two black stars, fanned out and snapped in their wake. The breeze stirred the Pennsylvania general's beard, and sunlight danced in his smiling eyes as he doffed his hat to the Eleventh. The men cheered him heartily.

Negley, a wildflower in his lapel, boomed, "Good morning, Michigan men!"

"A damned fine morning, sir!"

"We scare off them Johnnies, sir?"

"Find us some Rebs, General!"

James smiled broadly to himself as he watched the group of men gallop up the marching column. Dust swirled after them, but no one complained of its choking effects. Things must be safe if the division commander was going to ride with the vanguard.

Partway across the cove, the Eleventh forded a small, winding creek, and James thought of the Prairie River, thought of his father sitting alone on its banks. He wondered what his father was doing right now. Was he tending the store? Or did the mercantile sit, neglected? Perhaps he should write to him, even if no reply ever came.

"Chickamauga Creek, boys," Hart announced. "That's a Cherokee word."

Nate asked, "What's it mean, Sarge?"

"River of death," he replied matter-of-factly.

Nate exchanged an uncertain glance with James. "How you know that?"

"Some civilian told the Captain."

"Some Reb, sure," Jeremy added skeptically. "It'll be a 'river of death' all right…for the Johnnies. This here division ain't to be trifled with. Right, boys?"

Gunfire from the head of the column interrupted their collective agreement, startling them.

"Holy God," someone said.

"Hope the Rebs didn't shoot Negley," Elias said.

What a target Negley would make, James considered. Big man on a big horse.

"Mebbe it's just some of that cavalry from yesterday," Nate offered hopefully.

"Must be more than that," May said as officers shouted orders to deploy the brigade into line of battle.

The Eleventh completed the maneuver with practiced ease, and James found himself in the front rank of the double line as they advanced through the broken landscape. Ahead, skirmish fire continued to pop in the clear morning air. They passed through a tall, ripe cornfield which threatened their cohesion, but the lines were quickly dressed on the opposite side. The land opened upon a crossroads where one small house sat. Ahead, the Seventy-eighth Pennsylvania climbed a knob, gunfire and puffs of powder smoke punctuating their drive against the Rebels, who fell back before them. Apparently, the hill's vantage point allowed a fresh, unsettling view of what forces lay before them, for soon Sirwell's brigade withdrew. Then the entire division fell back to the woods near the house, west of a north-south road.

James hunkered down with his comrades to await further orders. He heard little of the speculation around him, instead tuned to the hidden skirmishing ahead in the tangle of woods and rocky knolls. His skin felt clammy, and he hoped no one noticed his unease. He wondered again of the whereabouts of the rest of the army.

From the left flank, excited calls arose. Men got to their feet. Words tumbled his way along the line.

"Pap Thomas is here!"

"He'll know what to do."

"Good ol' Pap. Figures he knew we was in trouble."

Down the road in a tornado of dust came Major General George Thomas, commander of the Fourteenth Corps, and his staff. This was James's first close look at Thomas, and he eagerly edged toward the road with his comrades, felt his confidence rise with this man's appearance. Pap, as the boys called him, trotted past, a large man, built wide and impressive, like a small mountain. His low brow and piercing eyes made him appear irascible when, in truth, James had heard Thomas was good-natured and unexcitable, a professional soldier who had not forsaken his country for his rebellious home state of Virginia. Thomas said little as he rode, head up, gazing toward Dug Gap, concern on his broad, bearded face. He raised an acknowledging hand and smiled at the men who called out to him, continuing toward the house where Negley and his staff awaited.

James's anxiety eased. Seeing Thomas assured him that the

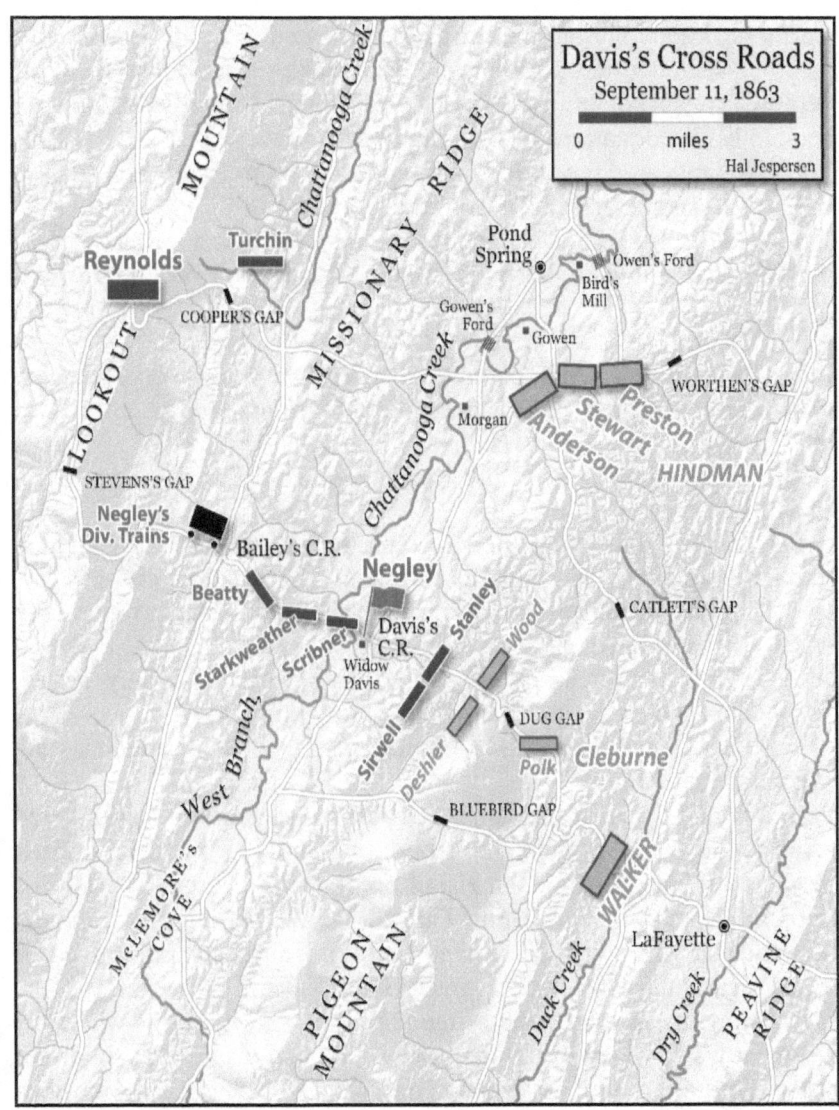

Davis's Cross Roads
September 11, 1863

0 miles 3

Hal Jespersen

division would not be trapped here in McLemore's Cove and forgotten by the rest of the army.

The brigade deployed forward, close to the foot of Pigeon Mountain, astride the road leading from the crossroads to Dug Gap, while Sirwell's brigade was positioned on their right flank. As darkness drew over them like a frayed blanket, the skirmishing along their front died off. The jovial mood that had been present that morning had been replaced by a quiet one. James sensed no dread from his comrades, just wariness as they lay on their arms, not allowed to build fires. Earlier they had seen couriers gallop away from Negley's headquarters at the Widow Davis's house near the crossroads, then Thomas had ridden off, back to his headquarters, or so rumors reported.

May appeared out of the night and sat next to Elias, who handed him a canteen and asked, "What's the word, Davy?"

"Well, from what I can gather we're in for a scrap. Rebs cleared out Dug Gap and came through. That's Cleburne's division ahead of us."

This drew several moans.

"That ain't all," May continued. "Hindman's division is out there somewhere. And maybe Buckner. We're outnumbered about four to one, I wager."

"Can't be no Rebs left in Chattanooga if they're all down here," Elias said.

"Hear tell Baird's division is coming up to support us," Langdon said from somewhere in the near darkness. "A forced march."

"They'll be exhausted by the time they get here," Abner said. "And we'll still have only two divisions."

"And the other corps are God knows where," Jeremy added. "Rosecrans should not to have split the army up so."

"Didn't have much of a choice, as I see it," Langdon said. "Damned mountains."

With the dying of the sun, a deep chill set in, and James shivered beneath his blanket where he sat, staring into the night, the black obstacle of Pigeon Mountain rising before him, mirrored by that of Lookout Mountain behind him. This all had the feeling of a trap, and he hoped morning would see them either significantly reinforced or withdrawn to the safety of Stevens's Gap.

James guessed it to be around three in the morning when the regiment was ordered to fall in. Skirmishing had resumed to the front, somewhere in the thick woods, occasional flashes from muzzles punctuating the gloom. Colonel Stoughton moved down the line, speaking quietly to his officers, then he led the regiment to the right of the whole line which wheeled left to face Hindman's threat from the north. The Union forces bent in a southerly angle to keep Cleburne from swinging behind and cutting them off from Stevens's Gap and the rest of the Army of the Cumberland. When the Eleventh halted and dug in, the black emptiness on their right flank unnerved James.

"Someone must have confidence in this outfit," he observed to Nate as they scratched out a protective hole in the cool earth. "We're the end of the line."

"Or," Nate answered with a tired grin heard more than seen, "someone don't like us."

Fatigue finally began to slow James's movements and thoughts. When he settled into their hole, Nate sat close, wide awake, gun across his lap, alert to any possible breath of movement in the forest to their front. Satisfied with Nate's vigilance, James drifted to sleep.

***

"Wake up, James. Wake up." Nate's voice sounded from far away, insistent, nagging. James refused to respond, for he dreamt of home, of a warm bed, of merchandise neatly lining store shelves. His father was there behind the counter...

"Come *on*, James." Shaking now accompanied the words. "Langdon will kick you into tomorrow if you don't get up. We're shiftin' again."

Slowly James's head cleared, and he opened his eyes to the dim forest, to the dark blue of uniforms all around, everyone stirring. The angry pop of muskets from the unseen skirmish line jarred him clear of all lingering fatigue. Through the trees, morning sunlight flashed over Pigeon Mountain, streaking the sky orange and blue.

"Cap'n says the Johnnies are tryin' to turn the flank and get behind us," Nate explained. "Have to stop 'em."

The men of the Eleventh struggled through the undergrowth, redeploying even farther to the right and now to the rear as well. The broken, hilly ground isolated them among the pines and cedars. James could see nothing but wilderness. The crash of more concerted musketry erupted all the way down the division's line. James and the others rushed to throw up breastworks of logs and brush. On either flank of the regiment, sections of artillery were manhandled into place, a most welcomed sight. Then James and his comrades crouched behind their cover, muskets at the ready, eyes peering into the receding shadows, searching for any telltale movement.

But no attack came. Occasionally James saw movement to their front but nothing more than fleeting figures, men firing from behind trees, probing to find any weakness in the line. Out of sheer frustration, he and a few others fired their weapons at some of these darting shadows, but they had no hope of hitting anything other than an innocent tree. Rumors floating along the regimental line brought news of the arrival of Starkweather's and Scribner's brigades from General

Baird's division, though no one here in this deserted place saw any reinforcements. News that Pap Thomas had returned to the field buoyed the men.

"I don't get it," James said testily in the breathless, smothering afternoon. "Why don't they come? Get on with it."

Nate grinned. "Reckon the Rebs know who they're facin'."

"Or else," Elias said, "they *don't* know. Maybe they fancy there's more of us than there is. They probably figure no one division would be fool enough to blunder this far without—"

"Look!" Jeremy rose, only to be yanked down by his brother as a bullet whirred past and struck a pine.

"You damned fool!" Abner said.

"But it's General Negley!" Jeremy persisted. "Him and his staff."

James followed his pointing finger through the trees to see the large man dismount behind the line and return Colonel Stoughton's salute. For some time, the officers parleyed. Stoughton, expression grave, swept his hand over the regiment's position, but at this distance James could not hear his words. Negley listened intently, his eyes drifting over the vigilant men of the Eleventh, touching upon the cannon closest to him, then sweeping over the surrounding ground.

Lieutenant Stephen Marsh of Company A approached the officers, saluting. After listening to the junior officer from Leonidas, Negley nodded and followed Marsh to a small rise, Stoughton at his side, Negley's staff following. There, Marsh sized up the trees then, removing his hat, he began to climb the tallest of them.

Jeremy cried, "What the hell is he doin'?"

"Tryin' to get shot," Abner answered, though admiration rang in his words. "Sharpshooters will pick him off, sure."

May watched with a small, proud smile. "He's trying to get a good look at this God-awful country. No one can see what anyone's doing."

Marsh drew the attention of nearly everyone in the regiment as he climbed ever higher. Sharpshooters tried to cut him down like a squirrel, twigs and leaves sprinkling to earth when bullets came close to their target. Marsh, unperturbed, clawed his way up until he reached a vantage point. From there he scoured the horizon, shading his eyes from the sun while everyone below held his breath, waiting for a bullet to find Marsh.

"Sir!" he called down to Negley. "There appears to be a large force on the left flank! Looks like they'll try to turn us and get in the rear!"

As Marsh descended, the sharpshooters continued their frustrated fire, answered now by some of the regiment to discourage them. Yet

62

soon Marsh stood safely before his superiors, shaking Negley's hand, grins all around. James shook his head in admiration and disbelief.

A moment later one of Negley's aides galloped off to the north.

Once Negley rode away, along with his staff, Officer's Call drew company commanders to Stoughton's side. James turned his attention back to the forest and reloaded.

Soon Captain Lane returned to the company, moving along the line, crouched, explaining, "Hold tight, lads. We need to give the rest of the division time to reform to the rear. We just have to hold a while longer, then it'll be our turn."

As Sirwell's brigade pulled out of position to the left of the Eleventh, Stoughton led his men through the woods at the double quick to rejoin the rest of Stanley's brigade. The Rebels' firing increased, but the regiment's redeployment seemed to take them by surprise and left them shooting at very little. James heard the shouts of Confederate officers off in the timber, urging their men on in the chase.

At last word came for Stanley's brigade to withdraw, none too soon for James, who could see the Rebels plainly through the trees now, ragged lines, brilliant flashes from muzzles. Bullets struck the trees around him with a variety of unsettling sounds. At the quick step, the brigade retreated from the forest, back across the lane in front of the Widow Davis's house, back across Chickamauga Creek. James considered refilling his canteen to quench his raging thirst, but instead he scrambled to keep up with his squad as the line swept across an open field. Beyond the field, a low north-south ridge rose. It was atop that ridge that the line halted behind a fence, the men quickly dismantling the rails to use as breastworks, everyone shouting and rushing to secure the position.

The Eleventh was on the right of the line, the Nineteenth Illinois on the left, the Eighteenth Ohio in reserve. One company of the Nineteenth trailed over to a barn on the right flank while another company from the Zouave regiment found excellent cover behind a stone wall on the left flank. A battery of the Fourth Indiana from Starkweather's brigade stationed guns on both flanks and behind the Eleventh. Forty rods in front of the right wing stood a large cornfield, tall and concealing. About the same distance off the left was a stand of woods and the stone wall. Behind Stanley's brigade and to the left, Beatty's brigade occupied an even higher ridge. James felt confident here, no longer buried in the blinding woods but now with a clear field of fire between them and the creek.

"Everybody down, boys," Captain Lane shouted, pistol in hand.

"Hold your fire until you hear the order. Remember to aim low."

James's breath caught as Confederate skirmishers appeared on the far bank of the creek, gray shadows below the skirting trees. They crossed over to the near bank and paused there, some of them firing toward Stanley's line, puffs of smoke marking their positions. Blood rushed like a river in James's ears, and the voices around him receded to a foggy distance.

High-pitched howls raised the hair on the back of his neck and sent a sharp chill down his spine. The roll of hooves drew everyone's attention to the left front where Rebel cavalry poured through the trees toward the creek like demons, their eerie keening freezing James, terrifying him, urging him to run.

"Looky there!" Jeremy gestured toward the thirty-odd gray horsemen. "They're after those two boys!"

Two Union infantrymen, apparently left behind during the withdrawal, raced toward the shallow water and charged into it, unmindful of the surprised Rebel skirmishers down to their left. Water flew high, one stumbling face first. A well-timed volley from the Illinois troops behind the stone wall knocked nearly every Rebel from the saddle. Riderless horses wheeled away from the water and charged back toward the trees.

Nate's excited voice drew James's amazed attention away from the creek. "Here they come! Through the corn! See their guns?"

Sunlight glinted on the musket barrels approaching in line through the cornfield, the men momentarily hidden, giving the rifles a disembodied effect. Someone shouted a warning, and another long Confederate line emerged from the woods beyond the creek and pressed forward into the field, flags waving in the breeze, hundreds of throats giving voice to that terrible battle cry. Along the Eleventh's line, officers ordered their men ready, and James slid the barrel of his musket along the top of the breastwork, took, aim, hands trembling, mouth cottony dry.

"Fire!"

The whole line erupted in a deafening crash of musketry, producing a wall of powder smoke. The Confederate line staggered, men fell, the Rebel yell stopped.

James flinched with the concussion from the Indiana artillery, the ground shaking. His ears seemed muffled, his senses dazed. Never had he experienced field pieces going off so close. Shocked by the noise, he could not move. He stared at the carnage wrought upon the Rebel lines, great gaps torn in the formation. The survivors dropped to their bellies, returned fire.

On the right, canister fire shredded the corn and among it the advancing Rebels. Men crumpled, dropped their weapons, others disappeared in a cloud of bloody gore. Cornstalks trembled and twitched from musket balls while others lay crushed beneath fallen bodies.

"Keep up your fire, Keenan!" Langdon cuffed him on the side of the head as he moved along the company line, bringing James back to his senses.

He lost track of time as the Rebels kept trying to advance and the brigade stubbornly held off the superior numbers. Smoke enveloped everyone, rolled across the open ground between the lines, masked the creek. The men of the Eleventh hung grimly to the task. James's fear had died away, replaced by determination to keep the attackers at bay. He was aware of little except the methodical loading and discharge of his weapon. Vaguely he heard Nate now and then, great agitation in his voice, his brogue more pronounced, nearly as thick as his father's. His blue eyes blazed bright and wide amidst the black powder smeared on his face from tearing cartridges open with his teeth. James tasted the same upon his own lips.

Confederate cannon appeared in the bloody cornfield, brought forward by stalwart hands. Behind those, fresh infantry pressed in great lines of gray and butternut. The Fourth Indiana shelled them with terrible effect, but the lines advanced, steady, undaunted, until they stalled within twenty rods of the Union right flank. There the Rebels lay or crouched, firing away at the defenders as their cannon fired over top of them.

Instinctively James ducked, felt a push of displaced air followed by a horrible cry. Sergeant Lovette of Company A writhed upon the ground only a couple of rods away, both legs torn off above the knees. James stared at the mangled bone and flesh as Lovette's comrades bore him away to the rear.

Nate tugged his arm. "What's wrong? Are ye hit?"

James fought to keep from vomiting.

"James!" Nate punched his shoulder.

A wave of anger swept over James, outrage over the loss of Lovette. There were others, too, he realized, being carried to the rear, wounded, others remaining in line with minor injuries, crimson gashes upon arms or heads. With fresh resolve, he turned back to the enemy, reloaded, fired.

The Eighteenth Ohio rushed forward from their reserve position, the small regiment taking position in support of the artillery on the right flank. Their appearance momentarily halted the Confederate advance from the cornfield, but the Rebel cannon raked the Ohioans. Through the smoke, James could see little of the bloody result, but he heard the screams. He kept his focus on the Rebels still pinned in the open field, reloaded time after time.

James could feel the right flank giving way before ever seeing the confusion that gripped the Eighteenth.

Someone cursed and shouted, "Where the hell did the artillery go? They pulled out from the left!"

Glancing that way, James saw the cannon now limbered up and withdrawing. From behind him, he heard Colonel Stoughton hail Captain Waggener of Stanley's staff. "What the devil's going on? Who ordered the artillery to withdraw?"

"I'm not sure, sir."

"Where's Colonel Stanley?"

"He's on the right, sir."

Stoughton put spurs to his horse.

Moments later, through the smoke down to James's right, he heard, "Fall back! Fall back!"

The disintegrating Eighteenth Ohio withdrew first, then the Nineteenth while the Eleventh held on, keeping up a blistering fire. At last Frank Lane's voice found James through the noise and confusion. "Fall back, men! Fall back!"

With the rest of the company, James darted for the rear, but next to him Nate suddenly stopped.

James called, "Come on!"

"Me knapsack!"

"Everyone's left 'em. Come on… Nate! Get back here, damn it!"

"Me Bible's in it!" Nate shouted over his shoulder as he raced toward the abandoned position.

James halted. Lieutenant Hicks and a couple of others also darted back with Nate. Cursing, James followed them. The Rebels in the field now came on with a howling rush as did the Confederates from the cornfield. James raised his musket and fired over Nate's hunched form. Down to one side, the enemy crossed the breastworks and surrounded James Ensign from Company A. *Jesus*!

Back through the smoke Nate ran, a grin on his darkened face, his and James's knapsacks over his shoulder. Together they raced after the Eleventh.

The Confederates gained the ridge as Stanley's brigade moved by the left flank into the road beyond. A deafening volley from Sirwell's and Beatty's brigades from the rear ridge slammed the attackers to a surprised, bloody halt. The Southerners withdrew behind the ridge, no doubt unsure exactly what lay before them now.

Baird's division reinforced Negley's men, but the fighting subsided as night closed in, bringing an unnatural quiet. To James's great relief, the Union forces withdrew to Stevens's Gap.

CHAPTER 7

The lowering first-quarter moon appeared almost white in the frigid night sky. Lying on his back on the cold Georgia ground, Nate stared upward at its mysterious surface, at the distant stars, and thought of home. He shivered in his blanket and folded his arms close against his chest, blew on his stiffening fingers. Even the nearby fire offered little relief. The few soldiers still awake around the circle of light sat mainly in silence. Jeremy and May spoke in drowsy voices, but he did not try to collect their words, his brain too fatigued to put forth the effort.

For the past week, since the fight at Davis's Crossroads, the regiment had had little rest. Even tonight, half of the Eleventh was on picket duty, the other half, including his squad, having just come in from a detail to extinguish girdlings the enemy had lit to reveal the Federals' locations. Their only reprieve had been the day after Davis's Crossroads, but that restful day had been followed by constant vigilance against the probing enemy, hours of picket details, of being called into line of battle, ready to fight at a moment's notice. When General McCook's First Division had relieved Negley, the brigades marched northward ten miles up McLemore's Cove toward Chattanooga, now in Union hands, and went into camp here, near Crawfish Springs. It would seem Rosecrans was trying to concentrate his far-flung army to meet the Confederates who massed to the east of Chickamauga Creek. After Davis's Crossroads, it was apparent that the Rebels were not retreating southward as many had thought; they meant to fight.

Although Nate knew morning was nigh, sleep eluded him. Perhaps his unrest had something to do with the rumors swirling around. Yesterday Union and Confederate forces had collided somewhere to the northeast of here, lost among the tangle of forest. Too far away for Nate and his comrades to know any clear results. Some said the Rebels had driven the Union forces before them; others reported the opposite. Either way, come morning, everyone expected much more than the scrap at Davis's Crossroads.

Giving up, Nate stood, blanket wrapped around him. James lay nearby, silent and unmoving, coiled in his blanket, his back to the fire. Nate thought of those who were gone—the Eleventh had suffered three killed and thirteen wounded at Davis's Crossroads. How many more to come? He shivered and shuffled toward the next fire.

Elias Cooper sat close to the small fire, as wide awake as Nate but for a different reason—he was writing a letter. Not an easy task, Nate knew, for the former miller could read and write no better than he. Concentration dug furrows into Elias's high forehead and tightened his mouth around his dying pipe. Rubbing his rust-colored beard, Elias turned to Nate, who settled next to him.

"How are you, lad?"

Nate nodded. "Tolerable."

Elias produced one of his characteristic smiles, slight but warm, just enough to raise his round cheeks beneath his small, kind eyes.

"Why aren't you asleep?"

Elias grunted. "Soon as I fall asleep, they'll be getting us up anyway, so I thought I'd write a quick letter to my family. Not coming too easy, though."

Nate considered Beatrice Cooper and her three children—a girl and two boys; a fine family. Then memories of his own family seeped in to torture him as his gaze wandered over the field where the brigade's campfires twinkled. How could he ever tell his family about the things he had experienced these past two weeks? No wonder his brothers' letters home had lacked combat details.

"There's a right big fight comin' on the morrow, ain't there, Elias?"

"Reckon so." He pulled contemplatively on the pipe. "Wilder's and Minty's cavalry found lots of Johnnies north of here, they say." He patted Nate's shivering shoulder. "Don't fret, my boy. You'll do fine, just like you did at Davis's Crossroads. You're cut from the same cloth as Ryan. And let me tell you, he was as scared as the rest of us before our first big fight."

"Ryan?"

Elias nodded. "Sure." He almost grinned. "But don't never tell him I told you so."

Rocking backward, Nate wrapped his arms around his drawn-up knees. "Never knew Ryan to be afeared of anything, 'ceptin' Da' maybe." He hesitated. "Everyone thinks I'm like Ryan. I'm not, though. Not really."

"Just the same, makes us feel better to think so."

Nate fell silent, and Elias went back to writing his letter. He remained next to the older man, felt some of the uneasiness ebb. Since joining the Eleventh, Nate often found solace in Elias's presence, just as many others did. And tonight he needed that assurance more than ever.

***

Nate managed about an hour's worth of fitful, shivering sleep before he awoke to the distant crackle of musketry and the throb of cannon to the northeast. Anxiety instantly energized him. He expected to see the regiment falling in to march, but around him all was calm, most of the men still sleeping, only the officers moving about, downing their first cups of coffee. Elias sat up in the frosty morning, ears attuned to the faraway fight, a serious expression on his face but no apprehension. Their eyes met, and Elias gave him a wan smile.

"Well, my boy, sounds like the Army's in for a long day. We'll have the fight we've been expecting, sure." He groaned and stretched. "Best boil some coffee whilst there's time."

By eight o'clock, Stanley's brigade, along with Sirwell's, was on the march, the roar of battle to the northeast unceasing among the endless forests. Each man steeled himself for what was to come, only to find delay when the brigade halted again a short distance from where they had camped. There they remained into the afternoon while anxiously listening to the distant roar of battle and watching smoke and dust billow above the trees.

The thunder of cannon and roll of small arms kept Nate's eyes in the direction of the conflict. Often he got up to walk about, saying little to those veterans who talked easily, trying to while away the painfully slow time.

To Elias, Nate lamented, "I wish we knew what was goin' on up there."

"Don't fret. We'll find out soon enough."

The night's chill had been driven away by an angry sun that pressed suffocating heat down upon the waiting troops. Nate thought he would go mad before orders finally came in late afternoon, calling the men back onto the narrow road where they formed in column of march. No one faltered as he took his place in line. The strain of waiting lifted from them like a heavy curtain. The stalwart, ready faces of his comrades gave Nate new confidence. He exchanged a brief nod with

James next to him.

They marched north about three miles, toward the howl of shells and rattle of muskets from somewhere in the masking forests. Nate tried to hide his growing unease, reminded himself how well they had performed at Davis's Crossroads, tried to glean confidence from the experience.

Beyond a farmhouse, the regiments took a lesser road that peeled off to the northeast, a wooded hill rising on the left. The brigade band struck up "Red, White and Blue," its strains bolstering Nate's steps and easing some of his tension. Judging from the battle sounds, they were now behind the Union right and headed for the center.

"That must be Rosecrans's headquarters," May said, pointing to the farmhouse where the general's flags gently fluttered.

Suddenly animated, Jeremy gestured. "Looky yonder, boys! That's ol' Rosey hisself!"

Each company brought their arms to shoulder in salute as they passed headquarters. Nate craned his neck to see the commander of their army. William Rosecrans was a handsome man with a high forehead and heavy-lidded eyes; his long nose crooked slightly downward at the bridge, reaching to a trim mustache and beard. His appearance was decidedly unmilitary for a man of his importance—black trousers, a white vest, and a plain blue coat. As he returned the Eleventh's salute, he smiled like a proud father. Nate straightened his back, squared his shoulders, and marched as if on parade, thankful for the moment's morale boost.

The regimental colors dipped, and Rosecrans's voice carried over them: "Make it warm for them, Michigan boys."

A cheer erupted from the men.

Rosecrans's blue eyes sparkled as he added, "I know you will."

As they continued down the gentle slope, Nate looked at James, who grinned, the first such happy expression he had seen there all day.

Onward they marched, closer and closer to the fighting, which the thick forest still concealed. Then, on the left, the trees opened upon a deserted tan-yard and a large field. The odor from tanning hides mingled with the drifting waft of powder smoke. Ahead and to the right, Nate spotted Federal troops filtering like shadows from the tree line, straggling, running across the road, confused and without order. A shiver trickled down Nate's spine.

Langdon mused aloud, "What the hell's happened?"

Excitedly Jeremy said, "Johnnies musta broke the line."

All conjecture ended with orders for the brigade to form into line of battle, facing east along the road. Before them, new shadows flowed here and there among the thick undergrowth, moving mainly at a northwesterly angle. These pursuing forms bore the paler shades of gray and butternut yet resembled the broken Union forces in their fragmentation. Nate's breath caught as he hurried to load his weapon.

"Fix…bayonets!" Colonel Stoughton's voice rang out as he steadied his nervous mount behind the regimental line.

The clank of metal on metal chilled Nate as he secured his bayonet to the barrel of his rifle. Could he actually use such a thing on another human being?

"Shoulder…arms!"

Nate's whole body trembled with a strange mixture of fear and excitement. He glanced at James next to him. The young man was pale, hair wet and limp, gaze buried in the trees, face slicked with sweat even though the sun had retreated well into the west, taking the day's heat with it.

"Charge…bayonets!"

A growl went up from the line as the men took a step, guns thrust forward, weak sunlight brightening hundreds of weapons.

"At the quick step…march!"

They moved forward into the jungle-like growth. The gray ghosts wavered several rods away, fired stray shots.

Captain Lane called, "Hold your fire, boys. Wait for the order."

The heady scent of pine and cedar mingled with the drifting waves of blue powder smoke. Pinecones crunched underfoot on the tinder-dry ground. Sudden thirst overwhelmed Nate.

"Keep that line dressed!" Major Bennet ordered from atop his lathered horse, directing with his sword.

Easier said than done, Nate thought as he closed on James to his left. The bushes scratched and plucked at him as he struggled over fallen timber. Still he could not see beyond the trees. Rebel skirmishers fell back before them, slowly, reluctantly.

Finally they reached the other side of the woods to find a rolling field with the ruin of dead and dying men strewn amidst the corn stubble, casualties from both sides. A Confederate line of battle advanced across it, flags flying, a sense of energy and confidence in the Southerners' steps, a result of driving the previous Federal troops away. But now, at the appearance of this fresh wall of blue, they hesitated as if surprised to find new opposition.

The daunting sight momentarily froze Nate, but then came the clarion notes of the bugle, the screams of officers, "Charge!"

With a roar, the blue line leaped forward. A few of the Southerners opened fire, but the effort lacked concentration. The surprised Rebel line shivered then fragmented, men first trickling to the rear, then more fleeing as if afraid they faced more than two brigades.

"They're running, boys!" Stoughton cried, sword waving. "They're running! After them! Push them!"

Nate could barely breathe, but he pressed on up the slight rise that stretched the length of the field. The sight of the fleeing enemy thrilled him. He felt outside himself, sounds from his own throat unfamiliar. If comrades fell around him, he took no notice. He ran ahead of the line, then the rest of the company surged to catch up. Once at the top of the rise, a north-south road at the far edge of the field came into view. *Get to them, get to them before they cross that road and take cover in the trees.*

Captain Lane led Company D, urging his men onward, sword raised, his face flushed with excitement. The regimental flag flowed out behind Corporal John Day as he raced, the blue banner bright and alive in the late afternoon sun. One glance its way infused Nate with courage.

The Confederates melted into the woods across the road, then turned to fire at the exposed brigade. Down the backside of the slope the Union troops flowed, taking cover in a ditch on the west side of the road. Dead Confederates choked the trough. The earlier work of cannon. Nate tried to contain his revulsion and keep from vomiting over the sights and smells, men shredded by canister, body parts strewn like a sickening puzzle, the ground stained with blood. The sheltered Confederates now poured an organized fire at their pursuers, pinning the brigade amidst the ditch's slaughter. Next to Nate, James stared around him, face gray. Nate gagged and coughed, glanced down the line at his grim companions, who ignored the grisly mess around them. Langdon and others used the bodies as breastworks.

"Keep firing, men!" Stoughton shouted above the din, his mounted form somehow defying bullets.

Everyone's breath labored after the sixty-rod run. Nate's thirst nearly choked him, but there was no time to reach for his canteen. Instead, he reloaded his musket, a more difficult task with the bayonet affixed, though he dared not remove it.

Time blurred. He was unaware of how long they stayed there among the butchered, but it was long enough for merciful darkness to settle in.

Gunfire died away, the smoke thinned. Unearthly night sank

down, filled with heartrending cries from the wounded scattered across the field and in the surrounding woods to the front and either flank. The bodies of the dead bloated and reeked. Haunting sounds carried above the trees from along the twisted lines of the two battered armies.

"Fall back to the trees," Hart said, touched Nate's shoulder, moved on.

Fatigue crashed down upon Nate as the brigade withdrew across the field and reformed in the ghostly woods that they had passed through seemingly a lifetime ago. A wind picked up from the north and brought numbing cold. The men set about building breastworks of logs and rails, quiet now, the earlier excitement long faded and borne away on the horrid cries of the wounded.

Pleas for water and aid echoed from across the battle-scarred field. A forlorn voice called for a friend, repeating the name over and over until Nate thought he would go mad.

"Can't we go out to help some of 'em, Sarge?" Nate asked Langdon from where he shivered behind their breastworks.

"We've got orders to stay put. Go wandering around out there and you'll get lost or captured or shot."

Nate frowned and clenched his jaw. He glanced at James, who huddled next to him, teeth chattering, eyes wide. From somewhere in the night another man wailed, long and clear. Nate covered his freezing ears.

CHAPTER 8

James's eyes fluttered open to the first traces of morning sunlight. He did not move, did not want to know where he was. Had he actually slept? No, he must have just dozed for a time, for he still felt exhausted. The reason for his fatigue returned to him, shattered his illogical hope that he were someplace else.

With no fires allowed, the night had been too cold for comfort or rest. They had made the best of it, sharing blankets and body heat by lying close to one another; Elias lay snug against him on one side, Nate on the other, Abner and Jeremy beyond him. Nate's impetuous retrieval of their knapsacks at Davis's Crossroads had proven fortuitous, for they, unlike many others, at least had their blankets. Though reluctant to leave what little warmth his comrades offered or incur their grumbles if he vacated his spot, the prodding of James's empty stomach eventually got the better of him, and he squirmed out of place. Amidst tenuous sleep, Nate gave a whimper of discomfort. Elias's irregular snores broke off abruptly, and he raised his disheveled head to peer about, as if hoping their situation had miraculously improved.

A heavy fog shrouded the earth. James looked down the line to the right, unable to see farther than the length of the next company. What units protected the brigade's flanks? From last night's rumors, it appeared that the entire army had been shuffled like a deck of cards and dealt out haphazardly so that little structure remained, units mixed and divisions scattered. At least their division had retained cohesion.

Nate stirred, then struggled to sit up, stiff and pale. His teeth chattered, but he managed a smile. "'Tis the Sabbath. Maybe there won't be no fightin'. Hear tell Rosey's a devout Catholic."

"Praise be," James said sarcastically as he searched his haversack for a bite of hardtack. "I don't fancy the day of the week matters a lick. This fog lifts, there won't be no holding back."

Corporal May came down the line of breastworks. "We got the Johnnies with their backs up against that there creek."

Groggy but sanguine, Jeremy reminded them, "River of Death. Recollect what I told you boys?"

Braced on one elbow, Abner smashed his brother's hat down over his eyes. "We do."

Water details returned with nothing, for the dry weather had parched the nearest accessible creek. As the men ate cold rations, skirmishing rattled to the north.

"So much for the Sabbath," James said.

"Well," Jeremy grinned, "if you're gonna die, reckon it might as well be on a Sunday."

Langdon listened to the gunfire for a time, then sagely said, "Longstreet's out there somewhere."

"Longstreet?" Abner echoed. "He's in Virginia."

Langdon shook his head. "His corps reached the field late yesterday. That's what the prisoners have been saying."

Jeremy snorted. "Why, I don't believe *them.*"

The rising sun burned away the fog, its warmth welcomed after the frigid night. Here among the trees, however, a chill persisted. The crackle of skirmishing now rang out on the far side of the field's crest. James wondered about the Confederates somewhere beyond that rise of land and dusty road. What if Longstreet's veterans *were* out there? Longstreet. Gettysburg. Uncle Pat. He withdrew his uncle's pocket watch. Half past seven.

Soon orders filtered through the ranks for Negley's division to withdraw from the breastworks and form in column of march along the road behind their position. The skirmishing to the north had expanded to the full-throated roar of battle.

Nate asked Langdon, "Where we headed, Sarge?"

"Hell if I know. From the sounds of it, we're needed on the left."

From his place in the column, James looked toward their abandoned position in the woods. Their skirmishers had not been withdrawn yet from the field beyond the trees, and the disconcerting pop of their rifles could now be heard.

"Who's supposed to relieve us?" James asked no one in particular. "We've left a gap in the line." A cold sensation like a winter wind breathed down the back of his neck. He hunched his shoulders, thought of the mangled corpses in the ditch yesterday, wondered if he would ever forget them.

General Negley and his staff, along with Captain Willard of General Thomas's staff, rode along the left side of the column at the trot, the division flag snapping in their wake. The pallor of Negley's face did nothing to bolster James's morale. Since Davis's Crossroads, the general had been gravely ill, but the Pennsylvanian had refused to stay out of the saddle, determined to share the hardships with his men as he always had. But by now the ravages of fever and diarrhea had reduced the large man so much that his uniform seemed loose, his face gaunt, his eyes dull. With the crash of cannon and gunfire to the north, some spark of life had returned to his gaze, his head up, alert. Yet, as he rode, he ignored the men's calls, and James knew Negley's reticence was not driven by indifference to his men but rather by physical weakness.

The soldiers waited, some impatient, others content to stand there all day. Some, like Elias, took the time to light a pipe for a last smoke. Others simply leaned on their muskets and exchanged conjectures about what might be happening out there amidst the forest.

"Ain't that Rosey?" Jared Taylor asked from the rank ahead of James.

A group of officers came barreling down the road in a swirl of dust, Rosecrans's flag prominent above them. The idle chatter in the ranks stopped, and all eyes and ears strained forward to the head of the regiment where Negley sat his horse next to Colonel Stoughton and Colonel Stanley. Rosecrans drew rein next to the officers and hastily returned their salutes, his face a harried red hue.

Rosecrans sharply questioned, "General Negley, has General McCook relieved your troops in the front line?"

"No, sir, there's been no one to relieve us."

The crimson flush deepened to a plum color, and Rosecrans's eyes widened with startling fury. "Can you not hear the skirmishing back in that field, General? You should not have withdrawn your men before your relief arrived. You have left a gap in the line, sir. You will send Sirwell's and Stanley's brigades back to the breastworks at once." He waited for no explanation from his flabbergasted division commander and instead barked at Captain Willard, "General Beatty is in reserve yonder; send his brigade to General Thomas. Once Sirwell and Stanley have been relieved, they will follow."

Willard put spurs to his horse.

What little color had survived on Negley's cheeks now drained away. Immediately he turned to Colonel Stanley to give the order. In an instant, the two brigades formed into line of battle as the reports of muskets sharpened beyond the trees.

"Forward, men! Forward!" Colonel Stanley shouted as he urged his horse along the rear rank. "At the double quick!"

77

There was no time to fix bayonets. The race was on to recover the breastworks before the enemy could reach them. The brigades plunged back into the snarl of trees and undergrowth, the Eleventh surging forward to take the lead. Through the woods, James saw Confederate skirmishers push aside the Federal skirmish line, followed by a solid line of Rebels cresting the hill, headed for the abandoned works. The Eleventh crashed onward and barely won the foot race to the breastworks. Guns came up in unison. From less than fifty feet away, the Rebel yell from hundreds of throats shattered the air, smudged faces contorted.

"Fire!"

James's gun kicked against his shoulder. A wall of smoke from the volley blocked his vision.

"Reload!"

Through the cloud, a few Rebels staggered forward. The rest of the brigade opened fire, stifling the tattered battle cry of the Confederates and cutting down the men closest to the breastworks. What few rounds had been fired by the enemy had done little damage. When the smoke thinned, James saw the Rebels' hasty retreat over the hill. The brigade cheered. Someone clapped him on the back. He stared in amazement, breathing hard in the crisp air. Amidst the field's corn stubble, rows of men lay where the volley had mowed them down.

Elias panted, "Didn't fancy I could run so fast."

The corpses before James failed to produce the same horror as they had yesterday. Instead, he found himself thinking of their canteens, for if the Rebs had their backs to the creek, they would have plenty of water. He trailed out among them. When he looked directly upon the bullet-riddled forms, his stomach rebelled more than his mind. His emotional transformation almost frightened him. What had happened to him overnight? Perhaps lying in that ditch full of them yesterday had changed him, made him view these bodies as simply a part of the landscape, as were the trees or the roads. If he had seen these dead elsewhere—Burr Oak maybe, someplace meaningful—maybe they would affect him with the appropriate horror.

He turned away from the gore and sightless eyes and quickly gathered several canteens and carried them back to his squad. His companions looked upon his generosity with surprise, some like Elias and Nate thanking him, others like Jared Taylor and Abner staring oddly, as if expecting him to keep the canteens for himself. Their disappointing response irritated James. Well, they would thank him later, he wagered.

From the trees behind them, Negley demanded, "Where the hell is Wood?"

Captain Alfred Hough, a member of Negley's staff, replied, "He's still west of the Dyer field, sir."

"Tell him he's to relieve us. Get him up here as fast as practicable. By God, we're needed on the left!"

Hough and Willard galloped off to the west.

The division remained in line of battle, guns at the ready should the Rebels again attempt to carry the position. The cacophony of battle to the north grew, the roar of cannon like thunder, shaking the very air. Frightened birds streaked across the blue sky.

Nearly an hour passed before Stanley's brigade was relieved. The regiments fumbled back through the trees again and formed upon the road. Sirwell's brigade remained at the breastworks, awaiting its own relief, but Negley would delay no longer, wanting to avoid another dressing down by the commanding general. He led the brigade up the road, the division artillery rumbling behind.

The noise of battle swung upward in full force, a constant, furious sound that astonished James. Smoke rolled heavenward. The forest seemed to amplify every volley and shell burst. The shriek of ordnance and shouts from thousands of voices echoed distantly, as if from another world, a world that James feared would soon engulf him. Being thus blinded by the forest agitated him. How could he prepare to fight what he was unable to see?

As the brigade continued along the dusty, narrow road, a captain intercepted General Negley. Though unable to hear the officer's words, James could plainly see the animation with which he conveyed his message. In turn, Negley spurred his horse down the length of the column. A moment later word traveled through the ranks that Negley had taken the division's artillery and vanished back down the road.

"Where the hell is he taking the guns?" Abner asked.

Within minutes, Brigadier General John Beatty, who commanded the division's First Brigade, charged down the road from the north and reined in at the head of column. To see the frazzled brigadier alone without his command concerned James, but he kept his anxiety to himself. Something was very wrong. Wild thoughts jumped through his mind as Beatty jabbed a finger northward, spewing words at Colonel Stoughton that James had no hope of hearing from this far down the column. Had Beatty's brigade been destroyed? Would they reach the left too late?

Orders quickly flew along the column, and Captain Lane echoed,

"At the double quick—march!"

With his heart in his constricted throat, James sprinted forward with the others. Out of the corner of his eye, he saw Nate touch the breast pocket where he kept his Bible.

Judging by the crashing roll of battle to the right, they were near the northern end of the Union line. Here the brigade filed left off the road into line of battle, struggling through the confusion of trees and underbrush. The Eighteenth Ohio made up the left wing while the Eleventh Michigan formed the right, the Nineteenth Illinois to the right and rear in reserve. All faced north, while to the east, barely seen through the trees and smoke, an open field revealed blue regiments and batteries hammering away at a foe hidden somewhere in the forests to the east and north.

Captain Lane's voice drew James's attention back to the business at hand. "All right, boys. Make short work of this underbrush. Pile it up in front. Those Rebs won't see us till it's too late."

In no time, the regiment cut down saplings and brush for breastworks, working as a desperate team, everyone grim-faced and often glancing to the north or east, all ears strained toward the veiled battle. All realized the gravity of this position, protecting the left flank of the whole Union army. As they worked, regiments from Beatty's thinned brigade—ragged, weary-looking soldiers—marched down the road, past Stanley's line, then eventually filed into line behind them, regimental flags from Illinois and Kentucky hanging limp upon their staffs.

Soon after the Eleventh finished their work and scrambled behind the camouflage of tangled undergrowth, bullets from unseen Rebel skirmishers began to whir over their heads and patter through the leaves like drops of rain.

Colonel Stoughton, dismounted now, walked confidently along the line, ordering men to keep their heads down and the colors to be dropped. His emphatic voice soothed James. "Boys, we've got them. Let every man take aim as if he were shooting at a target, and be sure and not waste a bullet. Aim at their legs and you will drop their front rank. No troops in the world will stand and have their front rank shot down. As soon as you fire, we will charge and capture the balance."

Wild voices called from in front of the line, "Don't shoot! Hold your fire!" Blue-clad soldiers darted toward them, frightened and apparently hard-pressed. James guessed them to be skirmishers from Beatty's regiments. They never broke stride but came on, shoving aside entangling vines and branches until they clambered over the breastworks.

One panted to Stoughton, "Rebs right behind us, Colonel. At least a brigade."

The shrill Rebel yell shattered the air. Everyone's attention turned forward again, muskets at the ready, bayonets now fixed.

Undaunted, Stoughton continued. "Pay strict attention to orders, and we will make those fellows sing a different song."

"Yeah," Jeremy muttered from the left side of James. "A funeral song."

Langdon crouched next to James and grinned, muddy eyes alight. "Scared, Keenan?"

James scowled and ignored him, heard someone's ragged breathing and realized it was his own. He clamped his mouth closed and concentrated on the matted landscape before them.

"Don't plan on running once the shooting starts, Keenan. I'll be watching you."

"Seems to me you should be watching the Rebs instead, Sergeant."

Langdon laughed, harsh and humorless. "I know what direction *they're* going."

The Confederates came on at the double quick, a formidable, multicolored wall of screaming men, obviously unsuspecting of anything more in front of them than the skirmishers they had scattered to the four winds. Closer, closer. James stared down the barrel of his musket, knowing at this distance the Eleventh's volley would be murderous. But where the hell was the order? *They're almost on top of us—*

"Fire!" Stoughton shouted, and the regimental flag arose just as the guns of the two front regiments volleyed a terrible hail of death.

"Charge!" Stoughton bawled, his order echoed by line officers.

The brigade rushed forward with a triumphant, deep-throated roar. Before them, the Rebels' front rank lay like a windrow, unmoving and bloody while the survivors stood but an instant, staring at the droves now pouring toward them. The Confederates broke for the rear, many discarding guns, blankets, anything that impeded them in their frenzied stampede. Yelling wildly, James bolted after them with his company, felt no danger now, only an incredible rush of energy as he vaulted over the fallen enemy, bayonet thrust forward. Trees blurred past, bushes swatted and scratched. He tripped over a log, regained his balance, ran on, loath to be left behind. Smoke blotched out the morning sun.

Some of the Rebels stopped running, exhausted, and tossed up

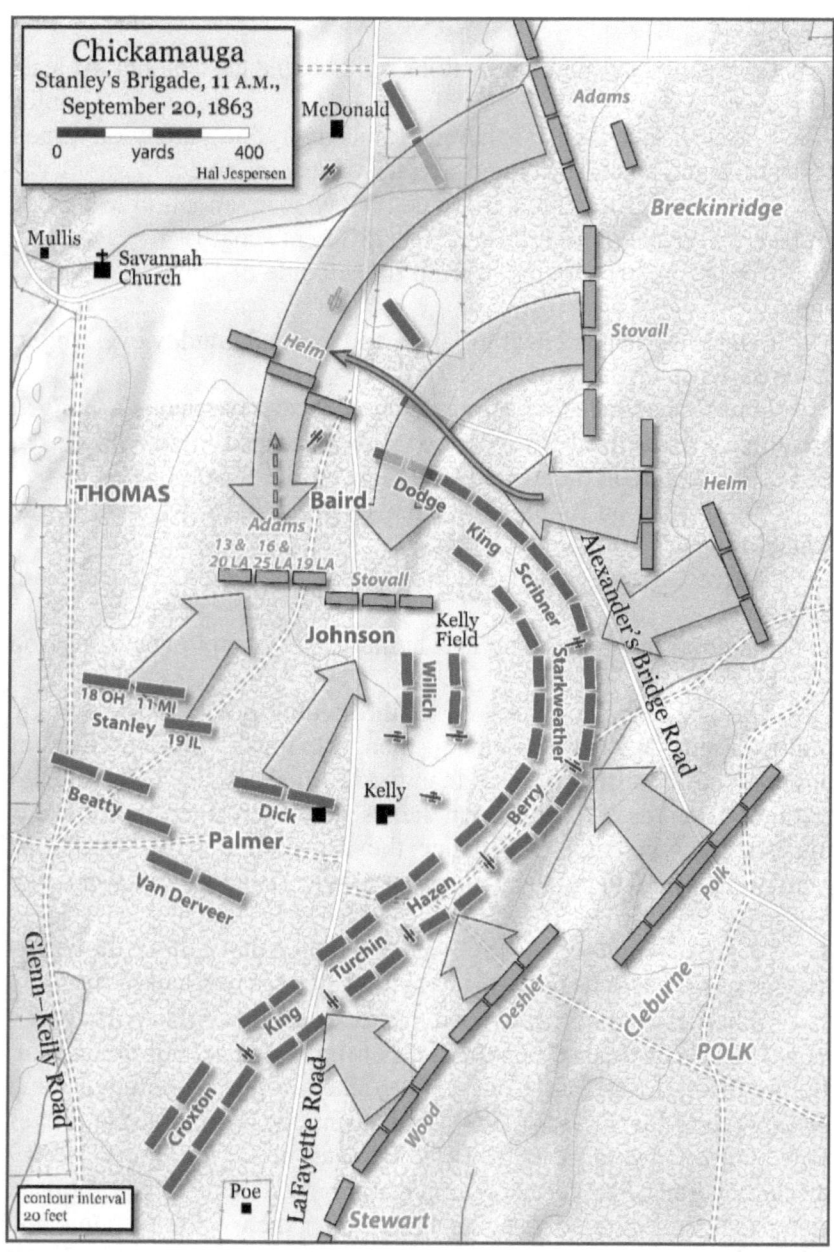

Chickamauga
Stanley's Brigade, 11 A.M.,
September 20, 1863

McDonald

0   yards   400

Hal Jespersen

Adams

Breckinridge

Mullis

✝ Savannah
Church

Helm

Stovall

THOMAS

Baird

Dodge

Helm

Adams

King

13 & 16 &
20 LA 25 LA 19 LA

Scribner

Alexander's Bridge Road

Stovall

Johnson

Kelly
Field

Willich

Starkweather

18 OH 11 MI

Stanley

19 IL

Beatty

Dick

Kelly

Berry

Palmer

Van Derveer

Hazen

Polk

Glenn-Kelly Road

King

Turchin

Cleburne

POLK

Croxton

LaFayette Road

Deshler

Wood

contour interval
20 feet

Poe

Stewart

their hands in surrender, but James kept on. He caught sight of a
Confederate brigadier general, wounded on the ground, surrounded by
Lieutenant Hicks and men from Company E. A general! They had
captured a God damned general! He pushed on with his squad. Hell,

they'd be in Chattanooga soon!

The woods opened, and they pushed the survivors across a large farm field. The brigade halted there, winded, and fired gleefully after the shattered enemy. They cheered themselves hoarse, hats tossed in the air.

Abner howled, face slick with sweat and grime. "Talk about skedaddlin'! That there's the definition! Run, you rabbits, run!"

James grabbed Nate's shoulder. "We captured a general. Did you see?"

Panting, May bent over and grinned. "Did you see Hicks? He has the Reb general's sword." He laughed. "He came charging after us with a sword in each hand. By God, what a sight!"

They exchanged excited, breathless stories, oblivious to the savage battle still raging, now to the southeast. All that mattered was the exhilaration of success. How far had they run? Certainly far beyond the left flank of the army. James watched the demoralized Confederates as they retreated across the large field, their battle flags no longer daunting, the horrible Rebel yell now silent.

Soon officers called out orders for the regiments to fall back into the woods and reform. Somehow out of the chaos of mixed units, Stanley's regiments regained command structure. The brigadier placed his men facing north once again, and the men hurried to throw up new breastworks. Still the storm of battle thundered to the south and east, blanketed in smoke and unearthly noise. Distant cheers, mixed with the Rebel yell, threaded through the crash of small arms.

Stoughton paced the length of the regimental line. "The Rebs will be back, boys. Keep a watchful eye."

As the men waited, they continued to relive the recent charge, each giving his own version of what he had seen.

"Who was the general we captured?" Nate asked.

Hart limped down the line, his hip no doubt protesting the recent run. "Brigadier General Daniel Adams; Hicks told me. That was his brigade we drove; boys from Louisiana."

Elias, resting with his back to the breastworks, said, "Looks like General Beatty's rounded up some fresh troops."

James followed the man's gaze to see Beatty directing a brigade into line of battle behind Stanley's men.

May squinted through the trees at the newcomers' flag. "Dick's brigade. Hell, they belong to Van Cleve's division. Wonder what happened to Beatty's regiments? I never saw 'em again after we charged."

Langdon grumbled, "Whole damned field seems to be one big mess. What the hell ever happened to Negley?"

James peered over the breastworks into the dense foliage, saw no movement. Would the Louisianans rally and try to regain their honor or would fresh troops challenge Stanley's men? He downed half of the warm water in his canteen, slaking his burning thirst. The sun was approaching its zenith, and even here in the forest the day's heat pressed down, the night's cold a half-forgotten memory. James closed his eyes, tried to rest. His heartbeat had finally returned to normal, and the tapering of excitement reminded him what little sleep he had in the past week.

He glanced along the regimental line. A detachment had been sent to the rear with the prisoners captured during the charge—haggard young Louisiana boys who resembled so many of James's comrades except for the humiliation of defeat etched in the grime on their faces. He almost felt sorry for them, wondered of their homes and families. Then he considered the Eleventh, gaze roaming the length of the small regiment, thankful to see that they had suffered no apparent losses during the charge. But what was yet to come? Surely the Rebels would test them again, especially here in the vulnerable flank position.

Sudden gunfire from the unseen skirmish line drew everyone's attention forward. James squinted through the leaves and vines, grip tight upon his musket.

"Get ready, boys!" Colonel Stanley's voice arose from somewhere down to the left, his encouragement picked up by the rest of the brigade officers.

The skirmishers darted back, eyes wide, mouths open for air as they reported a determined force wheeling toward them from the north and east. James thought he could see the enemy's skirmishers amidst the timber, but everything to their front blended together in the drifting battle smoke. The fighting in the field to the east rose to a crescendo, the ground shaking. James flinched when a stray bullet struck a fallen log in front of him. At ragged intervals, unseen Rebel artillery to the east rent treetops asunder above Stanley's lines, sending limbs crashing to all sides.

"I can't see a damned thing," James said through clenched teeth. "Where the hell are they?"

May cautioned, "Wait for it. Don't shoot till you have a target."

Muzzle flashes blossomed through the foliage, dozens of them, the men carrying those rifles still concealed by the fog, their motions mere blurs. These were not coming on in a headlong rush like Adams's men had; these Rebs apparently knew Stanley's position.

Suddenly they were there, drab-hued shapes coming on in a stubborn, determined line, battle flags protruding with splashes of color.

Stoughton commanded, "Wait for the order to fire, men!"

The tide broke. The Rebels pitched into a run, as if held back too long, voices rising above the storm of battle. Sunlight through the trees glinted on bayonets. James leveled his sights on a large Confederate.

"Fire!"

The volley's blast stopped the Southerners in their tracks, but these men did not break and run. They found cover wherever they could, behind trees or on the ground, and kept up a steady fire as they inched forward.

James reloaded without thinking, conscious only of the ever-closing enemy and the bitter taste of black powder as he tore cartridge after cartridge with his teeth. They had to hold this position. If they broke, the Union line would be struck from the flank and rear. To either side, his squad coolly stuck to the task, no one shouting, no one abandoning his position, his precious link in the line.

Major Bennet's voice broke through the musketry. "They're working around to the left, Colonel! Do you see them?"

Like Stoughton, James glanced to the left, but he could see little, just more smoke and the ever-impenetrable foliage. Stoughton called to Colonel Stanley.

James half expected the brigade to charge the bold attackers, but instead word came to withdraw firing, to fall back to the support of Dick's brigade. Maybe then they would attack; they would have the strength of two brigades. After all, they could not completely withdraw from this position without inviting disaster on a grand scale.

Nate and Elias remained steady on either side of James as they withdrew in an orderly line, firing as they went, holding the Rebels at bay. Langdon coolly picked his targets, cursed the abandonment of their breastworks as bullets clipped the leaves around his head. Beyond him, the Dell brothers moved in a crouch. Blood trailed down Abner's rawboned face, but he paid the wound no heed. Not all remained standing, however. Down the line, a bullet hit Captain Childs of Company H in the midsection, doubled him. His legs gave way. The smoke rolled over and blocked him from James's startled eyes. Captain Briggs clutched at his right leg, face contorted, and only the assistance of his sergeant kept him on his feet. Together the two of them struggled on, no one wanting to fall behind. Another bullet struck Billy Bishop, aide-de-camp to Stanley, and spun him about, his pistol tossed high. He fell, rolled, did not move.

"God damn them!" Captain Lane cried. "Where the hell are they?"

At first James did not understand what Lane meant, but then realization dawned on his scattered wits, bringing fear with it—Dick's supporting brigade had vanished.

CHAPTER 9

All was confusion. Stanley's brigade halted, tried to close ranks near where Dick's brigade had been. James frantically reloaded, glancing left and right for some sign of their vanished support, but he could see nothing except the ranks of the Eleventh shrouded in battle smoke. The shouts of officers and noncoms, the cries of the wounded, all jumbled together and drowned by the scream of shells overhead. What had happened to Negley and the division's artillery?

"Fall back!" someone cried, Stanley perhaps.

Again the regiment withdrew firing until Stoughton halted them and directed a volley that checked the enemy, lost in the smoke and trees, only their battle flags visible. James glanced about to make sure all in his squad were still standing, still together. Elias struggled to bind up a flesh wound on his left arm with a dirty handkerchief. James hastened to tie it for him. The older man, barely recognizable behind the veil of filth, sweat, and gunpowder, winked and nodded in silent thanks. James could only guess how much the injury pained him, for Elias would surely never say.

The position of the sun puzzled James; he had expected it to be lower in the west, for had they not been fighting all day, for hours on end?

Once more the brigade fell back, often passed by dozens of dazed stragglers from the fight off to the east, a fight that sounded closer, more constricted. These men, some unscathed, others streaming blood, did not stop in their flight, nearly unseeing in their efforts to escape. No amount of oaths and threats from the brigade officers could stop them or rally them to their ranks. Incredulous, James realized that the Rebel line no longer appeared to be pressing the Eleventh, the gunfire tapering off and swallowed by the greater roar from the east.

"Where the hell are they?" Jeremy shouted, looking to the north where the enemy had been just a moment before.

A frightened, shrill voice from somewhere near: "Maybe they got

87

around behind us."

With a twinge of panic, James glanced to the south, but what could anyone see and understand in this soup?

Erect and soldierly, sword in hand, Colonel Stoughton stood just behind his men, all of whom struggled to catch their breath in the heavy air. Stoughton's eyes gleamed but showed no fear, no alarm. He conferred calmly with Stanley and Beatty; Beatty, a brigadier without a brigade to command. Where had his regiments gone? Scattered? Destroyed? Most likely mixed in the flotsam of other units. As Stoughton listened to his superiors, his free hand stroked his long sideburns. James marveled at his fortitude, found strength by focusing on the officer.

"Look at the Colonel," he said to Nate. "He looks like he's listening to testimony in court."

"Aye. He'll get us outta this mess, sure."

Orders came quickly now, and the regiment marched by the rear rank through the woods in a southwesterly direction.

"Something's wrong," Langdon muttered, briskly chewing and spitting tobacco juice. "I don't hear nothing from the southeast. Nothing but those damned Johnnies screeching."

"Sounds like the fight's to the southwest, don't it?" Abner said.

The men now spoke with lowered voices, as if in fear of being overheard by the enemy, increasing James's uneasiness. Federal artillery somewhere ahead of them now, firing from an elevation. Perhaps they were headed there. Maybe they would be reunited with Negley and the rest of their division, along with the artillery. When he considered Negley's poor health, James wondered how the man could possibly be holding up.

The forest before them opened upon a cornfield perhaps six hundred yards long. Out amidst the cornstalks, several tattered Union regiments were formed in line of battle on the rising ground, a most welcomed sight for Stanley's men. Four cannon to the left of the defenders roared in a deafening display, their projectiles aimed to the southeast. Beyond those first regiments, James saw other units farther along a rugged, heavily forested ridge that rose behind the cornfield and ran north and south. He could make out regimental colors, Federal flags, upon a spur of land jutting eastward from the ridge.

Several officers sat their mounts near a tiny cabin nestled just back of the ridge crest, near the southwest corner of the cornfield. One had a pair of field glasses clapped to his eyes, peering south along the base of the spur where the Rebel yell echoed from the forest. Musketry rattled above the cannon fire, powder smoke drifting upward along the fringes of the hill.

"Ain't that our corps flag?" Jeremy said. "Up near that house?"

A large blue flag flapped from a staff near the humble cabin, fringed in gold with a black eagle upon its field.

"And ain't that Pap Thomas hisself with those glasses?" Some of the fatigue lifted from Abner's face as all who heard his question strained to see the distant officer.

There was little time to gawk and speculate. A mounted staff officer raced down the slope toward Stanley and Beatty, who rode at the head of column. James was unable to hear the orders relayed to the brigade commander, but an instant later Colonel Stoughton's clear, sharp voice rang over the ranks of the Eleventh, ordering them back into line of battle, a maneuver the men completed with practiced, unthinking precision.

"Battalion, forward! Double quick, guide center—march!"

Now in the front rank of the regiment, James could better understand the situation before them as they raced toward the hill. Rebel battle flags worked their way steadily up the slopes, some nearing the crest. Powder smoke arose south of the hill, foretelling another prong of the Confederate attack hidden by the curve of the spur and the trees. The Federals holding the hill appeared to be few. *Surely not enough*, James thought, the moment's urgency infusing him with a reserve of strength he never dreamed he had. A road curved down from the ridge and passed near the cabin. The regiment flowed across it, past the cabin, and up the hill, no time to load muskets, bayonets thrust forward. Two field pieces on the crest of the hill belched fire and iron over the Union defenders, then fell silent to allow Stanley's cheering brigade to charge past, the artillerymen urging them onward. James voiced his own hoarse cry.

Colonel Stanley, leading them with Colonel Stoughton, suddenly jerked and reeled in the saddle, his shoulder torn open. The horse staggered, sending him to the ground. Stoughton pushed on, urging the men not to falter at the sight of their wounded brigadier. James forced his attention back to the crest of the hill. He could see the Union line better now, thinly manned and stretching to the right, up along the eastward curving lip of the hill. The Rebels far outnumbered them, smoke and flashes from hundreds of muskets ascending amidst the trees, ready to engulf the defenders.

"Charge!" Stoughton and Major Bennet roared as one.

With a savage cry, the brigade surged forward to strike the Rebels' exposed right flank. The shock of their appearance staggered the Southerners, many scrambling and tumbling backwards at the sight. The Eleventh struggled through the trees on the eastern slope, tried to maintain order. Captain Newberry fell before Company E, his men passing over his inert form. The regiment managed a ragged volley as the Rebels melted away.

At last the Eleventh halted to watch the enemy retreat to the south and east, across ravines and through tight thickets until the foliage and smoke concealed them. The men caught their breath, many dropping to their knees in exhaustion, the heat of the day drenching them in sweat.

When James tried to ram another cartridge down the hot barrel of his Springfield, the ramrod met resistance. He shoved harder, cursed.

Langdon staggered past. "Piss down the damned barrel, Keenan. Don't you know nothing?"

James scowled after him.

Elias grinned starkly. "He's serious, boy. It'll unjam the barrel."

James decided to ignore that suggestion; no need to be caught in a compromising position should the Rebels suddenly counterattack. Besides, considering his thirst, he doubted he had anything to piss.

"Fall back," Major Bennet ordered. "We'll reform on the crest of this hill, boys."

James took account of his ammunition to find only thirty cartridges left. And God only knew where their division ordnance train was. Or where their division commander was. The artillery on the hill did not belong to Negley's division, so what had happened to the Second Division's guns?

The Eleventh filed into position at the top of the hill, the artillery behind them, the Nineteenth Illinois forming on their right, the Eighteenth Ohio, barely one hundred men now, placed in reserve near the battery. More troops had arrived on the Union left, extending the line across the cornfield to the tree line, units from the Twenty-first Corps; James could easily see the bright red, white and blue flags that denoted their corps affiliation. To the right, up along the edge of the spur that rose to meet the larger ridge, other ragtag Federal infantry units extended the line until it was lost to James's sight in the timber.

In this lull, news and rumors began to flow from unit to unit, company to company. Jeremy, having vanished in a futile search for ammunition, returned, his whole being animated. "They're sayin' the entire right flank caved in. What's on this here hill is all that's left of the army. Sheridan, Davis, even Rosecrans—they're all skedaddlin' up the Dry Valley Road for Chattanooga. All we've got here is bits and pieces to hold back the Rebs. But Pap Thomas is still here, by God, and he won't give up this hill."

"I can't believe it," Nate murmured. "Why would Rosey run? How could he just leave us?"

They tossed out opinions, grave but still determined to do their part to stave off the complete destruction of the Army of the Cumberland. James kept his feeling of stunned despair to himself.

Corporal May asked, "Anyone heard anything about Colonel Stanley?"

"Some fellas carried him back to the house yonder," Jeremy replied. "That's where the doctors are workin'. Colonel Stoughton's in charge of the brigade now."

Musketry renewed on the south side of the spur, pressed closer, higher along the rising ground on the right, much stronger this time, as if the Federals' stubborn resistance infuriated the enemy, keeping them from a victory so close to completion. The Eleventh's acting commander was now Lieutenant Colonel Melvin Mudge, a Quincy man who had been with the regiment since its birth. Mudge moved along the line, fatigue and excitement a bizarre mixture upon his face as he gave orders to the remaining officers.

"All right, boys," Captain Lane called out. "This ain't over yet. On your feet."

James's head swam, and nausea rose up with a freezing chill, but somehow he plunged forward with the regiment along the slope toward the south, toward the heavy firing. Confederates there among the trees in line of battle, pressing once more upon the Union defenders who fragmented before the larger, determined force. The reality of the crucial moment struck James like a blow to the chest—this hill had to be held at all costs. If the Confederates controlled it, they would consume whatever was left of the Federal forces here, then fall upon the rest of the Army of the Cumberland on its retreat to Chattanooga. The army would be lost, and Chattanooga would be back in Confederate hands.

The Eleventh poured a withering volley into the ranks of Southerners. The crash reverberated in the trees. Men dropped by the score. Some of the surviving Rebels began to fall back. One color bearer advanced, wagging his battle flag aloft, unwavering gaze latched upon the Union line. James aimed his musket in the color bearer's direction but was powerless to pull the trigger on such a brave man, mesmerized by his defiance amidst the hail of lead.

Major Bennet's voice rang out. "A captain's commission to the man who captures those colors!"

Several men leaped forward, including Langdon, but the commission would have to wait. Bullets riddled the color bearer. Langdon and the others bolted for the flag, but the Rebel wheeled as he fell and threw the standard back down the hill to his retreating comrades. On one knee he wavered, then slumped to the ground.

Stoughton's brigade swept forward in pursuit. With barely enough strength to stand, James trailed in their wake, passed the dead color bearer, could not look at him as unexpected emotion welled up. To counter this, he thought of those in the Eleventh who had been killed and wounded this day by that man's fellow soldiers.

Down the hill the screaming Eleventh and Nineteenth Illinois swarmed. James tripped on the loose soil, grabbed a sapling to stay upright, continued without thought, only a desire to remain with his comrades. A volley from below halted the line. He caught up with them just as they climbed back up the hill, firing as they withdrew.

Nate panted, "Too many of 'em down there for us. Orders to go back to the top of the hill."

Once there, General Beatty helped Stoughton place the exhausted men. Musketry had died down, giving the regiments time to construct breastworks along the crest of the east slope.

"Snyder went down in that last charge," May said in a subdued tone. "Got hit in the right side."

"I saw him," Abner said bitterly of the regiment's sergeant major, whom many credited with General Adams's capture.

"Captain Newberry's dead," Nate quietly said.

James glanced along the line at the stalwart but saddened faces. How many would be left by the end of this day? He looked upon them now with a fresh perspective. Except for Langdon, he gave thanks for each and every one of them, regardless of any past grievances. Even Nate. The boy's very appearance seemed different. True enough, he still had that unique light in his gaze, however dimmed by today's events, but any bravado lingering from Davis's Crossroads had been extinguished, lost somewhere in the blood and battle smoke of this day. In turn, James wondered what others now saw in him. The begrudging looks many had given him just this morning were nowhere to be found.

"Those are Longstreet's boys out there," Major Bennet said where he had paused behind James. "That's who we're up against."

The confirmation of the morning rumor brought fresh discussion, but it was short-lived, for a shout went up along the line, and Lieutenant Hicks cried, "Colonel! Here they come again!"

Bringing his musket to bear along the breastwork of fallen timber and rocks, James spied a strong line of Rebels advancing up the hill once more, firing steadily as they came…closer…closer. Longstreet's men, veterans from the Army of Northern Virginia, men his Uncle Pat had fought. Perhaps the man who had killed his uncle marched in those very ranks before him.

Lieutenant Colonel Mudge ordered, "Fire at will!"

This time the regiment's stubborn efforts failed to slow the enemy's advance. James's chest tightened as the Rebels came nearer. He struggled with his musket as it continued to jam. His comrades, faces smeared with black powder, stared with glassy concentration down the hill, firing, reloading, lips swollen from lack of water. The water he had gotten that morning was long gone.

Fifteen minutes of gunfire and smoke covered the hillside until finally the Rebels withdrew to lick their wounds and reform. James waited while they drifted away, then he tossed aside his fouled musket in disgust and stood.

Nate grabbed his arm. "Where you goin', James?"

The concern on Nate's face surprised him. James wavered like a reed in the wind, near collapse, muttered, "Need water and ammo…and a gun."

"I'm goin' with you."

They crossed the breastworks and moved among the dead and dying. In their rush, they used knives to cut free the cartridge belts and canteens. Moans from the wounded Confederates scratched through the occasional pop-pop of sharpshooters' guns. James realized he did not even flinch at the crack of a gun or wince at the cries of the injured, nor did he pay any heed to the dead; they had killed Newberry, wounded Stanley, and so many more. The Eleventh was dwindling. Was it only a matter of time before Longstreet gobbled the balance?

Empty canteens. *Damn it.*

He and Nate scrambled back up the hill with their burdens and quickly distributed the cartridge boxes into eager hands. As Colonel Stoughton strode past, he gave James an appreciative nod, a faint smile reaching the corners of his eyes. Sharpshooters' bullets clipped the air about the officer, but Stoughton ignored them.

Abner groaned. "Dear God…here they come again. Jesus, there's so many…"

Stoughton's voice carried across the brigade. "Hold your fire until you hear my order, boys. We'll give 'em the same medicine we gave Adams's men. We'll fire by volley then charge."

James shivered at the thought, for he lacked the strength for another headlong run. He might make it down the hill, but would he be able to climb back up?

The dense Rebel line of battle advanced, flags held protectively amidst the snatching undergrowth. The sun through the trees caught the gold fringe of some of the banners, brightening them among the shadows. The Southerners howled as one massive wall of bone-chilling din. Some of the Eleventh's men shouted back epithets and invitations for them to keep coming, which inexorably they did until only about twenty feet from the breastworks, struggling against the grade of the hill. A shout from the Eleventh's officers loosed a murderous volley.

"Charge!"

The regiments leaped over the breastworks, bayonets leading.

Through the curtain of battle fog James plunged, a fresh windrow of casualties before him. He stumbled over one of them, lost his balance, began to fall. A Rebel reared up before him. Unable to catch himself, James gritted his teeth, slammed into the man. Together they crashed against a sapling, glanced off, and tumbled to the ground. They lost their muskets, rolled several yards down the hill. Desperately James scrambled to his hands and knees, the brigade disappearing below him into the trees. He stared into the startled blue eyes of the young Southerner, who struggled to one knee. A terrible, indecisive second passed. The Rebel dived for a musket. James sprang on top of him. They wrestled on the body-strewn ground. Each grappled for the other's throat as they slipped downhill, struck a bruising tree trunk. The Southerner smashed something against James's head, knocked him away into a warm, dead body. Barely looking, ears ringing, James snatched the dead man's musket, prayed it was loaded, fired. The enemy's dirty face vanished behind the smoke.

James fell to a sitting position against the corpse, stared at the gory mess in front of him. He looked down the hill after his comrades, their ragged, hoarse cheers lost in the trees. He staggered to his feet, glanced up the hill, the ground thrumming beneath his feet from artillery fire, shells shrieking overhead, tearing through trees. Mechanically he trailed after the Eleventh.

He came to the road at the base of the hill. A Union soldier sat there in the dust, his back to James. Cradling a wounded comrade, he sobbed and rocked to and fro.

"Jeremy...Jeremy... It's gonna be all right."

Horrified, James sank next to Abner, who glanced at him with swimming eyes, tears streaking the mask of filth on his angular face.

94

In his arms lay his brother. James turned away from the sight of intestines protruding around Jeremy's bloody, clutching fingers. The boy's face glowed a ghastly ivory, eyes bright with pain and shock, rolling and wet with tears.

"They shot him. They shot my brother. Right in front of me." Abner wiped the red hair from Jeremy's eyes. "I kilt the bastard, Jeremy. I blew his God damned brains out."

Jeremy stiffened, clenched his teeth, breathing ragged. "Oh...God...Abner..."

The regiments trailed back up the hill, exhausted but triumphant. Nate trotted over, dragging his musket, followed by May and Elias. Nate's expression collapsed. He took off his hat and knelt next to the siblings. His eyes met James's, filled with tears.

Abner clutched Nate's arm. "Help me. Help me get him up the hill."

"Jeremy," Nate said softly. "Can you hear me?"

The boy nodded shallowly, closed his eyes. He coughed, and blood trickled from the corner of his mouth.

Abner swore, sobbed. "Please, Nate...Elias..."

"Jeremy," Nate continued. "We're gonna pick you up."

"No," he whispered through cracked lips. "Hurts."

Abner insisted, "We're not gonna leave you here."

"Hurts," Jeremy repeated, weaker this time, as if from a deep sleep. "Where's Mama?"

Langdon halted next to them, glanced at the wounded boy. "Leave him. We gotta get back up the hill before the Rebs reform."

"Fuck you, Preacher," Abner snapped.

"He's gut-shot, you fool. Just a matter of time. Now move!" Langdon continued upward.

Nate touched Abner's arm. "C'mon, Ab. You take him under the arms. James'll help. Me and Elias will catch his legs."

When they lifted Jeremy, the boy's eyes flew open, and he writhed against their hold before fainting.

"C'mon," Abner insisted with a frightened glance into the trees.

They carried Jeremy all the way to the cabin, now a field hospital. Eager to leave its crowd of misery and stench behind, James tugged Nate toward the door, but Nate stopped.

"Colonel Stanley. How are you, sir?"

Stanley lay on a makeshift cot, one shoulder bandaged. The fifty-three-year-old man looked much older than his age. Pain furrowed his high forehead, but when he saw Nate and James, a weak smile found its way through his dark, blood-spattered beard. Seeing his brigade commander alive eased some of James's anxiety over Jeremy.

"I'll be on my feet in no time, lads," the brigadier rasped. "How does the brigade fare?"

"We're holdin' 'em, sir," Nate said. "Just now pushed 'em back down the hill again. Colonel Stoughton ordered another bayonet charge."

Stanley gave a single nod of satisfaction. "You tell that colonel of yours not to expose himself so. I warned him earlier."

"No stopping that, sir," James said.

"You're probably right." Stanley managed a smile before sinking deeper against the cot. "But you boys best get back now. We need every man."

"Yes, sir."

They stepped outside into the relative quiet, leaving the moans and cries behind them.

"Looky there," Nate said. "Pap Thomas."

Surrounded by staff, General Thomas sat his horse a couple of rods away. He struggled to hold field glasses to his eyes while at the same time trying to control his fractious mount. His hands shook, and his beard was uncharacteristically ruffled.

Nate asked, "What are they watchin'?"

James peered to the north. His heartbeat skipped. "That dust cloud yonder above the trees. See it?"

"Who do you fancy it is?"

"Don't know. Hope it's ours."

Thomas spoke to his staff. "Take my glass, one of you whose horse stands steady. Tell me what you can see."

A man in civilian dress next to Thomas had a glass of his own. "General! I can see the U.S. flag!"

"Do you think so?" Thomas demanded. He turned to an officer from Negley's staff. "Captain Johnson, ride forward and ascertain the identity of that approaching column."

Neither James nor Nate had any desire to leave until Johnson returned under a hail of sharpshooters' bullets to report the arrival of Major General Gordon Granger's Reserve Corps.

Relief relaxed Thomas's broad shoulders, and the general stroked his disheveled beard back into order and, with a curse directed toward Braxton Bragg, regained his usual composure.

The appearance of reinforcements shot new energy through James, and together he and Nate rushed to report the good news to the brigade.

***

Heavy gunfire erupted on the right flank of the Federal line, somewhere back on the ridge, lost to Nate among the trees. It was in this direction that Granger's brigades plunged, immediately swallowed from sight. Within minutes, the ridge exploded in a clash of arms, nearly due west and, alarmingly, behind the Eleventh's position—the direction of the Dry Valley Road and the escape route to Chattanooga. A short time after Granger's arrival, Colonel Ferdinand Van Derveer's brigade from the Fourteenth Corps's Third Division arrived and took a position somewhere in the tangle of forest behind Stoughton's brigade. For the moment, no Confederates showed themselves below the hill where Stoughton's men kept vigil, but everyone maintained his position at the breastworks. No one dared leave this protection, for Rebel bullets still clipped the air, and artillery shells from the south screamed unceasingly.

Buoyed by the reinforcements, Nate rested against the breastworks, exhausted, thirsty, and painfully hungry. He listened almost disinterestedly to the unseen brawl to the west, simply relieved to have a minute of respite while someone else did the fighting. Next to him rested the Enfield rifle he had taken off a dead Rebel to replace his own gun. James stared beyond the breastworks in the opposite direction. Sometime during the day, the former storekeeper had lost his cap. Most of the men of the Eleventh wore slouch hats, but James had remained distinctive by wearing a forage cap, as if wanting to emphasize his differences. His sweat-darkened blond hair hung in dirty dishevelment, draped over his glassy eyes as he stared across the dead Confederates littering the slope below.

He appeared to sense Nate's attention, but he did not turn his head. "You kill anyone today?"

Nate frowned at the ludicrous question.

"I mean, look him right in the eyes and kill him?"

"So much smoke and shootin', I don't rightly know who killed who. Why?"

"I did."

"When?"

"The charge when Jeremy got shot."

His expression and the hollowness of his voice unnerved Nate. "What happened?"

97

He believed the story James related, for he could see it all reflected on his comrade's face, especially when their gazes finally connected. A sheen coated James's eyes, but Nate was unsure if grief or exhaustion lay behind its cause. Perhaps both. James stared at him for so long that he felt uncomfortable and wondered if James wanted him to say something, something that would absolve him from what he had done to that Rebel.

Lieutenant Colonel Mudge tramped along the line. "Stay sharp, lads." He gestured to the east. "Something's going on down there. The Colonel thinks they'll try us again."

Elias pulled back from peering over the breastworks, then tapped out his pipe and shoved it into a pocket. "Sounds about right," he laconically said. "Looks like Bragg's whole damned army's comin'."

The men gripped their rifles anew, attention down the hill. Stoughton and Bennet, along with Beatty, paced behind the brigade line, offering encouragement and words of patience. Nate did not see the Rebels at first, so much did their earthen hues blend into the underbrush, but then the flags appeared—crisp, whole flags; fresh troops, hundreds of them, advancing with the staunch eagerness of raw recruits, enthusiastically ignorant.

"Wait until they get close," Stoughton calmly advised. "We'll fire by volley. Hold tight now."

James scrabbled through his pockets and cartridge box. "Four damned shots. That's all. Four. Christ."

The hill reverberated with the Rebel yell—demons howling toward them. Despair sank like a weight into the pit of Nate's stomach, and for the first time he wanted to run. He forced himself to think of Jeremy, the eagerness always in his voice, remembered the boy's prophetic words from earlier that day. And, somehow, he remained with his gun aimed, grip tight, eyes stinging from sweat. The sun was finally slipping toward the ridge behind them, but night would not come soon enough.

Canister fire from the Union batteries ripped the Rebel line, punching great, bloody gaps, but still the Southerners came on. Stoughton gave the order, and the brigade opened a murderous fire. Nate rushed to reload, everyone doing the same, then firing at will. Smoke masked the enemy lines for a moment, but muzzle flashes revealed the Confederates' obstinacy. The continuous reports of muskets so deafened Nate that he could not even hear his own rifle, as if cotton were stuck in his ears. He felt the gun's kick but was unable to distinguish its smoke, for a bluish-gray fog blurred the entire area.

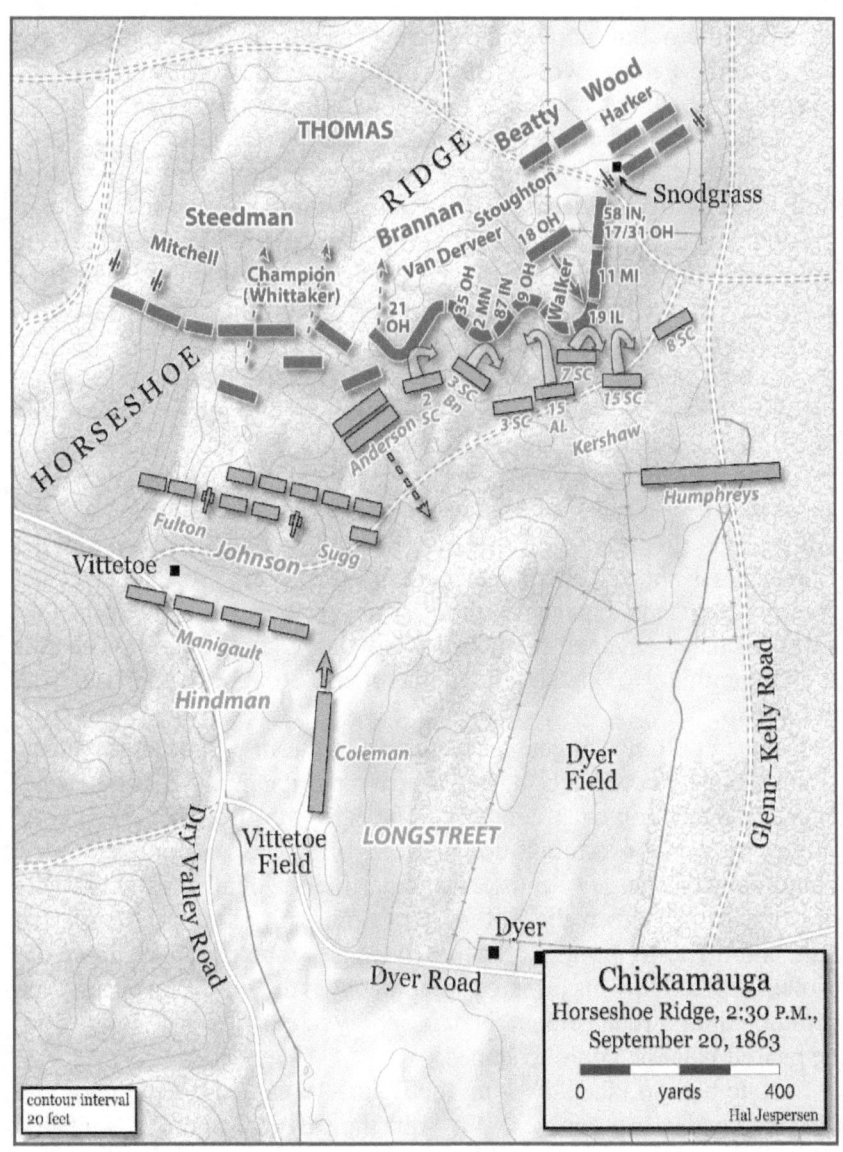

THOMAS

Wood

Beatty

Harker

RIDGE

Brannan

Stoughton

Snodgrass

Steedman

Van Derveer

18 OH

58 IN,
17/31 OH

Mitchell

Champion
(Whittaker)

21
OH

35 OH

2 MN

87 IN

19 OH

Walker

11 MI

19 IL

8 SC

HORSESHOE

2
Bn

3 SC

7 SC

15 SC

Anderson SC

3 SC

15
Al.

Kershaw

Fulton

Sugg

Humphreys

Johnson

Vittetoe

Manigault

Hindman

Coleman

Dyer
Field

Glenn–Kelly Road

Dry Valley Road

Vittetoe
Field

LONGSTREET

Dyer

Dyer Road

Chickamauga
Horseshoe Ridge, 2:30 P.M.,
September 20, 1863

0   yards   400

Hal Jespersen

contour interval
20 feet

The response of the nearby Federal battery concussed the air, the breastworks vibrating beneath his gun barrel. Cartridge paper fluttered through the air like butterflies.

Each time the Confederates faltered reinforcements pressed forward until finally they were within reach of the breastworks. The Alabamians' color bearer went down. A second man picked up the flag, only to be shot. Yet another lifted the flag. He too was killed, the staff sheared in two, but more willing hands carried the banner a few steps closer to the Federal works. Bullets cut the man down. Smoke rolled over the scene like a curtain at the end of a tragic play.

"Nate!" James cried. "Look out!"

Nate ducked below the breastworks as a dark form passed over him to collide with James. Their bodies thumped against the hard ground. James struggled wildly with the Confederate. Frantic, Nate rammed home a ball. James pinned the Southerner with one hand and smashed his free fist down, drove the Rebel's head against the earth.

"James, get away!"

Like a cat, James sprang to one side. Nate fired, and the ball tore off the side of the Rebel's face. Unthinking, Nate turned back to the oncoming line. James scrambled next to him, reclaiming his musket.

The Confederate flag down to the right had reached the line, surrounded by a mass of soldiers who poured a deadly, point-blank volley into the flanks of the two Federal regiments. Men on the Eleventh's right and the Nineteenth Illinois's left fell back, yet the enemy could not advance without suffering enfilade fire from both sides, so they remained there with their flag within a hundred feet of the Eleventh's. No one could dislodge them. Stoughton's brigade was cut in two.

Nate could no longer see the break in the line through the dense smoke, but he could feel it, could sense the danger. No one seemed capable of pushing back the threat. The Eleventh fired like a machine. James called for ammunition. The world was nothing but one continuous discharge of musketry and artillery. Small fires among the dry underbrush down the hill added to the pall. Confederates darted here and there, trying to pierce the line at a second point. James swore violently and threw his jammed weapon down the hill like a spear, then scrambled for a replacement. Nate's supply of cartridges dwindled, but he passed what he could to James.

Nate had no idea how long the Rebels remained lodged upon the hill. It seemed like forever. Why did the night not come? Soon the Eleventh and Nineteenth would be driven back, ammunition exhausted; all along the line men called out for cartridges. Yet if they caved in, what would become of the rest of the line on this hill or on the ridge behind them or out in that cornfield?

A roar erupted behind him. He jumped and spun about in fear of an attack from the rear. A rush of blue plunged through the smoke toward the ruptured line. The colors of the tiny Eighteenth Ohio cut through the gloom of failing sunlight. Bayonets gleamed. The

Southerners all along the line withered beneath this fresh onslaught, their colors finally fell. Men ran, others died, while many surrendered. The bulk of them fell back, left Stoughton's brigade in command of the breastworks again. Ragged, insane cheers broke from the parched throats of hoarse defenders. A wild release of energy.

Nate stared about him, incredulous. Elias, May, James, Langdon, and Abner; all looked back at him with amazement. He broke into relieved laughter, the sound ringing so strangely amidst the scene, but he could not stop, not until he heard a voice down the line, deep and raspy, singing—for the love of God—singing the "Battle Cry of Freedom"!

The entire line joined in, and when they emphasized, "*Down* with the traitors, *up* with the Stars!" Nate was certain the whole battlefield could hear them.

***

An eerie, incongruous quiet settled over the hill. The sun had dipped below the western ridge, leaving behind smoke from the battle and from brush fires that blinded Nate to anything beyond a dozen paces. Few of the living spoke, too weary and hoarse. Only the officers crept about, checking on their men. For all Nate knew and could see, his brigade could just as easily be the only unit left on the field, but then an occasional musket would fire from somewhere, answered by another, assuring him that others remained.

Nate dragged himself over to Abner, who had just returned from the field hospital. He settled next to his friend and put an arm around his shoulders. "How's Jeremy?"

Abner rolled his lips together, closed his hazel eyes, slowly shook his head. Nate's throat tightened as Abner began to silently cry.

"I was supposed to look out for him, Nate. I promised Ma. What am I gonna tell her?"

From the other side of Abner, Elias softly hushed him, took hold of his hand, squeezed it.

After a time, Abner collected himself and managed to ask, "Will you help me…help me bury him? I can't leave him to the Rebs if we withdraw."

Nate nodded. "Let me check with the Cap'n."

Other Burr Oakers, including James, joined them behind the cabin where they hastily scraped out a shallow grave. Nate held his mother's Bible, but it was too dark by then to read, so instead he led them in a brief prayer. Instead of the fresh grave before him—it was little more than a dark scar upon the ground—he saw Jeremy on his family's farm, hanging from his knees in the rafters of the barn, laughing, or swimming in the mill race, once pretending that he was drowning, just to frighten Abner half to death. So many other memories, jumbled together, so foreign here in this somber, foreboding place.

The little group floundered back through the smoke and darkness to their lines. As they arrived, Hart informed them that the brigade had just received orders to withdraw.

"Withdraw?" Nate echoed. "After all this?"

James grumbled bitterly, "Withdraw to where?"

"Chattanooga, I reckon."

Gunfire erupted on the farthest hill behind their position, muzzle flashes reflecting against the dark sky, the sounds sharpened by the cooling night. Nate and the others quickly took up their arms, waited, held their breath. But nothing came of it, and again the firing died off.

Someone whispered loudly, "We've gotta get outta here."

Major Bennet's shadowy figure passed along the ranks, softly calling, "Fall in."

***

Moonlight and stars filled the placid satin night sky while fires burned alongside the dusty road, offering a contrast of heaven and hell. The long, ragged, demoralized column of blue-black shuffled northward, the battlefield half a mile behind. The survivors moved with vacant eyes and heavy feet. Nate stared at the wreckage they passed alongside the road—limbers, wagons, played out men, wounded men, dead men. He tried to shut out the cries for help from the wounded or the sobs of someone lost in the bordering darkness. Soldiers called out their unit numbers, separated and disoriented. How had the Eleventh remained intact? He hung tightly to his comrades, though so exhausted he wanted to drop down into the dust.

He knew he would never forget the pleadings and weak protests from the untold number of wounded back on that hill when they had realized they were to be abandoned to the enemy, for there were no wagons or ambulances to transport them. Among those left behind was Lieutenant Colonel Mudge, who had been shot in the left arm. Gallantly he said he would remain behind with the other casualties of the Eleventh, perhaps some forty men, and make sure they were treated humanely.

The whole world seemed a disaster. Never before had the Army of the Cumberland been defeated. Many swore bitterly that if reinforced they could have held the hill for as long as it took, but of course there were no reinforcements—the rest of the army had deserted them. Though all took pride in the stubborn defense they had fought against Longstreet's men, it all rang hollow, especially when so many were now missing from the ranks.

Elias limped along next to Nate. Somewhere during the day, a shell fragment had ripped his right thigh—a bloody wound but not deep. Blood had seeped through the bandage as well as through the makeshift bandage on his left arm. His sack coat was gone, and he shivered in the cold night.

"Why don't you take me coat?" Nate asked.

Elias waved away the offer. "Feels good after that damned sun today."

A lie, but Nate did not press the issue.

Softly Elias said, "Jared Taylor got captured. Lieutenant Marsh told me."

"Dear God," Nate breathed. "Jared... He and me brother Matthew was best of friends. They used to go huntin' together. I'd go with 'em sometimes, when they'd let me."

He dropped into miserable silence, reflected upon all those lost this day. How had he not only survived but emerged unscathed? Jared, another Burr Oaker, another prisoner of the Confederacy, like Ryan. What would Ryan say about this day were he here? Would he be proud of how his younger brother had fought? How ashamed he would be to see them all now, crawling toward Chattanooga with their tails between their legs.

The click of James's pocket watch snapped Nate's eyes open, and he bumped into Sam Britton ahead of him in the column. Befuddled, he looked around in the darkness, glanced up at the stars, tried to get his bearings. The moon had moved since last he had looked.

Elias chuckled. "Asleep while marching, eh, lad? Well, I reckon you're a veteran now, if you can do that. Didn't believe me when I told you about that a month ago, did you?"

"No. Fancy there's a parcel of things I seen and done durin' the past days that I wouldn't have believed a month ago."

"Well, you've seen the elephant, sure. And a damned mighty big one he was."

Nate murmured, "I pray God I never see him again."

From somewhere nearby in the dark of midnight, May hoarsely

said, "They may have whipped us, but we've still got Chattanooga. That's what Rosey was after."

"We may have it now," Langdon said gravely, "but don't wager Bragg will let us keep it none too easy."

PART III

CHATTANOOGA

"When those fellows get started,
all hell can't stop them."

-- Major General Gordon Granger

CHAPTER 10

Dear Katie

there is a meen october wind blowing thru Chattanooga as i rite this letter makes my hands cold but i wont stop things is still vary bad here we ar on quarter rations and hav ben for some time all i have ate since yesterday is three crackers it is horrible to see the horses and mules dying as they are evry day now boys ar so hungry some steel from the animls gards ar posted to stop this but it is hard I even herd of a dog being ate but dont know if that is true rebs still all around us on the mountins and ridges cannons from moccasin point trade shots with reb batterys on Lookout mountin dont amount to much more then nois tho sad news genral Negley is no longer our division commander he is on leeve of absence and they say ther will be a cort of inquery about his conduct at Chikamawga we got reinforced by two corps from the army of the Potomac led by genral Hooker them paper-coller soljers aint done much to help just mor mouths to feed we ar all trying to keep our spirits up we miss Jeremy something fierse Abner is getting along but he is not the same maybe if we had something to do besides set arond and be hungry then he wud buck up wish we could break thru the rebs and head up into Tenessee but things dont look promising do tell Hether to rite to James he never has got much mail and i know it pains him tho he dont say you know James

The cold wind ruffled Nate's letter, and he paused in his writing to set aside the stub of pencil and rub his eyes. He searched the slate gray autumn sky in vain for a hint of the sun. Did the sun shine upon Burr Oak? Did the wind pull the red and gold leaves from the trees around his family's house and send them skittering across the porch? Did they swirl in dizzy circles for the cats to chase? Or was it dark and cold there, too? He could almost smell his mother's cooking, making his stomach pinch.

Around him stretched the camps of the Army of the Cumberland, here amidst the fortifications surrounding the small town, fortifications like Fort Negley, built after the retreat last month. Thousands of tents, white, gray, and sad in the half light. Blue figures moving in idleness among company streets. Very few officers dared drill their men since so many were weakened by meager rations. A gloominess pervaded the ranks of Rosecrans's army, not only because of their recent defeat but because of the perimeter of enemy guns upon the hills and mountains, besieging them for the past month.

Despite the dire situation, Nate found beauty in his surroundings. The broad Tennessee River snaked from the northeast, past the western edge of Chattanooga, then curled briefly westward around the northern tip of Lookout Mountain before meandering southward alongside the mountain's western face, down past Bridgeport, where, seemingly a lifetime ago, the Eleventh Michigan had paused on the march to gaze upon the bridge there. Lookout Mountain rose eight hundred feet above the river across from Moccasin Point, south of the city, rearing up at a forty-five-degree angle, rugged and majestic, marked by limestone outcroppings and wearing a quilt of autumn colors. To the east of the city, Chattanooga Valley had been virtually denuded for fuel by soldiers, both Northern and Southern. The fifteen-mile-long north-south Missionary Ridge rose beyond the valley, covered by ragged timber with outcroppings and ravines, some three hundred feet above the valley floor. On all these heights, the Confederate forces of Braxton Bragg glowered upon their famished foe. Conflicting rumors had the Confederates reinforced, had them thinned, had them hungry, had them strong and ready to wait forever until Rosecrans's men starved. *Well*, Nate thought as his stomach sent up its common protest, *it won't take near forever*.

Corporal May's excited voice carried down the company street, pulling the attention of everyone lingering about the tents, for it was rare indeed to hear anyone so animated these days. The noncom came at a brisk pace, face flushed. By the time he stopped near Nate's tent, several other Company D men gathered around in a curious, hungry, hollow-eyed circle. Nate hoped, as they all surely did, that May had news about rations. They neither cared for nor desired anything else.

"What is it, Davy?" Abner asked the breathless corporal.

"Rosey's been relieved of command!"

"What?" they chorused.

"It'll be announced at rollcall this evening."

Abner muttered, "I can't believe it."

Others voiced disappointment, some satisfaction.

Nate asked, "Who's replacin' him?"

"Our very own corps commander."

As pleased responses arose, easing regret over Rosecrans's loss, Nate grinned. "Why, Rosey's been fine by me, but Pap Thomas is a first-rate choice."

The despondency that had draped Abner's face since his brother's death lifted slightly. "Well, poor Rosey had his chance for glory but came up short, and here we sit. Now this army won't be retreatin' no more."

May's enthusiasm tempered. "That might mean being hungry for a spell longer. Pap won't give up this town."

They all frowned, but Nate insisted, "We can tough it out. Right, lads?"

Though not effusive in their responses, all agreed. Amidst further speculation and gossip, Nate noticed James coming briskly down the company street. The young man ignored the excited gathering just outside his tent, focused instead on his haversack held oddly close to his chest as he glanced to either side. He was mere steps away before his attention went to his comrades, and he faltered, as if regretful that he had arrived just then.

"James," Nate cried. "Did you hear?"

"Hear what?"

"Pap Thomas has replaced Rosey."

"Well, I'll be damned. Thought it was just a rumor."

May said, "General Grant is coming up from Vicksburg. He'll be here soon to take command of everything—the Army of the Cumberland, Hooker's troops, and General Sherman's, whenever they finally get here."

As the men discussed these latest, astonishing events, James ducked into his tent. Nate folded up his letter and tucked it into a pocket, spent a few more minutes with May and the others. When the gathering broke up, men hurrying off to spread the news, Nate crawled into the tent to find James covering his haversack with a blanket.

"What you up to, James?"

The young man glanced at him, almost alarmed, but then his expression relaxed, and a startling grin flashed across his pale face. He put a finger to his lips for silence, then unburied his haversack and opened it, pulling forth two large wrapped items. As if to tantalize Nate, he took his time peeling away the wrapping, revealing just a small square of each, but it was enough to widen Nate's eyes and set his mouth watering.

"By God, James, how'd you come by those?"

"James King has some connections with division commissary."

James King was a quartermaster sergeant in the Eleventh, a Three Rivers boy who had been with the regiment since its forming, respected and well-liked. During the battle of Chickamauga, he had driven a wagon of rations out of Chattanooga for the regiment, and Nate would never forget the sight of King on that wagon after dark on the second day of the fight.

Nate's mouth watered so much that he had to swallow twice, his stomach howling. The bounty of meat made him dizzy, and he could barely concern himself with what James must have paid to acquire such rarities.

"Well…James…when you gonna eat 'em? I mean, you gonna eat it all at once? The steak and liver both, I mean."

Confusion clouded James's expression. "They're not just for me. I got them for the squad."

Nate stared. He expected James to laugh at him and tell him he was lying, that he was going to keep the meat for himself.

"Go scrape up some wood and start a fire. I'll stay here." James covered the meat again with the blanket and patted it possessively. "Don't tell anyone but our squad. Not enough for the whole company; barely enough for us."

"They'll smell it, sure. Once it starts cookin', the whole regiment will be swarmin' us like bees."

"Then we won't cook it long. Now hurry up. Go."

Nate built the fire not in the usual pit but instead behind the tent, so it was less conspicuous. Once it was burning, he surreptitiously gathered his squad, and soon the beefsteak and liver sizzled upon the fire. Everyone crouched around, as close as they could get, eyes glued to the darkening meat as if beholding some priceless artifact, only looking away long enough to see if a hungry pack of their comrades was about to descend upon them. No one spoke, all mesmerized and salivating. James had grown almost morose, the original excitement strangely gone now, as if he were reflecting upon something else. But how could anything else be in a starving man's mind but the scent and sizzle of that meat?

"What the hell is this?" Sergeant Langdon's question blanched the faces of those around the fire. Horrified, Nate found the sergeant standing just behind him. Langdon jabbed a finger toward the fire. "Where'd that come from? There's been no meat ration issued."

No one spoke, each man's gaze jumping to the next. Nate knew if Langdon found out that James had been the one to acquire the meat, they stood a greater chance of losing their feast.

"I bought it," Nate blurted, getting to his feet.

Langdon's eyes narrowed. "You just told me the other day you sent your pay back home, Calhoun."

Inwardly Nate berated himself. Some of the others around the circle stood, as if to provide a united front. No one would give up that meat without a fight.

James climbed to his feet, jaw set. "I traded for it."

"Traded what? You don't have anything to trade." Langdon stepped closer to James. "More likely you stole that beef."

"Like hell." The precious nearness of the frying meat appeared to embolden James.

The rest of the squad stood, some with fists clenched. Hunger, Nate saw, outweighed their fear of Robert Langdon.

Seeing their cohesion, frustration swelled in the sergeant. He snapped, "I'll be back with the Captain. We'll see what he has to say about stealing."

Langdon stalked away, and everyone looked at each other and then quickly down at the meat.

Elias said, "Looks about done to me, boys."

"I like mine a bit bloody anyways," Abner said, his small grin contagious.

Nate had never tasted anything so delicious in his life. True enough the portions were small, but it seemed like a bountiful feast all the same, especially to their shriveled stomachs. No further words were spoken as everyone wolfed down the glorious beef. After the last swallow, Corporal May raised his canteen in a toast to Ulysses S. Grant and Pap Thomas.

The food and skillet were long gone by the time Langdon arrived with an irritated Frank Lane. Langdon glowered as the squad snapped to attention. They remained impassive until Abner belched, then all nearly collapsed in laughter.

"Attention!" Langdon roared.

Somehow they managed to comport themselves. Nate had to bite the inside of his cheek to keep from giggling, overcome with near delirium over the wonderful sensation of warm food in his belly.

"Sergeant," Lane said, looking a bit relieved now, "I see no food here."

"Captain—"

"Corporal," Lane said, turning to May. "Where is the meat to which the Sergeant referred?"

"I'm sorry, sir. There's been no meat here. The Sergeant must have been mistaken."

Langdon's face flushed purple.

"Very well," Lane said. "As you were, men." He returned their quick salutes. "Sergeant," he said darkly and turned to leave. Langdon glared at them before he trailed after the officer.

The squad held its composure only a moment longer before all melted into convulsive laughter.

***

Evening brought rain, chilling and oppressive. The men could either sit in the wet by their sputtering fires and try to gain some warmth from the flames or sit in their tents for protection and be cold. Nate and James chose the latter. The rain failed to dampen Nate's spirits, however; he could still taste the steak and see Langdon's enraged expression.

Through the dim candlelight, Nate said, "Wonder what Langdon will do to get back at us."

James kept his eyes on the small book he read. "After what we went through last month at Chickamauga, nothing Langdon can do can be that bad."

Nate nodded. "That's a fact." He continued reading his Bible but occasionally chanced a look James's way. The gloominess he had detected at the fire earlier had returned to the former shopkeeper, revealed in the way James avoided his eyes since they had entered the cramped tent. Nate grew curious, wondered if perhaps James had indeed come by that meat in a dishonest way. Even a month's pay would have been insufficient to satisfy the greed of some commissary sergeant.

"What you readin', James?"

"A book Jimmy Dorn got from a fellow in the Nineteenth Illinois."

"What kinda book?"

"One you're too young to be reading." He turned a page.

"I'm nigh unto nineteen summers. Lemme see."

James shook his head, his long blond hair straggling into his gray eyes.

"C'mon, James."

"What would your mother say?" James flicked a taunting glance his way.

Nate scowled and leaned back on his elbow. As he listened to the patter of rain on the canvas, he considered his messmate with a critical eye. Though James appeared engrossed in the novel, Nate could tell it was but a ruse.

"Jimmy Dorn trade for that there book?"

"No. It's borrowed."

"Lot of tradin' goin' on."

James lifted the book higher to conceal his face, but Nate could see his forehead and the furrows etched there.

"Did you trade somethin' for that beef?"

"None of your business."

"What's so secret? Nothin' to be ashamed of. 'Twas a right nice thing you did. I think so anyway."

"Good. Now leave me alone."

"You should be proud of yourself."

Suddenly the book came down. James's stare was hard, but Nate could tell his anger was aimed more inward than at him. "Proud?" James gave a sharp laugh, started to say more, then caught himself and scowled.

"Nothin' to be so peevish about. Don't know why you're bitin' me head off. If you reckon I'll think poorly of you if you stole that beef, you're wrong. We're all crazy hungry."

"Yeah? Well, I don't see you trading your mother's Bible for food." He quickly lifted the book back up. "Now, shut up and leave me alone."

The self-loathing in James's words struck Nate with sudden realization. Now that the meat was gone—it having been a momentary thing—the machinations behind it appeared to eat at James worse than the physical hunger had. Nate could see the truth now, could feel James's shame and regret, regardless of how much his generosity had garnered a bit more friendship from the squad. James had given more than money for the beef. And Nate knew of only one item of value his messmate carried.

CHAPTER 11

James shrugged deeper into his greatcoat as the orange sun crept over the ragged crest of Missionary Ridge. His breath hovered in white clouds before him, and he hoped the weak November sun would bring some warmth, at least enough to take the dampness from the rifle pit where he huddled. He flexed his stiff fingers, glanced along the picket line to the other drowsy men of his squad crouched in their gopher holes, here beyond the outer works of Chattanooga. Many looked to the south, toward the somnolent slopes of Lookout Mountain.

Yesterday, while serving as pickets for their division, the men of the brigade had all strained to see through the high clouds of fog ringing Lookout's heights, where General Hooker's men struggled to wrest the mountain from Confederate hands. Yet few in the valley below had seen more than the flash of muskets and artillery, the cannon's reports thundering against Missionary Ridge and Waldon's Ridge to the northwest, bouncing back and forth like a storm. The weather's shroud had added to the strange, detached feeling James had experienced while he watched, a witness to history being made so near yet seemingly above the very clouds themselves. In the afternoon, some said they had seen the U.S. flag upon the mountain, but James had not been one of them, and none of the rumors circulating through the brigade could confirm nor deny who held the mountain by nightfall.

James's stomach cried out for breakfast. How he longed for coffee and warm food. But at least this hunger lacked the desperation of a month ago. Shortly after James had traded his uncle's watch for the beef, General Grant had initiated the first step to bring relief to the besieged army—he sent two brigades to drive the Confederates from Brown's Ferry, west of the city. That successful operation had opened what everyone called the Cracker Line, a supply route that allowed an unimpeded flow of everything from food to mail to reinforcements in the form of General William Tecumseh Sherman's Army of the Tennessee from Vicksburg, some seventeen thousand strong.

In October, the Army of the Cumberland had been reorganized. With General Thomas's promotion, Major General John Palmer commanded the Fourteenth Corps. The Eleventh Michigan now belonged to Brigadier General Richard Johnson's division. Their brigade was led by their own Colonel Stoughton while Major Bennet commanded the Eleventh; though Lieutenant Colonel Mudge had been exchanged by the Rebels, he still had not completely recovered from his Chickamauga wound. The regiment was now brigaded with battalions from six Regular Army regiments as well as the Nineteenth Illinois and Sixty-ninth Ohio.

With all his troops reorganized and supplied, Grant moved forward in his plan to break the Confederates' hold on Chattanooga. Northeast of town, Sherman's men had stealthily crossed to the south side of the Tennessee River two nights ago to threaten the Confederate right flank. To distract the Rebels, that afternoon the Army of the Cumberland, minus the Eleventh Michigan's division, had made a brief demonstration in front of the Confederate center.

James would never forget the grand spectacle. Nearly twenty thousand men had formed in broad Lookout Valley, a staggering display of martial might with bands playing, drums beating, bugles calling, flags flying, and sunlight playing upon thousands of muskets. Then, as one, they stepped forward at the double-quick, and soon the afternoon air crackled with gunfire as the Rebel pickets in the valley opened fire. Little time passed before the Rebels fell back to the base of Missionary Ridge, their comrades on the crest staring down no doubt in complete bemusement at what had just transpired below. Atop the ridge, the Rebels scurried to shift their positions, strengthening their threatened center but weakening the flanks. James's heart had swelled with pride and a bit of redemption for Pap Thomas's boys; after all, it was widely said that General Grant considered the Army of the Cumberland a used up, ineffective force. Everyone itched to prove him wrong.

The following day, November 24, Sherman's men had attacked the Confederates near the north end of Missionary Ridge, where the Chattanooga and Cleveland Railroad passed through a tunnel. But it appeared Sherman had run into more opposition than he could handle, and the fighting had died off into a stalemate. Meanwhile, James had listened to "Fighting Joe" Hooker's boys grappling with the Rebels for possession of Lookout Mountain, which anchored the left of the Confederate line, while the Army of the Cumberland maintained the ground captured the previous day, including a prominence known as

Orchard Knob. Union cannon now glowered atop the hill, which stood more than halfway across the valley.

James tugged the collar of his greatcoat higher. The regiment was still not on full rations—supplies were steady but certainly not sufficient—so his coat hung from his shoulders with enough room for a second thin man. He looked off to his left where Nate sat in his rifle pit, musket near, a piece of paper in hand. Feeling a pang of envy, he guessed Nate to be reading one of many letters he had received from home over the past month.

"All these letters," the boy had bemoaned just yesterday, "but nothin' about Ryan. I hoped someone would've heard from him by now, but…" He shook his head.

"Well," Elias had offered, "the Rebs probably just don't let 'em send mail out like they should."

This failed to console Nate, and James could see and hear how much the boy itched to get at the Rebels again. James, on the other hand, was in no hurry.

James reached for his uncle's watch, but then remembered, frowned. Familiar shame rolled over him. He never should have allowed himself to succumb to the temptations of hunger and relinquish Uncle Pat's watch. What would his uncle have said to him? And, even more important, what would his father say when he returned home without it? Would he tell the truth or make up a lie about how it had been lost, perhaps in battle?

A rumbling to the south drew James's attention. At first, he thought the deep sound that of thunder, but there was no reason for such on this frigid morning. His ears had not deceived him, however, for the other pickets also sought the source of the rumble.

From down the line, First Sergeant Hart's voice rang out. "Look there, boys! On the mountain!"

Now James recognized the rolling noise as it swept across Lookout Valley—cheers and shouts from every Union soldier there, as well as those left in the works around Chattanooga.

"The flag!" voices cried. "See it on the face of the mountain? Someone's waving it!"

"I see it!" James called. "Hooker's boys really did it!"

Abner crowed, "The God damned mountain is ours!"

***

That day brought the renewal of Sherman's attempt to turn the

Confederate right flank. The roar of cannon and small arms shattered the morning, and great billows of smoke rose into the crisp blue sky. During those hours, when James and his comrades could see nothing of Sherman's fate up the valley, their brigade was relieved of picket duty. The Eleventh, only two hundred forty-four enlisted men and eleven commissioned officers, replenished cartridge boxes and drew three days' rations, a directive that indicated this would be no mere reconnaissance or simple demonstration. Carlin's brigade rejoined Johnson's division from detached service with General Hooker. In the open valley, Carlin's regiments formed in line of battle to the right of Stoughton's brigade, anchoring the Army of the Cumberland's right flank. The division's Third Brigade remained entrenched in and around Chattanooga.

Not to be outdone by their fellow Cumberlanders who had tramped out upon the plain so smartly two days ago, Colonel Stoughton's brigade marched in style, ranks perfectly dressed. The band played "Cheer, Boys, Cheer," which they most certainly did, giving vent to days of pent-up energy. Next to James, Nate nearly shouted himself hoarse during the short march. The left wing of the brigade was comprised of the Nineteenth Illinois and Sixty-ninth Ohio in the first line of battle, supported by the Eleventh as all flowed forward to connect with the right flank of General Phil Sheridan's division. The brigade's right wing, composed of the Regular Army battalions, closed with the left flank of Carlin's brigade. Rebel cannon atop Missionary Ridge continued to duel with the heavy guns from the Chattanooga forts, some tossing projectiles toward the fresh wave of troops, but most shots flew beyond the Union lines.

Reaching a belt of timber, the advance halted to await further orders.

From among the prone ranks, James eyed the open sweep of land before them. "They don't mean to send us across that, do they? It has to be at least half a mile to that ridge."

"Can't attack the center," Elias said. "It'll be like Pickett's charge at Gettysburg, sure. 'Cept this time the shoe'll be on t'other foot."

First Sergeant Hart said, "Don't worry, boys. The Captain says we only have to take the rifle pits at the base of the ridge. That'll draw the Rebs' attention away from Sherman to the north. He's not making much headway today."

"Again," Abner scoffed. "Sherman's boys need us to bail 'em out. We'll be sent to slaughter to save their bacon."

"But look yonder." James gestured toward Missionary Ridge.

"The Johnnies have another line of breastworks halfway up, then there's the main line at the top. And look at all the artillery up there."

The exhilaration of the morning was fast wearing off with the rising warmth of afternoon.

Rebel troops shifted along the crest of the ridge, headed toward Sherman's unabated fight. *Good,* James thought, *maybe that'll weaken the center; fewer guns on us, if Grant ever lets Pap's boys do anything.* Hopefully, Hooker would engage the Rebels' left flank down the valley. Yet no sounds of battle reached his ears from that direction. *Damned Easterners.*

Somewhere between three and four that afternoon—James had to guess by looking at the sun—a wave of excitement swept down the line from Grant's headquarters on Orchard Knob to the north. Something was about to happen; everyone sensed it.

Major Bennet strode along the line, passing orders to the company commanders and speaking encouragement to the men. His total lack of animation drew James's attention, stirred something unsettling in his breast. Bennet had an odd look about him, a slight pallor and tightness to his face. His steps came with an odd hesitation, like a man trying to remember something important.

"We'll be moving soon, boys," Bennet said as he drew near James's squad. "Six cannon will fire from Orchard Knob; that'll be the signal."

James asked, "Are you all right, sir?"

Bennet dragged a sleeve across his sweating forehead, met Nate's gaze with a wan smile of forced assurance. "I'm hale, James. It's just this infernal waiting."

"I know what you mean, sir."

When Bennet continued down the line, James murmured, "Something's not right with the Major."

Nate frowned, glanced furtively after Bennet, then leaned toward James so no one else could hear. "Last night, Colonel Stoughton gave James King permission to rejoin his company for today's attack. King said when he told Bennet, the Major said, 'James, you are a little fool. A lot of us will die tomorrow on that ridge. I shall not come out of battle alive.'"

Shocked, James stared from Nate to Bennet where the officer now stood in discussion with Captain Patrick Keegan, the Eleventh's senior company commander. With a grave expression, Keegan listened to a calm but fervent Bennet. A moment later Keegan shook his head decisively, taking a step back, his hands raised between them, as if to refuse something offered.

"James." Nate's quiet voice drew him back, and for the first time that day, the boy appeared almost grave, perhaps drawn into such a disposition by Bennet's premonition. From his sack coat, he withdrew his Bible, hesitated before continuing softly, "If somethin' happens to me, promise you'll send me Bible to Katie. I reckon she'd feel kindly if you put a lock of my hair in it...where I keep hers."

Indignation stiffened James. This was no time to be hearing men left and right talking about their demise. "Damn your hair, Calhoun. Put that thing back where it belongs." He turned away with the false pretense of retying his brogans.

The sharp report of the guns on Orchard Knob, ringing above the continuous crash of Sherman's fight, sent a shockwave through the regiment and silenced every tongue. Then the bugles blared, and with those notes, the command, "At the quick-step...forward...march!"

Into the open field sprang the Army of the Cumberland with a determined cheer, a line nearly two miles long, the divisions of Baird, Wood, Sheridan, and Johnson. Drums and bugles set the pace, kept everyone in a long-strided, determined step. Glancing to either side, James's breath caught in his throat at the magnificent sight. A double line of skirmishers from the front regiments darted ahead, followed by double, sometimes triple ranks of marching, well-dressed lines in the November sun, like a broad blue wave with a crest of silver steel washing toward the ridge. The worn battle flags seemed fresh and new. The music of bands stirred James's soul. Glory and pride drew a grin to his lips. He forgot about Bennet's presentiment and instead exulted at his part in this drama, could not imagine being elsewhere. Energy radiated through his muscles, lightened his steps with newfound confidence. Officers shouted from atop dancing mounts while men in the ranks yelled, swept up in the power of the moment.

For an instant James could believe this were all just one grand parade for the Rebels to admire from atop that bristling ridge. What could stop this bold force? Let Grant see them for what they were worth, for certainly he had never beheld a more glorious spectacle. Pap Thomas's face must be shining with satisfaction as he, too, observed from Orchard Knob. Indeed, James felt as if the whole world held its breath in admiration.

Then that world exploded as the long line of batteries atop Missionary Ridge opened fire.

CHAPTER 12

Nate kept his eyes upon the crest of the ridge. There smoke from the artillery hung like a storm cloud, yellow flashes stabbing through, the air shuddering as the Eleventh Michigan pressed onward. Ahead, a line of rifle pits scarred the earth, the tops of Rebel heads just visible, aimed gun barrels burnished by the afternoon sun. The voice of artillery, both Northern and Southern, all but drowned out the musketry. Under strict orders, the brigade did not return fire. Desperately Nate wanted to break into a run, to cross the open ground as quickly as possible, but he managed to restrain himself, focused instead upon the regiment's color guard. The movement of the guard gave life to the flags in the near-breezeless air, the silken fabric rippling like the surface of the ocean. How many of those men would be left once the Rebels started to single them out as they always did? *Brave men*, Nate thought distantly. *Braver than me.*

"At the double quick!" shouted the officers.

The men needed no further encouragement. They charged forward with a shout, heads down, shoulders hunched as if into an oncoming storm. The double quick resembled a headlong run, for all knew if they stayed out in the open much longer, few would be left to take the rifle pits.

The Confederates abandoned the first line of thinly defended pits, firing final shots before falling back to the defenses at the base of the ridge. There they joined others, and the combined forces sent a fresh hail of bullets at the attackers. Still the Union line held fire, officers and noncoms continually demanding discipline while men in the ranks fell. Crossing the abandoned works, the Federal lines lost cohesion, but on the opposite side, the men quickly dressed lines, rushed toward the ridge.

Closer, closer. Nate's chest hurt with the effort of the race, for he, like so many others, still felt the physical toll of long weeks of privation. Somehow he heard James's labored breathing next to him, no one able to give throat to any sort of shout now. The ridge loomed

120

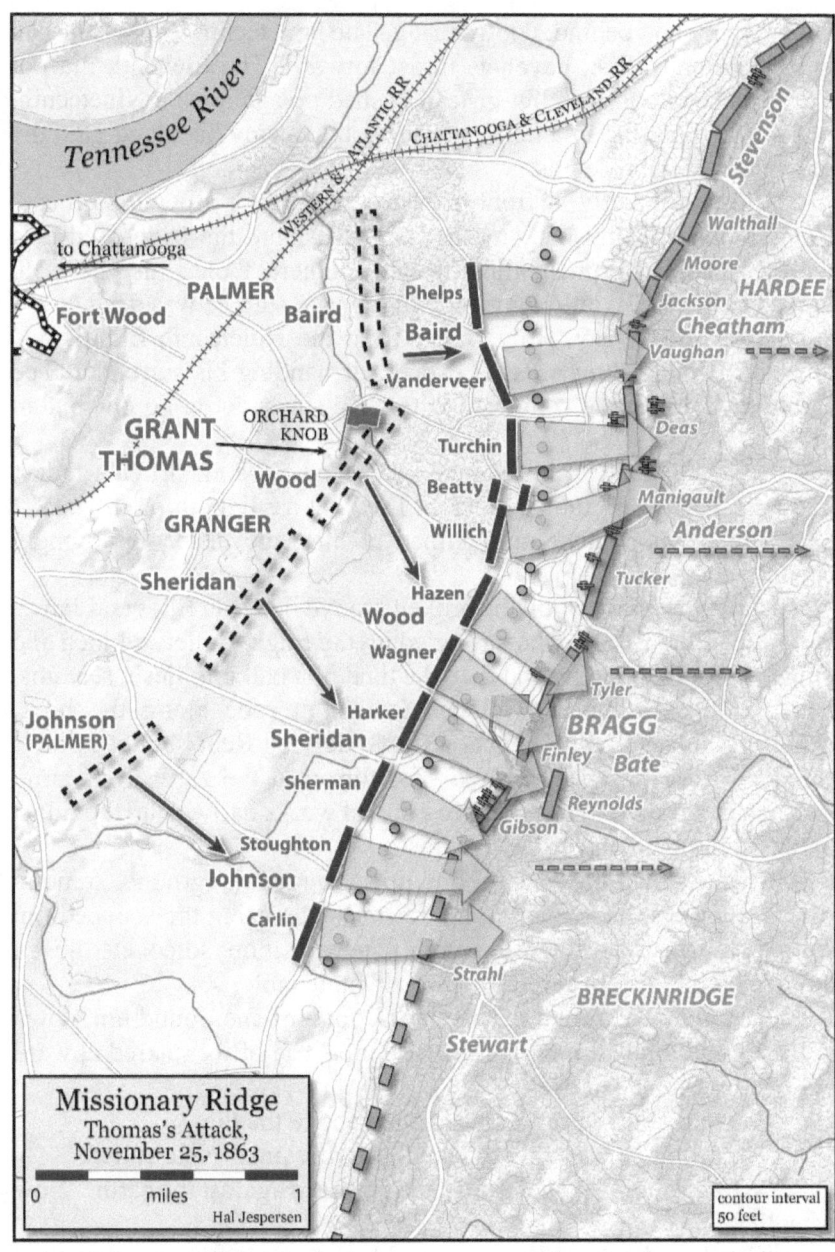

Missionary Ridge
Thomas's Attack,
November 25, 1863

0   miles   1

Hal Jespersen

contour interval
50 feet

above them. He realized many of the cannon high above were unable to depress their muzzles enough to efficiently target the attackers. All the more reason to continue forward.

The next rifle pits…steps away. Some of the Rebels fled upward.

Others remained behind, coolly firing. The Nineteenth Illinois clashed with the enemy first, bayonets thrust forward. The Eleventh did not check its headlong rush but instead pushed up against the Nineteenth, ranks intermingling in an effort to force the enemy back and gain the protection of the rifle pits.

A Rebel directly in front of Nate fumbled for a percussion cap. Nate clubbed his musket, smashed the stock into the frightened face with a sickening crunch, flinging the Southerner onto his back. He looked at the Rebel only long enough to make sure he was dead.

A few feet away, Billy Butler from the Nineteenth Illinois had leveled his musket on a Rebel officer, demanding his surrender. The stubborn Confederate countered with, "I'll surrender to no one but an officer."

Butler laughed. "You damned Rebel, we are all officers today. Take off that sword double quick or I will let daylight through you!"

With several other guns aimed at him, the officer grudgingly capitulated.

Nate threw himself on the broken ground between Elias and James and fired at the Rebels who struggled up the ridge. Bullets whined and pinged around him; now and then the thud of a ball into flesh; screams, oaths. Officers shouted. Colonel Stoughton rode along the lines, exhorting his tangled regiments' efforts, defying Rebel bullets. Shells shredded trees like paper. Solid shot furrowed the earth. Retreating Rebels disappeared into yet another line of works halfway up the ridge. Others scrambled onward to the crest.

Up and down the Federal line, men hugged the ground, some in rifle pits, others, like Nate, on the reverse side, using the scooped-out earth as a breastwork. The Eleventh's new position, so coveted just a moment ago, now appeared dangerously untenable.

Nate glanced around in search of Captain Lane, found him down to the right, huddled in one of the rifle pits. The officer stared upward with wide, frightened eyes.

"We can't stay here!" James yelled above the din.

"Hart said we was only to take these rifle pits," Nate called.

"We took 'em," Abner said, cheek pressed against the earth. "Now what?"

"Can't go back," Elias said. "It'd be murder to cross that field again."

"Where's Colonel Stoughton?"

"Down the line yonder. I think I see his horse."

Langdon shifted along the line, leapfrogging over prone men, face beet red as he instructed the soldiers in their firing.

Nate called, "What're the orders, Sarge?"

"Orders?" Abner cried. "Who's to give orders?" He swept a trembling hand around him. "Everything's a God damned mess." A bullet struck in front of him, spattering him with dirt. He glared upward at the unseen enemy.

"I'll talk to the Captain," Langdon shouted and continued to the right.

Nate reloaded and steadied himself against the damp mound before him, fired upward at nothing distinct. A bullet whizzed past his ear, tugged the blanket roll on his back. He rolled over to reload, cursed the intrusive bayonet affixed to the barrel but unwilling to remove it. Amidst the rising battle smoke, shells slashed streaks against the blue sky. Slowly his strength returned, and his breathing eased. Dear God, they would be wiped out if they stayed here. Damn Grant for his suicide orders. What did he care if the Army of the Cumberland was sacrificed for the sake of his pet—General Sherman?

Langdon returned, expression harsh.

"What's goin' on, Sarge?"

"The Captain thinks we should stay put, but Hicks and Coddington think we're supposed to take the crest. Others say the orders were just these rifle pits."

"Christ Almighty," Abner gritted out as he frantically reloaded.

James vehemently swore a streak of foul words that Nate had never heard him use before.

Major Bennet shouted something unintelligible from down the line. Still alive…

The men maintained their fire. The noise of battle now blended into one continuous roar. Smoke obscured the face of the ridge to left and right. Nate could see nothing beyond the regiment. Were the divisions of Sheridan, Baird, and Wood also pinned down? Or had they advanced or maybe retreated? Was Stoughton's brigade isolated? Nate ripped another cartridge open with his teeth and spilled its content of powder and ball down the barrel of his Springfield.

Then, like a thunderclap, a voice sounded above the clamor of battle, oddly clear and sharp, demanding and confident: "On up the ridge!"

The color guards of the Nineteenth Illinois and Eleventh Michigan rose simultaneously. As if physically tied to them, with no choice, no second thought, Nate rose with them. The whole line sprang forward as "Up the ridge!" echoed from all around, repeated by officers and enlisted men alike. On the heels of the Eleventh's color guard, James darted ahead of Nate, who scrambled upward, scraping and bruising himself on the rocks. Nate glanced to his right, did not see his captain, looked over his shoulder. Lane remained in the rifle pit. Nate turned forward again, forced the image from his mind. Above him, the top of the ridge was a wall of blazing rifles. They had to get there; they had to silence those guns.

The flash of muskets deep in the battle smoke all along the face of the ridge revealed a universal push, however jumbled and uncoordinated. All around Nate, men struggled over rocks and fallen logs. First Sergeant Hart led Company D, shouting and waving a sword. The higher they climbed, the more exposed they were to enfilade fire from all along the crest. In the confusion, regiments mixed, some led by officers, others led simply by brave men who seized the moment. Lines formed, then disintegrated as men were killed, wounded, or simply halted from exhaustion.

The brigade swept into the second line of rifle pits, flushed the handful of defenders. Before turning to flee, a Confederate shot Major Bennet, only to be killed by a bullet to the head. Horrified by the unmoving body of his commander only a few feet away, Nate stood momentarily paralyzed. Under the murderous fire, some of the men clung to the rifle pits, but Nate pushed on, afraid that if he stopped, he would never continue, like Frank Lane. "Get to the top," he kept muttering, though he thought the words were only in his throbbing head. *Stop them from killing us. Avenge Bennet. Show Grant and Sherman, Hooker...*

The regimental colors struggled ahead, and the Eleventh trailed behind in a flying wedge, fanning out like migratory geese.

Something tumbled down the rocks with a clatter.

"Nate!" Elias cried. "Look out!"

Nate jumped sidelong, stumbled, fell in a painful heap as a lit shell sizzled past, exploded, sprayed him with rock and dirt. He looked up in deafened shock. The Rebels were rolling down their shells, fuses lit.

He caught up to Elias, who had sought cover behind a tree. Both pushed forward. Around them, the climb had seemingly turned into a race, each regiment, each company trying to reach the top first. Nate's breathing grew more and more labored in the heavy air. As his hearing cleared a bit, he detected the gasps of those surrounding him. Sweat cocooned him in a web of dripping moisture. He was so damned thirsty.

To his left, a man cried out, tossed his gun, blood spurting from an arm. George Gillett. Another Burr Oaker.

"George!" Nate reached to keep him from tumbling downward, but a second ball slammed into the young man's chest, flung him from Nate's grip. He was dead before he hit the ground.

A bullet struck Nate's canteen, tugging the strap. Water trailed down his leg as he clawed upward again. He drank a large, quick swallow, then tossed aside the worthless canteen and joined Elias in a depression, only a few rods from the summit. So close. Here the ridge rose at a much sheerer, daunting angle. He could see the Rebels on the crest now, hear their officers. The rocky lip of their shelter gave him and Elias considerable protection. Men collapsed all around, mouths open, clinging to whatever cover they could find. The whole line faltered.

Nate peered through the smoke. "Major Bennet went down, so Keegan's in command of the regiment now. Can you see him?"

"Last I saw," Elias replied, "he was wounded."

"Then who's in command?"

"Captain Bissell."

Nate peered through the thick pall for Bissell, saw him on the ground, left hip and back bloody. Lieutenant Charles Coddington of Company A was with him, bent down as if to listen. Apparently Coddington was in command now. They were losing officers just when they needed order for the final push.

Nate saw James forward near the prone color guard, just a rod or so to his left. John Day, who had carried the regimental flag across the valley, was not with them. The banner, nearly severed from its staff, was in someone else's care now.

The Rebels along the crest to the right continued their deadly enfilade fire upon the brigade's exposed flank.

"Where the hell's Carlin's brigade?" Corporal May yelled. "We'll be shot to pieces!"

Nate reloaded and stared over the lip. A Rebel battery of six guns stood to their right, supported by infantry. They could be pinned here forever. He waited for a clear target, then fired. The Rebel slumped behind the breastwork.

A sharp blow to Nate's chest threw him backward, stole his breath. He struck the ground hard, strangled out a cry as rocks bruised him. He rolled against a tree.

Elias scrambled down, grabbed him, and hauled him back to the cover of the depression.

"Nate...Nate, where you hit?"

Dazed, he could not answer, tried to comprehend, gasped for air.

His chest burned. Frantic with dread, he groped for the wound, paused at the front of his sack coat where the fabric had been torn. Fingers shaking, he managed to unbutton his uniform, almost afraid to see. Beneath his breast pocket, his flesh had already turned an ugly purple— only a bruise. Amazed, he looked further. Nothing. He stared up at Elias's astonished, dirty face, then touched the torn fabric again, felt bulk beneath it, remembered. Slowly he pulled out his Bible and gaped at a spent ball buried among the torn pages.

A huge shell from the Union siege guns in Fort Wood wailed overhead, exploded somewhere above them. Nate tried to shut his ears to the dying shrieks of men. He rubbed his chest and put the Bible back in his pocket, muttering a prayer of thanks.

Elias gave him a wan grin. "Too bad Ryan didn't have your luck, lad."

"We're almost there," Nate panted.

But no one moved farther. Everyone clung to the face of the ridge, deafened and dazed by the noise, choked by the smoke. Exploding caissons shook the ground, showered debris.

Near the color guard, Lieutenant Hicks yelled encouragement to the men gathered around, perhaps a hundred strong, but Nate was unable to hear the young officer's exact words. The regimental color bearer rose, others with him, but a bullet ripped away half his skull. In that strange instant, the men of the Eleventh stared in silence as the dark blue flag with its defiant eagle fluttered to the ground, dirty, torn, and spattered.

From the knot of surrounding men, someone dived for the flag and raised it high, screamed like a madman, "C'mon, Michigan!" James, his face so transformed Nate barely recognized him, waved the banner in a circle, sprang forward. The Eleventh rose with a roar, a blue force of connected, resolute power. They charged upward behind James.

Nate bolted after his comrade. He was only a couple of yards behind when James's right leg suddenly went out from under him. Falling to one knee, James swore, grabbed his bleeding calf with his right hand, braced the flag against his chest with his left.

"James!" Nate staggered toward him.

Cursing, James tried to stand, fell forward onto his hands and knees. The impetuous Lieutenant Hicks caught the flag before it could fall to the ground, bore it onward. Next to him, Lieutenant Coddington carried the national flag up the ridge.

Nate slung his musket over his shoulder and grabbed James under the arms, pulled him behind the protection of a fallen log. James ground his teeth, cried out, tried to stand. Nate hauled him back down.

"What the hell ye doin', James?"

"Gotta get to the top," he coughed.

"Been shot, ye have, ye crazy fool. Stay down."

Again James tried to rise, using the log as leverage. Angry and frightened, Nate dragged him back. James turned on him, grabbed him by the collar with both hands, amazingly strong. The insanity of battle glazed his eyes, teeth starkly white against his dirt- and gunpowder-blackened skin.

"I'm going to the top. The whole regiment's there, damn you. Lemme go."

"Ye have to go to the rear."

James's grip tightened. Tears spilled unnoticed down his cheeks. "Help me to the top. Please… All this way…"

Nate frowned, glanced upward through the smoke to see the Eleventh's flags flowing on the crest. Somewhere up there, jubilant voices wildly shouted, "Chickamauga! Chickamauga!" He turned to James, whose hold loosened as shock wore off and debility rode in.

"You have to let me bind your wound first."

Weakly James nodded, but his gaze remained on the crest where the battle raged on without them. Nate reached for his knife and cut away the lower portion of James's pant leg. Between strong gulps, James swore. A bloody mess of a hole in his calf, the exit wound ugly and tattered.

"Clean through," Nate reported. Quickly he used the torn cloth as a tourniquet.

James spoke near a whisper. "Hurry…"

"Are you sure you can do this, James?"

The young man nodded, gaze still fixed on the flags around which men celebrated by throwing hats into the air, yelling, and cheering.

Against his judgment, Nate stood and carefully hoisted James with him. He draped the wounded man's arm around his shoulders, saw his face pale. Expecting a bullet every treacherous step from Rebels who still resisted somewhere above, they made it the final fifty feet to the top. The Confederates had abandoned the battery and fled down the eastern slope. The whole Rebel army was a tangled mass of retreat, while along the narrow crest, the Federal celebration neared pandemonium. Smiling and laughing at the delirious moment, Nate looked at James's exhausted but shining eyes, then helped him sit against the wheel of a captured cannon, the barrel of the three-inch ordnance rifle still smoking. Nate looked around for May or Elias or

Abner but could not see them in the chaotic mix of the brigade. He started to stand but James held his arm.

"Don't go," James croaked through parched, split lips.

"James—"

The grip tightened, and slowly James shook his head. For the first time, fear shined through the pain in his eyes, though Nate was unsure of what he feared. He knew then that he could not leave him, pursuit of the Rebels or no pursuit.

Order began to return. Bugles recalled men. Colonel Stoughton—now on foot, for no horse could have climbed that slope—shouted to his subordinates to reform the brigade. Langdon rushed by but altered his course when he saw Nate.

"On your feet, Calhoun. We're going after the Johnnies."

"Can't leave James, Sarge. He's wounded."

Langdon seemed to recognize James for the first time. He scowled. "The hell you can't. Now move."

James said nothing, but his hold on Nate's hand grew painfully tight, his defiant stare on the sergeant.

"I said get up, Calhoun." Grabbing Nate by the collar, he stood him on his feet. "You won't use Keenan as an excuse to shirk your duties."

Nate shoved the larger man away, brought his gun in front of him. Not respecting a wounded comrade was crime enough, but accusing him of shirking...

From behind Langdon, Colonel Stoughton demanded, "What's going on here?" The fast-failing sunlight showed intolerance on his begrimed face.

"James is wounded, sir." Nate gestured with his chin, kept his eyes on Langdon.

Stoughton's gaze softened, and he crouched next to James, a bloody sword in one hand. "Is it broken, son?"

"No, sir," James managed to reply.

Stoughton offered a small, warm smile. "You showed uncommon valor down that hill, James. It won't be forgotten."

Nate said, "He wants me to stay with him, sir."

Stoughton momentarily rested a hand on James's shoulder, then he stood and gave Langdon a pointed stare. "The lad can have anything he wants, Sergeant."

Langdon's jaw clenched. "Yes, sir."

"See to the men of your company."

Langdon glowered at James, then turned away.

128

The always-exuberant Lieutenant Hicks bounded over, still carrying the wounded flag, his entire being full of glorious energy. Others came with him, everyone drunk on victory.

"There he is! How is he, sir?"

"A bit worn at the moment, Lieutenant, but Nate's going to see to him."

Hicks crouched in front of James whose eyes trailed over the tortured banner. The smooth-faced lieutenant cradled the flag so its folds stayed clear of the ground. "I wanted to make sure you knew it got up here, James. Without you, it might not have."

James reached out a trembling hand, touched the gold fringe, caressed the blue field, closed his eyes.

"You woulda been first on the ridge if you hadn't got shot, I wager. But ol' James King beat us to the glory, blast him." The boyish officer grinned. "Went and got shot just like you. Broke his arm."

As Hicks continued, Stoughton drew Nate aside. "Get him down the hill if you can. It'll be a long, cold night on this ridge; not a place for a wounded man."

"Yes, sir."

Stoughton looked past him to James, and his expression softened even more. "It appears the regiment had him pegged wrong." He raised his voice to Hicks. "Re-form your company, Lieutenant."

Nate thanked the colonel and wished him luck, watched him hurry away with his staff.

Hicks patted James's shoulder, then stood to smile at Nate. "Take good care of him. We'll be back directly."

Nate smiled tightly and nodded. Hicks and the others rushed into the swirling blue mayhem.

Nate shared a drink from James's canteen. "Think you can make it down the ridge?"

Sleepily James replied, "Not yet. Rest first."

Nate settled next to him and listened to James's labored breathing. He watched the regiment re-form and advance down the eastern slope, disappearing from view. Gunfire continued at intervals to the north and south on Missionary Ridge, shouts and cheers intermingled, but no Rebel yells. The sun had set beyond Raccoon Mountain, and darkness crept up from the valleys, swept over the retreating enemy and pursuing victors.

"Nate," James said faintly. "Whatever happens…don't let 'em take my leg."

His words drifted away, one voice among the hundreds of

wounded whose cries all around them seemed suddenly louder and more terrible than any of the battle sounds of that short, triumphant afternoon.

***

The flag. James could still feel the staff in his hands, the weight of the banner, hear its living rustle. In slow motion it fell. Desperately he wanted to catch it, preserve it, but he could not let go of his damned leg, oddly curious about the warm, sticky wetness between his fingers. His own blood, pouring out, draining him. Hicks took the standard. James watched it flow toward the obscure summit, wanted to bury his face in its folds. Nate dragging him away from the bullets, the flag. The tightening agony of the tourniquet hammered home reality to James's dulled wits. But he had to get to the top; he had come so far.

"James. Let's stop a minute. Gotta loosen the tourniquet."

Struggling out of his haze, James mumbled, "Why?"

"Gotta let the blood down there now and then or else they'll have to cut it off, sure."

James remembered the moment he had been shot; it had felt as if someone had thrown a brick against his leg, kicking it out from under him. At first, he thought someone had tripped him in the rush or that he had stumbled over something. Then the pain sliced into his consciousness.

"James?"

He shook his gaze clear again, found Nate staring at him for a long, uncertain moment, the boy's hands poised near the bloody rag as he awaited permission. Battling his habitual mistrust, James gritted his teeth and nodded. Nate loosened the knot, and James stiffened against the hot pain and sucked in his breath. Blood trickled down into his brogan, taking strength with it. Staring off into the night sky, he tried to think of something pleasant, but nothing came. He closed his eyes. Something warm and comforting enclosed his left hand. He thought of his mother, squeezed his fingers tightly, realized, opened his eyes, released.

"'Tis all right," Nate murmured, taking his hand again. "Squeeze as hard as you fancy." He grinned palely in the moonlight. "Just don't break no bones."

James tried to laugh but instead produced only an embarrassing whimper.

"All right, then," Nate said at last. "That's tolerable. But we'll

130

need to do it again in a wee bit." He tied the tourniquet, frowned. "Sorry."

"It's all right," he gasped. "Let's go."

During their continued descent of the ridge, they often tripped and twice fell. James bit his lip so hard to keep from screaming that he tasted blood. Out of necessity they stopped frequently. While James rested, Nate trailed off into the dark to give water to the wounded and dying spread along the slope, both Union and Confederate, using whatever canteens he could find. While he waited, James drifted off. When he awoke alone in the ghostly night with nothing but the wails of wounded all around, cold fear gripped him until Nate returned.

"James, you all right?"

He stared dumbly into Nate's worried eyes.

"We're almost to the bottom. Can you make it?"

The top. The bottom. Which was what?

Nate frowned. "We'll set a spell longer." He sat next to James, remained quiet for a time while James closed his eyes. When he finally spoke, his words drew James back to clarity. "Reckon you'll get to go home for a bit."

"It's not that bad."

"Bad enough for a furlough."

"I'm not going."

Nate studied him through the thin darkness. "If I was you, *I'd* go home."

"Well, you're not me." He thought of Nate's brush with death—the boy had shown him the wounded Bible, Katie's picture torn, the lock of hair scattered. Nate had not traded the Bible for food.

"Your pa will be proud of you once you tell him what happened."

James muttered, "He won't believe me."

"'Course he will."

James glanced at him, then to the valley below. "Truth be told, he reckons me for a coward, always has since the start of the war."

"No man will dare think you a coward after today."

With a skeptical grunt, James struggled to stand. "Let's go."

When they reached the base of the ridge, James spied lights flickering in the distant trees across the open field, the trees where long ago the brigade had stepped off. He remembered Bennet's drawn face. Dead now, as predicted. The lights seemed unattainable as he and Nate hobbled toward them, past dead horses and men, gray and brown lumps in the early night, the air choked with hideous smells and sounds.

They stopped halfway to loosen the tourniquet again. Afterward

James could barely stand on his one good leg. The world spun. The diamond-sharp stars in the clear sky swirled closer. The other night the moon had been swallowed by an eclipse. The veterans watching it had claimed that it boded ill for the Rebels, for the Confederates were, after all, closer to the moon, being up on that ridge.

He just needed to rest a little longer, then he could go on. Damnation, why had he gotten shot? Shouldn't have grabbed the flag…but had to get the boys to the top. "Chickamauga! Chickamauga!" Who had been yelling that? *Hope Grant heard those voices, damn him. Bet he never treats the Army of the Cumberland like second-class soldiers again.*

For a moment, the pain eased but then returned with savage force when he focused his eyes on the stars again, so he closed them, a distant buzz in his ears, getting louder. His head swam, and nausea twisted his stomach. Someone called his name. Then the ground rose to greet him, soft and wonderfully cool.

***

Pain like he had never known before in life. Torturous. Shooting up his leg into his body, jerking him to consciousness. Someone pressed him down.

"Get off!" he rasped.

Nate's frightened blue eyes, candlelight bronzing his face as he restrained James. Trees above them; beyond the naked branches, a fat moon in a cold sky. It must be cold—it was late November—yet sweat soaked James's shirt.

"They're almost done, James. Lie still."

A field hospital. An unearthly chorus of agony around him, moans and shrieks, the stench of blood.

"Hold him still, soldier."

His leg! Still there. A surgeon, probing, poking, not even looking at his patient, apron smeared with gore.

"You'll not take my leg, damn you."

The short, balding man glanced up as if amused. "No need to, lad. Your friend here did a first-rate job. We'll bandage it up and send you into Chattanooga. 'Fraid you'll have to wait, though; lot worse cases going back first."

Nate held a bottle to James's lips, commanded, "Drink this."

The bite of whiskey gagged James, for he never drank liquor, not after watching it ruin his father. His father…

With the whiskey's dull warmth working its way through him, he managed to endure the rest of the doctor's brief treatment and the binding of his wound. James took another swallow, thankful for the way the alcohol seeped through him and made the pain almost endurable. Exhausted, he lay back and stared into the night sky. A scream from nearby caused him and Nate to flinch. James did not want to stay here. This was worse than being alone somewhere. Men lay all around, most on the ground, many without even a blanket beneath them. He at least had that, for he and Nate had gone into battle with their blanket rolls slung over their shoulders. Now he lay on his, and Nate draped his own over him.

"Don't need it," James insisted. "Hotter than hell."

"You need it."

James tried to argue but words failed him. He abhorred this weighty fatigue yet also welcomed the escape it provided. The whiskey relaxed his rigid muscles. Shivering, he tried to struggle back, to make sure Nate would stay, to thank him, but the old wall reared up around him. He felt Nate's now-familiar hand. James closed his fingers, had to concentrate to do so, tried to grip, could not, drifted away from the nightmare sounds.

***

Awake or asleep? Cries and moans for relief. Someone wanted water, another wanted his father, another called a woman's name. A dream or reality? His voice or others'? A soft voice, a man's voice, close but not right next to him.

"Where were you hit, my son?"

A dry, strained answer: "Almost up."

"What did you...? No, son. I mean what part of your body did the bullet strike?"

Clearer, almost excited: "Almost up to the top."

James heard the rustle of a blanket.

The animated, strained voice continued. "Yes, that's what did it. I was almost up. But for that I would have reached the top." The man's breath rattled in his chest, forced faint, dying words, "Almost up."

James drifted, heard his own moans, powerless to stop them. Someone touched the dressing. He rolled from his stomach to his side, wanted to get away. Some place quiet. No tormented voices, no dying words. Home. *No, can't go home. If I leave the regiment, will they forget what I did? Did it really all happen? Stoughton said...wouldn't be forgotten.* Dear Stoughton…alive while Bennet lay dead on that ridge. James twisted against the pain in his leg. Maybe they should have cut it off.

He awoke, cold, stiff, feverish. Morning sunlight trickled over the frosted crest of Missionary Ridge. Had he been up there once? No Rebel flags flew there now. It had been so long ago. What had ever possessed him to take that flag? He felt drained, like a wet rag twisted to dampness but not spread to dry. *Must have lost more blood than I thought.* Powerful thirst. He looked around at the wounded, tried to puzzle out who lay asleep and who lay dead. The blue, stiff ones…they were the dead. He looked at his hand. White, shaking in the bitter morning cold.

Nate? James rolled over, winced. The boy was nowhere in sight. James's empty stomach ached but not from hunger; he had no desire for food.

"Nate." Was that his own voice? Didn't sound like him. Sounded like his father after a long night of drinking. "Nate." Why did he call the boy? Surely he had returned to the regiment. But without Nate how could he stop the surgeon from taking his leg?

"For God's sake…Nate."

He gave up, shut his eyes, close to tears but unsure why. So damned thirsty.

"James?"

Nate knelt next to him. Blood stained the boy's torn uniform.

"Thought I heard you call."

"Water."

"Aye. Just filled your canteen."

"Where you been?"

"Helpin' bring the wounded in. Not enough hands 'round to help. Our boys are out chasin' the Rebs still." He braced James's head while he drank greedily. Afterward, Nate lifted the blanket from James's leg, frowned. "Another ambulance just came back from town. Let's get you on it. Our corps has two churches set up in town for our wounded. Best to get you indoors."

Suffering men already filled the ambulance, but Nate badgered the driver to allow James next to him with another soldier, half his head swathed in bandages. Their effort to haul James up took his breath away, started his leg bleeding again.

He looked down at Nate, located his voice. "Where you going to ride?"

Almost apologetically Nate smiled and shrugged. "I best be gettin' back to the regiment…if I can find 'em. Don't want 'em thinkin' I run off with the Johnnies."

James nodded, the fear of being alone hollowing out his stomach again. He imagined worse horrors awaited him than those of the field hospital. "Give the boys my best."

When the mule team lurched forward, James's eyes widened with pain. He clutched at the seat and watched Nate grow smaller as the wagon bounced onto the road toward Chattanooga, a mile away. He raised his hand. Nate waved back. The boy no longer looked so young.

CHAPTER 13

Nate's gaze slipped away from the candlelit letter he was writing and rested upon the daguerreotype Katie had recently sent to replace the one damaged by the Rebel bullet two months ago. A smile lifted the corners of his mouth as he drank in the sight of his fiancée. He closed his eyes and imagined the softness of her skin beneath his fingers. He still felt homesick whenever he looked at her likeness or read a letter from home, but no matter the pain, he would never discourage the memories.

He glanced around the little hut that he now called home. On the hard-packed dirt floor, Abner, David May, and Elias played a spirited game of cribbage. James lay on his bunk below Nate's and read *Harper's Weekly*, his right leg elevated by his knapsack. The five of them had built their winter quarters as a team effort, finding wood plentiful for the simple but comfortable cabin. A variety of material—hardtack boxes, barrel staves, and saplings—made up the bunks, which they cushioned with straw or leaves from oaks and pines. The hardtack boxes also provided furniture—the table where Nate now sat, as well as the chairs. A chimney made of barrels kept the dwelling comfortably warm. Occasionally the barrels would catch fire, one such occurrence last week. Nate grinned at the memory of May waking up with a howl to find his blanket on fire and his toes singed. They had doused the small conflagration in short order while Abner snored through the whole affair. In retribution the next night, May and Nate lit a couple of matches between Abner's toes while he slept. They burned almost all the way down before Abner's eyes popped open and he set to dancing around their quarters, cursing them thoroughly as all fell about the place in hilarity.

Many of the men in the Eleventh's winter camp near Rossville, Georgia, had christened their new homes. Theirs was called the Burr Oak Burrow, though May protested, being from Noble in Branch County. However, majority ruled. At Christmas they had incorporated

136

a little tree—kept away from the troublesome chimney—and decorated it with all manner of things. Somehow the pitiful evergreen made the holiday bearable, yet Nate had experienced his worst bout of homesickness. His companions, however, helped him endure, just as he helped them. They all looked forward to the spring campaign simply to erase the boredom of camp life.

Nate went back to writing.

James leg is coming along tolerable well   all most like new   i reckon the cold wether makes him hurt considerable but he dont say so much for the "sunny South"   not much hapening heer just camp dudy i reed evry nite from the new Bible ma sent and mark the page with yore new likeness   i try to git James to reed with me but he says no James and me hav kind uv become frends since Mission ridge   i still dreem about wen James took the flag and about that clime up the hill some say if we had pushed the Rebs more after Mission ridge then we could have used them up but insted they got away so now we wait for spring to fite   the five uv us all look out for each other   still miss Jeremy considerable   Ben Hart is home recruiting as you might know   has he stopped by to see my parents   Frank Lane is still captin but he didnt show hisself well at Mission ridge so the boys aint too happy with him James sed he will teech me how to better reed and rite   he is very good at it so you see i am to lern more than how to be a sojer   James got a letter from his father about a month ago   just one small page poor fellow but i think it ment the world to him   dont kno what was in the letter   James dont share   Abner sed his mother sed the news of James carrying the flag was all over town   no one could believe it just lik you sed   well it did happen i saw it   must end here becuz we ar off to hav a first rate treet sneeking out uv camp to a place down the road whare there is to be a dance with som of the boys from the regiment and som local girls   nun of them will be as pretty as you im sure

The cribbage game had broken up, and everyone eagerly prepared for the dance. Hair combed, hats beaten clean of dust or ash, buttons buttoned and shined, brogans brushed off. Soon they snuffed out the candles and stole outside into the January night where a light blanket of freshly fallen snow brightened the Eleventh's camp.

Corporal May led them from hut to hut in the darkness, all crouching low when the crunch of booted feet drew near. Voices carried outward from the orderly rows of shelters, laughter and the glow of lanterns and fireplaces shining through cracks. The secrecy surrounding the progress of their little band amused Nate, so thirsty for something thrilling was he. The burst of excitement made him giddy, caused him to giggle at May's serious expression. Abner clapped a hand over his mouth and gave him a shake. Nate bit his hand. Abner swore, which in turn drew another laugh from Nate. May elbowed him backward into James.

At the picket line, they hunkered behind a large tree and waited for the sentry, who paused in the night.

"Who goes?"

May hissed, "For God's sake, Lyon, move your ass. You'll make us late."

"Late?" the twenty-year-old drawled insouciantly. "Don't fancy it being fair, me pulling guard duty whilst you boys get the girls."

"C'mon, Mel," James urged. "Let us pass and we'll bring you back a girl."

"Sure you will." The sentry paused. "That you, Keenan?"

"Yeah."

"Best look out. I hear tell Preacher Langdon will be at that there dance."

Nate glanced at James, saw the tightening of his jaw but no further reaction.

May tried again. "Hurry up, Lyon. Move on. We're freezing."

"Now, Davy, don't rush me else I'll be telling that Hannah of yours that you've been stepping out on her." With a chuckle, his dark shape trudged on, and the five sprinted into the night.

* * *

May led them east through Rossville Gap, which cut through Missionary Ridge, well south of where the Eleventh had fought two months earlier. About two miles beyond the gap, May headed north through a dark wood, somehow finding his way with little but the snow as illumination. James's toes tingled with the cold and his healing leg dully throbbed, but he gamely kept up with the others.

Soon they reached a clearing where the remains of a small house provided a sad, dark scar amidst the pristine snow, stripped and partially burned by one army or the other. The barn northwest of the house, however, promised anything but ruin, aglow from within and humming with music. Happy voices and laughter rang through the still, crystalline air. Nate let out a yip and broke into a run. James grinned and limped after the others.

138

Inside, a double row of lanterns strung from dusty, cobweb-draped beams splashed light over the crowd of soldiers and eight young women. At one end of the barn, a decrepit wagon served as the bandstand where men from various companies of the Eleventh played a reel on tin whistle, banjo, guitar, fiddle, and harmonica. At the other end, an old stove had been rigged with a tin chimney that funneled smoke through an opening in the wall, its glowing front providing warmth.

The participants of the dance heartily welcomed the newcomers, shoving mugs of beer or warm cider into their hands. Bright faces, laughter and song, everyone looking young again as they had in Michigan before the war. The local girls swooped from partner to partner in a breathless whirl, none overly pretty or dressed in anything more than tired, everyday dresses but all made attractive simply by their femininity. Owing to the sparseness of partners of the opposite sex, many of the men wore rags tied around one arm to signify a "lady." So soldier danced with soldier, and enjoyment spilled over into the darkness beyond the walls, the boredom of winter quarters and the bloody struggles that had preceded it banished from thought.

In deference to his sore leg, James waited until a slow melody played before he ventured into the dance floor fray and only after enough spiked cider had thoroughly warmed his body and his confidence. He conjured his most dashing smile for the young woman who had just danced with Abner, catching her eye as he stepped over.

"Would you so honor me, miss?"

Her brown eyes widened, and she smiled, somehow sultry and arousing for one so young. Abner started to protest the incursion as the dark-haired girl took James's offered hand.

"Recollect, Ab," James said with a wink, "you're a married man." He turned away.

"Yeah? Well, your leg hain't gonna hold out for long, James Keenan, then the lady will be a-needin' me again. I can go all night."

"That's not what I heard," James said over his shoulder, then smiled at the blushing girl.

"I declare," she said, "I ain't never seen such a handsome Yankee. What's your name, sojer?"

"James." He kissed her hand, and her eyes sparkled in response. "And yours?"

"Elmyra. You may call me Myra."

"Well, Myra, shall we dance?"

She giggled and allowed him to waltz her out among the others as

"Lorena" swelled up from the band. Although the crush of bodies upon the dance floor allowed for little movement, James did not mind; in fact, for the sake of his leg, he was grateful. Besides, the tight quarters gave him an excuse to be closer than normally accepted. Myra wore soft gloves, thin enough to convey her gentleness, a welcomed sensation to him after so many months of harsh living. By God, a lifetime. To look into a woman's eyes, feel her body against his, hear the music of a light voice…he had not realized how tiresome men's company could be, living a soldier's life with nothing tender nearby. In fact, as they talked of trivial things, he had to make an effort to mind his language, a problem unknown back home, for his parents had never allowed cursing. Home. He remembered the dance before he had left Burr Oak, an evening that at the time had meant little to him; now he often revisited that sweet memory in the boredom of winter camp.

When the song ended, young Amos Gilbert stepped over to claim Myra for the next song, but she turned a coquettish smile on James and said, "I'm gonna set this one out." Then she took James by the hand and led him through the throng toward the back door of the barn.

Outside, several men stood or crouched around a fire—a serious group of gamblers tossing dice, smoking, and drinking against a black backdrop of trees. The cold air felt wonderful against James's sweaty skin, and the scent of the fire pleased him. Then he recognized the blocky shape of Robert Langdon. The sergeant's firelit gaze touched upon the girl then slid to James, chilling him. James turned away and led Myra around the corner of the barn.

When they were out of sight of the men, Myra stopped and pressed her back against the side of the barn. The music and voices from inside easily passed through the slats, causing them to smile. James draped his sack coat around the girl's slim shoulders.

She murmured, "I needed some air." She studied him in the moonlight, her lashes dark against her skin.

James smiled. "You don't mind dancing with Yankees?"

"I ain't from around these parts; most my kin is in Tennessee, and they's Union folk. My ma and pa sent me down here to my cousin's last summer to get away from the war. 'Course that was afore all you boys come over them mountains last fall and pushed Braxton Bragg into Georgia." She shrugged. "T'other gals…they don't much care what color uniform a boy wears if'n he can dance. Now if they's folks found out they was dancin' with Yanks…well, that might be a different story." She grinned and brushed James's hair back behind one ear. "You got a gal back home, James?"

"Well…sort of."

Myra cocked one sable eyebrow and considered him further. She raised a slim finger to touch his mustache, his lips. "Ain't you a-hankerin' to kiss me?"

He would have liked to do much more than that, but he settled with taking her in his arms and answering her question.

***

Nate wasted no time in imbibing wholeheartedly to keep warm as well as to enjoy himself. He managed to steal one of the girls long enough for two dances, but then Abner claimed her, and so he had to be content with one of his soldierly comrades as a partner. Once tired, Nate retreated for another mug of beer while he regained his strength, having grown soft these past weeks.

He gave voice to nearly every song, a voice not as true as he would have liked and even less so the more he drank. At home he had been allowed alcohol only on special occasions, though his brothers sometimes deigned to allow him to sneak a nip or two with them when they were fishing the Prairie River. Since joining the army, he found the temptation often at hand, but he feared any indiscretion might be communicated to his parents, so he remained virtually a sober citizen, especially since neither Elias, James, nor May were married to drink. If any of them got tight, it was Abner, especially since Jeremy's death, a weakness they readily forgave.

Following a brief break, the musicians regained the stage, having been refreshed by their grateful audience.

"'Fisher's Hornpipe'!" Nate requested just as James and Myra returned from outside, faces flushed. "C'mon, James! Let's show 'em how it's done."

"Looks like James is too tired to dance," May teased, drawing hoots and catcalls from the crowd.

Elias added, "Been gone a long spell, lad."

The banter continued, drowning out James's red-faced defense. Myra giggled behind her hand. Nate sprang forward and towed his reluctant messmate into the middle of the dance floor. James tried to decline the invitation, but when Myra urged him on, he grinned and turned back to accept Nate's challenge, much to the raucous approval of all present.

As the musicians launched off into the hornpipe, the crowd closed in tighter, feet stomping and hands clapping. The barn vibrated with

141

life. Nate's feet moved fluidly, his steps confident from many an evening of song and dance among friends and family throughout his life. To his surprise, James matched him nearly step for step. Nate had seen enough of James at town dances to envy the smoothness of his waltzes, but he had never known him to possess the agility he now displayed. If the effort pained his leg, he concealed it. Instead, a competitive light flared in his eyes, steely with determination, no doubt to impress the girls, who unabashedly cheered him on. Sweat dampened James's low brow, but otherwise he looked strong as the unspoken duel progressed, the song rolling on and on, quickening to heighten the pressure. The men and women howled and called to each of them.

At last James began to lose step. The crowd responded, some shouting encouragement to him, others to Nate to finish him off. They roared as James capitulated, bent over, hands on his knees, panting. He waved a surrendering hand. Nate and the musicians finished with a flourish, then the onlookers rushed in to clap the dancers' backs and shove celebratory drinks their way.

* * *

James could not find Myra anywhere. He looked throughout the barn, including the loft where he interrupted an amorous couple. Myra had disappeared shortly after his dance with Nate, gone by the time he had finished another mug of beer. He had been a fool to dance like that, but at least the alcohol dulled the subsequent ache in his leg as he stepped outside. Several Company D boys still huddled about the fire, smoking and playing cards, but Langdon was no longer among them.

"Hey, Thornton," he said to one Burr Oaker. "Seen Myra? The dark-haired girl I was out here with a short while ago."

"I seen her," John Coe offered, pointing. "She walked off yonder with the Preacher."

A flash of jealousy made James draw in breath, but a quick foreboding overrode that emotion, and he spun on his heels and rushed around the corner of the barn. He saw nothing out of place in the night, no shadows lingering alongside the structure. Intently he listened, peered across the clearing toward the woods. No one.

A girl's scream, abruptly curtailed, froze James's blood. He broke into a dead run toward the ramshackle house a hundred yards away. Shouts arose from the fire circle left behind.

He burst across the doorless threshold into the blackened ruins and

142

staggered to a halt. On the hard-packed floor, two dark shapes struggled. The girl's outcries were muffled by the hand of the silent man who straddled her, determined in his efforts to pull up her dress. In the moonlight, Myra's terrified eyes reached for James.

Langdon looked over his shoulder just as James dived upon him. They tumbled across the room, broken boards and half-demolished furniture crushed in the onslaught. The scent of old ash filled James's nostrils. He squirmed and clawed for a grip, but Langdon shoved him away. They scrambled to their feet, and just as quickly James barreled headfirst into Langdon's chest, wrapping his arms around him and driving him against an interior wall. He pummeled the man's stomach, robbed the sergeant of air. Surroundings blurred, time reversed to Burr Oak, to that horrible day of discovery, and his blows came harder. Langdon grunted, hands scrabbling at James's back until he caught hold of his shirt and yanked it over his head. Thus blinded, James struggled, arms tangled in the sleeves. He swore. A knee to his groin flashed agony throughout his body, and he crumpled. A kick to the ribs tumbled him, gasping, across the debris. Just as he whipped the shirt free, Langdon charged. James ducked low, caught the sergeant's legs, toppled him. His knee struck something solid. He groped for it, fought to remain atop Langdon, raised the brick above his head.

"James! No!"

Nate's voice caused a miniscule hesitation before the brick smashed down, thumping into the frozen earth where Langdon's head had been a second before. James cursed again, aimed a fist for the blurred face, but someone grabbed his arm, dragged him off. James battled to break free. He ignored the jumble of voices now around him, saw only Langdon, who got to his feet and glowered at him, fists clenched, lips bloody.

"You bastard!" James snarled. "How many women have you done this to?"

"James!" Nate next to him, emerging through the fog of the nightmare memory.

"I'll kill you, God damn it! I will!"

Langdon only stared back, small eyes hard but for once revealing a hint of alarm.

Someone said, "Get the hell outta here, Langdon. Now. Or we'll turn the boy loose."

Langdon hesitated, then slipped past Myra, who cringed against the wall, quietly crying against Elias's shoulder. James made a final lunge and broke free, but Nate and May grabbed him again. He struggled to be released.

"James, stop! We can't let you go."

Slowly, inevitably the hopelessness slipped in, unlocked his muscles, bringing fatigue with it. He shrugged off their hold and staggered away toward the back of the building, into a dark cloak of shadows. His entire body ached, his leg burned. He stumbled, fell to his knees, buried his face in his hands.

***

Nate waited for the others to drift from the house, escorting the trembling girl. Elias gave him a knowing nod before he left. Nate watched them retrace their dark steps across the thin layer of snow toward the barn, voices fading. He considered following them but instead remained behind, anchored there by the faint sobs drifting through the broken house. Unsure of his course of action, Nate gathered up James's forgotten shirt and the sack coat that had once graced Myra's shoulders, then made his way toward the disturbing sounds.

James's bare skin glowed among the shadows of the second room or what was left of it. A cloud drifted across the moon, burying them in blackness. The sobs trailed off into ragged breaths.

"James," Nate called softly, hesitantly, stopping several feet away.

From where he sat against one wall, James moaned, "Oh, Christ. Go away."

"I brung your shirt and coat." He stepped closer, tossed the garments into his lap. "You'll catch your death."

Stiffly, James shrugged into the gray flannel shirt and buttoned it. Reappearing, the moon filtered gray light upon his shaking hands. Self-consciously he wiped at the wetness that slicked his cheeks, then struggled into the coat. Nate wavered, reluctant to leave James alone out here in the cold; God only knew what he would do if left to himself when so distraught. Yet neither did he want to mortify him by staying. At last he settled next to him.

James waved a hand. "Leave me alone."

Gently Nate commanded, "Just shut your noise for once." James trembled violently, offered no further resistance, much to Nate's surprise. "You hurt?"

"Just bruised."

"What about your leg?"

"It's fine." He swiped away the last of the tears.

For the first time, Nate saw James as a mere boy like himself, just as lonely and homesick…and often afraid. They sat in silence for some time, the night growing colder, the distant music in the barn drifting to them like something from his mother's music box.

James murmured, "Is Myra all right?"

"Seemed so; just mighty scared." He hesitated. "Did Langdon…?"

James shook his head. "He would have."

"Good thing you came along."

James gave a cynical snort. "Didn't come along when I needed to…for my mother."

The remark surprised Nate, especially the deep regret and self-incrimination behind it. Never had he considered the possible guilt James felt for his mother's death. How could he when he knew nothing of the truth of that day? More than the usual curiosity stirred him, for he now realized James's fight with Langdon had been about much more than rescuing Myra. Carefully he considered his words before venturing, "What happened back then, James? Back home, I mean."

James scoffed. "You mean you don't believe what Abner and everyone else says?"

"I'll believe whatever you tell me."

With surprise, James studied him for a long, uncomfortable moment before staring down at his hands. "I don't rightly know what happened…what *really* happened, I mean. My father was there, of course, but he was so drunk he probably couldn't tell me if he wanted to. Never has." He frowned. "Things weren't going so well with my folks at the time because of different reasons, one being Pa's drinking. Ma never talked to me about it, of course, but I knew she was troubled. That's when she started going to Preacher Langdon, seeking his counsel, I figured. He was a different man back then, or so we thought. We used to go to church, all of us, every Sunday. Some folks started talking because of how regularly my mother and Langdon were seen together. Of course my father heard the talk, and he started thinking crazy things, accusing her." James grimaced as if he choked on something horribly unpleasant. "She told him he was wrong but said she would tell Langdon that she would no longer ask for his advice. The day she told Langdon, she came home a mess—her bonnet gone and her hair mussed, her dress torn. Before I could ask her anything, she went straight to her room and shut the door. I heard her crying. That wasn't like her at all; I'd never seen her cry."

When he failed to continue, Nate feared he never would, but at last James drew in a long breath and pressed on. "I went to find Pa. He had been drinking. I should have known better than to tell him then. I expected him to get angry, but he didn't; he just told me to go back home to check on Ma, so I did." He drew his knees up as if to make himself a smaller target for the deepening cold. "When Pa came home, he had blood all over his hands and shirt. Scared my mother and me half to death. He was saying crazy things, kept repeating Langdon's name, saying he'd killed the bastard. He said Ma had to go to Uncle Pat's place. She tried to talk some sense into him, but I could see she was terrified. He hitched up the team and pulled her out of the house. I tried to climb onto the wagon, but Pa shoved me off and whipped the team into a gallop. I ran to fetch Mr. Bordner's horse and rode after them."

James's breath shortened, and he wrapped his arms about his legs, stared vacantly off. "I found them out the road toward your farm, by the bridge. The wagon had overturned into the river. Pa managed to get to the bank. Maybe he was thrown there; I don't know. He was so drunk but…" He rocked forward then back, shook his head. "Jesus, Nate… I found her under the wagon, her neck broken…dead before I ever got there."

Nate frowned and slipped an arm around James's shoulders, unnoticed.

"I couldn't wake Pa. For a minute I thought he was dead, too, but then I saw that he was still breathing. I rode back to town to get help as fast as I could. By then they had found Langdon beat nigh to death in the church. When we got back to the bridge, Pa had somehow pulled Ma out. He was sitting there on the bank, holding her, crying. He kept saying he'd killed her. Of course he didn't mean it like everyone heard it. And Langdon being busted up didn't help my pa. If not for Uncle Pat talking folks down, I think they would've charged him with murder. In the end, her death was recorded as an accident, but the stories started. I wanted to leave Burr Oak, but Pa wouldn't listen; said he'd be damned if Langdon stayed a preacher while his wife lay buried in the church's graveyard. Everyone started talking about Langdon then. Guess some of that you can blame on me. I told everyone who'd listen what I knew of the good reverend. He had fooled us all. I always wondered if something like that had driven him from his previous community as well."

He wiped at the fresh wave of silent tears, his nose running.

"I'm sorry, James."

"Sorry for what?"

"For all of it. For listenin' to other folks. My ma always said your father was innocent, but I wouldn't listen. Reckon I didn't want to."

"Well," James said weakly, "you weren't alone." He dragged a sleeve across his eyes. "You won't say anything about this to anyone, not even Elias?"

"But…don't you think folks should be set straight?"

"Why would anyone believe me now?"

"Well, things is different now, since Mission Ridge and all."

The old cynicism twisted James's lips. "Some things don't change, Nate. Me carrying that flag may make folks think differently about me, at least for a while, but it won't make them think any differently about my father."

A sudden rush of running feet pushed them into silence. Then May's voice, quiet but insistent from the ruins of the next room. "Nate! James! You here?"

Nate hurried toward the sound of the corporal's voice. "What's wrong?"

"Provost guards are coming," May said. "Gotta skedaddle."

PART IV

ATLANTA CAMPAIGN

"One from the abode of the damned
could not have suffered tortures more horrible
or more revolting."

-- Private John Downey, 11th Michigan Infantry

CHAPTER 14

Ringgold, Georgia, May 6, 1864

Dear Father,

To-morrow we have orders to march against the Rebels so I thought I should write you since it is hard to say when I will have another chance. We just arrived here four days ago. I am sitting on a hill just now, overlooking the Fourteenth Corps' camp spread in the valley. It is a grand sight and gives me confidence about the upcoming campaign. We have been drilling nonstop since March—battalion drill, brigade drill, target practice. I have become quite a good shot. With General Grant gone to fight in the east we have General Sherman to lead the campaign as you might know. And quite a force he has. Besides the whole Army of the Cumberland, he now has General Schofield's Army of the Ohio and has turned command of the Army of the Tennessee over to General McPherson who they say is a good fighter. We have nigh 100,000 men. But this time we won't be fighting Braxton Bragg. The Reb army is now commanded by Joe Johnston. I do not think it will matter who leads them. Sherman wants Atlanta and her railroads and with such a force as this I do not see how anyone can stop us. We have received some recruits since our fight last November. The Eleventh has close to 450 men and officers now, the biggest regiment in General King's brigade. We are the only volunteer unit in the Second Brigade now, the rest are Regulars. They have even taken the Nineteenth Illinois from us and just to-day sent them to Turchin's brigade. We hate to see them go because the two regiments have been together since '62.

"Hey there, soldier. Can you tell me where I can find the camp of the Eleventh Michigan Infantry?"

James looked up from his letter, shaded his eyes with his hand. Before him stood a lanky fellow with a close-cropped, reddish beard, his eyes the color of the sky above him. For a long moment James peered at him, for the natural good humor in the soldier's eyes stirred a faint recognition. A second soldier arrived, panting as if he had run to catch up. This young man also seemed familiar to James, but not as much as the first.

In his Irish brogue, the bearded stranger asked, "Say, don't I know you?"

James kept his attention on the infantryman as he got to his feet.

"Why, James Keenan! I'll be damned." Incredulous, the first newcomer swept off his hat to run a hand through his thick red hair in a familiar old habit.

"Brian Calhoun." James spoke the name with shock but little enthusiasm, for in Burr Oak he had disliked Brian even more than Nate.

They stared at one another, at a loss and now uncomfortable until the other soldier spoke, offering his hand to James. "I'm Charles Rose. Come looking for my brother Dan, Eleventh Michigan."

Brian put his cap back on. "Looks like we're both in luck, Charlie. Accordin' to me little brother's letters, ol' James here belongs to the Eleventh. Reckon he can tell us both where to find our kin."

James glanced down at the sea of tents and men below them, an incredible array of military might, everywhere activity in preparation for tomorrow's march. Smoke curled from thousands of cook fires. The scent of the noontime meal stirred James's hunger and reminded him of the time. He had heard the dinner call a while ago, ringing up from the valley on hundreds of bugles, drums, and fifes.

"I'll take you to our camp. Reckon it'll be worth the walk to see Nate's face." As they descended the hill, James added, "I thought your regiment was still up in Tennessee."

"We was, until we got orders to rejoin Butterfield's division. Reckon you boys need all the help you can get." Brian tempered his grin when James tossed a defensive glance his way.

"We did just fine on our own at Mission Ridge."

"Aye, so I hear tell. So, how's soldierin' been treatin' the likes of James Keenan?"

"Well, everything's still attached."

"A damned trick, that. Sure, but you and Nate are still fresh as daisies. I've been at this business a spell longer."

Reflecting upon the past ten months, James felt anything but fresh.

After directing Rose to Company A's street, James and Brian headed for Company D where they found May, Elias, Abner, and Nate gathered near their cook fire, all conversing with expressions bright in anticipation of tomorrow's march. The winter had been long and dull, and though all knew of the dangers ahead, they still welcomed the campaign, for only through hard fighting would they ever see an end to this war and a blessed return home.

Nate smiled up at James but only glanced at the soldier with his messmate before looking back to the fire. A mere instant passed, enough to form a thoughtful frown, then Nate's attention darted to Brian, who grinned. With a shout, he leaped up and threw himself into Brian's embrace, almost bowling him over.

Nate's countenance fairly glowed as he inquired, "Where the devil did you come from?"

After explaining, Brian told Nate, "'Fraid I don't have much time, little brother. We'll all be marchin' on the morrow. Have to get back to me unit. Had a devil of a time gettin' permission to come as it was."

Disappointment marred Nate's expression but quickly vanished as he introduced Brian to his comrades. They heartily welcomed him.

"I have somethin' here," said Brian, reaching into a pocket as all sat down to share their meal. "Somethin' you'll all be interested in readin'. 'Tis a letter from Ryan."

"Ryan?" they chorused, and Nate snatched the wrinkled paper.

May asked, "He's alive, then?"

"Aye. At least he was when he wrote that back in January. I just got it the other day. Don't know what took so damned long. Fuckin' Rebs. He was at Belle Isle then, you see."

Elias frowned. "Then he's in Andersonville now, poor lad."

"Aye," Brian said. "In this cursed state."

Nate read the letter aloud, a letter that told of hardship, privation, and illness but did not dwell upon them. When he was through, Nate thoughtfully folded the letter yet did not surrender it. He had paled and his eyes had lost the spark of a moment ago.

"Don't look so down, lad," Brian said. "If anyone can survive prison, 'tis Ryan."

Distantly Nate nodded, stared into the fire. "He's still alive. He has to be."

All looked uncertain, for they had heard horrible stories about the Confederate prisons, but James figured no one wanted to mention them now with the two brothers in their midst.

Brian forced his smile to return and his voice to lift. "Here, now. How 'bout some of that stew afore I have to make the long journey back to the Nineteenth? And tell me, little brother, what you've been up to these many months."

As the men ate, the gloom lifted. Talk flowed more easily. Both brothers reacquired a stronger flavor of their homegrown brogue, often laughing at asides regarding their siblings. James listened with interest to Brian's narrative of the fight at Thompson's Station in March '63 when most of the Nineteenth Michigan had been compelled to surrender.

"Not me, by God." Brian thumped a fist against his chest. "I skedaddled outta there as quick as a hare, I did. One Johnny got a bead on me but just missed."

Nate in turn described the Eleventh's battles. When he spoke of James carrying the colors at Missionary Ridge, Brian raised an eyebrow and gestured with his tin cup of coffee. "You told me of it in one of your letters, sure. But I figured you meant a different James Keenan, certainly not the tightfisted merchant of Burr Oak."

Everyone laughed except James, but he had little opportunity to bristle much before Nate spoke for him. "The same man. 'Twas a sight, to be sure. Right, lads? He got shot for it, too. Don't recollect if I told you that. Show him, James."

"Shit, Nate—"

"Go on. Show him."

Self-conscious, James lifted his pant leg to reveal the brownish, leathery skin where the ball had done its damage.

Brian's eyebrows shot up. James figured his fellow Burr Oaker had doubted the contents of Nate's letters. Brian's reluctant nod of respect pleased James, but he hid any smugness.

Brian lingered for almost an hour after the meal. Nate tried every tactic possible to convince him to remain longer, but duty called, for all of them, and soon the brothers walked away up the company street, arms around each other's shoulders, steps slow and prolonging their time together. Soberly James watched them, wondered if Nate would see Brian again...or any of his brothers. He thought of the letter he had started to his father. His only family. Yet perhaps his long-suppressed desire for siblings had been better served unanswered, because now, unlike Nate, he had no brothers with worrisome fates, especially one in the unenviable position of Ryan Calhoun. Regardless of Nate's bravado, James had little belief in the prospect that Ryan, or anyone, could survive ten months as a prisoner of war.

CHAPTER 15

Shells screamed over Nate's head, exploded beyond the prone battle line of King's brigade on the tree-covered ridge. Shattered limbs of pine and oak moaned and crashed to the ground amidst Scribner's brigade, held in reserve. The Georgia clay beneath Nate vibrated from the earnest and deadly work of artillery from all sides. In front of the Second Brigade, the land fell away into an open slope that dipped to a meandering creek before rising back up again on the opposite side to another wooded ridge. It was there amidst the trees and breastworks that Joe Johnston's army was making another stand, protecting the Western & Atlantic Railroad, which ran behind the Confederate lines. Powder smoke from Rebel artillery and small arms blanketed the ridge. Though Nate could see little beyond the flanks of the brigade, he knew the whole of Sherman's force was arrayed along this position, stretching for miles, cannon fire thrumming to both north and south. The Second Brigade's position appeared to lay near the center of the Union line.

Nate pressed his cheek against the ground but found little relief from the broiling afternoon heat even here in the shade. Every inch of clothing stuck to him. Sweat escaped the saturated band in his slouch hat and trickled down to sting his eyes; wiping it away was fruitless. Regardless of the crash of cannon, he knew if he closed his eyes, he would fall asleep, but with the prospect of soon being called to his feet and sent across that narrow, marshy valley, rest was an impossible dream. Some men along the line did sleep, however, for everyone was exhausted beyond comprehension, and even the threat of battle failed to enliven them.

One of them was Captain Lane, at his post on the right of Company D. Nate frowned, a bit unnerved by the sight of his company commander with face to the ground, eyes closed, jaw slack. Nate berated himself for his lack of charity, however, for he knew Lane was sick, judging by how often he left the column during yesterday's sweltering march to attend to nature's cruelty. So many had fallen out of ranks, yet somehow Lane had remained, pale and reticent, almost furtive, leaving Nate with a troublesome lack of confidence. Others in the company had murmured concern last night, knowing that another fight was coming. Since Lane's less than stellar conduct at Missionary Ridge, the men treated him differently. No overt display of disrespect but neither did their bearing toward him contain any warmth. In turn, instead of being angry or wielding his authority in retribution, Lane had become withdrawn. Nate felt sorry for him, tried to still offer him some bit of friendship, yet with this long campaign stretching before them, he knew simple friendship would be insufficient to sustain Lane or erase his past actions. Some wondered aloud if Lane should be relieved, but who would replace him when the company had no other officer?

They had been on the march only a week, covering less than thirty miles, but it felt as if an entire month had passed. On May 7, they had marched southeast from Ringgold, skirmishing with Confederates at a place called Tunnel Hill, driving those few defenders back to the Rebels' main line atop a north-south prominence called, appropriately, Rocky Face Ridge. For the next five days, the Union forces battered away at the fortress-like Confederate position, the Eleventh Michigan under artillery fire much of the time. A gap in the ridge faced the First Division's position, a place known as Buzzard's Roost, but no amount of demonstrations by Palmer's corps, or any other corps along the Union line, could compel the Confederate forces to abandon their impenetrable position. In the end there was no need, for Sherman sent elements of McPherson's Army of the Tennessee to exploit the Confederate left flank far to the south, a movement that eventually led Johnston to withdraw his forces from Rocky Face Ridge and fall back upon their current defenses west of the town of Resaca.

The day's oppressive furnace heat finally claimed Nate, and he had just begun to drift into sleep when a furious rattle of musketry to the north shook him back to consciousness. Momentarily hazy, he looked around, startled that he had succumbed. Next to him, James's attention remained on the U.S. Regulars in the brigade's first line of battle.

"That's Baird's boys going in," Langdon said to no one in particular from his place behind the Eleventh's rear rank. "Get ready."

Within minutes, the men of the brigade's first line rose to their feet on command, readied themselves for the advance. To their left, the brigades of Van Derveer and Turchin advanced from the safety of the trees into the long green swale, flags flying, a band's music lost amidst the men's cheers. Nate thought of the Nineteenth Illinois and wished he had the strength to cheer on his old comrades. Instead, he watched in silence as King's U.S. Regulars stepped off, the orderly ranks soon dipping below sight down the slope.

Next the command, "Attention, battalion!" rang out from the officers of the Eleventh.

Like tired beasts of burden, the men lurched to their feet. They dressed ranks and fixed bayonets with little said. Nate had to think about every move he made, things that normally came automatically after these many months of drill and soldiering. He reminded himself of the impending danger, his instincts dulled by heat and fatigue. With a quick shake of his head, he focused forward on the trembling afternoon heat waves, wondered distantly where Brian was in all of this, prayed for his safety.

Nate looked to the right where Captain Lane should be but instead found him behind the lines, a few paces to the rear with Sergeant Hart. The perplexed expression on Hart's face drew Nate's interest. Hart's solid stance seemed to be blocking Lane from going to the rear.

"Step aside, Ben," Lane said without authority, more like a pleading friend.

"Where you going, Cap? We're about to advance."

With hollow eyes, Lane looked beyond Hart into the protective trees beyond Scribner's men. His agitated fingers toyed with the hilt of his sheathed sword. "I've been in front as long as I care to be."

Hart's jaw tightened, his stare steady upon the officer, who refused to meet his gaze. "Haven't we all, Frank?"

Lane attempted to step around Hart, but the sergeant grabbed his arm.

"Damn it, Cap..."

Lane's pallid face dripped sweat. He attempted to infuse authority into his tone but fell short. "Let go of me, Ben."

"Cap, I know you're feeling poorly but this ain't the time—"

A shell wailed directly over their heads, exploded amidst the front rank of Scribner's line, tore men apart, screams piercing the air. The sight disintegrated any scrap of resolve Hart's words may have instilled in Frank Lane. With a wild, shoving lurch, he broke free from the noncom and rushed for the rear. Hart shouted after him, swore. Nate stared in disbelief, glanced around to see if anyone besides the file closers had noticed Lane's flight, but thankfully everyone else's attention was focused forward as Carlin's brigade on the right advanced down the slope and out of Nate's sight.

The hills opposite King's position exploded in a well-concerted

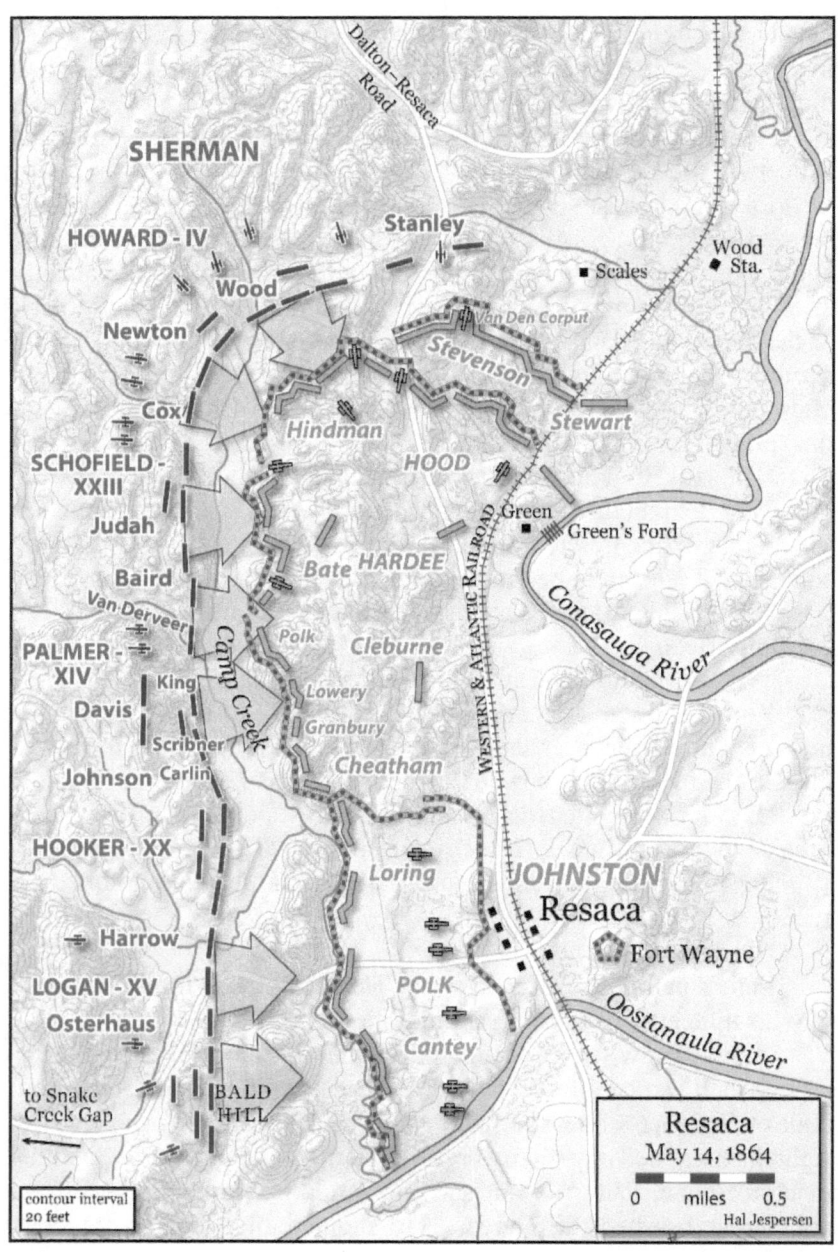

Resaca

May 14, 1864

0 miles 0.5

contour interval 20 feet

Hal Jespersen

volley of smoke and flames as the Rebels there homed in on Carlin's regiments and the U.S. Regulars. Soon the rest of King's brigade was ordered forward to support the first line. Out of the protective darkness of the trees into the glaring sunlight. The earth shuddered with the concussion of cannon. Nate could now see a Rebel battery of Napoleons to their left front on the ridge, only some four or five hundred yards distant, wiping holes in Turchin's and Van Derveer's ranks.

Oddly enough, Nate felt little fear. Perhaps the exhaustion overrode it; perhaps after surviving previous battles, the fear had simply taken on a different shape, something not quite so immediate, more beneath the surface, still there but quiet, like a morning mist skimming just above a pond's surface, not enough to cover the water but enough to alter its color, its texture.

He tried to put Lane's desertion out of his mind, but several times he glanced to the right where the company commander should be; instead of their captain, he found First Sergeant Hart. The noncom's sharp blue eyes caught Nate, and in that fleeting instant, Nate could feel Hart's anger and grief as deeply as his own. Nate gave a small nod to let Hart know how much he appreciated his sense of duty, especially at such a dire time.

Advanced farther than King's men, Carlin's brigade had reached the boggy creek and attempted to press onward, but the narrow, banked waterway disorganized the lines. As the men ran forward in determined disarray, bayonets thrust before them, the Napoleons targeted them. Grape and canister felled men by the dozens, staggered the advance.

Closing with the first line of King's men, the Eleventh Michigan halted and prepared to fire to suppress the Rebel musketry. The slope's gradient would allow them to fire over Carlin's brigade. The brigade's volley crashed, smoke thrown forward in blinding sheets. Quickly they reloaded. When some of the powder smoke lifted, Nate saw Carlin's men valiantly advancing in the brief respite King's volley had afforded them. But the enfilade fire from the Confederate battery to the left raked Carlin's lines, shattered the advance. Carlin's men had little choice but to fall back to the creek where they took refuge behind the east bank's natural breastwork. A carpet of blue choked the distant slope in the wake of the withdrawal, dead and wounded by the dozens, like a herd of cattle Nate had once witnessed struck dead by a single lightning bolt.

King's brigade held their ground, the men now ordered prone. As the regiments kept up a steady fire, Nate expected they would press forward to the creek, then perhaps charge in concert with Carlin's regiments. But mercifully no such orders came. Down to their left, Turchin and Van Derveer had no better luck, nor did the Federal troops farther north who tried to assault the Rebel works. Those who made it beyond the obstacle of the creek soon came tumbling back to the protection of the banks; others retreated farther, back up the slope. Nate looked over his shoulder and to the south where a division from Hooker's corps remained under cover of the trees. No fools there. Hooker's men, but which brigades? Was Brian's regiment among them?

The troops still along the creek kept up a steady, furious fire all along the Union line, a line that bent to the east, toward the left flank. Rising battle smoke beyond that bend told the story of fighting well beyond where Nate could see up the narrow valley. Smoke to the south as well, from both sides, thunderous cannon fire and crackling musketry. Soon a fresh voice joined in the duel—two 10-pound Parrott rifles from Dilger's battery, First Ohio Light Artillery; the guns had just been brought forward along the ridge just north of where Nate lay. With these sending missile after missile across at the Rebels, driving some off, King's brigade withdrew under heavy fire back to the ridge.

As they stepped into the blessed shade, Nate collapsed, breathing hard, the taste of gunpowder bitter in his mouth. How long had they been out there? He looked around, pleased to see that the regiment had not suffered much. Surely nothing like Carlin's poor fellows. They would have to wait until the cover of darkness to make it back from that damnable creek.

Nate half-expected to see Captain Lane. Surely he would have realized his mistake and collected himself enough to return to the regiment. But Lane was nowhere in sight. First Sergeant Hart was down the line with Colonel Stoughton, listening gravely. Stoughton's face was flushed, his muscles tight, as if suppressing something with great effort. Hart drew himself up and saluted, then spun on his heels to return to the company, his expression so grim that Nate could not turn away. Hart came along the lines, offered congratulatory words for the company's cool behavior under such galling fire. He appeared distracted, perhaps still thinking about his conversation with Stoughton.

"Sarge." Nate took hold of his arm to stop him. "Where's the Captain?"

Other curious faces turned Hart's way, more questions. Hart looked at none of them as he moved down the line. "Frank's gone. I'm in command of the company now."

***

160

For the next ten days, General Sherman's forces continued to outflank the Confederates, driving them on the second day of battle from Resaca, across the Oostanaula River south through Calhoun, Adairsville, and Cassville, then over the Etowah River, ever closer to Atlanta. The Army of the Cumberland snaked across the Georgia landscape, land that for a time was level and fertile, crops of wheat sown in the brick-red soil, making Nate think longingly of his family's fields. The Fourteenth Corps saw little of the Rebels during this time, but other elements of Sherman's forces engaged Johnston's men near Rome and Cassville.

May 26, 1864
Georgia

Dear Katie

Heer i set in the Georga woods waiting for the corps to resoom march im still hoping to git news on yesterdays fite that i heer Brians outfit was in sotheast of heer sum place called new hope church i cud heer it when we was helping the 20th corps train over a creek which was tuff because the land has becum wooded and hilly the 4th corps relieved Brians corps and i heer tell we are to relieve the 4th corp now i am worried about Brian i saw him three days ago when his regiment marched past our camp but only had time for a quick word its odd to think on how ther is three Calhoun boys in this state so clos together but still far apart i hope Ryan heers news of Sherman coming Uncle Billys crusaders thats what Brian called us as soon as we capture Atlanta i hope we can free the thosands of Union prisoners they say ar at Andersonville thats southwest of Atlanta i cud bear that march just fine just to see Ryan agin well must go they ar sonding assembly

"Doesn't sound like the Johnnies are planning on retreating this time," James said once they resumed the march along a rough road. A violent storm late yesterday had settled the dust, but the wagon trains had gouged ruts in the soft ground.

Abner added, "I hear tell we're only about fifty miles or less from Atlanta. Reckon Jeff Davis told Johnston he'd best stop fallin' back or he'll run out of places to retreat to. Our big runnin' fight won't have nowheres else to run to."

"A fight for some of us," Langdon growled. "The ones of us that didn't turn tail and run."

Ben Hart, now wearing the single bars of first lieutenant, scowled at Langdon. "There'll be none of that talk, Sergeant. Captain Lane will be back."

"At the end of a rifle barrel maybe," Langdon muttered.

"You've been in enough battles to know how things can play on a man's mind," Hart continued. "But for the grace of God, what happened to Frank could have and may still happen to us, perhaps even to you one day, Sergeant. So, I'd watch your tongue."

Langdon spat a stream of tobacco juice at a nearby tree, said nothing more. James exchanged a glance with Nate, then gave their new company commander a nod of satisfaction.

Hart ignored the acknowledgement—always careful not to engender a division on the subject—and faced forward again, limping gamely along. Nate knew his bum hip alone did not lame him; last night's rain pestered the rheumatism that occasionally flared up, a lingering debility courtesy of the freezing battlefield conditions at Stones River in '62. Colonel Stoughton had offered his horse to Hart earlier that day, but the new lieutenant respectfully declined. Perhaps Hart felt compelled to accept no favors or show any weakness because of Frank Lane's desertion. They were, after all, both from Bronson, and Hart had enough pride in his hometown to be driven to restore its honor, to set an example high above anything Lane had. Surely Hart worried what the good people of Bronson would say about the cowardice of one of their own. He would not want to offer a second example, and because of this, Nate had no doubts about their new commander. The boys all agreed that Hart had deserved a commission long ago, though Nate suspected Hart had turned down promotion in the past. But here in the middle of a brutal campaign, Benjamin Franklin Hart had at last taken up the mantle, and who better for the job?

As they marched into the afternoon, distant skirmishing rattled in the masking forests to the southeast. They passed hospital tents, and often the column gave way to tired ambulance drivers bringing more wounded in from yesterday's fight. With dread, Nate looked into the faces of those inside—shattered, dazed, bloody men, some near death, others alert enough to trade brief words with the passing column. They said their corps—Hooker's Twentieth—had shattered itself against General John Bell Hood's corps; lost well over a thousand men. Nate's heart sank with each demoralizing word.

"Nate! Nate!" Dan Rose from Company A came running down the column, the twenty-year-old's voice pitched with excitement. "A fella just told me the Nineteenth's hospital is right over yonder. I got permission to go look for my brother. Wanna come with me? Maybe they can tell you about Brian."

Before Nate could open his mouth, Ben Hart waved a hand at him. "Go ahead, lad, but don't tarry."

They found Charles Rose with several others from the Nineteenth. Battered, exhausted men, some asleep, the less severely wounded awake and eager to exchange news. Charles had been shot through the left hand. His middle finger had been amputated, the remaining digits heavily bandaged, but even this failed to lessen the boy's joy at seeing his brother.

Nate, however, could waste no time on others' happiness. "What about Brian? Is he all right?"

Charles frowned, looked down then forced his attention back to Nate. "I wasn't very close to him, but…but I saw him go down."

Nate stared in silence, afraid to hear more.

"I don't know how bad it was," Charles continued in a tone that revealed little optimism and perhaps little truth. "We was in a warm spot. Everything was a mess; you know how it is."

Weakly Nate said, "But he ain't here."

"That don't mean nothing," Dan insisted. "He could be in a different hospital."

"I have to find out."

Nate searched the other hospitals of Butterfield's division, to no avail. Hundreds of men; haunted faces. Blood and stench. Worn surgeons and stewards, none with the patience or time for his questions. The ambulances kept coming. Nate, more and more frantic, scoured them as well, interrogated the befuddled, impatient drivers. Why had no one seen Brian if he had been injured? Surely he had not been left upon the field of battle to die a slow death. Surely he was not out there, dead and forgotten.

Darkness began to creep in. The distant skirmishing had faded away; he did not know when, had long ago forgotten about anything beyond his search, thinking not even of his duty to return to the regiment. At last, deeply alone, he headed down the road, knowing not where he might find the Eleventh but at a loss to do anything else.

In the last of the twilight, a voice found him; James appeared before him, gray eyes clouded with concern beneath the brim of his forage cap.

"Nate, where the hell have you been? Ben is madder than shit."

Barely hearing him, just relieved to have a friend near, Nate said, "I can't find him. Charlie Rose said he was wounded, but no one knows where he is."

James took him by the elbow and urgently guided him off the road to let a battery rattle past, the horses lathered and muddy, the men equally so, one of them cursing.

"What can I do?" Nate asked. "What if he's out there dyin' 'cause he can't help hisself? I don't even know where to look for him in this God-awful country."

With a slight shake, James brought his rush of words up short. "It'll be dark soon. We have to get back to the regiment. We've been deployed behind the Fourth Corps. God damned hills and woods; we'll be lucky to find our way back this late, but I promised Ben I'd fetch you."

"Damn it, James, I've gotta find Brian."

James frowned, spoke quietly, no anger, only uneasiness. "We'll find him tomorrow. All right? We'll both look."

"You don't understand—"

"I understand, damn it, but you'll get in trouble with the Lieutenant. You do that now and you'll never get a chance to look tomorrow."

At a loss, gnawed by mosquitoes and frustration, Nate stared off into the pine forest, wished he could see beyond the hills and ravines to where his brother might be. Color and light drained around them, falling to gray. Wagons moved past, wagons belonging to their corps—ammunition, food—the mules' coats sweated black beneath the harness. Twenty days' rations, Stoughton had said four days ago. All regimental wagons turned over to the division. An army traveling as light as possible, carrying the war deeper and deeper into the South, leaving dead men, wounded men, lost men in its wake.

James slipped his arm around Nate's shoulders. His warmth and strength broke through Nate's fog, allowed him to think, to feel. James was right; he could do nothing in the dark. So he slowly nodded, and together they headed down the road.

***

Morning light accentuated the ragged, torn treetops around the open field where Johnson's division had spent the night behind hastily dug entrenchments. In column now, the men stood, frowzy and yawning, some talking in low voices, speculating on what the day might hold. According to rumors, the Rebels were still out there, waiting for them amidst the forests and hills.

James fully awakened as aides galloped up and down the column. He was not yet alert enough to fear the day. Abner and Elias were speculating on what their orders might be. Next to him, Nate stood in worried silence, fingers restless upon his musket. His anxiety, James knew, had nothing to do with the division's inevitable orders but instead with his brother's situation, the damnable not knowing, the helplessness. Nate's request to return to the hospitals earlier had been denied by Lieutenant Hart. Always ready for a battle, Nate now appeared detached from the prospect, an unpreparedness that disturbed James.

To distract himself, James pulled a worn, wrinkled envelope from his pocket, a letter he had received a week ago. He had read it multiple times every day since. The second letter from his father since Missionary Ridge. Although short and stiff, the words did convey concern for his safety and claimed everyone had confidence in Sherman and expected the capture of Atlanta soon. Two sentences interested James even more than the solicitude expressed: *I walked past our old house on Main Street the other day. It needs some paint, I think.*

It was the first time in years that his father had mentioned the family house. Whenever James had brought up the topic, his father had always grown angry and loud, telling him to drop the subject. Now James wondered what had made him write of it, especially referring to it as "our" house instead of as Uncle Pat's house. Was he actually going to take some interest in their old home? The very possibility lifted James's spirits.

"Where we headed, Lieutenant?" Corporal May's voice drew James back to the forest road when Hart limped back from Officer's Call.

"Our division's going to the left with Wood's division and McLean's brigade," Hart replied. "Try to turn the Johnnies' right flank."

"In this God-forsaken country," Abner said, "how the hell we gonna *find* the right flank?"

"General Howard's in command since we've got Wood's boys from his corps. Reckon he must know where we're going," Hart said with little confidence.

"Hey, Nate!"

Everyone turned at the clarion call of Dan Rose, running down the column. Rose, breathing hard, slid to a halt next to Nate.

"As I was leaving the hospital, I just heard. Your brother...they found your brother."

165

"What?" Nate clutched Rose's arm.

The brigade bugle blared Attention.

"Is he hurt bad?"

James held his breath for the answer, caught Rose's fearful glance.

"They—they don't expect him to make it. Shot in the neck."

Nate's eyes shut; he swayed. James put a sustaining hand on his shoulder as the bugle sounded Forward. The distant head of the division column began to march into the trees, expanding and contracting like a snake beginning to stir. No bands played today.

"Gotta get back to my company," Rose said and rushed away.

As the Eleventh stepped off, Nate snapped out of his shock, his attention latching onto Hart. "Lieutenant…" He started to break ranks, but James instinctively grabbed him. "Did you hear Dan? I need to go to me brother."

"Permission denied." Hart's face was set, but James saw the struggle there, the memory of Ryan Calhoun. "This ain't the time, Nate. I'm sorry."

"Please, Ben. I won't be gone long. I promise."

"I can't let you go. Not now. After…if I can."

Nate started toward Hart, but James and Elias restrained him.

"You go on, boy," Langdon goaded. "Take one step outta ranks and I'll have to enforce the Lieutenant's orders. You ain't getting out of this fight."

Quietly, evenly James commanded, "Don't, Nate. For God's sake…"

Nate looked only at their company commander marching just ahead of him. "Damn it, Lieutenant. Please…"

"Nate." James's grip tightened on his shoulder, shook him. "Ben's just doing his job. We can't spare anyone."

Nate made another attempt to break free. James jerked him back, unnerved. "God damn it," he hissed. "You step out of line and Langdon will shoot you. Hear? What good will that do anyone?"

At last capitulating, Nate shoved away James's hand and stared into the impossible tangle of forest that soon enveloped Johnson's division.

CHAPTER 16

The pop-pop of skirmish fire echoed somewhere ahead, hidden by hills and forest. The trackless wilderness reminded James of Chickamauga except for the rolling nature of the land. The hill upon which they had halted sloped away on the left to a creek. At least here they had shade. There was, however, no escape from the humidity; its weight seemed to press the oxygen out of the air to make simply drawing breath an effort. Judging by the sun's angle, it had to be about four in the afternoon, an observation that came with the usual twinge of guilt over his uncle's watch, followed by an unwitting motion to touch his father's letter in his pocket. Although it felt as if General Howard's forces had marched halfway around the world today, they probably had not marched more than two or three miles to reach this position. Now they waited, the division formed in column of brigades with Scribner in front, then King's brigade, then Carlin. To their right, Wood's division deployed in the same way; beyond those units, McLean's brigade.

"Column of brigades," Abner observed. "I hear tell that's how Hooker's boys advanced t'other day when the Rebs chewed them up so bad." Then he glanced at Nate's troubled expression and said no more.

May added, "Just be glad Scribner's in front, not us."

The calls of brigade bugles rang through the trees, and the officers of Wood's division began to bark out commands. None of the officers were mounted, their horses useless in such thick undergrowth.

"There they go," Langdon stated coldly as Hazen's brigade stepped off alone and almost immediately dropped from view down the front of the hill.

James, whose attention often rested upon Nate throughout the day, allowed his gaze to wander forward and watch the flags of the Twenty-third Kentucky, furled and carried over the bearers' shoulders to protect them from snatching branches, slip away below the edge of the hill. Almost instantly the distant ridgeline across from the Eleventh's position erupted in massed musketry, a blaze of guns that sparked through the foliage where nothing else could be spotted. Soon the deep-throated roar of cannon fire from the right front shook the very air around James's head, startling birds into flight in protesting waves from the tall trees.

After several minutes of suspenseful, unseen violence, Elias drawled, "Don't sound like we're turning anyone's flank."

"Sounds more like we run smack-dab into a hornet's nest," Abner added as he watched the thick waft of blue battle smoke rising, torn by tree limbs.

Half an hour passed. Some of the men tried to rest, hats over their eyes; others sat in strained silence, tuned to the unreadable sound of the battle beyond their sight; others offered conjectures as to how things fared and when they might be sent into the fray. Confederate shells howled above, ripping through trees, occasionally raining down fragments. To James, it sounded as if Hazen's regiments had spread out, some veering off to the left. God only knew what sort of terrain they had encountered. Some thought they could see far across the ravine that separated the two forces, over to a cornfield, claimed blue battle lines and flags pressed forward there. Just maybe, James thought, Hazen's boys were indeed outflanking the Rebs.

Soon, to their front, bugles called out, and the men of Scribner's brigade rose to their feet and dressed their lines. A ripple of anticipation ran through the Eleventh's ranks. Excited comrades rousted those who had managed to doze. James glanced at Nate, who stared vacantly ahead, uninterested in the bullets that clipped the leaves above them or burrowed into tree trunks with disturbingly sharp *thwocks*.

Within minutes, Scribner's brigade advanced down the hill to the left of where Hazen's brigade had vanished. Soon the crash of their guns added to the continuous cacophony, the shouts and screams of men intermingled. General King's brigade marched forward about a hundred yards to occupy the position that Scribner had just vacated. There the men were again ordered down.

Colonel Stoughton ignored the bullets whining around him as he moved along the regimental line. "Dig in, boys. We're to hold this position. Get yourselves the best protection you can." When he noticed Nate, he drew near, crouched, and laid a hand upon the boy's shoulder, surprising him out of his miserable reverie. Stoughton offered a small, consoling smile. "I'm glad you're still with us, Nate. I'm sorry to hear about your brother."

"Thank you, sir."

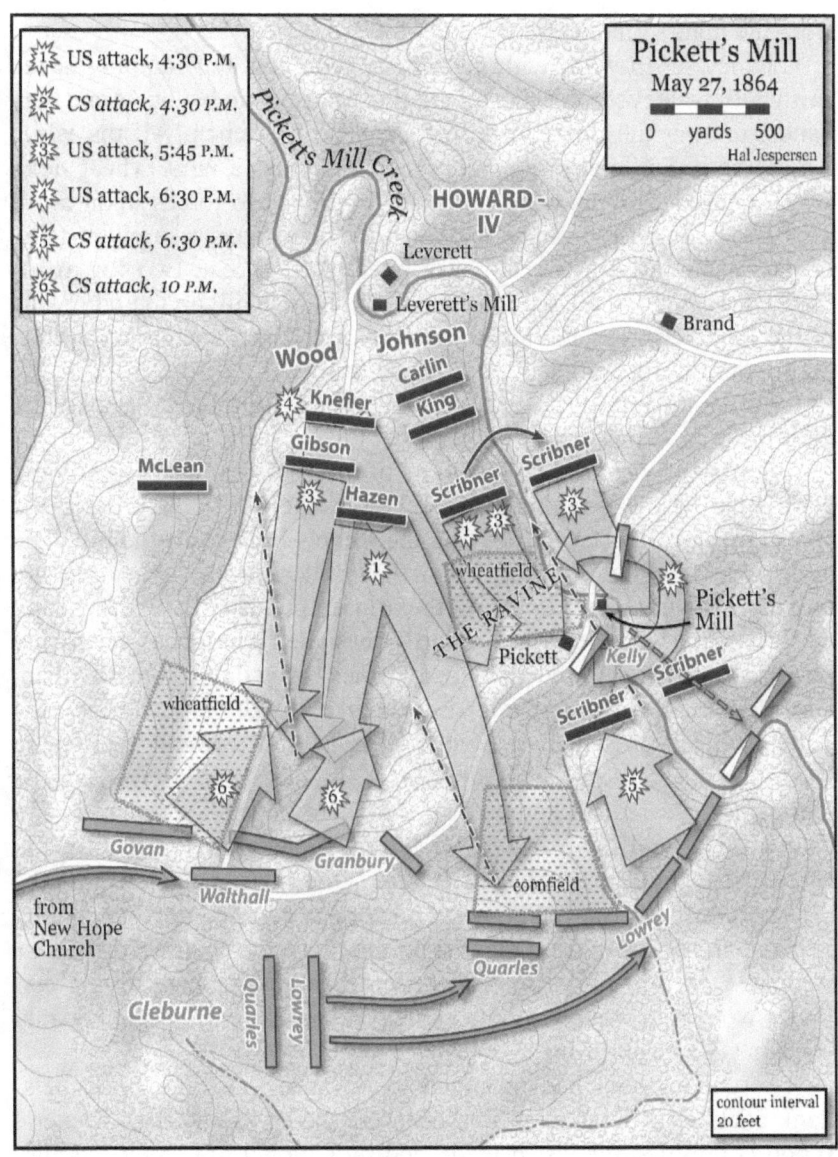

Pickett's Mill
May 27, 1864

0   yards   500

Hal Jespersen

1 US attack, 4:30 P.M.

2 CS attack, 4:30 P.M.

3 US attack, 5:45 P.M.

4 US attack, 6:30 P.M.

5 CS attack, 6:30 P.M.

6 CS attack, 10 P.M.

Picketts Mill Creek

HOWARD - IV

Leverett

Leverett's Mill

Brand

Wood   Johnson

Carlin

Knefler   King

Gibson

McLean   Hazen   Scribner   Scribner

wheatfield

THE RAVINE   Pickett's Mill

Pickett   Kelly   Scribner

Scribner

wheatfield

Govan   Granbury

Walthall   cornfield

from New Hope Church   Lowrey

Quarles

Cleburne   Quarles   Lowrey

contour interval 20 feet

"Keep an eye on James there." He winked. "Don't need him grabbing the flag and getting himself shot again, do we?"

"No, sir."

"How's that leg, James?"

"Fine, sir," he lied.

Stoughton patted James's shoulder once before straightening up to continue along the line. James watched him go, felt foolishly aglow

169

from the man's kindness, especially toward Nate.

James set to work with the others, scooping and scraping at the earth with whatever tools they could find, most using bayonets and bare hands, tossing the dirt in front of the shallow trench. All the while below them, Scribner's regiments pressed across a large wheat field. Two hundred yards beyond the field, Confederate forces upon a hill kept up a galling fire from behind trees and breastworks, surely missing no target among Scribner's dense lines. As the lead two regiments reached the edge of the woods beyond the field, a hill on the other side of the broad creek to the left suddenly erupted in a staggering volley, raking Scribner's brigade with enfilade fire.

"We ain't turnin' no one's flank," Abner grumbled. "Looks like they're about to turn ours."

Scribner reacted quickly. Three of the four regiments in column behind the two lead regiments marched by the left flank, crossed the creek, firing as they went, driving the Rebels back from the hill. The three Federal regiments reformed on the left flank of the Thirty-seventh Indiana, struggling into line until the brigade presented one wide front.

As time crawled and King's brigade continued feverishly fortifying, General Wood advanced his next brigade. Colonel William Gibson's six regiments marched staunchly into the breach along the same path Hazen's men had gone. Within half an hour they came streaming back along with dozens of bloody men from Hazen's regiments, chewed up somewhere out there beneath murderous fire from artillery and small arms. Men bore wounds of all kinds, struck in every conceivable part of their bodies. One man staggered past the Eleventh, his lower jaw shot away, his tongue hanging down, wagging as he went, his entire front black with blood. One captain reformed his company, only to find a meager dozen men answer his rallying cry. James wondered what in God's name was out there to do such deadly work in such a short time.

Scribner's men had managed to advance, pushing the Rebels' flank back toward a distant hill bordering the creek. By then, General Wood committed his last brigade, led by Colonel Frederick Knefler. Like the two brigades before them, these six regiments vanished off to the right, swallowed up by forest and ravine. Artillery roared even more ferociously now. No cheers of determination rang up from the Union forces. Only horrible, distant screams above the gunfire, echoing from somewhere far below the Eleventh's position as the sun drifted ever downward behind them, shooting the shadows of trees out toward the wheat field.

By then, the shattered remnants of Hazen's brigade had reformed to the right rear of King's brigade. To Hazen's right, Gibson's dazed regiments rallied what was left of their brigade. Still Scribner's men continued their fight to the front and left of King's position while Knefler's men fought on the right.

James slumped down in the shallow trench and listened to stray bullets clip the trees, the screams of nearby shells. He bemoaned the Federals' lack of artillery, yet how could batteries have gotten through this damned jungle? The Rebels must have access to a road. He thought he would go mad waiting and listening. Why were they not sent to at least aid Scribner? What kind of disaster was out there in that wilderness? Darkness, merciful darkness would soon fall. If King's brigade was not sent in now, surely they would not go in at all.

More and more wounded drifted and staggered back from the front, men from each of Wood's brigades, all with stories of slaughter, of Patrick Cleburne's Rebel division on a ridge, well-protected, of a bottomless ravine where Union casualties piled up, raked lengthwise by canister fire, men trapped there between steep hills. Knefler's brigade would have no more success than the other brigades, and by now the firing was so murderous that they could not even withdraw without suffering even more casualties. Hundreds of men, James figured, would never come back to this hill, had already been murdered, hundreds more maimed, some unable to even crawl back out of that hell.

There would be no turning the Confederate right flank, James thought, not with Cleburne's veterans protecting it. Cleburne was the best general the Rebels had. He had fought a stubborn rearguard action at Ringgold Gap after the Confederate defeat at Missionary Ridge, a brave scrap that may well have saved the entire Rebel army.

Night at last arrived, sweeping up from the east and turning the landscape black and even more foreboding. Gunfire continued to flash, though slackening. Fires glowed evil reds and oranges among the distant pines where the discharge of weapons had sparked the tinder. The smoke covering King's brigade thickened; James's eyes watered. Cries from the wounded agitated Nate, driving him even deeper into brooding silence, so uncharacteristic that his mood troubled James as much as the echoing pleas for help and mercy all around.

Two hours slipped past. More wounded stumbled up the hills, dark shadows among the darker shadows of trees. James shifted his weight, settled deeper against the cooling earth, wished he could sleep. On one side of him, Elias silently smoked his pipe. On the other side, Nate gave a sudden, muttered groan and got to his feet.

"Get down," James snapped.

"Goin' to piss."

The hair on the back of James's neck prickled, and he exchanged a long look with Elias. "Best keep an eye on him," the man murmured around his pipe. "He ain't thinkin' right."

James scrambled after the dark lump.

***

No one stopped Nate; he was just one among many shifting about in the dark. He could be anyone—an aide searching for one of the brigadiers or for General Howard. Howard…shot in the foot, someone had said. General Johnson wounded by a shell fragment. Hundreds gone down that hill, never to return. How had the Eleventh been spared? He stumbled onward, heart pounding, afraid someone would stop him before he could completely melt away into the trees.

"Damn it, Nate." A hand clamped down upon his shoulder, spun him around. "Don't be a fool. I know where you're going."

"Leave me alone, James. Go back to the boys." He pulled away.

"You'll get turned around and lost in this damned country. Brian wouldn't want you to get shot for him."

"I said go back." He struggled on through the underbrush, afraid James might call out for help.

"Damn it, stop. How the hell you gonna find your way?"

Nate hurried on, searched through the torn branches above for the winking stars. James caught up again and this time grabbed him with greater force, turning him back, their faces close.

"God damn it, Nate, they're going to think we're running, just like Frank Lane."

"Ben'll know where I'm going. He shoulda let me go this mornin'. All we did was sit around all day, watchin'. Well, I did me duty; 'tis high time I see to me kin. Now let go, James, before I have to slug you."

"How do you even know he's still alive?"

"Don't you recollect when you was shot? You didn't wanna be left alone. That's how Brian feels. I helped you that day, James. I know you ain't forgot. So, I'm askin' you one last time to let me go in peace. Go on back to the regiment and tell the Colonel I'll be back as quick as I can."

Slowly James's hand dropped away, and Nate wheeled to resume his march, still unconvinced that his friend would let him go. Last year's fallen leaves rustled disturbingly loud beneath his feet as he plowed onward, dropping down into a ravine and struggling up the opposite side. When he heard the uneven gait of someone to the rear, he spun.

"By God, James, don't you listen?"

"Pipe down." James stopped next to him, the night too dark to see his face. "If you're going to do this crazy thing, then I'm going along to keep you out of trouble and bring you back."

A long silence stretched between them, broken by a burst of gunfire from back in the direction of the battlefield. Both instinctively crouched, attention to the rear. Flashes shot up into the sky. Distant, ghostly howls from Southern throats.

Nate whispered, "Sounds like an attack."

"Not at night." They continued to listen to the frightening, prolonged noise. "Well…it is Cleburne. Maybe…"

Nate said a silent prayer for the regiment, then started off again, bearing southwest by the stars, James following close. As he picked his way along through the broken landscape, he thought of Burr Oak, considered how he and James had never socialized back home but here they were now, never separated since leaving Michigan except for the short time James had spent in the hospital. Would all that change once they returned home? Only way to find out was for them to survive this.

They spoke only when necessary, too tired and uneasy. Nate hoped the army had not shifted during the day, that the Nineteenth Michigan's hospital was in the same place, that Brian was still alive. If only he had come earlier… But truth be told, he had feared Langdon, feared him more and more since that night near Rossville. The closer his friendship grew with James, the more Langdon resented him. When he had nearly left the column that morning, the gleam in Langdon's dark eyes had halted him more than anything James or Hart said. He had known that he could not go to his brother until he received Hart's permission or darkness fell, whichever came first.

When they stopped to rest, James panted, "Why don't we swing southeast? We'll run into our lines, then it'll be easy to know where we're going."

"No. Someone might get the wrong idea and arrest us."

James laughed humorlessly. "The wrong idea? No, the right idea—we're absent without leave, by God. Hart and Stoughton are going to kill us both."

"I'll worry about that later. If it was *their* brother, things would be different."

173

"Maybe."

The ominous, concerted gunfire far behind had died off, replaced now by stray shots to the southeast where nervous pickets blazed at shadows. Nate used the sounds to guide them as they continued.

James's steps dragged slower and slower until he fell behind. Nate was just about to stop again when the trees opened upon a narrow road that ran south. A wagon train, pale canvas glowing in the night, floppy-eared mules shadows against the tree line.

Nate startled one of the half-asleep drivers when he spoke. "I'm lookin' for the hospitals of Butterfield's division."

Displeased, the man cleared his throat, grunted, "Follow this road to the next one. Not far. All the hospitals you want, sonny."

Nate returned to James, who sat on the side of the road, too exhausted to even swat at the persistent insects. "You stay here. Catch up when you can."

James struggled to his feet. "No. He said it's not far. Let's go."

They pushed on and soon struck the east-west road that led back to Owen's Mill where the Eleventh had crossed Pumpkin Vine Creek. Had that truly been just yesterday? Time ran together. How long had Brian been injured, bleeding unattended? Lights shone through the darkness. Canvas. Murmuring sounds of misery; stench, death. They passed more wagons, ambulances, asked directions. Nate jogged ahead, forgot James.

Only a few feet from the entrance to the tent where he had visited Charles Rose, a scratchy, harsh voice slammed Nate to a halt: "Calhoun, Brian. Nineteenth Michigan Infantry."

Nate spun to the left, saw a wagon there, a driver, another man standing nearby who ticked off more names. Two other men lifted a body into the wagon, no care in their movements. Like a bottle uncorked and turned upside down, everything drained out of Nate. He floated forward, nothing beneath his feet. This was no ambulance...

James grabbed him from behind. "Nate, don't—"

Nate jerked away, attention pinned to the wagon. He could not have come all this way only to be too late. He stumbled closer, stared inside at the bodies that filled the bed like grotesque cordwood. Lantern light spilled over the ghastly exhibition. Pale, bloody, sightless faces turned to the stars. A flutter of red hair.

A strangled, animal-like utterance slipped past Nate's lips. He reached for his brother's hand. "Brian." Fingers cold, rigid, and blue, no longer human. "Brian...Brian."

A gaping, mangled wound had covered his neck and collar with

174

crusted, thick blood. Not even a bandage; they had been waiting for him to die. A wound so horrible Nate distantly marveled at how Brian's head could still be attached, how he had survived at all.

His knees buckled. He clung to the wagon, tears on his cheeks. His brother's form blurred.

"Here now," a voice rasped from afar. "Get back from there, boy. We hafta get goin'."

The reek of death gagged Nate. He could no longer hold himself up. Hands supported him, gently tried to draw him back. Sobs choked him. He had gotten here too late…too late.

The man spoke gruffly again. Another pried his fingers loose. The slap of reins. The wagon lurched away. Nate started mechanically after it, but arms wrapped around him, held him in place. He had no strength to resist.

"No…no…" He heard himself say the word over and over; he could not stop, he could not hear anything but that single word, on and on.

CHAPTER 17

James wanted nothing more than to get Nate back to the regiment. The boy had fallen into a deep, silent shock, a silence far more disturbing than the wordless agitation that had gripped him throughout the day. Common sense told James to wait until morning before beginning their trek back through the wilderness. But the thought of remaining anywhere near those nightmarish hospitals infused him with enough energy to lead Nate back up the road. His days spent wounded in that Chattanooga church still haunted him, lying among so many men far worse off than he, an experience he feared repeating more than he feared death.

He looked up through the trees, cursed his navigation. Unlike Nate, he had not been taught about the orientation of moon and stars, and any advice he sought from his grieving comrade went unanswered. The boy trudged along dutifully, and James had a feeling the only thing that motivated Nate now was an intense desire to return to the front lines and kill as many Southerners as he could.

James searched for something to say, anything that might somehow soothe his friend, but what could anyone say to alleviate the sorrow he had witnessed back there? He had little experience in consoling others. When his mother had died, his father had chosen solitude in which to grieve, leaving him to the same. News of Uncle Pat's death had only produced similar results.

Fatigue mounted the farther they traveled. Often they stumbled over rocks and downed branches. James's leg ached. He paused several times to get his bearings but had to admit they were probably going in circles. Perhaps they should just hunker down and wait for morning, yet the desire to return to the safety of the regiment pushed him on. Nate seemed equally determined, shaking his head when James suggested stopping for the night. They crossed one stream, and James vaguely remembered doing so on the journey to the hospital. Or had it been two streams that they had crossed? *Damn it*. There had been a stream to the left of the brigade. Should they go back and follow the one they had just crossed? Or should they look for a second stream? If only he could remember…

In time they struck another creek. Was this the same as the first? Had they made a circle? Did the one creek curl back on itself? Or was this the second? Unnerved, James decided to follow this one, hoping that he was traveling east and not west. Surely they could not have traveled far enough to double-back on Pumpkin Vine Creek?

Exhaustion and anxiety slowed him as they followed the twisting waterway, and finally he called for a halt. Like it or not, he doubted he had the strength to find the regiment tonight.

"Gotta keep goin'," Nate maintained in a flat tone.

"Let's just rest for a bit. Just a bit."

Reluctantly, Nate settled next to him, leaning against a tree. *Maybe*, James hoped, *if I sit here and rest, I'll think clearer; I'll remember the way. Should have paid more attention when following Nate out, but all I could think about was keeping up with him. Damn it all.*

He looked upward at the tree. The top seemed ragged, perhaps torn by artillery. If so, they were getting close to their lines. Perhaps this was the right stream. He closed his eyes, sighed, relished the cooler night air, listened to the murmur of the waterway.

He whispered, "Hey, Nate. Remember the buckeye tree back in Burr Oak?"

Nate said nothing, motionless, but James knew he was awake.

"Just outside my store. Folks used to gather under it on hot days, read their mail, gossip." He trailed off, for the very thought of the tree and what it represented relaxed him, pulled him away from the unsettling night sounds and into a restful sleep.

He dreamt of his father, saw him under the tree reading his most recent letter. He looked much younger, though, as he had when James was just a boy. Then his father left the buckeye tree and started up Third Street, hauntingly empty. He turned left onto Main Street until he reached their old home. The two-story house appeared as it had six years ago—a bright white coating of paint, flowers planted in window boxes and swinging in pots hung on the porch where a comfortable chair rocked in the breeze. Before his father could reach the front door, it swung violently open. Robert Langdon stood in the doorway, a bloody bayonet in his hand.

James awoke with a start. Immediately he sensed a void in the night—Nate was no longer next to him.

Jumping to his feet, he scanned the darkness, heart pounding, fear coursing through him. The woods were disturbingly quiet. He thought he heard voices, muffled and distant, off to his right, almost behind him. Had they gone too far? To call for his comrade would be foolish and could draw a bullet. But damn it...

Downstream he heard movement along the far bank but was unable to tell if it was coming toward him or moving away. If they had gone too far to the left, if they had gone too far to the east... James rushed after the shadowy form, slipping on the bank, silently cursing his clumsiness. Then he heard voices, unfamiliar, low, and harsh. Pickets? But whose? James crouched near a tree, fumbled for his musket, but what good would it do him? He could not shoot blindly.

The sound of a struggle. Shadows tussled. Muffled oaths, splashes. James recognized Nate's voice, clear now, alert. "Run, James!"

Down the creek a gunshot flashed. Its brief illumination revealed two Confederates with Nate between them, on his knees, the boy's white face turned in his direction. The shot struck the tree next to James, made him flinch and sink ever lower, heart hammering.

Several shots rang out from the hill to James's right and rear.

"Hold your fire!" he shouted.

He heard them then, felt them, the heavy presence in the night, flowing down off the now-familiar hill, the clatter of accouterments, the soft commands from officers. No more shots. None were needed. The Rebels quickly vanished into the farther darkness as Union forces splashed across the creek behind James and climbed the opposite hill.

James stared down the creek where he had last seen Nate. Nothing there, only the peaceful passing of water toward a left-hand bend. Dear God, he had lost him. Pain tightened his chest, labored his breath. Frantic gasps. His vision blurred.

"No, God damn it, no," he muttered.

"Who's there?" a Northern voice rang out from behind.

James bitterly cursed himself, wanted to weep. He had led them too far, beyond the Union flank. Why had Nate gone ahead of him? Walked right into them...

"James Keenan," he answered, the name echoing with accusing singularity. "Eleventh Michigan."

"Get your ass back up that hill, son."

The voice trailed away, returned to the flow of men splashing across the creek several hundred feet behind James, lengthening the Union flank. *If only we had come this way a few minutes later*, James lamented, staring back down the creek. He realized it then—the creek to the left, the hill to his right rear, a field opening to his right…the wheat field Scribner's men had crossed. The Eleventh was where he had left it…so close… Anguish crushed him to the ground. His trembling fingers let his musket fall, and he buried his face in his hands.

***

James found King's brigade manning the same trenches on the hill above the wheat field where he had left them. It had been Carlin's brigade crossing the creek to take a position on the hill opposite, anchoring the far left of the Federal line. Scribner's bloodied brigade now lay behind King's, and Wood's shattered division stretched off into the night to Scribner's right.

Damning Patrick Cleburne and all the Rebels under his command, James groped his way along the line until he found his company. Lieutenant Hart rose from where he had been resting against a tree, half asleep. Now quite awake, the officer loomed so close that James thought their noses would touch. The lieutenant's anger shot through the night like an unseen blow.

"Damn it, Keenan. What the hell's wrong with you? Bad enough Calhoun takes off, but you—"

"I couldn't just let him go off alone, Lieutenant. He wasn't thinking straight."

"Neither were you. God damn it, don't you realize you could be court-martialed for this?"

"I wasn't running off," James protested weakly. "I went along so I could bring Nate back."

"Then where the hell is he?"

James felt it then—the weight of every man's gaze along the Eleventh's line. Unseen in the night but felt all the same, curious, expectant.

Langdon's blocky shape drew near, the glow of a cigar stub bobbing when he growled, "The Lieutenant asked you a question, Keenan."

James could look at no one, unable to speak for a long moment. Damn it, he would not cry again, not here, not in front of Langdon.

"We went to the hospital and found his brother, but it was too late. Nate was broken up about it, of course. He wasn't paying much attention to anything on the way back. He…he ran into Reb pickets. We came up along the creek and went too far. They got a hold of him

179

before I knew it."

"How'd you get away?" Langdon asked.

"Be quiet, Sergeant," Hart snapped. "I'll ask the questions here."

"We stopped to rest. I fell asleep. Nate got ahead of me. I don't know why he went on without me. Like I said, he wasn't himself after seeing his brother."

Silence blanketed the company. The weak cries of a wounded man somewhere in front of the line scraped at James's nerves. He saw Brian's dead face in the wagon. They should have stayed there until morning.

"You fucking coward," Langdon said. "Why didn't you go after him?"

"Leave it, Sergeant," Hart ordered coldly. James could not read his tone—disappointment at least—when he said, "Go back to your squad, Private. I'll see what the Colonel wants to do with you."

James remembered Stoughton earlier that day, the kindness in his voice, the faith he had in his men. Perhaps neither Stoughton nor Hart would censure him, for both knew well enough that he would punish himself far beyond what any military court could decree.

When James returned to his squad, he expected some sort of judgment, something along the lines of Langdon's remarks, but mercifully the men said nothing, and the night hid what lay in their eyes. Surely the more time elapsed the more they would feel Nate's absence as they still felt Ryan's, and then the old animosity would return.

Elias offered a cold cup of coffee as James settled next to him in the hollowed-out earth. The older man briefly patted James's arm.

"Don't fret about it, lad. Nate'll be all right. And don't worry none about the Colonel. I told him it was my idea for you to go after the lad. He understands. 'Course he can't come right out and say it's all right, now can he? But it's not like the regiment went and did anything whilst you was gone. Sat here and watched Scribner's and Wood's boys come tumblin' back, bloody as all hell. Cleburne attacked Knefler right after you left, after dark, would you believe? Damnedest thing. God awful slaughter." He paused to light his pipe, allowed the match life long enough to reveal his sympathetic expression. "You did the right thing, lad. No shame in it, hear?"

James finished the coffee in one long gulp, handed the cup back, nodded appreciation before Elias blew out the match. But as he lay back against the trench, he knew he would never forgive himself. And Langdon would make sure no one forgot.

CHAPTER 18

Nate awoke from an exhausted doze and peered around the smelly interior of the rocking boxcar. At least a hundred Union prisoners shared the space, too crowded for more than a few to recline; men taken during the battles of New Hope Church, Dallas, and Pickett's Mill—the fight he had left behind. No talking now, only an occasional cough. Men slept or stared off into space, miserable in their capitulation. How long had it been since he had been captured? One day, two? Three? Everything was a vast, demoralizing blur.

He stared vacantly at his bare feet. The damned Rebs had taken his socks, brogans, blanket, everything except his pants, shirt, sack coat, canteen, and hat. One had tried to pilfer his slouch hat, but a punch to the nose dissuaded the Alabamian. The thief stood taller than he, and this fact, coupled with Nate's audacity, had amused the other Rebels. They laughed and told their comrade to let the little Yank keep his damned hat. They also allowed him to keep his new Bible and Katie's picture, though first he had to suffer their crude remarks as they passed the photograph among their grubby hands.

With a sinking heart, he thought of Katie, wondered of her reaction once she heard the news. Surely Lieutenant Hart or James would write to her, to his family. His poor mother. She would probably hear of his capture at the same time she learned of Brian's death. *Dear God.* As clear as yesterday, he remembered his father warning him that he did not understand what lay before him. Imprisonment had not been one of the things Nate considered when he had enlisted.

Thank God James had not been captured. There was at least that. When Nate had left their resting place beside that creek, he thought James awake, heard him mumbling something about his father, about Langdon. He told James it was time to move on, thought his companion followed him, but his own senses had been too fogged to pay much attention…until he heard those hard voices, those Alabama boys from Cleburne's division. They grabbed hold of him before he could react,

181

too stunned to flee until it was too late. He called for James to run, relieved his friend had not followed him. If he had been the cause of James's capture, he never would have forgiven himself. No doubt he was back with the boys of Company D. Nate wondered of their reactions to his capture. How he missed them. Those men were his family. Would he ever see any of them again? Looking around the boxcar, he felt horribly alone; most of the men had a comrade or two captured from their same outfit.

Ryan. Nate prayed that his brother still lived; he refused to believe otherwise. He would be in Andersonville. They would be reunited, and together they would escape. He grinned. *Them Rebs might be able to hold one Calhoun, but they won't be able to hold two. I'll be back with the boys in no time, and Ryan with me.*

Nate closed his eyes, saw Brian. He would have to tell Ryan about their brother. Perhaps he should refrain. No, Ryan would know something was wrong; he would see it on his face. Nate had never been able to hide anything from him.

His stomach clenched in a spasm of hunger. If only they had something to eat. He had had nothing since that morning, and then only a few bites of cornbread, hours ago. And his canteen was almost empty.

Before he could fall asleep, the shriek of the engine's whistle pierced the air, and the cars shuddered, then slowed. The men stirred, grumbling and swearing. Uncertainty poked Nate's hollow stomach. Maybe they would get rations now. Several minutes passed. From outside came the shouts of Southerners. The latch clanged, startling Nate, pushed him back against another man. The large door protested, then slid away to reveal a squad of armed guards.

"Y'all git out," an old sergeant ordered.

Warily the prisoners complied. Around the depot rose tall trees, many of them aged, scraggly pines with most of their foliage near their tops, stark against the cloudy sky, the air perfumed by their spicy scent. A few small shanties squatted near the rails, but otherwise the country appeared stark and unfriendly. An elderly man and a small girl in a shabby dress looked on from the depot, silent, apathetic.

"Fall in!" the sergeant barked.

As they marched in a ragged column up a road to the northeast, Nate noted a haze hovering in the distance, washing the blue from the sky. A large structure through the trees. A sound—a low buzz, barely heard above their tramping feet. Then the breeze shifted and carried to them a noxious odor. He and many of his companions wrinkled their noses and grimaced.

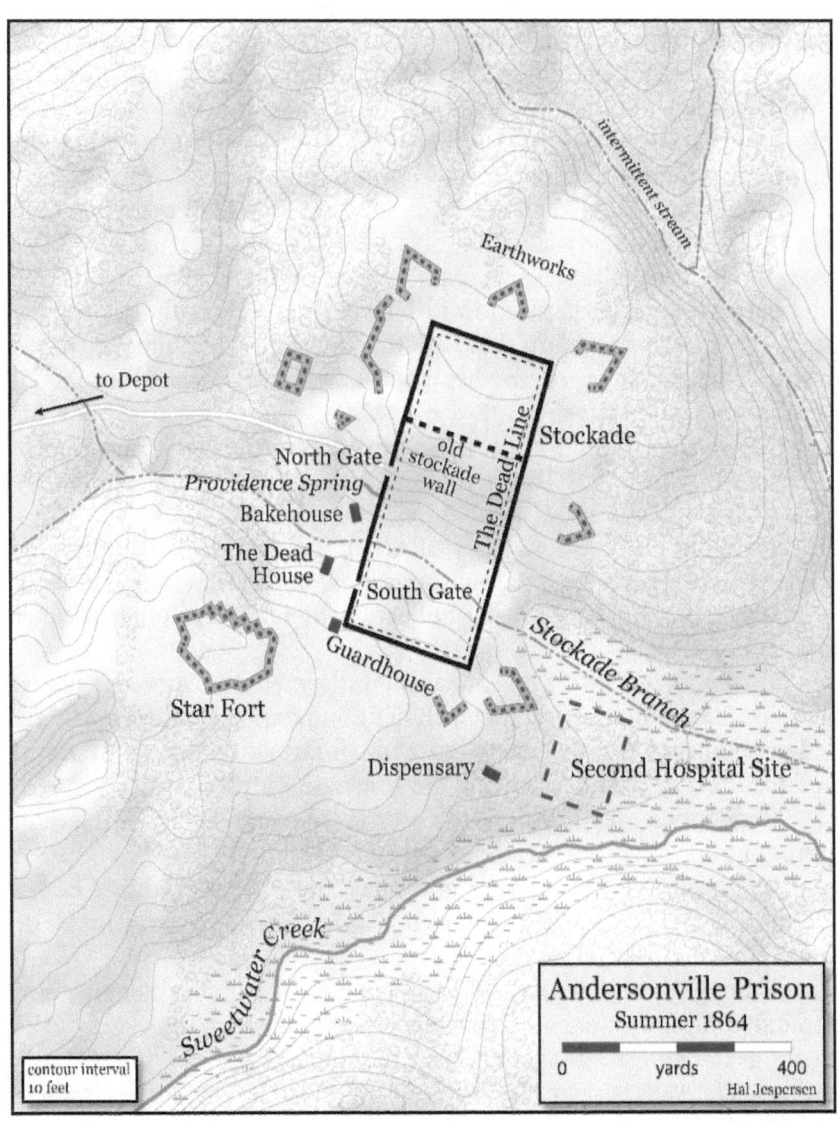

Andersonville Prison
Summer 1864

0   yards   400

Hal Jespersen

contour interval
10 feet

Someone behind him asked, "What the hell's that stink?"

"Don't rec'nize it?" one of the guards, a squeak of a boy, answered sarcastically. "That thar's the smell of Yankees. Y'all find out soon enough."

The prisoners glanced at each other with growing unease.

When the forest at last fell away to either side, they came within full view of the prison. A huge pen, a parallelogram made of squared, vertical pine logs set on end, reaching fifteen feet high, the palisades stretching north and south maybe ninety-five rods on ground that sloped down in the middle. Along the top of the stockade walls, sentries manned small platforms at intervals of perhaps ninety feet, awnings protecting them from the relentless Georgia sun. Surrounding the prison, a wilderness of forest.

Cold fear tightened Nate's throat. A wild urge to flee gripped him, but to where could he run?

When they halted near a massive gate on the northwest side, the undulation of the ground allowed Nate to see across the top of the stockade to the southern slope of the interior. Although he stared intently, he failed to comprehend what he saw beneath the pall of smoke from small fires.

"This ain't right," one of the prisoners protested to no one in particular. "Those look like niggers in there. We're white soldiers, by God. What's the idea—?"

Nate did not hear the reply of the nearest guard. He studied the moving herd of humans, untold thousands, beyond the wooden wall, crowded there amidst a trashy collection of tents and other meager shelters.

As their names were taken, he paid little attention. Someone poked him, said something about a detachment number, a squad, a mess. He did not bother to ask the man to repeat the information, too mesmerized and terrified by what lay beyond the stockade wall.

Suddenly a gray horse passed in front of Nate, the leg of the rider jarring him back toward the other prisoners.

"Sergeant! Get dis brizner into line," the rider barked in a heavy German accent. "Vat is de matter vit' you? You must vatch dem all de time!"

Nate gawked upward at the captain. The man's small form reminded him of a rodent. One glance from his sharp, blue-gray eyes made Nate shrink away, back to the others without the guard's prompting. A dark, wiry beard covered most of the officer's face, mouth small and cruel. His right arm hung in a sling, the other held the mare's reins. A formidable, ugly pistol hugged his hip. Something foreboding and unrelenting permeated the foul air. The foreigner gave them all a quick glare, then rode southward.

"Who the hell was that?" someone asked.

A guard grinned. "Captain Henry Wirz. Commandant of this here prison. And a right friendly fellow he is." The man laughed.

The heavy wooden doors yawned before them, and the guards prodded them inside, then closed the doors. Now they were in a small enclosure with another gate facing them, its wicket closed. The prisoners looked at each other in bewilderment as the guards stepped forward to the interior gate. When these doors opened, an overpowering stench slammed into Nate—stale, furnace-like air, and burning pine. The guards' bayonets poked them forward into the stockade, then the Southerners left, the doors closed and barred.

An incorporeal voice announced, "Fresh fish!"

Hundreds of faces stared at Nate and the other new arrivals, instantly forming into a crescent wall of grotesque cadaverous figures. Not black slaves. But were they really once white Union soldiers? Perhaps those Rebs back in the forest near Pickett's Mill had killed him and he had gone to hell. This could not be a prison. It looked and smelled like some charnel house where rot and decay ruled. And the inmates…they were scarecrows at best. A dark substance like pine tar smeared their faces. Ratted hair, shaggy beards, eyes large and sunken. Their clothes—some had next to none—hung in tatters. Had they once been uniforms? Some wore forage caps, others no hats at all.

This had to be a nightmare.

A prisoner asked, "Where you boys from?"

To hear words from such specters seemed unnatural, disturbing. The crowd pressed closer, surrounded the gaping, paralyzed group. Horrified, Nate backed away, bumped into his equally disbelieving, repulsed comrades.

"Jesus," someone behind him muttered. "Look at 'em, for Christ sake."

"What the hell's happened to 'em?"

"They look half-dead, starved…"

The inmates paid no attention to their reactions. "What's the latest news, boys?"

"They's Westerners. Hey, when's Sherman gonna lib'rate us wretches?"

They clamored for information until one of the newcomers from Hazen's brigade told them of the fighting near Dallas.

"Where in hell's that? How far from here?"

"Maybe twenty-five miles northwest of Atlanta."

This set the prisoners buzzing, and several ran off, shouting the news, stirring more languishing men to their feet.

For as far as Nate could see, men stood, sat, or reclined in pure idleness. Good Lord, how many? There could not be more than sixteen acres inside the barren, treeless stockade, all congested with a haphazard collection of shelters. Some prisoners appeared to have no shelter whatsoever. The north end of the stockade, in which they stood, sloped much steeper than the south side, providing Nate with a view of a swamp at the foot of the two slopes, running east and west. Sinks stood at the farthest end of the stream, if that were indeed a stream...or had once been before this place had been erected.

As the fellow from Hazen's brigade rattled off more news of the campaign, Nate's gaze roamed in terrible fascination across the prisoners near them. He had never seen men so filthy, so underweight. No, they were beyond underweight but...why? Were they not fed or able to even wash and care for themselves?

One prisoner caught Nate's attention, for he wore a brimless forage cap that displayed a battered corps badge on the top—a white trefoil: Second Division, Second Corps, Army of the Potomac. The same division in which Joseph Calhoun's Seventh Michigan was brigaded last Nate knew. He was unable to tell how old the fellow was. Shirtless. Ragged pants worn off just below the knees.

The man's feverish eyes swung to Nate. He stepped forward, bringing with him an offensive odor. "What outfit you with, boy?"

"I...um...Eleventh Michigan Infantry." He gestured to the man's cap. "Might you be from the Seventh Michigan? That's me brother Joseph's outfit."

"He captured, too?"

"Not last I knew."

"Well, *I'm* not from that outfit, but I got some chums from the Seventh Michigan. Captured at the Wilderness. Maybe they know your brother."

"Another of me brothers was captured last summer in Tennessee—Ryan Calhoun. Ever hear of him?"

"Last summer?" The man peered heavenward. "Sure he's still alive?"

"Well...no. But I aim to find out."

"Maybe them Seventh Michigan boys know of him."

The prospect of finding Ryan buoyed him. "Would you take me to 'em?"

The fellow gave an incongruously white grin, a couple of teeth missing. "Follow me."

The idea of leaving the other newcomers unnerved Nate, for he felt akin to them even if he did not know them; at least they were like him. This shriveled waif of a man...who was he? Could he trust him? Nate could not even bring himself to ask for a name. Instead, he decided to follow the prisoner, praying he would help him find Ryan in this pest hole. Would Ryan look like these others? How could anyone survive here? How would *he*?

The slow-moving man led Nate down an east-west pathway, perhaps ten feet wide, which served as some sort of street. Other, smaller paths led north and south from that avenue.

"This here's Market Street," the guide explained blandly. "Buyers and sellers gather here, as you can see." He gestured to the strange collection of hawkers along the sides of the path. Voices, advertising their wares, blended together in a grating song—someone had a comb for sale, another some onions, another said he would repair shoes in exchange for food, someone waved a watch for sale, reminding Nate of James's watch, traded for food during those hungry days before Missionary Ridge. Now he had a feeling he had never really known true hunger.

Soon they turned down one of the smaller paths and headed south. Silent specters watched them weave their way among the tangle of tents and listless men. Most lay on the bare ground or beneath shelters made from all manner of flotsam, shading shallow holes dug in the earth, holes that reminded Nate of the ones his dog used to dig back home in the yard to keep cool. Clouds of flies buzzed. He stared in horror at the dozens of men so obviously close to death, sights that often brought him to a stupefied halt. Many had swollen lower legs, so distended that they wore no pants or shoes. Toothless gums protruded beyond parched lips, skin tight and translucent. Painful coughs rang out. Open, oozing ulcerations on young and old alike. What caused such agony? What was wrong with these men? How long had they been prisoners? Dear God, no one had warned him...

He stumbled over a man sprawled outside one tent. Unnerved, he snapped, "You damned fool! Why don't you get out of the way?"

He realized the man was not asleep. He was stone-cold dead, his eyes only halfway closed, as if death had come suddenly, without a final warning. Cracked, blue lips invited flies. The fuzz upon his shirtless chest suggested a young age, though the rest of his scrawny form looked like that of one older, his dark skin laced with lines. Lice by the hundreds ruled his lifeless body. Nate shrank back when he noticed the boy's left arm, recognized the sight and stench of gangrene. A squirming mass of maggots covered the rotted flesh.

Someone rushed over, shoved Nate aside. "We saw him fust," the inmate snarled in an unrecognized accent.

"Yeah," a second man, with feral eyes, growled. "Beat it."

Nate could only stare, wide-eyed and open-mouthed, as the two carried the corpse away. He jumped at the laconic rasp of his guide's voice: "They'll be able to get some wood with that, if'n they's lucky."

"What?"

"Carry someone to the dead-house. You know, outside the pen."

No, Nate almost said, *I don't know*. He hurried to follow the wiry fellow. "You make it sound like someone dyin' is a—"

"A common thing?" The man looked over his shoulder with a macabre smile. "Oh, 'tis common, by God. Too damned common. Hundreds have been 'paroled.'" He chuckled. "Dead, you see."

"Jesus, Mary, and Joseph." Nate concentrated on his companion's back, tried not to look too closely at the living dead whom he passed.

"Here we are." The man halted near a dug-out area of earth over which a blanket had been fashioned at an angle with crude poles. Beneath its shade, three men played cards with a smudged, frayed deck. "Hey, Johnny Blair. Have here a Michigan boy. Fresh as fish can be."

The three men looked up. Something sparked in their eyes. One stood with a smile on his grimy, mustached face. He looked to be in his forties. He shook Nate's hand. "What outfit, lad?"

"Eleventh Infantry."

"Where from?"

"Burr Oak. You was with the Seventh?"

"That's right. Captured at the Wilderness, me and Byron Cusick there."

"Me brother Joseph's in the Seventh. Company K. Joseph Calhoun. You know him?"

Blair exchanged a surprised look with Cusick, a look that bespoke of better times, better memories. "Sure, we know him. Fine fellow."

Excitement pushed away some of Nate's fears. "How was he the last time you saw him? Was he well?"

"Fit as could be," Cusick assured him, still seated. He appeared to be about Nate's age, pale and unwell for only being captured earlier in May. "Here now. Have a seat and tell us all the news, Burr Oak."

"Yeah," the third, a man whose pants displayed the yellow stripe of cavalry, added. "What's the word on exchange?'

"Don't know nothin' 'bout that." Nate refused to sit on the ground. Lice. How he hated those little bastards. "Reckon exchange wasn't a concern afore yesterday."

The foursome's laughter lacked the genuine mirth Nate was accustomed to hearing.

"Well, I'll tell you plain," the cavalryman said, "that's one of the main topics in this here pen."

"That and food. Damned little of neither."

Nate shifted his weight. "Much obliged for your invitation to sit, but your friend fetched me here 'cause I'm lookin' for one of me other brothers. He's from the Eleventh Michigan, too. Captured at Elk River last July. Ryan Calhoun."

The three frowned at each other. Nate barely breathed.

"Ryan," Cusick mused. "Irish lad, taller than you; older, too?"

"Aye, he is. Hazel eyes, hair the color of mine."

Blair laughed. "Hell, hoverin' 'round these here pine fires turns everyone's hair black, and their skin, too."

"I bet I know him," the cavalryman said. "Good scrapper?"

"Well…used to be back home. Could lick all us boys, even Matthew, who's the eldest and biggest."

"Sure, must be him. Recollect, Johnny, the fellow who pounded one of the Raiders t'other night. Not five rods from here, over yonder."

The others put in their opinions, agreeing, but Nate understood none of it, deafened by impatience and eagerness.

Blair grinned. "I didn't know he's Joseph's brother. Well, I'll be…"

The man who had brought Nate from the north gate sat down. "Mind showin' him the way, Johnny? I'm not feelin' too powerful well."

"Sure. Finish my hand, will you? I could use a walk. C'mon, Burr Oak."

They wound their way through the tents and shelters, northeast across Market Street until they reached a shelter constructed with two blankets supported by six sticks. Beneath the awning's meager shade, a thin, sinewy fellow lay on his back on the scooped-out ground, arms behind his head for a pillow, torn and faded slouch hat over his face. Two other men crowded beneath the protection, the smaller of the pair playing "Johnny Has Gone for A Soldier" on a battered recorder. But when they saw Nate and Blair, the song ended, and suspicion hooded their raccoon-like eyes.

Cheerily Blair said, "Howdy, gents. Brought someone here to see one of you. Just came in from Uncle Billy's fight. Says he's one of the Calhoun boys from Burr Oak."

In one quick movement, the man on the ground jerked away the hat and sat up. His face, like so many others here, had been blackened by the fires, high cheekbones accentuated by hollowness. Although heavily stubbled, he sported only a mustache. Hair the color of coal fresh from the earth stuck together by pitch into wild patches. Nate

189

stared, unsure, afraid to believe. The man scrambled from beneath the tent. The others watched closely.

"Dear God…Nate," he said near a whisper.

Nate did not care how dirty or infested his brother was—he threw himself into his arms. Neither uttered a word as they embraced. Nate's shock and isolation since capture, his ten months of worry for Ryan, his grief over Brian welled up, squeezed tears between his eyelids. He did not want to cry, for he knew how Ryan felt about public displays, yet the tears were undeniable. Perhaps if he clung to his brother long enough, he could hide them.

But there was no deceiving Ryan. He held Nate at arm's length, gave him a gentle shake. "Hey, now. I'll be havin' none of that, boyo." No real rebuke in his tone; in fact, a small smile in the corners of his lips. "You always was the first to bawl over somethin', wee little Nate."

Nate swiped at the tears. He always hated it when one of his siblings called him little, but right now Ryan could call him anything he wanted.

"How in God's name did you end up here?"

"I joined the Eleventh last summer, right after I heard you was captured."

Ryan's scowl made him realize he should have avoided mentioning the timing, for now Ryan would hold himself accountable for his younger brother's present predicament.

Blair smiled at Ryan as if grateful for being able to see some happiness again. "Didn't know you was related to Joseph Calhoun."

"How do you know Joseph?"

"I was in the Seventh Michigan."

"Well, I'll be damned. How is Joseph, last you knew?"

"Like I told Nate, he was fine. Healthy and a sergeant now. A brave fellow through and through."

"Well, now, that sounds like me brother." Ryan held out his hand. "Much obliged for you bringin' Nate over."

"God knows I had nothin' better to do." Blair shrugged. "Well, looks like you two have plenty to keep you busy in the gabbing department, and I've got a card game to finish, so…"

Nate thanked him again before turning back to Ryan, who grinned and put an arm around his shoulders, turned him toward his two companions, who no longer looked so cynical. "Come and sit in our humble shebang, little brother. 'Tis a mansion, you'll come to learn. Here now, let me introduce you to me very best friends. They're both from the Twenty-fourth Michigan, Iron Brigade. Old-timers like me.

Captured at Gettysburg."

"Gettysburg," Nate murmured, thought of James's uncle, thought of James. He settled next to Ryan on the excavated plot of dirt.

"That stumpy fellow there is Jonas Whitmore."

Nate found the young man's handshake surprisingly strong, almost challenging. His long hair, perhaps once blond, was swept back from his forehead and square face, his furrowed brow hunched over small, intense gray eyes and small nose, his full lips smiling slightly, as if at a personal joke. He was smaller but sturdier than Billy Hathaway, whom Ryan next introduced. Billy was the handsomer of the pair, with crisp blue eyes, a straight, pointed nose, finely etched lips, and a strong chin and jaw line. His smile came more readily.

"Now," Ryan slapped his shoulder, "tell us. Tell us everything we've missed since rottin' away as a guest of our fine Southern hosts."

***

Nate began with his engagement to Katie, news that flushed Ryan and made him grin. Ryan himself had no such romantic ties, but he had never shown jealousy over any of his brothers' sweethearts. On the contrary, he enjoyed having such fodder with which to tease his siblings. While self-confident in all other things, Ryan had a streak of shyness in him when it came to the female persuasion, and some in Burr Oak viewed the handful of Irish in the community as less than equals, and this veiled prejudice influenced Ryan. Whenever forced to speak with one of the local girls, he was self-conscious of his brogue, sometimes attempting to conceal it, though he had little success. Now, after three years away from home, he had indeed lost some of their ancestral lilt, though Nate figured the erosion had been caused more by the absence from his family than by any conscious effort on Ryan's part to deny his roots.

After talking about Katie, Nate purposefully veered away from familial news, now unsure whether to reveal Brian's death. Instead, he told them about the battles that he and the regiment had fought since Ryan's capture, told him of Major Bennet's death, of Frank Lane's desertion and Ben Hart's promotion, about James and the others of Company D, about how much they still talked of Ryan and missed him. Ryan's face flushed again at this, and he tried to hide his smile of satisfaction and nostalgia.

"I read your letter to the boys at the start of the campaign," Nate explained. "The one you wrote back in January. Brian said Ma sent it to him and told him to send it on to me, but he brung it hisself."

"You saw him?"

Nate faltered, berated himself. "Aye, the day afore we started the campaign earlier this month."

Ryan grinned at Whitmore and Billy. "Brian was the last to join up before Nate. Our mother, God love her, was so dead set against it that she slept in his room. But got out of her sight, he did. Went to the privy one night and ne'er came back. Ran off to the Nineteenth's camp at Dowagiac in Cass County, the sneaky little bastard."

Nate stared down at his lap, at the wool of his pants, which already beckoned the lice, wondered how long it would be before his uniform hung in rags like everyone else's.

"Come now, little brother. How is it with Brian?"

Again Nate saw Brian's face in the wagon, felt his cold skin, smelled the blood.

"Nate?"

He did not want to tell Ryan, did not want to cry again. How he had cried that night by the hospital. James had supported him when he slipped to the ground and sobbed like a small child, like he had when his first dog had died and Ryan had been there to comfort him, the only brother to do so. Now he felt like that child again. How could that be when just a few days ago he had felt like a man, lying there on that hillside near Resaca, remaining at his post when men like Frank Lane broke and ran away? He needed to be a man now, he needed to find the strength to tell the truth. After all, if he were in Ryan's shoes, he would want to know.

He swallowed hard, spoke without looking up. "Brian was wounded at New Hope Church...just a few days ago, not sure now. I went to the hospital when I heard he was brung in." He faltered, his chest tightening.

Ryan's question, soft but urgent: "How bad was he?"

"Well...Ryan...when I got there, he...he was dead."

Silence...silence somehow amidst the dull hum of thousands of idle men around them, a sound unable to penetrate here. When Nate had mastered any threat of tears, he looked up, saw Ryan's dry stare somewhere off in the hazy distance, as if he were trying to see Brian, remember him. Three years ago, they had said goodbye, never to see one another again.

Jonas Whitmore gave Nate an almost rebuking look, then spoke protectively to Ryan. "I'm sorry, Scrapper."

Billy frowned, said nothing, shifted his weight.

At last, Ryan turned back, blinked, sniffed once, and smiled tightly. "Well, now. Dear Brian. God rest his soul." He crossed himself.

Ryan's brief, almost dismissive reaction unnerved Nate. True, he had not expected an outpouring of visible emotion but certainly something more profound, more tactile than a simple, single sentiment. Ryan reached over with a bony hand and closed Nate's gaping mouth. Only within the depths of his brother's penetrating, cautious gaze did he find the sorrow he sought, carefully guarded by a mature responsibility far beyond Ryan's years.

"Nate," he said quietly, as if they were alone, "survivin' is a damned hard thing here. As you can see, the lads and me have been doin' somethin' right to have made it this long. Most have not. We manage it by followin' rules, you see. Our rules. And rule number one is this: We don't speak of bad things if we can avoid it. We try to keep our spirits up." His close-set eyes narrowed. "Soon you will find, boyo, 'tis Brian who is the luckier of us three brothers."

Nate was too dazed to respond.

Ryan cleared his scratchy throat, straightened his spine. His voice took on greater authority, all emotion gone. "We have other rules, too. Anyone who didn't obey 'em was told to move elsewhere. First of all, we don't drink the water outta the damned creek. 'Tis poisoned by both the Reb guards and us wretches inside. Supposed to serve as drinkin' supply *and* sinks, believe it or not."

"But where do you get water, then?"

"There's a well t'other side of that there shebang." He gestured to the east. "We helped dig it. Ain't *much* better than the swamp, and even then, you don't drink that till you boil it. And, more's the pity, ain't enough wood around no more for many fires, so get used to not drinkin' much."

Nate looked toward the distant treetops. "But there's plenty of wood out yonder."

Whitmore, his voice much too deep to match his stature, grumbled, "May as well be as far as Michigan. Damned few wood details let out."

"Then why don't the Johnnies bring it in?"

Whitmore snorted a sour laugh. "As you can see, the Johnnies hain't too concerned with helpin' us out."

As Ryan continued, agitation crept into his tone, as if Whitmore's words had fueled some simmering anger, the type of temper he often displayed back home when his brothers failed to reflect his own strict work ethic. "The next rule is just as important. When Nature calls, get

193

your ass down to the sinks. We keep this area clean, by God. Sounds simple enough but simple things will become a chore, you'll find. Like keepin' clean. We try the best we can—shave, cut our hair, keep the graybacks down as much as possible."

Nate chafed under the harsh, almost accusatory orders. He had hoped after all this time that Ryan would see him as more than a boy to boss around. Saying nothing, he stared out over the patchwork of men and shelters on the north slope, then over to the southwest. There, beyond the stockade wall, cannon mounted on earthworks pointed their way. The tears from earlier hovered somewhere near.

"Nate," Ryan said, the hardness gone. When Nate at last turned back, Ryan frowned, said, "Come on," and stood.

He led Nate away, off through the tangle and noise and stench to the edge of Market Street. There Ryan stopped, his face pinched, that distant, guarded look returning.

"I'm sorry if I sounded a bit rough back there. 'Tis just…" His eyes misted. "'Tis happy I am to see you but…Jesus, I wish you wasn't in this God-forsaken place. I've seen many a man die in the past ten months. I don't want to see you go that way, and I don't want you to watch me neither."

Nate tried to smile, some of his confidence returning. "Won't let that happen, will we?"

Ryan shook his head, smiled self-consciously. Then he put his arm around Nate's shoulders, and they walked along Market Street, silent, trying not to hear the misery around them. Men studied Nate from all sides, some under shelters, some staggering by. They covetously eyed his uniform. His skin crawled as he remembered the two men fighting for the corpse. The dark undercurrent of violence, despair, and desperation—beyond anything he had ever known—frightened him.

When they reached the end of the street, near the east wall, Ryan pointed to a small barrier—rickety posts some three or four feet high, perhaps twenty feet inside the stockade. Sagging scantlings connected them along the top, the fence line paralleling the stockade wall for as far as Nate could see. Barren ground took up valuable space between the barrier and the palisades.

"That there's the Dead Line," Ryan warned coldly. "Don't go nowhere near it. Even touch it and one of them lamebrained sonsabitches up yonder will shoot you. That is, if their aim is any good. Hard to miss that close, though, even for them."

Nate nodded, glanced up at a dozing sentry beneath the roof of his perch. Just a boy really, not old enough to be at the front.

Again his stomach clenched like a hard fist. "Powerful hungry, Ry. When do we get rations?"

"Not till mornin', lad."

"Mornin'? I ain't had nothin' to eat since…" He stopped when he saw that apologetic, pained expression again. "Reckon I'll get used to it, aye?"

"No. Never get used to it. Just make do. I get an extra ration 'cause I'm sergeant of our squad. You see, the commandant has this half-assed way of organizin' us. We're divided into detachments of two hundred seventy, then divided into squads of ninety, then divided into three messes of thirty. Plays hell, though, 'cause so many die a day in here and so many new ones arrive, so the math never quite works. Over fifteen thousand in here now. We're squadded over every now and then. Anyway, 'tis me job as sergeant to see that each mess gets its proper share. That's why I get an extra ration. And I always save it for the three of us for supper. Well, four now. I'll get you into our mess."

"I can't take your extra ration away from your messmates. They need it worse'n me."

"Don't matter. We all share." He paused. "Used to be seven of us, helped each other through Belle Isle. Well, we left two there—dead, that is—and the other two are fresh graves out yonder, including Billy's younger brother."

"What did they die from?"

"Many things. Take your pick. Starvation, disease. Hell, I was about done-in last winter. So damned cold, it was. Scurvy's tryin' to get hold of me; lost a tooth the other day—damned bread. Need vegetables. That'd save a lot of us." He laughed dryly. "Fancy that— me, a farmer, dyin' for want of greens."

"You're not dyin'."

"Won't go easy. Fella's fine till it gets in his legs, then… Well, anyhow, the boys will probably have supper cooked by the time we get back."

They started up Market Street but did not get far before two men stepped out from behind shebangs on the south side of the street and came toward them. Large, rugged men, better fed than the masses around them. Their uniforms barely showed the rigors of prison life, yet the way they carried themselves bespoke of much time spent within these walls, men who had lost the army's discipline. Ryan took hold of Nate's arm in warning as the pair blocked their path. The stockier of the two, who bore a nasty scar down his right cheek, grinned at Nate, showing a tooth broken half off in front, but the expression held no friendliness. His smaller companion wore a snide grin and spoke with a harsh Irish brogue.

"Who's the fresh fish, Scrapper? If me eyes don't deceive, I'd hazard a guess he's kin to you."

A chill ran through Nate as Ryan stepped between him and the predatory pair. Around them, interested, fearful eyes turned their way.

"Step aside," Ryan growled.

"Nice clothes, runt," the man said, as if Ryan were nonexistent. "Care to sell any of it? Fella gets crazy hungry in here. You can buy food from the guards or sutler, but you need money. Give you greenbacks for that there sack coat, I will."

Ryan snorted. "The devil you say, Kevin Murphy. Since when do you *pay* for somethin' you're wantin'?"

Murphy put on a hurt look. "Are you suggestin' somethin', Scrapper?"

"Suggestin', hell! You're a murderin' thief, and no mistake. Everyone knows it. I'll tell you now—stay away from this here boy. Somethin' happens to him, won't matter how many of your God damned bullies I have to go through; kill you I will, and the pen will be the better for it."

To Nate's surprise, Murphy laughed in Ryan's florid face. "Why don't you let the lad answer me question, Scrapper? Come now, runt. Wouldn't you do better with food instead o' that coat? 'Tis warm already, to be sure, and only spring; won't be needin' a shirt even."

Nate glanced at his brother, then set his jaw. "Reckon I'll keep me coat."

Murphy tossed an unhappy look at his square-headed, silent companion, then sized Nate up. "Full o' yerself, I see. Scrapper's brother; no doubt about it now. Well, remember, runt. I gave you a fair chance. Next time, you'll listen to Kevin Murphy, I wager."

"C'mon, Nate. The smell's gettin' worse around here." As they passed, Ryan's shoulder thumped against Kevin Murphy. But Murphy held his ground, his dark chuckle in Nate's ear.

CHAPTER 19

As they made their way up the north slope, Nate wondered how Ryan could so easily find his way amidst this uncharted tangle. Nate often glanced over his shoulder to see if the two men followed them. He could not quell the uneasiness they had stirred in him.

"Who was those men, Ryan?"

"They belong to Mosby's Raiders."

"Mosby? The Reb raider who—?"

"He's named after the Reb, though to me this one's worse. Collins is his real name, and Kevin Murphy licks his boots, as do many others. Raiders we call 'em, among others. Cutthroats. The slime of humanity." Anger deepened his tone. "Disgraces to the uniform. Here the strong survive, and the damned Raiders are the strongest...and gettin' stronger. Kill a man for a blanket or less, they will. Killed Billy's brother, God damn them. They support each other. Most of their work is done at night, but they're gettin' bolder."

"Why don't no one stop 'em?"

"No organization. This place is a mess. Easterners, Westerners. Everyone suspicious of each other. God damned spies everywhere, for the Rebs and the Raiders. Can't trust no one. Everyone's afeared to put his neck on the line to try to put down the Raiders, 'cause if the Raiders hear about him, they'll kill him. But there will come a day, boyo..."

Holy Mary, Nate thought. *This place is horror enough without having to worry about being killed by our own men. Well, Ryan's made it this far; fancy I can, too. Murphy calling me a runt...*

Easily he had sensed the begrudging respect Murphy had for Ryan, a caution that had kept him from taking what he wanted right then and there. Whitmore and Billy clearly respected him, too. Nate's curiosity grew over his brother's life in this hellhole.

"Here now," Ryan said presently. "This'll make you feel more welcome. The boys who own the well with us, you probably know 'em. Might not recognize 'em—"

"Know 'em?"

"Aye. Eleventh Michigan boys. Captured at Chickamauga, most of 'em."

Nate brightened at the thought of old comrades, remembered his sorrow over their loss during that sad retreat to Chattanooga so long ago. If he had to endure this place, at least he would have friends.

"Hey, lads." Ryan hailed six men who lounged in and around a shebang made of half a dog tent, a couple of wool blankets, and a rubber blanket. "Where's the rest of the boys, Jacob?"

Grimy faces turned their way, and Nate tried to hide his shock at their appearances. Was that possibly Jacob Kessler, Lenawee County man from Company G?

"By God," another said, getting up. "Nate Calhoun?"

"Jared Taylor?" Nate stared at the twenty-seven-year-old Burr Oaker.

The others also got to their feet, smiling and welcoming. They introduced themselves again. Some he knew, like Jared, better than others: from Company H, George Griffin and Edwin Green, the eldest of the lot at forty-one and captured only last December; Corporal Ansel Rich of Company B; Henry Damon of Company A. Elmer Bradley of Company K and Napoleon Sprague of Company I were off somewhere, they said. They mentioned two others, Tindall and Wilson, who lived not far away.

"We've only lost one so far," Jared said proudly. "Don't know if you knew him, Nate—Oliver Brock from El's company. Died less than a month after coming to this shithole."

Nate frowned. "I recollect the name, but I didn't rightly know him."

Henry Damon, a farmer from Leonidas, said, "Sit down, Nate. Tell us everything you know. I just pine away for news. We all do. Any word of exchange?"

Ryan chuckled and clapped Nate on the shoulder, his dark anger over the Raiders banished. "Go ahead, little brother. I'll fetch you when supper's ready. He'll be in our mess, lads, so he's to use the well, mind."

No one objected as they urged Nate to tell them the latest news from God's Country.

***

Nate slept restlessly that night, crammed together with his messmates for warmth and to share the two blankets. After the day's intense heat, the biting cold dampness that had slammed down on the compound after sunset had surprised Nate. Occasionally one of his comrades would order, "By the right flank, spoon!" and they would simultaneously roll over and resume snoring.

He fell in and out of dreams. Dreams of Katie, his family, James and the others from Company D, of food—tables and tables weighted by it—of the street dance in Burr Oak last July. The scent of lilacs replaced the stench of the pen. The heady purple flowers on the bushes below his bedroom window would be done blooming now, shriveled and brown, but how he loved to lie awake on a spring night and drink in their perfume while listening to gentle, distant thunder.

In the last dream, his whole family gathered in the dining room—even Brian, looking as he had that day in Ringgold—seated around the table, talking and laughing. A holiday feast spread before them. He could smell each dish as distinctly as if it were the only one in the room. Chicken and corn and potatoes and gravy as hot as… The front door opened, and everyone turned, deathly silent. James stood in the doorway, eyes glazed, staring. Blood soaked the front of his torn uniform, a gaping wound in his neck. He wavered, began to collapse. Nate lunged to catch him.

"Raiders! Raiders!"

Nate jerked awake. Someone scrambled over top of him in the dark, stepped on his legs. Disoriented, he untangled himself from the blanket. Shouts and curses filled the heavy night. He tried to get up, but someone held him down, and he heard Billy Hathaway's voice in his ear. "Stay here, Little Brother."

Two black shapes wrestled a couple of yards away. A third man—he recognized the squat, square form of Jonas Whitmore—charged another shadow to the left, yelling savagely in the moonlight. The shadow fled. Whitmore halted and wheeled back to the other two, who struggled to their feet, grappling and swearing.

"Ryan!" Nate got to his hands and knees, but Billy's scant frame fell on him again.

"Damn it, boy. Stay put. Scrapper can handle the bastard. It's you they're after. Don't show yourself."

The Raider swung for Ryan but missed. Whitmore jumped him from behind, pinned his arms. Ryan kneed the Raider in the groin, drew a scream that made Nate cringe. Disembodied voices filled the air from all around.

"Give it to him, Scrapper!"

"Break the bastard's neck!"

"Kill him!"

Ryan's punch, deep into the man's exposed belly, drove out what remained of his air. The man doubled over, gasping. Ryan's knee met the Raider's face with a sickening crack. The man went limp. Whitmore let him fall. Ryan kicked him, but the form lay motionless. To Nate's surprise, his brother continued to kick the man, swearing as he had never heard him swear before.

Nate escaped Billy's relaxing grasp and ran at his brother, shoved him. "Stop it. You'll kill him."

Ryan stiff-armed him away with a growl and kicked the man again.

Jared Taylor's voice: "Leave him be, Nate."

But Nate grabbed Ryan by the shoulders. Again his brother shoved him back. "Get away from me. Damn it, stay outta this."

"He's out cold. You can't kill him."

"Can't I? Whit, gimme your knife."

Whitmore stepped forward, but Nate jumped between them, horrified. "You can't do this, Ryan. 'Tis murder."

Ryan hovered mere inches from Nate's face, teeth and eyes glaring white in the gloom, a stranger to Nate. What had this war, this place done to his brother? He was suddenly afraid to find out.

"What do you think they came here for, Nate? To rob us—*you*! And if he tried to kill you in the bargain, do you think his bullies would stop him? No one would give a God damn. Now, step back."

Momentarily numb, Nate watched Whitmore hand Ryan the small knife. But when his brother reached for the downed Raider, sense returned to Nate; he grabbed his sibling's shoulder and punched him in the face. The blow staggered Ryan, something no childhood punch had ever done. Somehow Ryan managed to remain upright. Nate lunged for his wrist, tried to pry the knife away from him. Ryan swore and struggled to break Nate's unyielding grip.

Someone shouted, "Hey, he's awake!"

"Don't let him run!"

Whitmore called, "Scrapper, he's gettin' away!"

Ryan, breathing hard, swung his free hand, caught Nate in the side of the head with a sledgehammer blow that broke his grip. Stars exploded before Nate's eyes. His legs gave way.

By the time he recovered his wits and got to his hands and knees, men had gathered in the dark near where the Raider had lain. They spoke among themselves, but he deciphered only Whitmore's deep voice. "Cool down, Scrapper. We can't let you go after him. They'll be waitin', mind."

Nate got to his feet, ears still ringing. Their displeasure with him felt as weighty as a wet blanket.

His brother quietly addressed the group. "'Tis all right, lads. I take responsibility for me daft little brother. Go back to your blankets. We'll watch for the sonsabitches."

With a note of admiration, Jared said, "Don't fancy they'll try again tonight. That there fella's in a world of hurt. Won't wanna try his luck again none too soon."

"Don't bet on that." Ryan sounded exhausted, utterly spent.

"Jesus, Mary, and Joseph," Nate breathed to himself. What had he been thinking, fighting his brother in Ryan's weakened condition?

Ryan returned to him, said nothing for a time as he stood before him, the rank odor of sweat mingling with the night's myriad smells. Nate shivered, then thought of how better clothed he was than Ryan.

The softness of Ryan's voice masked his anger. "Get back under the blankets with Whit and Billy. Somethin' like this happens again, I want you to stay put, stay with them. Hear?"

Swallowing in a parched throat, tasting blood, Nate glanced around at the others, who returned to their various shebangs. "*Will* it happen again?"

"Oh, aye. That it will. If not tonight, then some other night." He gripped Nate's shoulder so painfully that Nate tried to pull away. Ryan's words slipped to him in a dangerous whisper. "Don't you *never* lay a hand on me again. Hear?"

"But, Ryan—"

"Never." He gave him a shake. "Not here."

Nate backed away. Ryan stood resolute. Bewildered and hurt, Nate retreated to the safety of their dugout.

***

With his head still aching from Ryan's punch, Nate slept little, senses attuned to the surroundings, while at the same time trying to block out the moans and wails that occasionally sliced at him from various directions. Apparently, there was no peace in this place, day or night. He heard men talking, roaming about, taking advantage of the coolness. Ryan did not return to their blankets. Instead, Whitmore relinquished his watch and took Ryan's place beside Nate, falling asleep with astounding ease after those few minutes of sharp violence. Ryan was just a few feet away, sitting with his knees drawn up, head erect and listening, the faint moonlight falling palely across his bare head. Nate studied him, his emotions tangled, his heart aching, worrying over his brother's brutal transformation before he finally dozed off.

When he awoke just after a cloud-streaked sunrise, only Billy lay next to him. Dear God, it had not been simply a nightmare; he was still here. Billy's gaze was lost somewhere among the rays that fingered through the thin clouds in pinks and blues, a diaphanous display floating above this ugly landscape of brown and gray. A black cloud of crows called from above the unobtainable trees to the west. The outcry of Nate's stomach drowned out the raucous birds and their reminders of the peaceful woods beyond his family's farm, dark, inviting places where he and his brothers used to hunt.

"Where's Ryan and Jonas?"

"Went to the sinks. Our turn when they get back."

Sitting up, Nate stared off to the south, to the swampy area nearly hidden by the tops of the shelters falling away down the north slope. The pen was already alive, almost as if never fully asleep, men trudging about, talking, moaning, coughing, some in long, painful croups.

"They didn't come back," Nate murmured against the frayed, dew-damp blanket.

"No. Scrapper scared the bejesus out of 'em."

One corner of Nate's mouth raised. "Why does everyone call him that?"

"Most everyone's got a nickname. They call me Cowboy."

"Why's that?"

"Whit started calling me that back in the Twenty-fourth when I rode a mule one day; just a-larking, you know? Well, that blamed mule got stung by a bee what got caught 'neath the saddle. He set to bucking, but I hung on, game." Billy grinned straight teeth. "Whit said I shoulda been a cowboy."

"But…Ryan…Scrapper; does he fight a lot?"

"Only when he has to. They don't yank his tail much now; he's licked most of the ones dumb enough to try him. I reckon they couldn't resist, what with you a-coming along. New clothes. Maybe money or a watch or something."

"All I got is me clothes and a Bible."

"Well, they'll kill for the clothes, sure."

Nate shook his head, glad the sun would soon chase away the night chill. "Ryan stayed awake all night, didn't he?"

"Oh, yes. Well, we usually spell each other, but Scrapper wouldn't hear of it once those fellas came. It's all right; he'll sleep during the day. A lot of us do. Gets too hot to do much else."

"Sorry I'm causin' so much trouble."

Billy offered a thin-lipped smile. "Don't fret about it. Besides, I think you got here just in time."

"What do you mean?" Nate sat cross-legged with one of the blankets draped over his rounded shoulders.

Billy laced his fingers behind his matted head. "Well, I mean Scrapper." He gave him a sharp look. "And don't go a-telling him I said any of this."

Nate shook his head.

"We've been together a while now, as you know. Gone through hell, and I reckon there's more a-coming. Scrapper's held us together. Won't let no one go. The boys in our mess who've died, I'll tell you, Scrapper took it personal, especially my brother. Ryan was sick bad last winter. Whit and me didn't fancy he'd make it. But he hung on to spite the damned Johnnies and because of his family. He's told us all about each of you. Hell, the three of us knows everything about each other. I seen him really down for the first time, though, when we was brought here in March. Some of his interest in life's been slipping ever since, though he won't say it; respects our rules. But now, with you, he's got something here to live for. I know Scrapper well enough to know he'll get you outta this damned place alive. He won't give in to them and leave you behind. No, siree."

Nate frowned. "He got pretty cross with me last night. Told me to never touch him."

"You don't understand this place yet. It takes a short time; short 'cause you either learn or you go out that south gate yonder feet first with your toes tied together. There's a code here. Your brother is one of the few who stands up to Mosby's Raiders and the like. They hate him, but they also respect him. Why, once ol' John Sarsfield hisself asked Scrapper if he wanted in with 'em." Billy's blue eyes sparked with delight as he laughed and sat up to face Nate. "You can guess what Scrapper told Sarsfield. I wasn't there, damn it all, but I hear tell Sarsfield about turned purple and bust when Scrapper got done with his answer." The mirth died away. "You can't be showing Scrapper up or else word will get around, then they'll start trying their luck again. Like Kevin Murphy. You met him, right?"

"Aye."

"He's thick with Sarsfield and Mosby—Collins, that is. Ol' Murph got his ass whupped twice by Scrapper. Fool didn't know when to quit. Murphy's determined to get to him, figures he'll impress Sarsfield and Collins thataway. Now that you're here for Scrapper to worry about, Murphy will be at his best in the shit department. I guarantee he was behind last night's fun." He considered Nate's despairing expression. "You're giving your brother a purpose, so don't look so down. May be a dangerous one, but it's a purpose just the same. He might snap at you, but everyone does in this shithole. Like a buncha dogs caged up too long. Sometimes we three even fight each other; you know, just to *do* something. No one takes it to heart." He grinned. "Besides, Scrapper always wins."

They fell silent for a time, then Billy grunted and stretched. "C'mon. Let's get these here blankets back on the poles. Sun clears that fence, we'll need shade, sure enough."

Nate's stomach twisted horribly and made him wince. "When do we get rations, Billy?"

"After rollcall. That's at seven."

Nate wondered how he could wait. Last night's pitiful mouthful of coarse cornbread had done little but irritate his insides. Maybe this morning would bring something more substantial. He reached for his canteen and sloshed around the last of the clean water. The sound drew Billy's keen interest. Nate pulled the cork, took a swallow, and offered the last to his comrade.

"Much obliged for tellin' me about me brother."

Savoring the water bit by bit, Billy finally finished and handed back the canteen. He smacked his lips loudly. "Welcome to paradise, Little Brother."

CHAPTER 20

The dank smell of earth choked Nate. He could see nothing even if he opened his eyes, so he kept them shut to keep the dirt out as he worked. The tunnel was just large enough to accommodate an average man's body. Its walls pressed in like a grave, horrifying and suffocating. He worked on his belly, using a canteen half to scrape at the stubborn earth before him, longing for fresh air and light. Maybe another five minutes, then someone would replace him. He could make it, he told himself over and over. In the tunnel's solitude, his heartbeat rivaled the sounds of his feverish burrowing. He counted the beats, timed his digging with the rhythm, tried to think of a song to go with the beat, anything to distract. Moles, rats…he was akin to them, like the ones that the cats or dogs would kill and bring like trophies to the porch back home. His hunger pangs, however, pushed through everything. He used the pain as motivation, to dig faster, harder, to inch ever closer to freedom.

Using a bag fashioned out of a pant leg, he disposed of the soil he had excavated, then tugged on the attached rope made of strips of precious cloth. The scratch-scratch of the bag as one of the boys, topside, dragged it back. There, under cover of night, Jared or Billy or someone would conceal the bag beneath his clothes and amble down to the swamp where he would casually release it.

He imagined the other tunnel-diggers somewhere in the ground to either side, imagined he could hear them working, too. Because this scheme had been hatched well before he had arrived at Andersonville, many of the tunnels were reportedly already close to the stockade wall. The plan was to weaken the pine logs by hollowing the ground beneath them so that the prisoners could shove several over at once and break out.

"We'll capture the artillery," Ryan had explained that first morning of Nate's imprisonment. "The Plymouth Pilgrims will turn the cannons on the Reserves."

Billy said, "You know damned well them Reserves'll skedaddle without a fight, the cowards."

"Who are the Plymouth Pilgrims?" Nate asked.

"Fresh boys. Easterners," Ryan explained. "Came in not long ago, so they're stronger than the rest of us."

They spoke quietly of this beneath the shade of their shebang. The flame of hope in Ryan's eyes stirred Nate. Billy had told him how, whenever an escape plan was afoot, Ryan was a part of it whether here or at Belle Isle. And in this, the most extensive, his brother commanded a group of fifty, which was how the large numbers involved were broken down, all headed by trustworthy men, everyone involved sworn to secrecy with a blood oath.

During this discussion, Jonas Whitmore had said little, his hooded gaze often resting on Nate, making him uncomfortable. He suspected Whitmore was displeased that Ryan had shared the escape plot with even his own brother, considering he had just appeared in the pen the day before. Ryan and Whitmore had argued on their way back from the sinks that morning, the conversation abruptly ending just before they reached their shelter. Tension darkened Ryan's expression, and Whitmore had stalked off toward Jared Taylor's shebang, not returning until after rollcall. Hoping to allay his new companion's suspicion, Nate had volunteered to help with the digging, an offer that both pleased and agitated Ryan, for there was danger in tunneling. The other day, a cave-in had almost buried Billy, but they had managed to drag him out and revive him.

Nate dug with a vengeance on this his second hour-long shift. When he had gone down the well, he had tried to appear unperturbed to his comrades, but as he wriggled his way into the tunnel which projected away from the well, the fear rose up, and he had to fight to keep from going back. Even now he sensed panic somewhere nearby and started to count the seconds to distract himself. Then...blessedly...

"Time's up," a voice called down the tunnel. Jared. "Nate. Time's up."

Nate muttered a prayer of thanks, then inched his way backward, grunting and cursing the soil that clung to him, musty and stale, making him spit, though he had little moisture left in his mouth. Finally he reached the shaft, felt the welcomed flow of night air upon his cheeks as he climbed out. Putrid stockade air but appreciated anyway. Ryan awaited him at the top. Waning moonlight gleamed in his close-set, pleased eyes. Saying nothing, he clapped Nate on the back, put an arm around his shoulders, and led him back toward their shebang.

Wind herded clouds across the Georgia sky, scudding mounds of white and gray. Their fleeting shadows upon the landscape provided momentary relief to the sweltering inmates of Andersonville. From the sinks where he squatted like a sick bird, Nate watched the swaying pine tops beyond the stockade, closed his eyes, imagined their whispers and the cooling breeze. If only that sweet ripple could swoop down inside these walls and ruffle his hair, caress his cheeks, dry the sweat, vanquish the oppressive fetid air. He dreaded going down into the tunnel tonight but tried to sustain his courage with the prospect of escape, for it was almost time. Maybe just one more night, then he would be able to enjoy that breeze yonder.

Another fiery cramp burned his innards. The Rebels' cursed cornbread would soon shred his guts to a bloody mess. They ground everything together—husk and cob alike. The *Corn*-federacy, Ryan had said. Hell, the pigs back home had better fodder. If only their diet had some variety, at least there would be that, but Whitmore said not to hope for any such extravagance. Cornmeal was cornmeal, no matter how many creative ways they prepared it. Starvation would be slow, torturous, but cheaper for the Confederacy—one way to save bullets.

Ryan had said, "Wirz and ol' General John fucking-H. Winder hope we all rot in here. All the better for their bloody damned *Cause*."

At last Nate left the sinks, still trembling from cramps. He prayed they would not return soon. He passed over the swamp and its indescribable morass of human filth, trying not to think of all the slag that clung to his feet. The ever-swelling population of prisoners had rendered the sinks hopelessly inadequate. Sewage had choked the creek's flow to a trickle. The stench of the pen defied all belief, but the swamp in particular reeked worse than anything he had ever experienced or conjured. Going there was enough to make him sick. Indeed, the first few visits he had vomited what little food had been in his stomach. But he knew he needed to abide by the rules of his mess and make the trek whenever the urge struck him, and sometimes it struck damned fast. Darn near had not made it just now. Well, at least their shebang was high up on the north slope. Some poor wretches, unable to find room or welcome elsewhere in the crush, had settled along the edges of the swamp. Flies, maggots, and all manner of insects swarmed the area, added to the constant noise of the prison until he wondered if any other sounds existed in the world. Silence was difficult to imagine; even in the tunnel, he sometimes swore he could hear the voices and the footsteps of the multitude.

Ryan forbade Nate from traveling anywhere alone, afraid of Raiders, so one of their mess always accompanied him to the sinks. And since this was a frequent journey, they took turns. The other two guarded the shebang and their meager belongings. This time was Billy's turn, and now he waited like a faithful hound as Nate drew near. Crouched on the ground, the young man looked pale and feverish, which he was. "Comes and goes," he had explained earlier. "Someday it won't go, I reckon."

A subtle change occurred in the air. An increase in the volume of life struggling around them, a rising murmur, a small current passing from tent to tent like an overflowing river, a charge akin to a lightning strike. Men were getting to their feet, some running here and there, stopping near others as if spreading news, then moving on. Something nudged Nate in the pit of his stomach, like the feeling he experienced just before battle.

Billy stood, frowning, head cocked to the growing sound. "Something's wrong. Let's get back to the others."

They had traveled only a short way up the north slope when Ryan intercepted them, his brow stormy, a look that stirred Nate's unease to a new level.

Nate asked, "Why'd you leave Jonas?"

"Had no choice." Ryan's attention drifted to the south gate. "Both of you get back to him directly. And tell the lads to cover the well."

"What's goin' on?"

"The Rebs just took Baker outside."

Alarm shot through Nate. Billy swore.

Baker was the mastermind behind the escape plan.

Ryan said, "Sergeants have to report to Wirz."

Nate stared. "You can't go."

"Have to."

"No. If someone informed on Baker, Wirz might know about you, too."

"Cowboy, get goin'. Take him with you."

Nate grabbed his brother's arm. "No, Ryan, listen—"

"I'm goin' out, Nate, and I don't want you alone. Now, go back with Cowboy, damn it. They'll just come for me with a guard if I don't go. 'Tis easier this way, looks better." He pried away Nate's fingers. "I'll be all right. No need to fret."

Billy's hand rested on his shoulder. "C'mon, Little Brother. Have to get back to Whit afore someone takes advantage of him."

Ryan offered a quick smile that failed to ease Nate's rising fears. As his brother walked off, Nate could not take his eyes from him, unable to ward off the last living image of Brian walking away just days before he had been wounded. Then he remembered his brief encounter with Henry Wirz and the ugly pistol he carried. Jonas Whitmore had said Wirz had once killed a prisoner with that same pistol.

Nate's dread deepened to despair. "What will Wirz do to him if he knows about the plan?"

Billy gave him a gentle shake to break his gaze away from Ryan. "Don't worry, boy. Scrapper will be just fine. He's got more wits in his little finger than Wirz has in his whole brain."

***

Nate plunged into the crowd gathered at the north gate. Jonas Whitmore trailed close behind, an ever-present shadow since Ryan had been taken outside; no doubt following strict orders, an onerous task to Whitmore.

Indignant, fearful remarks rose from the prisoners near the gate. Someone was reading aloud from a posted order, but Nate wanted to see the notice himself. Some splintered off to spread the news throughout the pen. He elbowed and cursed through the malodorous throng until he made it to the front ranks. There he saw the paper Wirz had secured to the gate.

Not wishing to shed the blood of hundreds, not connected with those who concocted a mad plan to force the stockade, and make in this way their escape, I hereby warn the leaders and those who formed themselves into a band to carry out this, that I am in possession of all the facts, and have made arrangements accordingly, so to frustrate it. No choice would be left me but to open with grape and canister on the stockade, and what effect this would have in this densely crowded place need not be told.

"Nate!" Jared called urgently from the rear of the crowd.

Hoping he had news of Ryan, Nate threaded his way toward his friend, Whitmore in his wake. When they reached Jared, the young man's gray expression filled Nate with dread.

Jared said, "I was just talking to one of the sergeants who came back in."

Whitmore growled, "Where's Ryan?"

"Wirz is keeping him and some of the others outside for punishment, to make an example of 'em."

A wave of dizziness crept over Nate along with the persistent cramps. His head throbbed from the heat and lack of sleep. "What kind of...punishment?"

Jared glanced at Whitmore, who scowled and looked down.

"What *kind* of punishment?" Nate's question came stronger. "What does that mean?"

Jared tried to answer, failed, looked to Whitmore for help.

"No sense in lyin' to the boy," Whitmore grumbled then turned to Nate. "Hard tellin' what Wirz will do, but...there's the chain gang, the stocks. Other things. Wirz is creative."

"Isn't there anything we can do?" Nate looked at them in desperation, but they appeared resigned. "For God's sake, there must be somethin' we can do."

"Hain't nothin' you can do but pray," Whitmore said morosely. "That is, if you believe in that sort of thing. In the meantime, Scrapper told me to keep you outta trouble if he didn't get sent back in right away, and I aim to do that. Remember the rules, said he, and that's what we're gonna do, all of us. No more talkin' about Wirz and his shit. Scrapper will be back before you know it. Nothin' Wirz can do to him will stop him from tryin' to get all of us the hell outta here."

***

For the next several days, as oppressive rain settled in, an edginess permeated the stockade's population. Men discussed Wirz's threat every waking hour, but no one dared gather in any noticeable group for fear that the Rebel sentries or those manning the cannon in the redoubts would open fire. Meanwhile the tops of the stockade walls were reinforced with iron staples and pine cleats, lest the prisoners entertained any desperate hope of storming the walls. The tunnels undiscovered prior to Wirz's warning were subsequently found through the words of traitors—surely some of the Raiders—who used such tactics to gain favor with Wirz and other Rebels among the Georgia Reserves. Rewards most probably consisted of food, water, work details outside the pen, wood details, and many other opportunities to improve the chances of survival. The Rebel detail that discovered the tunnel Nate and his messmates had been digging not only closed the tunnel but filled in the well. However, as soon as the guards left, Nate and the others had set to work digging another well under cover of darkness.

"If this place goes to hell," Whitmore said over rations one morning, "and they open them cannons, we'll rush the damned gates. They may wipe a lot of us out, but they can't kill all of us."

"Yeah," Jared Taylor added. "Maybe we can get to the cannons before they can reload."

"How many men here now?" Henry Damon wondered.

"Reckon nigh unto twenty thousand," Billy answered.

"Well," Whitmore repeated, "can't kill all of us, by God."

From the highest point on the north slope, Nate could see over the southwest corner of the stockade to the earthworks there. Upon that hill, the chain gang moved listlessly in the gloomy rain, too distant for Nate to discern individual identities. Also on that hill were the stocks—foot stocks as well as spread-eagle stocks. The men who were restrained by the latter, their arms outstretched to either side, made Nate think of Christ crucified, a very unsettling metaphor indeed.

Often he visited the south gate, hoping for word from paroled prisoners who worked outside in the hospital or on burial detail, begging them to inquire as to his brother's fate, but no information came. Fruitlessly he even questioned a couple of the guards in their perches. One spoke civilly to him; the other threatened to shoot him if he came closer to the Dead Line.

"Y'all look the same to me," the Georgia Reserve sneered from behind his peach fuzz.

Nate tried in vain to ignore the dead who were brought to the south gate, most of the bodies completely stripped of clothing, arms folded across their chests, large toes tied together, displaying scraps of paper with name and regiment. Many were terribly emaciated. Others, recent newcomers to the prison, still held their flesh yet were just as dead.

He helped carry one corpse to the dead-house outside the stockade, and when the wagon and its slave crew arrived there to collect its macabre load for burial, he protested the callous way the bodies were lifted and stacked like cordwood. Only one of the slaves showed any care whatsoever, and that was a massive young man with a gentle face. He seemed detached from his fellows, almost distracted, occasionally glancing at the nearby Rebel guard, who stood with musket at the ready. When the big slave met Nate's gaze for a mere instant, Nate thought he detected compassion in those coffee-brown eyes. Perhaps this fellow could get information for him. But when he attempted to engage the slave, the guard cursed Nate and forbade the black man from talking to him.

As he shambled back to the gate, he reflected upon the slaves who worked around the stockade. Strong young men capable of a variety of physical work. Slaves, yes, but the Rebs fed them better than their white captives. Nate expected to feel resentment toward them for it, but considering their shared captivity, he found that he instead felt sympathy for them.

Someone always accompanied Nate during his visits to the gate, usually Jonas Whitmore or one of the boys from the Eleventh. Today it was Billy, who huddled in a crouch, trembling from his fever, which the incessant rains had worsened. No matter how often Nate insisted Billy return to their shebang, that he would be fine alone, the young man remained, offering a wan smile of stubborn duty until at last Nate decided, for Billy's sake, to give up waiting. Tired and eager to lie down, Billy went ahead.

"Can't lie down too much, Little Brother," the young man had said earlier. "Lay on the ground too much you get sores, then the sores turn into gangrene. Then you're gone up."

Nate's despondent, dragging steps caused him to fall behind. The rains had turned the ground to a slippery slough that clung to his bare feet and made walking a chore. He had already fallen earlier and managed to slime himself from head to toe, but at least the rain had helped wash the worst of it off.

Unthinking, he mounted the footbridge that led over the stream— Stockade Creek, most called it—edging past others crossing to the south side. No one spoke, too miserable and drenched to make the effort. Just before he stepped off the bridge, the distinctive noise of brogans on the planking caught his ear. As he was contemplating the luxury of having footwear, a hand clapped down on his shoulder, spun him around. Before he could react, a rock-hard fist rattled his teeth and knocked him off his feet. Men shouted and scattered. Someone yelled, "Raiders!"

In his urgent attempt to regain his feet, Nate slipped, half fell again, tried to push himself away, but the assailant grabbed him by the legs. He squirmed and kicked, recognized the ugly leer of Kevin Murphy's bodyguard. Behind him stood Murphy himself with a confident grin, saying, "Just get the coat, Pete."

The large New Yorker struggled to strip Nate of the rain-soaked sack coat, dodging flailing swings.

"Give it up, runt," Murphy said. "If you don't, we'll kill you, to be sure. Ain't much without yer brother, aye? Hear tell he's dead."

With a roar, Billy Hathaway charged back through the gray rain, scattering alarmed bystanders, and plunged into the fray. Nate's assailant ducked beneath the driving force and lost his grip on his victim. As Nate scrambled out of reach, the New Yorker reared back and flipped Billy into the mud. Laughing, Murphy stepped away to avoid being splattered. The New Yorker swore and turned on Billy, but a quick kick to his crotch dropped him to his knees with a howl. Billy scrabbled on all fours to get away, just as Murphy stepped in. Nate reached for his messmate, helped drag him to his feet. Murphy's clutching hands reached Billy's shirt, but the mire beneath his smooth soles claimed him. He fell with an oath, and Nate half-dragged, half-towed Billy out of range. Still cursing, Murphy scrambled after them.

The roar of a cannon shook the stockade, halted Murphy and most everyone within sight. All eyes turned heavenward as a shell sailed across the pen, close to the top of the palisades, then burst in the forest opposite. Instant pandemonium followed as many dived for cover in fear of another round, one with deadly intent. A rush of men over the narrow footbridge prevented Murphy from pursuit, and Nate took advantage of the panic to escape up the north slope with Billy. Many men stood in defiance, gazes toward the smoking cannon, some with upraised fists, shouting epithets at the Rebels.

As Nate and Billy hurried down Market Street, they kept their attention behind them for pursuers or another shell. If those gunners opened on the pen, the massacre would be unthinkable. There was no place to hide, but Nate wanted to get back to their comrades. If they were to die, they would die together. At least Ryan was not here for this.

The wretched thousands waited what seemed a lifetime for the next shot. Drums beat in the Rebel camps west of the stockade, and soon more troops manned the rifle pits and surrounding earthworks, officers' voices ringing out amidst the slackening rain.

But no second report barked forth from any of the artillery.

Nate found Whitmore with Jared Taylor and the other boys from the Eleventh, all staring toward the Rebel guns. Fearful faces on the south slope looked toward the redoubt beyond the stockade's northwest corner. A collective holding of breath. Crows called from far away, black dots fluttering above the distant trees. Time slipped past. The prisoners swayed together then, realizing this latest dumbshow had been nothing but a drill meant to intimidate them, they fragmented, wilted from the tension. Indignant shouts went up from every corner. Tightly-strung men yelled insults at their captors. Nate's knees trembled with relief, and he had to sit down to compose himself. *God, if it hadn't been a bluff...* Never had he felt so powerless.

He thought of what Murphy had said about Ryan, fought away the very concept that his brother could be dead, dead like Brian, far beyond his reach. Yet, staring toward the Rebel cannon, he considered that maybe, if Murphy was right, his brother was better off.

***

The rains poured down on the stockade. Hour after hour, day after day. The whole place steamed in the June heat. The holes the men lived in filled with water, and they had no choice but to lie in it. Mold grew on everything. Saturated blankets had to be handled carefully lest they fall apart. Nate had never felt so wretched. The continuous patter on his battered hat nearly drove him to insanity. One blessing, however, did come out of the misery—the rain provided drink and water with which to wash away some of the filth. Everyone put out pans and half canteens, anything to collect the sky's weeping.

Nate rarely went to the south gate since Murphy's attack; he did not want to tire his accompanying comrades or put them in further danger. So he remained close to his companions, venturing out only to the sinks or to Market Street. Jonas played his recorder, and they sang and talked of their civilian lives as well as their service before capture, doing their best to keep their spirits up regardless of the weather and Ryan's absence. Nate told them about Katie. The wet had all but ruined her picture there among the folds of his soggy, well-read Bible, the lock of hair long gone. He struggled to keep up his façade, for he did not want to break the mess rules and let down his friends. Though they all worried about Ryan, they rarely spoke of the situation. However, their eyes betrayed how much they missed him.

"Looky what I borrowed," Billy said one soggy evening as he tramped up to their shebang, a board tucked under one arm.

"What is it?" Whitmore eyed the wooden item with a predatory glint, perhaps hoping for fuel for their fires.

"It's a cribbage board. Ansel bought it off'n a fella. Let's have a game, Whit."

Whitmore glanced at Nate. "You know how to play?" When he shook his head, Whitmore continued. "Well, then, we'll show you how, then you can play the winner."

"Careful, though, Little Brother," Billy cautioned with a wry grin. "Whit cheats."

As Whitmore argued against his friend's claim, Nate smiled to himself. In the past couple of days, Jonas Whitmore's suspicion of him had begun to fade, perhaps driven off by sympathy over Ryan's fate. He had stopped referring to him as "boy" and had picked up on Billy's nickname for him, a moniker Nate accepted since he truly did feel part of a brotherhood here between his mess and Jared Taylor's mess. Some men in the pen turned against friends, either from accusations of thievery or some other survival instinct, yet Nate sensed a lasting bond between his comrades, a link forged and strengthened by Ryan.

As he watched Billy set up the board, an odd sensation tickled the back of his neck. The rain, of course. He swiped at the wet, shrugged his shoulders up toward his ears. But the tickle persisted, almost as if someone were brushing a feather back and forth. Then something stirred deep within him, like a flutter in his heart. Turning, he looked through the gray veil of rain, pushed the stringy, dripping hair from his eyes.

"Little Brother?" Billy asked. "You all right?"

A figure wobbled toward them through the surrounding murk, eyes wide and white as milk, mouth half open among a ragged growth of beard. Nate stopped breathing. The man wavered, staggered closer, reached out one hand, stumbled, fell into the mud.

"Ryan!" Nate ran to him, slid to his knees. "Ryan." He rolled his brother onto his back, wiped the sludge from his thin face. Ryan's swollen tongue prevented his mouth from closing. His tattered clothes hung on him. A ring of raw flesh encircled his neck, brown and gray and red. His wrists and ankles bore similar marks.

Whitmore paused long enough in his stream of curses to say, "He's been in the spread-eagle stocks."

"Cowboy, fetch him some water," Nate ordered. "Hurry."

Ryan's eyelids twitched then opened. His sunken hazel eyes focused on his brother. A smile touched his lips. When he tried to reach up to Nate's face, his hand fell to the mud, and unconsciousness claimed him.

"Whit, help me lift him."

By the time they moved Ryan, the boys from the Eleventh had gathered around. Billy handed Nate a battered tin cup half filled with rainwater. Gently Nate slapped Ryan's cheeks, whispered his name in desperation. Gradually his brother came around, groaning.

"Water, Ry. Here." Nate brought the cup to his mouth. He choked on the first swallow, then managed a small mouthful. Some trickled down his chin.

Whitmore swore again then said, "Don't look like he's ate or drank for a long spell. Fucking Wirz."

Nate cussed as he had never cussed before. He examined the puffy flesh where the stocks had restrained his brother. "Jared, fetch your rubber blanket."

Jared glanced at the others of his mess, for the blanket was community property. No one spoke.

"For God's sake," Nate shouted at them, "how much has he done for you, and you can't loan him your lousy blanket? Get it, damn you all, or I'll lam every last one of you!"

Ashamed, Jared scurried away and soon returned with the article. Nate snatched it from him and spread it over his brother. Ryan closed his eyes, nodded with a satisfaction that Nate suspected had more to do with his younger brother's resolve than with the blanket's protection.

"Cowboy, fetch that sliver of meat I kept from this mornin'. Make him some soup."

Billy obeyed without hesitation. Keeping a fire going would not be easy in this weather, but Nate knew Billy would manage. Most of the boys drifted away, talking among themselves. Whitmore, however, remained nearby on his haunches, full attention on Ryan's face. The small man's unbreakable devotion made Nate feel not so alone. Whitmore gave Nate a small, appreciative smile, true respect at last in his gray eyes, eyes that Nate realized for the first time reminded him of James Keenan.

Nate kept Ryan's wrists and ankles exposed to the rain, hoping it would rinse off the wounds. He remained sitting in the mud, his sibling's head pillowed in his lap. When the soup arrived, he fed the thin broth to Ryan, who then drifted off into exhausted sleep, his hand weakly holding Nate's.

CHAPTER 21

James squinted through the three-inch horizontal opening between the head log and the top of the earthworks, studying the Eleventh Michigan's latest position. Only fifteen rods of scarred red landscape separated the armies, a wasteland of shattered trees and rocks. Rebel snipers and artillery kept up a continuous monotony of contrasting arguments—the roar of field pieces sending shells wailing overhead to explode beyond the Second Brigade's entrenchments, accompanied by the singular, spaced crack of a distant rifle, sometimes followed by the dull thump of a bullet into the breastworks. No concerted shots or volleys.

Earlier that day, to the south, a battle had raged—Hooker's and Schofield's corps had engaged the Confederates—but now with evening soon to turn into night the firefight had ended. James had little faith that the Union forces had accomplished much, for the Confederates again held favorable ground after their retreat from the Dallas-Pickett's Mill line. General Johnston's defenses lay in the shape of a crescent, bulging westward atop a southward ranging string of mountains and hills. Formidable, twin-peaked Kennesaw Mountain anchored Johnston's right flank, which lay to the northeast of the Fourteenth Corps' position.

Following the battle of Pickett's Mill, the Second Brigade, commanded by Colonel Stoughton after General King replaced the wounded General Johnson as division commander, had remained in the same position until June 5, hunkered in lice-infested trenches, under constant enemy fire. When the Confederate army had resumed the retreat eastward, Sherman's forces followed doggedly, their supply line now preserved by having control of the Western & Atlantic Railroad. The Second Brigade had marched northeastward to the town of Big Shanty where it remained until June 10 before taking up the march south once again. Twelve days of constant marching, fortifying, and skirmishing in the heat and rain had brought them to the Kennesaw line where tonight they had relieved Whitaker's brigade of the Fourth Corps.

James settled back down in the trench, listened to the weary talk of the regiment. They virtually ignored the sporadic Rebel guns, knowing soon the annoyance would die with the setting of the baking sun. In less than a month, they had become like gophers—persistent diggers who had grown accustomed to the protection of trenches, earthworks, and head logs. No unit halted for more than a moment before throwing up defensive works, a strange new type of warfare that received mixed opinions from the men. As talented at entrenching as any outfit, the Eleventh could complete formidable works in less than an hour.

Because the bottom of the trench still retained water from the June rains, most of the men sat a couple of feet up on the red clay earthworks, many reaching into haversacks for any morsel of food to be found, then lying back against the dirt. The familiar hollowness in James originated not from hunger but from a continued sense of loss. It haunted him most during the evenings when the day's work lay quiet behind him and the men's spirits and strength renewed with a meal. Then talk would flow, jokes and stories, songs, memories—a camaraderie that was incomplete for James and stirred the oppressive guilt he felt over Nate's loss. Everyone missed the boy, and though no one except Langdon voiced blame, James suspected that others indeed shared the sergeant's views, perhaps more so as the days went by and Langdon's reminders continued. The void left by Nate's capture expanded with every casualty suffered by the regiment. Yet, as painful as Langdon was to endure, the man's barbs could never inflict more pain than James felt when he found someone other than Nate beside him. Sometimes he regretted the friendship they had forged.

"Leg hurt?" Elias's question jarred James, made him realize he had been rubbing his old wound.

"Nah, just thinking about Mission Ridge," he lied.

Sitting next to him, Elias filled his pipe, smiled wryly. "It's about time for us to do some more real fightin'."

"Yeah," Abner grumbled from the other side of James. "Boys are beginnin' to think Uncle Billy won't fight no more, just keep flankin'."

Well, James thought, *if there's to be fighting, bring it on. At least then I won't think so much about Nate.*

But he knew he was fooling himself, for in battle he would feel Nate's absence even more than he had during the skirmishes since the boy's capture. Davis's Crossroads, Chickamauga, Missionary Ridge,

Resaca; Nate next to him through it all, steady and dependable for all of them, as Ryan had been before him.

When James found Elias studying him, the older man returned his attention to lighting his pipe. Elias's old tentmate, Thomas Hodgins, had been killed back on May 31, so he now shared space with James. Elias snored, and the rattle reminded James of his father, yet the older man was a comfort, for he seemed to understand his despondency, knew when to offer opinions and when to keep silent, and never did he impugn James's integrity. Now Elias's brown eyes reached toward Lost Mountain beyond which the sun set with a final flare of brilliant orange and gold. His hair, the rusty color of Georgia clay, trailed from beneath his slouch hat. "Won't cut it till I'm tight in the streets of Atlanta," Elias had vowed. Considering the latest formidable barrier of nature before Sherman's army, he would be braiding his hair before getting drunk in Atlanta.

James's attention drifted over the regiment, stretching along the entrenchments in the smoke-tinged twilight. Worn, sun-burned or tanned faces. Weary eyes. Lieutenant Hart stood down to the right, talking with Captain Keegan.

How Hart had aged since Resaca! A man through and through, his youth long gone, stalwart in his duties and fiercely loyal to his men. The rain played hell with his rheumatism, but the Bronson man marched without complaint, only occasionally riding a horse. A damned good officer, worthy of two bars. More than could be said for poor Frank Lane who had been arrested at the beginning of the month and would face court-martial. Like Hart, the men of Company D took Lane's failure personally, wordlessly ashamed that one of their own had cast the black mark of desertion—desertion in the face of the enemy, no less—upon the regiment and its proud record.

Nate's loss had been a severe blow to Hart. He had bemoaned his decision to keep Nate from leaving the regiment when he had received word of Brian's wounding. Perhaps the boy would be with the Eleventh today if he had been more lenient. No one could convince the officer otherwise. James felt akin to him for his self-persecution.

To distract himself from his gloomy thoughts, James asked Elias, "You got a letter from your eldest boy yesterday, didn't you?"

Elias nodded, took the pipe from his mouth. "That I did." He reached into his pocket and pulled forth a small, round object, smiling at it. "Zack sent me this here compass. I told him how wild some of this country is, so he sent this and told me if I ever get lost, I'll be able to find my way home; easy to find north and all." He chuckled and tucked the silver instrument away. "That boy's nigh unto sixteen now and vows he'll join the army and fight alongside his pa. He's got his mother scared half to death. When she reminded him that he has to be eighteen, he said he'll be a drummer boy."

"I'm sure he won't get out of her sight."

Elias chuckled again. "I hope not."

With a sour glance at the rainwater below him, James wondered if it had been raining in Burr Oak. The crops would need it. In a recent letter, his father had written that Daniel Calhoun had not planted as many acres as usual this year because of Nate's absence. The elder Calhoun visited the mercantile regularly since he had no sons to run his errands, and James liked to believe that the friendship he and Nate had forged perhaps had some bonding influence on their fathers. They had never been at odds, like James had been with the Calhoun boys, but neither had they been particularly neighborly; had no reason to be. The letter had continued:

Mr Calhoun and his wife keep cheerful faces for the folks in town but I see the sadness in their eyes, especially Mrs Calhoun. Everyone was shocked to hear about Brian and Nate, and the news all at once. We have read about Andersonville, none of it good. The news has changed Katie Moylan in just these few days.

The rest of the letter went off into talk of politics, one of his father's favorite topics and one which had set him and Major Bennet so at odds back home. He wrote of President Lincoln's nomination, but the words about the Calhouns stayed with James longer than the rest. To hear his father express sympathy more than surprised him. Had the war and his son's part in it been responsible for these changes?

James studied the dirty faces of the company's Burr Oakers and tried to picture them back home. Unwittingly he murmured, "Nate's lucky he isn't in this mud hole, digging every day like a damned gopher."

Elias nodded. "Can't do much dancin' in this mess, sure."

Langdon's gravelly voice sliced through the soft evening. "Don't fancy that boy's doing much dancing where he's at. Probably about starved to death by now. Rebs don't feed prisoners too well, I hear." Langdon sloshed down the trench until he stopped in front of James. All conversations to left and right ceased. "We've all heard how it was with Lieutenant Platt. He was captured same time as Calhoun's brother, recollect. When he was released from Libby last month, he was nothing but skin and bones, they say. You don't see him back here for duty with the regiment, do you? Hell, no. He's up in Nashville on some damned general's staff. We won't see him again. And if it was that bad at an officers' prison, just think what Andersonville must be like. I've heard men die there by the score every day."

James's indignation and outrage propelled him, unthinking, off the embankment toward Langdon. His impetus, however, carried him farther than intended; he landed nearly on top of the sergeant, who lost his balance and fell into the mud. Laughter rang out in the ranks, the laughter of tense men. Standing over the sergeant, James could think of nothing to say or do, simply glad he had silenced the man. The dull glow of restless energy flamed into a warning in Langdon's eyes before he growled and sprang, driving James downward into the trench. On his back, James sank into the mud, the water lapping over his face. He gagged and coughed, struggled blindly against Langdon's weight. Men shouted around them, voices distorted, hollow. Then, abruptly, Langdon was off him, as if a great hand had plucked him away. James struggled to his feet, mouth open, breathing hard.

Langdon lay sprawled in the trench again, Elias standing over him, legs braced apart, fists balled. The sergeant stared up at him in astonishment, the entire company having gone silent.

"What the hell's going on here?" Hart stormed from above the trench.

No one answered for a long moment, then Elias calmly reached a hand toward Langdon, said, "The sergeant turned his ankle and fell, Lieutenant. I was just helpin' him up."

Hart's glare swept the faces of his men, stopped on James's dripping form. "I suppose Keenan fell all on his own, too?"

James discreetly spat out more water. "Yes, sir. Slipped in the mud."

Langdon ignored Elias's hand and sullenly got to his feet. "They're a pack of liars. Keenan jumped me."

The deepening evening failed to conceal Hart's annoyance. "And why would he do a fool thing like that, Sergeant?"

Langdon had never baited James about Nate in front of Hart, for the sergeant knew too well, as did everyone, the Lieutenant's own sense of guilt over Nate's capture, but Hart was no deaf fool; he knew everything that went on in his company. Langdon's narrowed eyes darted from his commanding officer to the stolid faces of the men around him. They all waited for Langdon's incriminating answer to Hart's question. A sniper's rifle cracked in the distance, but no one

221

stirred in response, not even Hart, who was partially exposed on the backside of the trench. Langdon fumed in silence.

Hart regarded them coldly. "I suggest you both watch where you're stepping next time." With that, he limped away down the trench.

Just loud enough for James to hear, Langdon growled at Elias, "You'll rue the day you defended that coward. There'll come a time when you're both going to be on the casualty list. And it won't be from a Reb bullet." He splashed back up the trench, removing his soiled coat, the blue chevrons covered in muck.

***

"Now see here, Key..."

Ryan's argumentative tone concerned Nate, but he dared not interrupt the meeting; his continued presence was more apt to be tolerated by the older men if he remained a silent listener.

Nate studied the two men who sat with Ryan and Whitmore in the late June swelter, men he had known for a month now, introduced early in his captivity by his brother. The taller of the two was Leroy Key, a twenty-four-year-old Illinois cavalry sergeant known throughout the pen for his calm disposition and intelligence. Next to him sat a Chicago Irishman named Ned Carrigan, reputedly the best fighter in Andersonville. Whitmore claimed Carrigan had been a prizefighter in civilian life and had once killed a man with one swing. Key and Carrigan listened respectfully to Ryan's argument against involving Captain Wirz in their plans to rid the prison of the Raiders.

Once Ryan was finished, Key voiced his reasons for acquiring Wirz's help: "If we do this without him knowing, then once fists start flying, he might think a revolt is at hand and double-shot those damned guns."

"If we tell him what we're about," Ryan countered, "he might arrest every last one of us what's on the side of right, just to avoid the blood that's sure to spill when we move against Collins and his bullies. Don't know about you lads, but I'm not up for another week in the stocks."

Nate frowned at the raw flesh of Ryan's left ankle where gangrene would surely soon appear, though Ryan's stubborn constitution fought against the murderous rot. The other wounds had mended tolerably well. If Ryan were anywhere but Andersonville, Nate figured they would be completely healed.

Ryan had lain helpless for days under the protection of their shebang, as weak as a newborn kitten. A dangerous time for all of them, for the Raiders knew of his condition. Kevin Murphy paid a visit during that time, bringing with him a half dozen toughs, but Nate, Whitmore, Billy, and the boys from the Eleventh chased them off. They had maintained constant watches.

The Raiders' boldness had swelled even more during June, along with their ranks. They robbed and murdered in broad daylight now. No one could stop them; the guards had no interest in the matter. Just that morning, the Raiders had made their biggest and most audacious attack, descending upon a group of newcomers just through the gate, who had no time or ability to respond. By the time the maelstrom of violence subsided, many lay dead, the rest bloodied and dazed. All had been thoroughly robbed. The whole pen was in a furor, but Wirz offered no aid; he simply threatened to withhold rations if the unrest melded into a threat of escape.

Whitmore had grumbled, "The Raiders don't give a fuck if rations aren't issued. They just steal and trade with the guards for whatever they want."

The Raiders' latest offense lay behind this meeting between Ryan and Key. Key was the mastermind behind the formation of a secret society known as the Regulators, in which Ryan was a captain, an organization made up primarily of Westerners because they trusted few Easterners, especially considering so many of the Raiders were from that region. Nate and those of his mess were a part of Ryan's thirty-man company, the growing organization able to muster close to four hundred men. But the Raiders had even more in their ranks, making the Regulators' task daunting.

During his debate with Key, Ryan's face flushed deep scarlet, as it did whenever his blood was stirred. Clearly, he and Key were not going to agree on this point of contention about Wirz, and to continue arguing only agitated him.

"Now, Ryan," Nate interrupted his sibling's latest point, "don't you think you've said your piece fair enough? No sense gettin' all hellfire riled up."

Carrigan and Key looked at each other and broke into laughter.

Key teased, "Ryan, I think your doctor is ordering you back to bed."

Flustered, Nate tried to counter and defend his position but failed to string two words together.

"Ease up on him, Sarge," Ryan chided. "If not for me little brother, I wouldn't be sittin' with you lads, sure. Why, didn't he tend me night and day for all that time and trade all his brass buttons to the guards for medicine?" He tugged open Nate's shirt. "And ripped his underclothes for bandages, he did. When he wasn't tendin' me, he was out scroungin' for somethin' for me to eat, Raiders or no. He's just as much a veteran of this place now as any of us, so ease up, I say."

The others chuckled and acquiesced. Sheepish, Nate said nothing more. Act as they please, he knew they had been just as worried as he about Ryan...and still were. *Ryan may act like he's as good as he was before Wirz's sentence, but he ain't. Probably never will be. He ain't got back much weight, and his leg pains him considerable.*

With his smiling eyes upon Nate, Key said, "I suppose Little Brother is right, Scrapper. After all, we've been sitting here too long as it is, especially in the daylight."

Reluctantly the others agreed, and Key straightened to a formidable six-foot-two height. They all shook hands before parting company, Key and Carrigan moving off in separate directions. To Nate's regret, Ryan ignored his advice to get some rest and instead headed off to Jared Taylor's shebang.

Jared's mess had recently been reduced by one. Back on the twelfth of June, they had taken James Ensign to the hospital. The hospital had once been located inside the stockade, but the need for more space led to its relocation outside the prison's southeast wall. Ensign, twenty-three years old and no doubt soon to be dead. Few men ever returned from the hospital, a place where victims of scurvy, dropsy, dysentery, fever, pneumonia, and crushing melancholy lay about with little shelter or medical care, the sheer numbers alone too great for the Confederates' meager provisions. Often men suffering from such ailments preferred to die inside with their comrades.

According to a prisoner who clerked for Wirz, over twenty-five thousand prisoners were here now, and though the stockade had been expanded ten acres beyond the original north wall just a short while ago, the crush remained unendurable. Nate's detachment had not been among those ordered by Wirz to occupy the prized new ground. His disappointment had turned to relief when he witnessed the dangerous stampede that ensued once a ten-foot gap had been opened in the old wall. Wirz demanded that the migration of these hundreds be completed in two hours. Any man not complying would have his shelter confiscated, but few needed such motivation to reach the other side. Unfortunately, a ditch left over from the excavation—five feet deep and three feet wide—awaited them on the other side of the opening. Nate had no idea how many had been injured while struggling through this obstacle during the rush.

Some of the prisoners had helped construct the new fence because they received double rations from the Rebels for their efforts. Nate had wanted to volunteer simply to acquire extra food for his ailing friends, but Ryan would not allow it. "We'll not help those bastards build our own cage," he had said.

Once the new section had been opened, Nate and his comrades had battled desperately for their share of the old stockade wall to use as firewood. Men fought one another over their claims, the strongest winning out as usual. Even the ends of the timbers underground had been dug up in a matter of hours by the fuel-starved inmates.

Another member of Jared's mess had also left them but he through his own designs. Henry Damon was out there somewhere beyond these cursed walls, breathing clean air, hopefully finding food and the strength to make it to Sherman's lines. He had escaped by bartering for a Rebel uniform, and two days ago had walked out of the pen with a Rebel detail, neat and slick as could be. Only God knew what had happened after those gates closed behind him, but whatever it was, Damon was no longer among the condemned. They all prayed for his safe return to their lines. Nate had asked Damon to contact his family to let his parents know that their sons lived but cautioned him against expounding on their prison conditions or Ryan's wounds.

Ryan returned to their shebang early in the evening, and just as he and Nate were taking down the blanket awning for the night, Jared dashed up.

"It's Key," he gasped. "Raiders—"

Without waiting for more information, Ryan rushed off at a skipping limp in the direction of Key's shebang. Nate followed, his mind spinning. If the Raiders had gone after Key, they probably knew about the Regulators.

They found Key unscathed, standing near his blanket-covered hole in the ground, other Regulators near him.

Ryan asked, "What the hell happened, Sarge?"

"Curtis came after me, him and five of his boys, your friend Kevin Murphy among 'em. They was sent, I reckon, by Collins. Said they'd heard about me recruiting a force to clear out the Irish. I told him it was nonsense. 'Well,' says he, 'you're getting up a band for some purpose, what is it for, if not to clean out the Irish?'"

Nate asked, "What did you tell 'em?"

"The truth."

Key's audacity left Nate speechless.

225

"Collins pulled a knife, so that's when I showed him this." He displayed a small pistol inside his coat.

Ryan grinned in admiration. "Where the hell you get that?"

"One of the Plymouth Pilgrims. I had a feeling I'd need some extra help." He drew Ryan closer and lowered his voice. "Plans must be changed. Meet me at Carrigan's shebang in an hour."

Later, when Ryan started for the designated meeting, Nate tried to accompany him, but Ryan forbade it. "The less you know, the better. What you already know is too much. I never should've let you in on any of this till the last minute."

"But, Ryan—"

"Tell you all you need to know later, I will. Now, stay with Cowboy. I need Whit with me."

In sullen anger, Nate obeyed, for he knew this was no time for another taxing argument. Whitmore gave him a conspiratorial grin and wink before leaving with Ryan. Nate sank to the ground. Damn it, he was healthier than Whitmore, whose symptoms of scurvy had become more noticeable, so he should be the one accompanying his brother. After nursing Ryan back to health, he had expected a bit more consideration, yet it was always Whitmore who got to attend Regulator meetings. When would Ryan stop treating him as a child?

Several hours passed, and darkness rolled in. Nate eventually dozed off while Billy watched for Raiders. He slipped in and out of dreams, always about the same thing—food, family, and friends. The Three Deadly F's, Whitmore called them.

Nate awoke with a start to find Billy bedding down tight against him and Whitmore settling on his other side with a grunt. Ryan sat a few feet away next to their neighbor's tent, alert, armed with a stout club. Nate wondered how he had acquired such a weapon.

"Got the Johnnies scared shitless," Whitmore said. "They know somethin's up. They've strengthened the guards."

"Damned fools," Billy muttered. "Not enough of us strong enough to try escape."

"None but the Raiders," Nate offered.

"Them? Huh!" Whitmore snorted. "They've got it made here. This is their kingdom. They wouldn't wanna leave outta here." With a wry laugh, he added, "They might fancy that on the morrow, though."

CHAPTER 22

The sun rose as relentless as always, indifferent to the coming events in the pen. It cared neither for Raiders nor Regulators, nor the thousands of others content to be mere spectators in the struggle for order and survival. The sun's only concern was to broil them all alive, unbiased as to whom it sent to an early grave.

Although Nate had slept little, he awoke feeling a strange energy. He could sense it all around like a sizzling current in the air, not just from his messmates but throughout the stockade. Not since being captured had he felt this type of spirit, the spirit of purpose. Today was about more than the basic, static, everyday struggle for life and sanity. Today he had the chance to play a role in determining his own fate and the fate of so many others already here, as well as those still to come. Perhaps what they did today would save lives, would make a lasting difference. A glimmer of hope for something resembling civilized existence once again, instead of the base culture of predator and prey.

Throughout the pen, the Regulators mustered their forces. As Nate gathered with the rest of Ryan's company, the Rebels stood ready next to their artillery pieces outside, the sentinels doubled upon their perches, the regiments turned out. Nate prayed that once all this started, the quick-triggered Georgia Reserves would not open fire on the masses.

Ryan hobbled his way through the gathered grim-faced men. When he reached Nate, he put one hand on his shoulder and said, "When we cross the swamp and close on 'em, I don't want you near me. Hear? I'll be with Key and the bigger fellas to take the leaders."

"But I'm just as tall as Sullivan and Sarsfield. I can take one of them. You know they'll be right there with Collins."

"Sullivan and Sarsfield outweigh you by half. Now, don't argue with me; this ain't the time, damn it. I want you on the flank. The others will break once they see the order of things. You smaller lads on the flanks need to keep 'em from escapin'."

Nate fingered his weapon, a spoon whose handle he had sharpened to a point with a stone. "I ain't so small."

"You heard me." With a stern look, Ryan moved on.

Nate sputtered next to Jared, who found amusement in the brothers' squabble, saying with a grin, "Just like back home."

When they moved out, they did so in silence. Most of the companies originated from the north slope and now wound their way through the disturbingly quiet pen. Idle men watched from every hole and tent with a mixture of hope and dread. All knew that if the Regulators failed, they all failed; the Raiders' rise to power would be unstoppable. They would be like dogs cowering in the shadow of the pack leader, heads down, tails tucked, groveling in the dirt. But even the hopeful ones spoke not a word, offered no encouraging cheer, perhaps out of caution for the Regulators' advance or perhaps for fear of retribution if the Regulators lost and someone told the Raiders that they had been on the wrong side of things.

Down the slope to the swamp, men filed on the east and west sides, heading for the bridges under the suspicious eyes of the Rebel sentries. The Regulators moved quickly, concerned that the Raiders would oppose them before they could cross the putrid sea of sludge, for if the brigands confronted them at the crossings, the Regulators would stack up and be kept from deploying. But to Nate's relief the Raiders did not appear, either too confident to believe any true attempt would be made upon them or too hung over from the pine-top whiskey they bought from the guards. Nate had heard them last night, carrying on into the wee hours on the south bank as they often did, a raucous, taunting orgy of drinking, singing, and dancing as well as other debaucheries which Nate chose not to contemplate. A celebration of their past day's rapine. A ludicrous, cruel contrast to the suffering around them.

Once the Regulators had re-formed on the south side, Jared tugged Nate's tattered sleeve and gasped. "By God, looky yonder."

Nate followed Jared's gaze back to the steep north bank. The odd sight startled him, and for a moment he could not comprehend what he saw. The ground rose from the creek like a natural amphitheater, an incline that put row upon row of prisoners directly above the shoulders of the ragged line in front. Up and up among the jetsam of the pen so that it looked like a perfect sea of sooty male faces, thousands and thousands of countenances seemingly sewn together into a patchwork of humanity.

Nate murmured, "Damnedest thing I ever seen."

"Reckon they got the best seats in the house," Jared said. "Time to start the dance, Little Brother."

The Regulators, armed with clubs and all manner of improvised weapons, swept forward through the tight maze of tents, many heading for assigned shebangs. The silence remained over the pen, as if the world held its breath, as if nothing existed beyond these wooden walls. Nate could not hear a single birdcall from beyond the palisades, not one shout or command from the attentive Rebels along the walls or beyond. The void contrasted so sharply with the usual, continuous hum that his nerves tightened to the breaking point. Already the sun's powerful frown sapped the men's endurance, but few had enough hydration in their bodies to produce much sweat. Nate passed through the unreadable spectators as well as the dead, the dying, and hoped they knew that this was being done for all of them. How many Raiders were there? Certainly as many as the Regulators, probably more, but some of the bystanders might lend Key's men a helping hand once they saw the strength and determination of their comrades.

A large tent in the middle of the south slope was home to the worst villains. Key, Carrigan, Ryan, and the rest of the Regulators' toughest, largest fighters concentrated there. By the time they arrived, the Raiders had mustered their own forces and awaited the bold attackers.

Nate's position lay upon the left flank, distant enough that the exchange of words between the leaders was lost when the two lines met. Nate stared into the hard eyes of the lesser Raiders confronting his squad and wondered where Kevin Murphy was in all of this. Was he hiding? Was he close to Ryan?

One of the nearby ruffians laughed. "You boys hain't meanin' to take us on? We'll whip you into next week."

Another barked, "Buncha puny bastards."

"Hey, boy! You ain't old enough to be away from your mother's tit! You're facin' *men* here. We'll chew up your scrawny ass and spit it out."

Nate's grip tightened on his dagger. Some of the Regulators snarled back at the taunting Raiders, but most saved their strength, for they knew this battle would be their one and only chance to reverse the tide. To fail meant only death, either quickly or slowly.

With a shout, the center of the Raider line sprang forward. In that first instant, Ryan wielded his club against the large form of Willie Collins. The two lines surged against one another like a tempest, and Nate lost sight of his brother.

Nate clashed with a man who was much taller but weaponless. The Raider had homed in on the knife and struggled to wrest it away, his grip like iron, twisting Nate's wrist. Crying out, Nate slammed a knee into the man's groin. The ruffian swore, let go, staggered back in white-faced agony. Nate advanced, yelling, swiped at him with the dagger, drew blood on his hairy arm. The Raider swung a blur of a fist, but Nate feinted out of reach then sprang forward and sledged a left into the man's midsection, knocked out his air. Jared's small club cracked against the man's head. The Raider dropped, unconscious.

A sharp blow from a new foe sent Jared reeling. Nate sprang on the assailant, bore him to the ground. Jared piled on top.

"Nate, gimme his arm!"

The Raider struggled and swore, but the two Burr Oakers managed to bind the man's hands behind his back with their cloth rope.

From the tangled mass of fists and weapons swirling around them, another Raider charged. He kicked Nate in the ribs, catapulted him away from their captive. Nate fell, unable to breathe, certain a rib or two had been broken. The Raider, small but well-fed and muscled, dived in just as Nate brought the dagger between them. The man's weight slammed down upon him and the knife. Pain in Nate's chest nearly caused him to black out, but the Raider's instant wail shocked sense back into him. Warm blood flowed over his hand and wrist. He twisted the dagger, shoved the attacker off. The man screamed, writhing and clutching at the impaled weapon.

Nate rolled onto his hands and knees, gasping for air, each breath filled with pain. Before his blurry eyes, the line of battle swayed back and forth until at last the Raiders broke and ran. The man confronting Jared suddenly turned and bolted. Many of the Regulators pursued their quarry, yet many, like Nate, were too spent.

Jared helped him to his feet, and they leaned on one another, panting. Nate looked indifferently at the Raider whose screams had died to a string of raspy pleas for help. Perhaps this was one of the villains who had killed a man not two rods from their shebang last week or reported a tunnel to Wirz or tromped to death a new prisoner near the north gate the other morning. Nate bent over him. The man's wide gaze latched upon him as he begged for aid. Nate pried the doomed Raider's slimy fingers from the dagger, yanked it free, listened to the shriek. He wiped the black blood on the man's sleeve, then turned to help Jared secure their prisoner.

From the north slope, a great cheer shattered the air, a triumphant roar that seemed to shake the earth and make the distant trees shudder. Jared and Nate stared at each other in amazement, then Jared grinned and shook his hand. The Regulators and the rest of the pen's population returned the cheer. Nate joined in as they all vented their stored-up tension from the past weeks, indeed from the day each had arrived here. An intoxicating, nourishing moment, a moment of power. Nate's ribs throbbed with the effort, but he did not care. He had never felt so liberated in his life.

***

When Nate awoke the next morning, every inch of his body ached, and the pain in his ribs had not subsided. Billy probed the tender spots and diagnosed only bruised, not broken, ribs.

"Where's Ryan?" Nate looked toward the sun already well above the east wall. He had overslept. Even his empty stomach had failed to rouse him at the usual pre-dawn time. "He go to get rations?"

"No. Word came not long ago for all the detachment sergeants to report outside to Wirz. Hard to say what's going on."

Nate refused to believe Wirz would feel the need to punish the Regulators; he had done nothing to suppress them thus far. The commandant should be thankful that the prisoners themselves had managed to suppress the Raiders.

"Since things has settled down," Nate said, "maybe Wirz has decided to issue rations. Don't reckon he'll give us what he kept from us yesterday, though. Damned fool. I mean, by God, we was too worn out after fightin' to rush the gates like he afeared."

"Well, I hear tell Wirz was about scared pissless yesterday. 'Twas safer letting the rations rot outside than open them gates with the whole pen in a right uproar. We was all feeling full of ourselves after what we did. Felt like I could take on every last one of them lamebrained Georgia Reserves."

Whitmore brought over a handful of splinters from some Maine boys as payment for well water. As he went to work lighting them, Billy scrounged the half pint of peas and a morsel of what passed as beef that they had saved for just such a shortage. Nate went to work putting up their blankets and his coat to block the coming sun.

By the time their meager breakfast was warm, Ryan had returned, moderate triumph brightening his countenance.

"Wirz said Winder's approved our request to put the Raiders on trial. We drew the names of twenty-four men to select the jury from."

"When's the trial?" Billy urged.

"Today. They want this over with as soon as possible."

Whitmore grumbled, "I say to hell with a trial. Let's hang the lot

231

of 'em."

"No," Ryan insisted. "Unlike the Raiders, give 'em justice, we will. We'll not sink into a lawless pack of hounds like them. We have plans to run this place fairly now, like it should be. We're all Union soldiers, for God's sake."

Reluctant, Whitmore nodded, touched the bruise under his left eye, a reminder of the Raiders' power. They all had bruises and cuts, but none of them minded.

A wiry boy hurried to their shebang, a cavalry forage cap at a jaunty angle on his matted head. One of Key's Illinoisans.

"Scrapper. Key wants to talk to you."

Ryan savored his last morsel, then followed the cavalryman in the direction of Key's shebang. Within minutes, he returned with a dozen others from his Regulator company.

"Jared!" he called to their neighbor. "Get the boys. We need 'em."

Whitmore jumped to his feet. "What goes, Scrapper?"

"They found where Murphy's a-hidin'."

Nate scrambled up, felt for the dagger tucked in his waistband.

"Billy," Ryan ordered as everyone gathered, "you and Ansel stay here. The rest of you follow me. No talkin', mind. We'll move right up. Hard tellin' how many Murphy's got with him. He won't go without a fight."

They marched down the north bank and across the bridge at the western end of the swamp. Off to the east, Ned Carrigan headed a squad armed with clubs, moving on a shebang. This would be a long, tiring morning for the Regulators, but the job must be finished and as many criminals rounded up as practicable. While they could not identify and arrest all the Raiders, they could punish enough of them to make it clear that their reign was at an end.

In the southwest corner of the stockade, Ryan's men halted near a shebang made of a single blanket. They formed a crescent barrier before it. Inside lay two men, one on his back, dressed too shabbily to be a Raider. The other, much larger, lay on his side, dressed in relatively new cavalry breeches and a calico shirt of red and white, wearing shoes with few holes. The scrawny fellow, Nate figured, was a cover, affording the Raider the appearance of being too lowly to be party to the murdering hordes.

The smaller prisoner stirred then sat bolt upright, eyes wide, when he saw the Regulators. "What in hell's this? I ain't no Raider."

The sleeping Kevin Murphy stirred, glanced up with bloodshot eyes. With an oath, he scrambled out from under the shebang, drawing a five-inch knife from his shirt. The other fellow leaped as far from Murphy as he could, paling. "You're a—?"

Ryan ignored the man, kept his cool gaze on Murphy's calculating eyes. The New Yorker's thick chest rose and fell quickly, reminded Nate of a badger he and his brothers had once cornered in their barn.

Ryan grinned. "Come quiet, Murph, or I'll rattle your teeth with me club."

Power surged through Nate as he gripped his weapon next to Ryan and said, "You won't get no help from your thickheaded bully neither. We tossed him on his ear yesterday."

This did not appear to be news to Murphy, for his scowl never altered. He flashed the knife at Ryan. "Have to kill me, Scrapper. And slice you from tip to tail in the bargain, I will. You needin' a whole pack of mangy curs to take me."

"No different than what you did to dozens yourself," Nate responded.

The Raider spat at him. "I shoulda let me cookie wring your neck last month. Fancy now I'll have to do it meself."

The crescent closed in on the burly New Yorker, some slipping to the rear to cut off any escape route. Nate and Whitmore maneuvered in front of Ryan, would not budge when Ryan cursed at them to let him through. The circle faltered when Murphy cut a swath with his blade. Sweating, eyes white and wild like that badger, teeth bared, Murphy snarled and lunged at Nate. Whitmore latched onto the Raider's wrist with the tenacity of a terrier. Murphy roared and swung him around in a circle, but Whitmore refused to let go. The crowd rushed upon Murphy and drove him down. Nate snatched away the knife. Murphy kicked and gnashed and swore, but too many bodies crushed him into immobility.

Once bound, they hauled him to his feet amid cheers from the surrounding neighborhood. Nate grinned at Ryan, who nodded approval.

Murphy, scarred face soiled and bruised, spat at the brothers. "Just you wait, Scrapper. Get outta this, I will. Then you best be watchin' night and day, for I'll kill you as sure as I'm born."

Showing neither fear nor complacency, Ryan regarded Murphy's hate-filled face and ordered, "Take him to the north gate, boys. Mind in case some of his pack try to get him free on the way."

Over his shoulder, Murphy shot, "I'll see you in hell, Scrapper."

CHAPTER 23

Nate felt the ill will as much as heard it. He shut his Bible, its pages and cover too warped, however, to truly close, then he left the blankets' shade to stand in the withering July sun and listen. Voices, deep and disturbed, shouts. The skin that sagged over his ninety-five pounds crawled with anxiety. Around him, others stood, looked toward the distant south gate, threw conjectures back and forth. Jared ran over from his shebang.

"What's going on, Nate?"

"Don't rightly know, but somethin's outta sorts, sure."

Ansel Rich wound his way through the crowded neighborhood, excitement on his scorched face. "Just came from the south gate," he called. "Wirz says the trials are taking too long, tying up his precious gate. The balance of the ones not tried yet are gonna be turned back in here."

Everyone within earshot sent up a howl of protest. Many hurried off in the direction of the south gate.

Urgently Nate asked Rich, "Did you see Ryan?"

"Yeah. He's with Key at the gate."

Nate rushed toward the south side, swearing at anyone who got in his way. Vaguely he remembered days before the war when he did not blaspheme. What would his parents and Katie think of him now?

A large crowd had gathered at the gate, making it impossible for him to get close. Angry faces, loud voices, fists waving. The mob pressed dangerously close to the Dead Line near the gate, the guards on the nearest perches watching fearfully with muskets half raised. Nate tried again to make his way through, but elbows and hands resisted his efforts. Men had formed a gauntlet over a hundred yards long that stretched away from the gate's wicket, many waving cudgels and other weapons. He hopped up and down, attempting to see over heads in order to spot Ryan.

The wicket opened to let the Raiders in one by one. They dashed down the double line of enraged prisoners. Most did not get far. Nate fought his way along the perimeter of spectators, able to see better now with the ground sloping gently upward away from him. Kicks and blows from fists and weapons poured down upon the Raiders running the gauntlet. One would fall, be pounded, stagger up, move on, only to be bashed down again, to get up, covered in blood, blinded, stunned. Nate stumbled to a halt. Horrified by what he witnessed, he could neither draw nearer to participate nor turn away as he desperately tried to recognize the tormented Raiders, afraid to see that one face. Many broke through the gauntlet, and some got away in this manner, but the vigilantes dragged most back, screaming and struggling, to be kicked farther along. Two went down under mobs of men and never stood again. Unable to distinguish comrades, Nate wondered if Whitmore and Billy were somewhere in there, exacting revenge; a boiling mass of murderous retribution. Somehow he knew Ryan refrained from participating, yet certainly his brother approved of the justice.

Still another figure tumbled through the wicket, paused as if in disbelief. A familiar shape. Prisoners kicked him into the mouth of the gauntlet, and Nate momentarily lost sight of him. But that brief glimpse…the yellow stripe of cavalry breeches. Dear God, they could not let him back in here! Frantically Nate began to fight his way through the layers of men in front of him.

Raiders were being pushed more quickly through the wicket now, drawing the attention of some away from Murphy, who had progressed a third of the way down the double row by the time Nate got within a hundred feet of him. A club crashed down on Murphy's head, dropped him to his hands and knees. Blood poured down his face, momentarily blinded him. He struggled up, bounced off his attackers, stumbled back, arms shielding his head. Then, with a desperate, Herculean effort, he slammed against two smaller men, broke through like a wounded bull. Nate bolted forward, reached the gauntlet, cursing the men not to let Murphy get away, but their attention was already up the gauntlet, urging on the next victim. Nate tried to pass through, received a thump on the head and an elbow in his tender ribs for the effort. In vain he watched Murphy vanish into the jumble of the south side.

***

"James. James, wake up."

The gentle voice tried to penetrate his nightmare. His father's voice? He struggled to leave the darkness, to abandon the images of

235

torn land, torn men, bloated corpses. Again he heard the screams of the wounded caught between the lines after the battle of Kennesaw Mountain, men burned alive when the dry ground cover had caught fire from musket and artillery fire. One of them reached out a charred hand, blackened face turned pleadingly toward him—Nate's face.

"Son, wake up." A strong hand upon his shoulder.

With a gasp, James awoke, sitting up in one swift motion, startling the man next to him.

"Easy now, lad." A familiar voice but, of course, not his father's, not here among the Georgia trees.

He stared at the man who had awakened him, blinked through the firelit twilight to make sure, disbelieving. "Colonel?"

A reassuring smile drifted across Colonel Stoughton's bewhiskered face.

James's senses raced back into place. "Colonel, sir. What are you doing here?"

Beyond the eagle insignia on Stoughton's right shoulder, the first hint of sunrise attempted to paint pink fringe along the tops of the trees, trees among which thousands of Confederate troops awaited them today—July 4, Independence Day. Around him lay gray clumps of his sleeping company, exhausted men who had come off picket duty just a few hours ago.

"I was sharing a cup of coffee with Lieutenant Hart when we heard you cry out." Stoughton remained on one knee beside him, making James self-conscious yet grateful for his presence, for delivering him from the recurring nightmare. Hart was not with him, but James could make out his shape nearby beside a low fire. The scent of coffee stirred James to greater awareness. "Thought it best I rouse you before you wake our Southern hosts over yonder. No need starting the war at this hour, eh?"

"Yes, sir. I'm sorry, sir."

"No need to apologize, James. Happens to all of us."

James found it difficult to believe that nightmares troubled a man of Stoughton's mettle. After all, what did he have to feel guilty about?

"Well, son, try to rest a bit more. We have a long day ahead of us."

An even longer one for a man with Stoughton's responsibilities, a brigade commander who was up before all of them or perhaps had never slept at all, but one who had taken the time to deliver him from that dark place.

"Thank you, sir."

Stoughton gave his arm a sustaining pat and rose to his feet. He started to turn away.

"I'm sorry, sir." The words fell from James's lips before he knew what he was doing. "I'm sorry about Nate, I mean."

Stoughton turned back with a troubled frown.

James faltered, cursed his impulsiveness, cursed the shame. "I walked him into those Rebs, sir."

Stoughton breathed a soft sigh. "You can't blame yourself for that, for any of it. My God, son, if we try to bear every tragedy in this war as something we personally caused...well, none of us would be sleeping at night. This war, James, that's what happened to Nate. Nothing more, nothing less. Remember the boy, honor his memory, pray for him. That's all we can do."

"I do, sir. I mean...well, I've never been one to pray but...I do...now. I just wish there was something more I could do."

Stoughton's small smile returned. He nodded. "You've done enough. We all have. Just maybe when we're through with this, maybe then we can get our boys back."

James tried to return the smile, failed. "I hope so, sir."

"Get some rest, lad."

"Yes, sir."

James watched Stoughton slip back through the trees to where his horse awaited. No brigade staff with him. Alone, taking the time to steal away to his old regiment, to check on his boys, like a father. James glanced around at his sleeping comrades. Brothers.

He wiped the sleep from his eyes, stared beyond these trees to their latest breastworks where the rest of the Eleventh waited for dawn, beyond that into the rugged wilderness. The Georgia landscape steamed from yesterday's heat, the veil of night having provided little relief. Everything stuck to his skin—clothing, dirt, woolen stench. The few birds that already called and sang would soon flash away with the first inevitable deep thud of artillery to the north, toward Smyrna.

Sleep refused to return, so he lay staring up at the fading carpet of stars and listened to Elias's snores. His guilt over Nate clung to him with a claw-like grip, a cold feeling that told him Nate's situation grew worse with each passing day. Hopefully Colonel Stoughton was right, and the sooner Sherman's forces defeated Joe Johnston's, the sooner Nate would be free. But would it be too late?

By full light, the entire brigade was back in the trenches, waiting. The artillery of both armies opened briskly, encouraging all to keep well below the breastworks. Word had it the Army of the Cumberland would be sent forward to assault this latest Confederate defensive position. Once again Sherman had flanked the Rebels out of their previous line, driving them back from Kennesaw Mountain and ever closer to the Chattahoochee River. Mere miles beyond the river lay Atlanta and its strategic rail hub. Like the Kennesaw line, these new defenses stretched from northeast to southwest, well-fortified by the Rebels, who had become as skilled as their Union counterparts at digging.

A rumble of hooves turned James's attention from the scrubby, shell-torn forest in front of their position. Behind the brigade line rode Colonel Stoughton and his staff. Sunlight flashed against the colonel's scabbard, burnished his gold buttons and the eagles on his shoulder straps, his uniform somehow neat and clean in this damned dirt hole. Stoughton's presence commanded the group. He rode superbly, back straight as if on parade, one hand on the reins of his eager mount, his other hand at rest against his thigh, his trim form moving fluidly with the motion.

"Keep your head down, Colonel!" Abner crowed then laughed with his grinning comrades when Stoughton smiled his appreciation and touched the brim of his hat. The group galloped away toward the right flank, the brigade flag fluttering above them.

"He's too good for this job," Corporal May said. "Should be leading a division."

"At least," Elias concurred. "Pap Thomas needs more officers like Stoughton."

"And fewer Frank Lanes," Langdon added.

This wiped away the buoyant expressions, and James silently cursed Langdon for it.

They ate a cold breakfast behind their breastworks. The broiling sun climbed higher. Most of the men talked as best they could over the furious noise of the artillery, others kept pensively silent, some pulling thoughtfully upon pipes or enthusiastically chewing tobacco. All of them calm, dulled almost into indifference after so many weeks of constant exposure to shot and shell.

Langdon reclined on the reverse slope of the trench, just a few feet down to James's left. The sergeant had his musket in hand, and when a pair of frightened ducks flew overhead, he sighted his uncapped Springfield upon them, tracking them as they raced over. Even when they had vanished, he kept the rifle to his shoulder, squinting along the barrel. In a smooth motion, he drew the barrel downward, moving the muzzle to the left, along the company line. No one paid attention to him except James, everyone accustomed to Langdon's close relationship with his gun; the man was endlessly cleaning it. The black muzzle halted, leveled upon Elias. A flash of panic froze James. Langdon pulled the trigger. The hammer snapped down on the empty nipple. Langdon lowered the gun with a look of satisfaction.

"Looky there!" Abner shouted. "Hain't that the Colonel's orderly?"

From down to the regiment's right, the orderly galloped madly their way, hat gone, hair flying. Below the pallor of his tear-streaked face, blood blackened the front of his uniform; but whose blood?

His shouts cut through the artillery's din: "I need a stretcher! A stretcher! Colonel Stoughton is terribly wounded!"

For a moment James could not comprehend the words. Surely that blood was the orderly's, not Stoughton's. Surely he had heard wrong. But the stunned faces of the regiment told him otherwise. No one spoke. Many, like James, sank back to the dirt, stared in silence. His throat constricted. Tears blurred the frantic rider to mere shades of black. He did not see the stretcher-bearers race away; he saw only the overturned red clay of the trench, red like blood. Jeremy's blood, Colonel Stanley's blood, Major Bennet's blood, Brian Calhoun's blood, his own blood, and now...

In time, the stretcher-bearers returned, carrying Stoughton. Several officers from the Eleventh rushed over, trotted alongside the litter, some speaking to Stoughton, who could say nothing in response. Down the regimental line he came, his right leg mangled, his face an ivory hue. His pain-racked gaze, unblinking, travelled over the ranks of his old regiment as if trying to remember each and every man, each and every tear-filled gaze. Onward he went, soon lost from sight.

David May wept openly. Abner stared grim-faced and hate-filled in the direction of the unseen Rebels. Elias held his dying pipe in his hand as tears coursed down to his beard. Langdon sat in stony, glaring silence. James did not care that the sergeant saw him cry. He was just grateful that for once Langdon said nothing.

***

Rain dripped from the sagging brim of Nate's tattered hat where he stood vigilant before the crowds near the south gate and the gallows. He caught the drops in his hand and licked them away. The brief downpour had momentarily tempered the fetid, dead afternoon air trapped within the pen. The north slope displayed the same crazy puzzle of thousands of expectant faces that Nate had seen when the Regulators first moved on the Raiders. The nearer spectators pressed close to the unwavering square formed by the Regulators around the gallows. They respected the newfound authority of the police force and refrained from trying to break through the elbow-to-elbow barrier, though many coveted the gallows boards more than they cared about what was about to occur upon that raised platform. Most of the Regulators carried new clubs fashioned with wrist straps. Nate, however, carried only his spoon dagger.

Next to him, fever-ridden Billy nodded toward the gun placements southwest of the stockade. "Look at all them civilians out yonder. Women even." He snorted. "Don't much care about us when we're alive but crowd around to see us die. 'Come watch the Yanks kill each other.'"

Whitmore, on the other side of Nate, said, "Sounds like you don't want them six to hang, Cowboy."

"Oh, they should hang, sure. Hang several times over for my brother alone. Just seems a damned shame we're stuck in here, killing each other instead of out there with the Iron Brigade, killing Johnnies."

"Don't pay to think on that." Whitmore rubbed his scurvy-sore arms. "Think instead on those Rebs yonder. Hell, them cannons ain't just loaded; the gunners got the lanyards in their damned hands already."

Among the drone of talk all around, Nate laughed nervously. "Hope none of 'em gets a twitch." His joke, however, fell flat.

Jared, stationed beyond Billy, said, "Hell, they've got the whole camp turned out. Even the cavalry and Turner's mangy pack of curs."

Nate shuddered at the thought of the dogs. One Rhode Island boy whom he knew had managed to tunnel out of the pen only to be caught by Turner's mongrels and torn so badly that he lived only a few days. Turner collected his bounty for his captures, alive or dead. Many of the would-be escapees feared the dogs worse than a Rebel bullet, Nate included.

From the mob of spectators, someone yelled, "Let's get this going!"

"Yeah! Bring the bastards in here!"

Other voices raised in anger, heightened by the long day's heat that made the stockade steam after the recent rainstorm. Some of those voices, however, spoke in contrast to the majority, those who were allies to the six condemned Raiders, those followers who had been released back into the pen's population. They posed the biggest threat to all of this going awry today, so the Regulators had stood ever vigilant, both here and amidst the greater population, since the wood for the gallows had first arrived. Was Murphy somewhere near, waiting to help his old comrades? Or had he died from those blows suffered during his gauntlet run?

Many prisoners, old Raiders and honest prisoners alike, had doubted that Key and his men or even Wirz would go through with the executions. Even now, with the gibbet complete, many men still voiced disbelief. The trials had brought lesser punishment upon the various offenders, saving the death sentence for the six leaders, who had since spent ten days in the stocks, awaiting approval from Rebel officials in Richmond before the executions could proceed. When authorization had finally arrived, Wirz had provided the materials, and the inmates had provided the carpenters.

From behind, a hand rested on Nate's shoulder, and he turned to see Ryan, who had come over from his station with Key near the gallows. His brother's grave expression had nothing to do with the pain of his deteriorating ankle wound. He put his other hand on Jonas Whitmore's shoulder, said, "Sounds from the reaction of them folks out yonder, they're bringin' the scum in. Stand fast, lads."

The gates groaned upon their hinges. Ryan returned to his post.

Whitmore muttered, "Here comes Death on a Pale Horse."

Captain Wirz, dressed very unmilitary-like in a suit of white duck, entered upon his worn-looking gray mare. Nate's attention did not linger upon the slim officer but instead upon the horse. In a brief flash, like those that teased his mind more and more frequently now, he saw his family's draft horses in the fields, felt the warmth of their sweaty bodies, smelled the dankness of their coats as he trailed behind them with the plow.

Next to the mare walked the solemn, familiar figure of Father Peter Whelan, his purple chasuble providing an incongruous splash of color in this drab hell. Whitmore had once grimly joked, "The Last Rites are his specialty."

Whelan had arrived at Andersonville in mid-June, and Nate often spoke with him, asked for his prayers, prayed with him, confessed his sins. The sixty-two-year-old Irishman lived on the post and, without fail, entered the prison and the hospital every morning and stayed throughout the day, ministering to his miserable flock. Sometimes Nate went with him on his rounds, holding the priest's battered umbrella to shield him from the withering sun as he knelt beside some poor wretch breathing his last. Deep admiration had grown in Nate. He considered

Whelan a saint, for who but a saint would willingly circulate among the putrid, rotting sea of humanity that was Andersonville? He never saw Whelan eat. The food he carried with him was given to the inmates. Often a trail of prisoners followed him about, especially when he first arrived in the mornings, begging him for whatever he had brought in that day. Whelan himself in no way appeared particularly healthy, and Nate feared the priest would contract any one of the numerous diseases in the pen.

Whelan's quiet brogue reminded him of his father, sometimes nearly brought him to tears, and always elicited torturous memories. Perhaps that was why Ryan rarely spoke with the priest, though Nate knew his brother's lack of interest also stemmed from something darker. His failing belief concerned Nate, for he viewed it as a fatal sign.

Behind Father Whelan and between two files of armed guards marched the six condemned, somehow still swaggering and unconcerned after all that had happened to them. Either the six men were fools, Nate thought, or they knew something the other prisoners did not. He tightened his grip on the dagger. Could it be their released followers planned violence to save them? But would they not realize the hopelessness of such an attempt, one in which many of them might be injured or killed?

"Jesus Christ!" Whitmore hissed. "The fucking Rebs didn't tie their hands."

The procession entered the Regulators' square. A hush fell over the masses. Wirz, looking pinched and melted, raised his scratchy voice and declared, "Brizners, I return to you dese men so goot as I got dem. You haf tried dem yourselfs und found dem guilty. I hef had not'ing to do vit it. I vash mein hands of eferyt'ing connected vit dem. Do vit dem as you like, und may Gott haf mercy on you und on dem."

As if eager to flee, he jerked the mare's head around and ordered the guards out with him. Nate thought of Pontius Pilate washing his hands after acquiescing to the Jews' wish to crucify Jesus. Well, these six were no holy men; more like the unrepentant thief who hung on one of the crosses beside the Savior. And Wirz was worse than ten Pilates, Nate was certain.

With one eye on the spectators and one on the condemned, Nate studied the six: John Sarsfield, Willie Collins—or Mosby, as Ryan and others always called him—Charles Curtis, Patrick Delany, John Sullivan, and Andrew Muir. As they watched the Rebel guards leave them to the bloodthirsty mob, reality dawned upon them.

242

Collins's face loosened in despair. "My God, lads, you're really not meanin' to hang us up there, are you?"

Speaking evenly, with Ryan by his side, Key answered, "Seems to be about the size of it."

The criminals began to speak at once, beseeching their fellow prisoners in such pitiful tones that Nate grew increasingly uncomfortable and questioned the true justice of the moment. Ryan, however, close to Collins, showed only a scowl of intolerance and loathing.

At last, Delany silenced the lot and said, "Let the priest talk for us," no doubt thinking Whelan's good standing among the prisoners, Catholic or otherwise, would afford them some slim hope.

Father Whelan closed his Bible and looked up for the first time since entering the pen. His great sorrow for these six was palpable, and again Nate thought him a saint, for only a saint could feel such emotions. True, Whelan had not directly suffered at the Raiders' hands, but how many times had he administered the Last Rites because of them? He tried to close his ears to Father Whelan's plea for pardon as the words sailed over the prison on fervent wings, that voice so like his father's. Surely Whelan understood that clemency would only lead to the pardoned returning to their old ways?

Nate closed his eyes and wished this were over.

A chant started, at first small and ragged, then it gained voices and volume, forming like waves on an ocean as a storm builds, and crashed toward Whelan, drowning his words.

"No! No! No!"

Whelan paused, and though hope began to drain from his sweating face, he continued more zealously.

The chant spread over the pen, rolling, rising, evolving, deafening, frightening.

"Hang them! Hang them!"

Nate's heart pounded painfully against his chest. He no longer heard Whelan or anything except the ferocious, guttural, primeval chant. Billy stood silent, but Whitmore joined the chorus of condemnation. Nate cursed this place, this realm unto itself, like an isolated island, its inhabitants sentenced and forgotten by the world. And so, they had formed their own way of living, if it could be called living, formed their own rules, harsh and without quarter, like savages. Although he hated to admit it, he was one of them. Had he not, after all, helped hunt down these men, fellow Union soldiers, who perhaps had been good citizens once, maybe had sweethearts, wives, children?

Had he not felt triumphant when he watched Kevin Murphy fall under the blows of clubs? Nate wanted to run away from the death chant, but where would he go? He wanted to weep for himself, for the six, for all of them and what they had become.

Shouts of alarm sprouted to Nate's right. Gasps and oaths went up from the spectators. Someone shrilled, "He's got a knife!"

One of the six burst through the square of Regulators, knocked several flat before charging into the crowd, slashing a knife at anyone within reach. Curtis! Men fell back against one another, stumbling, clawing to make way for the Raider's dangerous hulk.

A squad of Regulators pursued him through the tangle on the south side. Ryan and Key yelled for the rest of the Regulators to hold their positions. The five remaining thugs showed a spark of hope, but Ryan and the others closed tighter to dash their optimism. Nate held his breath, waited for the Raiders' cohorts to attack or support, but none stepped forward.

Distant shouts and screams came from the southwest, beyond the stockade wall. A commotion among the civilians crowded around and in front of the cannon. Wirz galloped that way, one arm flailing. The civilians fell away from the mouths of the field pieces.

"The cannons!" Nate shouted, taken up by others, warnings echoing all around.

"The sonsabitches are gonna shoot!"

"Jesus, run!"

The mass of prisoners melted into panic, breaking, struggling to flee in all directions but getting nowhere in the crush. Frozen by duty or fear, he did not know which, Nate maintained his position, as did the other Regulators. With a detached calm, he looked for Ryan, wanted to see him before grapeshot shredded them to bits. Still near the five other Raiders, Ryan glanced his way, no fear on his face, only regret. Nate closed his eyes, prayed, felt for Billy's hand, squeezed it in farewell.

Nothing. No roar from the guns. No musketry from the sentries; indeed, some of them had fled also. Nate finished his Hail Mary, surveyed the scene. As quickly as it had come, the panic diminished as everyone realized the cannon would have fired by now if so ordered. Nate sagged, his knees weak.

"It's all right, Little Brother," Billy said. "The gunners have more sense than Wirz, thank God. They can see the boys are running *away* from the fence, not towards it."

Ryan and Key called out for order, reassuring everyone, drawing them back.

Someone shouted, "Curtis has done gone in the swamp!"

"And he's stuck for sure," Whitmore crowed. "A shit covered in shit. Now, there's justice."

Curtis's predicament drew the prisoners' attention away from the silent cannon. Some began to laugh.

Jared asked, "Who the hell's goin' in after him?"

Someone did, and by then Curtis's run and subsequent mired struggle had so exhausted him that he offered no further resistance. Cheers went up. As the Regulators escorted him back up the south slope, prisoners again fell back, but this time they feared no weapon, only the human filth that coated the lower half of Curtis's body. Once inside the square again, he collapsed and begged for water as the police tied his hands behind his back like the others. Now all of them pleaded for the same, which Key allowed to be given.

"Damned precious stuff to give to the likes of them!" someone complained, followed by similar sentiments from the thousands.

Whitmore grumbled, "Good thing they ain't gettin' it from *our* well. I'd tell 'em to kiss my raggedy ass."

The Regulators prodded the six up the steps and to their tight positions near the nooses. Key glanced at a watch in his hand. Nate thought of James's traded watch. Maybe that same watch was somewhere in this very pen.

Key said, "Three minutes to talk."

Five of the six broke out in a jumble of pitiable words. Nate understood only a few sentences, not certain what came from whom or how much of it was truth. Yet what purpose would lies serve now? One talked of a family back home, another of how he had been an honest man before Andersonville, another said he might as well die because he could not live the way the rest of them did. On and on until Nate wanted to cover his ears. The spectators' responses tangled together, mocking the six. Then meal sack hoods muffled the Raiders' words.

Billy asked, "Ever seen a hangin', Little Brother?"

Nate shook his head.

Nervously, Jared laughed, "In Burr Oak?" but Nate could not react in kind. No doubt Burr Oak would have once hanged Seamus Keenan.

The nooses were tightened. He was unsure whether to watch, but he felt it was his duty, that he should witness what he had helped bring upon these six; he should not be a coward. But when he again looked over his shoulder, his attention instead went to Ryan, there beside the scaffold. Their gazes held as Key gave the signal, and the two executioners below the platform jerked their ropes and pulled the support planks away. Five men fell with thuds and snaps, but Collins's rope gave way, spilling him to the ground. Curses and groans went up from the crowd.

Two of the bodies swayed loosely on their ropes, necks broken, but the other three struggled against their bindings, twisting and turning. Sarsfield drew his legs up as high as he could, then straightened them with a horrible jerk, the veins in his neck looking to burst. Lightheaded, Nate stared downward, knew he would have vomited had he anything in his shriveled stomach.

Ryan and others surrounded Willie Collins and removed the sack. Collins gagged and coughed as he regained his senses. For an instant his bulging eyes touched Nate, then rolled to those around him. Blood ran from his ears, nose, and mouth. As they hoisted Collins to his feet, others worked in a frenzy to repair the rope.

"For the love of God, you can't put me up there again," Collins wailed. "Can't you see God is meaning for you to spare me?"

Nate glanced at Billy's frown, then back to Collins as they lugged him up the scaffold once again. He tuned out Collins's pleas, heard his voice but not the words, listened instead to the prisoners around him.

"Yeah. Hang him twice!"

"That's what he deserves!"

"Make it good and tight this time!"

"Strangle him like a chicken!"

"Like his hoodlums strangled Franklin last week."

"Hang him!"

"Quit your blubberin', Mosby! Take it like a man!"

This time Nate watched, for perhaps he had been meant to watch the first time and this delay had occurred because he had not. Now he would witness the punishment and not seek his brother's assurances. He remembered one of his mother's sayings—things once started must be finished.

Collins was soon in place, and again came the slam of dropping supports and human flesh. Nate watched the Raider's struggles, held his breath until certain the rope would hold, then when Collins's life left him, the six forms hung in silence like dead fowl in a poultry shop window.

CHAPTER 24

Like an unobtainable jewel, the city of Atlanta lay just beyond the grasp of Sherman's armies. After the Eleventh Michigan had been engaged during the July 4 fighting near Smyrna, Major General Francis Blair's Seventeenth Army Corps had worked its way around Joe Johnston's left flank, causing another Confederate withdrawal, this time across the Chattahoochee River, the last natural obstacle before Atlanta. Prior to crossing the wide river at Pace's Ferry, the First Division had welcomed the return of General Johnson, sufficiently recovered from his Pickett's Mill wound, and thus General King resumed command of the Second Brigade, which had been led by Colonel Marshall Moore since Colonel Stoughton's grievous wounding. James and the men of the Eleventh had been devastated to learn that Stoughton's leg had been amputated and that he would not return to the regiment.

After nearly two more weeks of fighting and life in the trenches, the men of the Eleventh could see the church steeples of Atlanta from their position west of the city. Sherman's forces embraced the outer reaches from northeast to west then south, grappling constantly with the Confederates. The most recent conflict had cost the Army of the Tennessee its bold commander, General James McPherson, a well-liked, hard-fighting Irishman, a loss that was felt among the ranks of Sherman's other forces as well. With the battle cry of "McPherson and revenge!" the men of the Army of the Tennessee had thrown themselves at the Rebels north of the city yesterday, but that brawl had accomplished little more than additional bloodshed on both sides.

During the month, the Confederate high command had endured a casualty of its own. On July 17, defensive-minded Joe Johnston had been replaced by aggressive, one-legged General John Bell Hood. James and the others of Company D had predicted that Hood would throw his army on the offensive. True to form, Hood did just that on July 20, suffering a repulse at Peachtree Creek, north of the city's heavy defenses. During the battle, the Second Brigade had been engaged on detached duty, sent to fill a gap in the Fourth Corps' line. Not until today, July 23, had they rejoined the division.

Each day put an even greater strain on the original men of the Eleventh, for their enlistments would expire in less than a month, and no one wanted to fall victim to a Rebel bullet or shell so close to escaping this madness.

James, glad to be reunited with the rest of the division, sat upon the rear facing of the entrenchments, for evening drew near and the Rebels' shot and shell had died away. Most of the men around him were quiet, fatigued from the arduous work of the previous days and the march back to the division earlier today. Elias sat on the opposite side of the trench, smoking his pipe, his face deeply tanned, his uniform ragged like everyone else's from living exposed to nature for nigh three months. Next to him sat Abner, pensive, his gaze lost somewhere in the dirt between his feet. He now wore a full beard, which sometimes looked gray, but how could that be at only twenty-four years old? The regiment stretched to either side along the trench line, dusty blue, completely accustomed by now to this cycle of fighting and entrenching. Even the recruits from over the winter were seasoned veterans. Good men all of them. Well, James considered, there had been poor Frank...

Captain Frank Lane had been found guilty of cowardice, absence without leave, and deserting his post in the face of the enemy. His sentence brought him before the regiment where he had been stripped of his rank. A sad, miserable day that no one wanted to remember or see repeated. Lane's shame would reach far beyond the Eleventh, all the way back to Michigan and his hometown where the court-martial findings were to be published. Seeing Lane's forlorn, disgraced figure there before the regiment had filled James not with mortification but with sorrow for Lane, an emotion that confused him. Men like Langdon condemned Lane for the black mark against their good reputation, but James realized with each passing day and every man lost that all he cared about was their solidarity and survival. Lane was but one man, a man who had done his duty to the best of his ability until, at last, he could no longer stand the strain and responsibility. James had little doubt that Lane had never dreamed when the war started that he would ever be anything less than a model soldier.

A sudden buzz of voices traveled along the trench line. James straightened, looking down to the left along the regiment's front, straining to hear. The boys of Company A seemed to be in a state of animation, all gathered around someone, but at this distance James could discern nothing. Others around him craned their necks as well.

"What in hell's goin' on?" Abner wondered for all of them.

From Company A on down the line, men stood as word passed, everyone turning toward the gathering. Soon the news reached Company D—Henry Damon had escaped Andersonville and returned to the regiment. James's incredulous gaze locked with Corporal May's, and he knew May was thinking the same thing as he—Nate.

May said, "Go on," with an urgent wave of his hand.

James bolted down the line until he reached Company A's position where the men had gathered in an excited circle, many asking questions at once. Pushing his way through, James found a gaunt figure that vaguely resembled Henry Damon seated cross-legged in the middle of the circle, dressed in a new uniform, dark hair freshly cut. His face belonged to someone ten years older—shallow cheeks and withdrawn gray eyes, sallow skin blotched by dark patches and pink patches as if scrubbed too arduously. His hands, bony and claw-like, clung possessively to a cup of coffee.

"But how in thunder did you make it all this way?" young John Downey, one of the Eleventh's recruits at the start of the campaign, questioned. "I hear tell that's nigh a hundred miles away."

"Traveled at night," Damon explained in a tired voice. "Got help from some darkies. Couldn't have made it without 'em, I reckon."

"Hank." James at last recovered. "Did you see Nate Calhoun there...in prison?"

Damon's attention rested on James as the men fell silent. Before Damon's capture at Chickamauga, he and James had not known each other well, and Damon had viewed him no differently than the bulk of the regiment had prior to Missionary Ridge. But now he regarded James in an oddly respectful way.

"James Keenan," he said, then paused as a small smile enlivened his countenance. "I hear tell you're a hero now. Carried the regimental colors up Mission Ridge. Nate told me all about it."

Warmth rushed to James's cheeks.

"Well," Damon considered his comrades, "I'll tell you boys this much. When I saw those colors today..." His words caught, and he shook his head. The men remained silent, some shifting uncomfortably. "I've never beheld a more beautiful sight. I can't explain it rightly. Can't explain any of it rightly, especially Andersonville. Nate's there, all right. Lived near him. Him and his brother."

"Ryan's still alive?" Dan Rose asked.

"Was when I escaped. He's been a prisoner a God-awful long

time. One tough lad to still be hanging on." Damon's tone darkened. "Things weren't going too well for him when I left, though. He was one of the leaders in an escape plan, but when the camp commandant found out about it, he rounded up some of the boys, Ryan being one of 'em, and punished 'em. Put Ryan in the spread-eagle stocks a hell of a long spell. 'Bout starved and dying of thirst when they threw him back inside."

Several of the men cursed the Rebels, vowed they would make them pay for what they were doing to the prisoners in their care.

"The stocks chewed him up, and in that place open wounds usually mean you've got a ticket on the dead-wagon. But that little Nate, he tended to his brother day and night. I wager Ryan made it through, thanks to him."

"Did you talk to him much?" James asked.

"Most every day. Damned little else to do in that hellhole."

"Is he all right?"

"As all right as anyone can be there. The boy's a tough one," Damon said with quiet conviction. "And he has his brother, or at least he did when I left."

James remained there until dark when Damon asked everyone's pardon so he could rest. Reluctantly James drifted back to his company and relayed everything Damon had told him. Damon was in no shape for active duty and thus would not remain with the regiment. Knowing this, James hoped to speak with him again in the morning. But what more could the man say? Plainly the prison had left a deep mark, a wound so painful that James suspected Damon would never reveal to anyone all he had seen and endured, for to talk of it would be to experience it anew. Maybe, James considered, he should not press Damon. After all, what would he gain besides more guilt for having caused Nate's incarceration in such a dreadful place?

Lying awake deep into the night, afraid to sleep lest Damon's stories stir up the nightmares, James stared at the sky, at the black expanse with its untold millions of stars, pinpricks of white and yellow light, distant and indifferent to all those below who gazed upon their mystery. He thought of his father, of Heather Cabot, of Nate, of the Rebels there in front of Atlanta, and of the Union prisoners in Andersonville and how they all looked upon the same sky as he. If only he could fly to those black heavens and let wings take him wherever he wanted. But where would he go?

To Andersonville, he decided without hesitation. He would find Nate, and they would return to Burr Oak together.

***

"You should go to the hospital, Ryan."

"No God damned hospital, Nate," Ryan growled, weakly wiping the sweat from his face. He lay under the meager shade of their shebang, the blankets so torn and full of holes that the late July sunlight easily found its way beneath. Nate's coat, worn but still in passable condition, served as Ryan's blanket, the wool quivering over his feverish form.

Exasperated and fearful, Nate turned to Whitmore, who sat, loyal and stoic, on the other side of Ryan. "Whit, talk some sense into him."

Jonas's response came a bit unclear, for he had lost several teeth to scurvy, and his tender, bloody gums had begun to protrude. "I ain't never been able to change Scrapper's mind for as long as I've known him, Little Brother. Don't reckon he'll let me now."

Gangrene had won the struggle for Ryan's left leg, the whole limb now black and useless, the rotted flesh around the ankle wound filled with wiggling maggots; there was no way to keep them out. The stench would have gagged Nate if the whole pen did not already defy the sense of smell. For several days, Ryan had been unable to eat, his form shrinking before Nate's eyes.

"Ryan," Nate tried again, "please—"

"No."

Nate struggled against the tears once more. In truth, he did not want his brother to leave for the hospital, not only for his own selfish reasons but because he knew, as they all did, that the hospital held nearly the same horrors as the pen itself. Over sixteen hundred patients crowded the hospital, and no indifferent brigade of Confederate doctors could hope to successfully or otherwise treat so many gravely ill men.

Bitterly Nate recalled the day when the Raiders had been hanged, for Leroy Key and several other Regulator sergeants had marched out of the pen after the corpses, allowed thereafter to live outside the stockade with Wirz's permission, to thus be protected from retribution from the surviving Raiders. When Nate questioned Ryan why he had not been included, he discovered to his great horror that his brother had declined the offer from Wirz. Though thankful for his own sake, Nate had vehemently argued with Ryan as to the wisdom of his resolve. If only Ryan had listened, maybe he could have received treatment for his wound and saved his leg and perhaps much more.

Billy tottered over from the shebang of the Eleventh Michigan's survivors where George Griffin and Edwin Green lay close to death. Slow and unsteady, he carried a tin cup of water. His fever was now constant, his breathing labored and ragged from congested lungs. He managed to conjure a smile as he sat near Ryan's shoulder. "Got some water for you, Scrapper."

"Don't want it."

Billy looked at Nate with growing concern. Whitmore did the same. Nate wished they would look somewhere else. Damn it, he was not the one with answers; he was not his brother. *He* should be looking to *them*, to Ryan. Leadership was not his to wield.

Nate ordered, "Drink the water, Ry. They went to the trouble of boilin' it for you."

"Let Cowboy drink it," Ryan mumbled, eyes still shut. "Needs it worse'n me."

Nate swore with such ferocity that Ryan looked at him with reproach. "Damn it, Ryan. You're goin' to the hospital...today!"

"The hell you say. Not gonna cut off me leg."

"They have to. There's nothin' else for it. 'Twill save your life."

"No help for that now." Ryan's bloodshot eyes slid shut once more.

"C'mon, Whit. Let's take down a blanket and carry him to the south gate."

Ryan raised himself on his elbows. "I may only have one good leg, but I still have two good fists, and use 'em to thrash you, I will. Leave me be, damn it."

Nate stood, hands and jaw clenched.

"No one comes back from the fucking hospital," Ryan reminded him. "What about James Ensign? You know where *he* is now, don't you? If I'm to die, do it among friends, I will."

"You're not gonna die," Nate snapped. "But you have to get that leg—"

"Leave me be," Ryan said with hoarse finality, then lay back down, grinding his teeth and closing his eyes, as if the faintest light pained them.

Nate turned to Billy, who shrugged, and Whitmore, who shook his shaggy head. With an oath, Nate struggled to his feet and stalked away down the north slope, the fire inside his stomach and bowels urging him through the press of the pen's population—close to twenty-eight thousand now—and to the creek. But fear for his brother overrode his own ailments. He had to get out of this place; he had to get Ryan out before he... Nate pushed away the image of his brother on that dead-

252

wagon. He would find someone working on a tunnel.

Millions of flies and gnats buzzed and swarmed in the trembling heat. He no longer made the futile attempt to swat them away. The whole month had been one continual blast from nature's furnace, bringing with it the untold torments of insects, day and night. Their noise blended with the pen's unending nightmare of sounds. Sometimes Nate purposefully lay awake in the thin minutes right before dawn, just to experience the brief time when the prison almost fell silent. Almost. Never before had he appreciated silence, and he knew if he was fortunate enough to survive, he would never be able to get the voice of this place out of his mind.

When he finally left the sinks, he made it only a short way up the north slope before a familiar scarred face loomed amidst the black cloud of flies, staggering him to a halt. The grin Kevin Murphy wore, while lacking the cockiness of old, still alarmed Nate. He had not seen Murphy since the New Yorker had been released back into the pen, had even figured the man had perished. Murphy's hollow cheeks and eye sockets betrayed the amount of weight he had lost, as did his shirtless torso, his ribs easily counted. The sun had burned and blistered his fair skin. He no longer wore shoes. The ex-Raider's appearance allowed Nate a twisted feeling of satisfaction.

"Well, Murphy, how does it feel to starve like the rest of us?"

Murphy's broken-tooth grin wavered only a little. "I'm makin' do, runt. Better than your brother, I wager."

Nate scowled. "Me brother's fine."

"Is he, now? Well, I hear he's doin' poorly." Murphy clucked his tongue. "Och, gangrene is a nasty business. Poison his whole system, it will. Slow agony. No stoppin' it. Too bad the Rebs didn't parole him to work outside with Key and the others who hanged me friends. Guess he wasn't important enough."

"He wanted to stay with me."

"A foolish thing, that, for now there'll be two dead Calhoun boys instead o' the one. I haven't forgotten what happened at the end of last month, spalpeen, nor who it was who caught me with his pack o' hounds, not man enough to take me alone."

"Just try somethin', Murphy. Sergeant Hill's in charge of the police, you know, and he'll have no mercy on the likes of you. Fine big Ohio fella like that could snap you in two. You best stay away from our shebang."

"I've been by. Didn't know it, did ye? I see you still have that fine coat amongst you. I could use that, you see. Damned sun like to scald me alive."

"Get used to it. I hear hell is a lot hotter."

Murphy chuckled. "Still got a gob bigger than the rest o' you, aye, runt? Well now, we'll be seein' how cocksure you are with your brother dead." He winked and moved away along the edge of the marsh's sludge.

***

James sprang over the breastworks, along with the rest of the Eleventh Michigan, crouched low, musket held at charge bayonet. The regiment, stretched out in a single rank to either side of him, pressed forward beneath the covering fire of Union artillery. Confederate cannon replied, but most of the shells sizzled far above James, their targets back amidst the main Federal line from where the bulk of the attack would soon commence. Across the scarred, barren ground, the Rebels opened fire from their first line of works some two hundred yards distant, musket balls whirring past James as he jogged along, Elias to one side, Abner on the other. Lieutenant Hart's voice pierced the explosive bursts of cannon fire, urging the men onward, demanding order, his sword always ready to motivate anyone who might falter. The regimental officers knew that some would require extra motivation as each day brought so many men closer to the end of their enlistments.

Behind them, the clarion call of bugles ordered the rest of the Second Brigade forward, a scene repeated all along the position held by the Army of the Cumberland, James figured. Orders had reached them that morning for a demonstration in force to be made by General Thomas's army. This was to occupy and confuse the Confederates while the Army of the Tennessee began the arduous process of marching from the far left of the Union lines to south of Atlanta near East Point, through which the Rebels' remaining two railroads passed.

James did not need to look behind him to make sure the rest of the brigade was advancing; he felt the presence of the Regulars' battalions, heard the shouts of the men and officers above the pound of artillery. Instead, he concentrated forward on the muzzle flashes beneath the head logs atop the first line of Rebel trenches. Although clouds shrouded the sun, the murderous heat that swarmed over the red earth in shimmering waves drew every ounce of moisture from James's pores, but somehow his focus remained cool, his hands as steady as his gaze. Distantly he wondered when he had acquired such aplomb. When had the shopkeeper become a true soldier? He held his fire as ordered, for he had no target, just the mounds of clay, the logs, and the blossoming muzzles of Enfields. Men fell wounded from the line, but he did not look to see who they were, did not want to know, especially now. He wanted nothing to cause him to falter. *Keep your eyes forward, forward, legs moving.*

Behind the Rebels' outer works, a battered forest protected the main line. Musketry rattled from there as well, adding to the deafening crash. James crouched ever smaller until his elbows brushed his knees as he moved. Behind him, the Regulars gave throat to their battle cry, a sound most impressive for battalions so reduced by weeks of fighting. All told, James figured the brigade barely outnumbered a single large regiment.

Within a few yards of the outer works, Hart's order echoed that of other officers, and the skirmishers went to ground, the whole regiment melting into the earth. Clinging to the red clay, James absorbed the crump of artillery through both earth and sky, the loose dirt in front of him trembling with each report. Union shells had found the range on the outer line of defenses and now ripped the Rebels' trenches apart. Screams filled the air. One shell tore a hole in the breastworks directly opposite James, tossed bodies like toys amidst a red cloud. *Head for that gap*, he told himself, and gauged how many paces away it lay, lest the battle smoke impede his vision during the charge. Safer to plunge through the opening and its carnage than to expose himself climbing over the mounds of dirt and logs.

"Wait for the brigade, boys!" Lieutenant Hart cautioned. "Hold the line! We need to go as one!"

Soon the brigade bugles blared the charge. The main force swept forward at the double-quick, withholding fire, the Regulars still howling, wild yells from hundreds of throats. James focused on the gap to his front, gathered himself. Wraith-like Confederates there in the smoke, hoping to plug the hole. When the Regulars reached the skirmish line, the Eleventh rose as one with a concerted roar to advance with them. Still no firing, just the crazed shouts from all around. Minié balls whirred past him, tugged on a sleeve, a pant leg, but he kept going. A shell exploded somewhere near. The concussion staggered him against Langdon, knocking them both over. Through his muffled hearing, Langdon screamed something at him. James recovered his musket, spat dirt from his mouth, clawed his way onward again.

The gap yawned before his squad, veiled in smoke. Some of the Confederates had begun to retreat to the main line. Abner surged ahead, reached the line first. He raised his musket to fire, but his body gave a jerk then reeled. He stumbled back, blood on his chest, expression wrapped in disbelief. His musket slipped to the ground as he listed backward, fell. Corporal May and Elias leaped past into the trench, disappeared from James's horrified view. The whole line flowed up the breastworks and down into the trench, pulling him along. Bayonets flashed, men at last firing at will. Bodies and rifles clashed in a tangle of screams and curses. James reached the gap. The trench roiled with hand-to-hand struggles. Elias stood above a young, wounded Rebel, bayonet poised, the Southerner's eyes wide and wild, empty hands upraised.

Next to James, Langdon raised his rifle, fired downward. But the ball tore not into the enemy but instead into Elias's back, collapsing him onto the stunned Rebel.

James stood paralyzed by disbelief. Langdon jumped into the trench, shoved Elias's body off the Confederate, then plunged his bayonet into the helpless man's neck. Spinning to the left, he smashed the butt of his rifle against the head of a Rebel who grappled with Corporal May, knocked him away, then bayoneted him.

May, breathing hard, looked gratefully at Langdon, then saw Elias. His expression collapsed. "Elias!" He clawed his way over the dead Confederate, rolled Elias onto his back as James slid down next to him, dropped to hands and knees, all strength in his legs gone.

Elias's vacant brown gaze reached up to James, his mouth open, blood trailing into his beard, into the long, rust-colored hair that he had yet to cut during the campaign.

Around them, the close combat ended, the Rebels having fled or surrendered or died in the trench. The artillery fire, however, continued, and once the retreating Confederates cleared the field of fire, the Rebels' main line in the trees resumed its deadly leaden hailstorm. Langdon had dragged Abner down into the protection of the trench, and the young man lay gasping, his eyes glazed while Langdon and the rest of the company blazed away at the distant Rebels.

May said to James, somehow heard over the crash of musketry, "He's gone," then recovered his musket and reloaded, his face a blank mask.

James ignored his own gun, powerless to look away from Elias, waited for the older man to revive. He had no idea how long he sat there, mouth hanging open until he was parched. No tears came, for he could not, would not believe what he had witnessed. A nightmare. Soon he would awaken. Soon Stoughton or Elias would be there to gently stir him, bring him back to consciousness.

"James!" David Burleson's voice. Burleson now Company D's first sergeant. "James!" Burleson's face loomed between him and Elias. "Are you hurt?"

James stared at him, unthinking.

Burleson gave his shoulder a shake, shouted in his ear, "I said are you hurt?"

James's gaze slid toward Langdon, who remained intent on his killing.

"Where's your rifle?"

The question made little sense, but in another instant, Burleson pressed a musket against him, jarring him.

"Get to it! We need to keep the Johnnies busy!"

But the enemy suddenly mattered very little. James stirred enough to convince Burleson that he had regained his senses, and the sergeant crabbed his way along the trench, checking on each man. James stared at his musket, then at Langdon. Had Langdon really done this? Or had his eyes deceived him? Had the sergeant been aiming at the Rebel and his shot went astray? No. His eyes had seen the truth; he knew. After all, Langdon had warned them.

Sudden fury welled up, blinded him to everything else around him, numbed him to the bullets flying above the trench, to the reports of the rifles, the shouts of officers, the pleas of wounded men. With an enraged cry, he fell upon Langdon, pummeled the unsuspecting sergeant, his mindless outcry all that rang in his ears. His vision tunneled, and he saw only Langdon's face as the sergeant struggled to fling him off. Other voices around them, May and Burleson, hands clawing at him, trying to restrain him. He fought against them, his blows still falling—short, ineffective blows now that the sergeant had recovered from the shock of the attack and grappled to defend himself and strike back.

Lieutenant Hart's voice roared through the din. "What in God's name...?"

Burleson and May flung James back against the trench wall. James propelled himself forward again at Langdon, but Burleson shoved him back, stiff-armed him to the ground.

"Keenan!" Hart bellowed. "God damn it, get a hold of yourself!"

Breathing hard through gritted teeth, James stared up at the officer, the rage still boiling, the frustration of being stopped nearly strangling him.

"Have you lost your mind?" Hart snapped. He crouched near on one knee, shoulders hunched defensively against the background of a leaden sky veiled by battle smoke.

"He killed Elias!"

Hart exchanged a confused glance with Burleson.

"I saw him," James insisted.

"You're out of your mind," Langdon snarled, wiping away the trickle of blood from his nose. "I'll have you up on charges, by God."

"Back at Kennesaw...he threatened us...when Elias defended me. You fucking bastard, Langdon, he has a family."

"Sergeant Burleson," Hart ordered, "get James out of here. Take him down the line—"

James grabbed Hart's arm. "Listen to me, Ben. Damn it, I know what I saw."

Hart leaned closer, muscles tight, his face boiled red. "This isn't the time for this, James. Go with Burleson. Now!"

"Damn it, Ben—"

"Now, I said! When this is over, I'll see to the matter. But right now, soldier, you have a duty to this regiment. Pick up your rifle and go with Sergeant Burleson. Do you hear me?"

The urgent light in Hart's blue eyes worked on James, settled him, assured him that Hart would keep his word. He was unable to tell if the officer believed his accusation—perhaps Hart did not want to—but there was doubt enough in his gaze. James's attention drifted back to Elias, and he thought of the man's children—Zack, Bart, and Mary—thought of his wife, Beatrice, imagined them receiving the news, just as the Calhouns had received the news about Ryan, Brian, Nate.

Burleson's powerful grip dragged him to his feet, both men still crouched below the lip of the trench. James met Langdon's burning, deadly gaze before he started down the trench, his grip tight upon the rifle.

***

With the diversion accomplished for the day, the Second Brigade withdrew under the cover of darkness. James helped carry Abner back to their lines. Abner, his chest bandaged and his arm blackened with blood and useless at his side, had bled himself pale. When James asked if he had seen Langdon shoot Elias, Abner, too weak to even lift his head from the litter, managed to roll his head back and forth.

"Passed out," he whispered. He studied James's frown, his gray countenance belonging to someone else. "Watch yourself. Langdon..." His voice trailed away into a moan.

James touched his shoulder, smiled his wan thanks. That damned pallor; he had seen it so many times, all too familiar. *Please, God, not both of them.* He murmured, "You'll be all right, Ab. You'll get to go home now. Mattie'll be glad to see you."

Abner tried to smile but broke into a painful, draining cough.

As Abner was borne away, James wondered if he would ever see him again. From their lines, Abner would be taken to the hospital at Vining's Station and then to the general hospital in Kingston. Their old rivalry over Mattie was but a vague memory, for after all these months, Burr Oak and its people seemed unreal, as if from another world, a dream world. Here, the only thing that mattered was getting each other through this alive. Then maybe, when this was all over, Burr Oak could again become reality.

James skipped supper, for he had no appetite. Although his fury against Langdon had not diminished, his grief over Elias overpowered his outrage and reduced his violent impulse to a background simmer. Losing friends to Rebel bullets was a bitter though understandable product of war, a potential result all had acknowledged upon enlisting. Yet Elias's death had nothing to do with war and everything to do with James and Langdon's feud, a feud in which Elias had no part until that night near Pickett's Mill. With his support of James, he had unwittingly condemned himself. James mourned the fact that he had accepted Elias's fellowship, fully aware that Langdon resented the man's stalwart friendship, and now Elias lay murdered, his children fatherless. Bitterly James regretted not killing Langdon back in the Rebel trench. Surely the sergeant would deprive him of a chance to make up for his lack of vision. Langdon would do to him what he had done to Elias at the very next chance because James had now cast the same cloud of suspicion over Langdon as he had among the people of Burr Oak after his mother's death.

By the time Lieutenant Hart summoned him, the emotions of the day had drained James, and he wanted only to fall to the ground and sleep. In silent misery, he followed Corporal May through a light, steady rain to a grove of trees where Hart and Burleson sat near a small fire. Across from Hart stood Langdon, hands clasped in front of him, expression sour but soldierly. Next to Langdon, May and James came to attention and saluted Hart. From beyond this tense circle, the calming murmur of camp tried to ease its way into the scene but was battered back.

"At ease," Hart said. He remained sitting against a tree, probably because his old hip injury troubled him after the long day. Glowering and displeased, he studied the three men for a long moment before speaking again. "You made a dire accusation against your sergeant today, James, particularly serious due to the fact that you expressed it in front of the entire company."

"Yes, sir."

"Since returning to camp, I've questioned the men, and there's no one who can corroborate your version of events. Sergeant Langdon denies your charges, of course."

"Damned right," Langdon growled. "Sir."

Hart's gaze flicked with loathing toward the sergeant, a reaction that told James much; Hart lacked the doubts portrayed by his obligatory words.

"So, this boils down to a case of one man's word against another's," Hart continued, "a private soldier and a non-commissioned officer."

"Yes, sir."

"No one can—or at least is willing—to even say which of you struck the other first."

The restless shift of Langdon's weight betrayed his effort to withhold an outburst.

"And because of this there is very little that can be done."

Rage swelled anew in James, and he stared in disbelief at the lieutenant. "But, sir—"

Hart held up a hand. "I am, however, relieving Sergeant Langdon from duty for a couple of days. He will be detached to brigade headquarters. Perhaps that will afford the two of you a new outlook on just what the hell is important here. You're supposed to be fighting the Rebs, by God, not each other. When the Sergeant returns, he will be assigned to a different squad."

"Sir," James persisted, "Elias was shot in the back. The back, sir. You know he was no man to show his back to the Johnnies."

Frustrated anger clipped Hart's response. "Damn it, James, what can I do?" He caught himself, rolled his lips together, and momentarily looked away into the heavy night. Sorrow conquered the anger, sheeting his blue eyes for an instant before he recovered. "Elias Cooper is dead, and that's a fact. A God damned unjust fact. If it was in my power to pass judgment on every man who's killed one of us, don't you think I would do it?"

Chastened, James dropped his gaze into the fire where a sudden explosion of sparks danced up into the night. So wrapped up in his own grief, he had failed to consider how Elias's death affected someone like

260

Hart, the man responsible for everyone in the company. When Bryon Liddle, a twenty-two-year-old in Company D, had been killed the same day Colonel Stoughton had been wounded, Hart had taken the loss personally and carried it with him ever since, as clearly as he carried his sword or pistol, a part of him forever now, always there in his eyes, as Elias would be.

Hart drew in a quiet breath, spoke now with heavy fatigue. "Sergeant Langdon, in the morning, you're to report to brigade headquarters. Understood?"

Langdon grumbled, "Yes, sir."

"The three of you are dismissed."

With the eyes of the company upon him, James returned to his blanket. Whispers and murmurs, conjectures and uncertainty. Would May and the others now avoid him, afraid such an association might one day find them with a bullet in their back? James liked to believe the boys of Company D were made of stronger stuff, would remember always what he had done at Missionary Ridge, but with only a month remaining in most of the men's enlistments, the pull of personal survival remained far stronger than the friendship of someone they might never see again. After all, Elias had been one of those men destined for home next month. James knew he should shun them all if he truly cared for their safety.

Lying on his side, away from any of the fires, he felt hollow, worn, and alone. Although the night was muggy, he shivered all the same, looked around him. Where was Jeremy or Elias or Abner or Bennet or Stoughton or Nate? Why was he the only one left? Why had he not warned Elias off? Why had he led Nate into those Rebs?

He forced his burning eyes shut. *I couldn't keep Elias from dying, but maybe…Nate…*

CHAPTER 25

James trembled, though the August night was like warm milk. A steady rain added to his discomfort where he hunkered behind a windfall near the brigade picket line. While he welcomed the rain's dark veil of concealment, the soaking worked on his resolve. He scanned the woods for the Eleventh's nearest picket, strained to hear if the man was drawing close to him, but the weather made such distinctions difficult. At last he spied the soldier some ten feet away, draped in a rubber poncho and leaning against a tree to find protection beneath its boughs. A match flared orange across his face as he attempted to light a pipe. James feared the picket would hear the pounding of his heart or the nervous rumblings of his innards. In an odd twist of memory, he recalled when he, Nate, and the others of his squad had run the guards to attend the barn dance last winter. A happy time, when they were all together.

He had been here behind the fallen tree several minutes as he battled within himself, urged himself to go, to stay, to return to the company. Whenever he nearly started back, he reminded himself of Major General George Stoneman's raid at the end of July. Sherman had sent Stoneman's cavalry division along with two other divisions on a bold raid toward Macon. The main objective was to destroy the Macon & Western Railroad, but Stoneman had a second goal in mind—to free the Union officers held as prisoners of war at Macon and then to dash even farther south to Andersonville to liberate the enlisted men there. This aspiration had distracted James from his grief for Elias and filled him with hope that soon Nate and the other prisoners from the Eleventh would, like Henry Damon, be free. On July 31, however, at the battle of Sunshine Church, Stoneman himself was captured along with nearly six hundred of his men, the rest of his brigades barely escaping. James had nearly wept when he heard the news. He knew then that he could no longer sit by and wait for a miracle, and so he had formulated a plan and secretly hoarded his rations in preparation for the journey.

Sherman's forces had spent days playing a massive game of leapfrog, edging ever closer to the railroad junction at East Point, south of Atlanta. Once Howard's Army of the Tennessee had completed its trek around Thomas's Army of the Cumberland, Schofield's Army of the Ohio passed behind Thomas's lines then Howard's. Then came Thomas's turn. By the end of August 3, Johnson's division lay on the extreme right of the entire Union force, the empty right flank providing James with an open gateway.

James felt in his pocket for Elias's compass, closed his fingers around it for strength, the feel of the small instrument helping to ease his fears. When he returned to the regiment, he would send the compass to the Cooper family and explain why it had not been mailed with the rest of Elias's effects. Maybe, he prayed, Elias would help him on his way.

A hundred miles lay between him and Andersonville. He would find his way there by following the rail lines. When Henry Damon had escaped, he had traveled northwestward from the prison and crossed the Chattahoochee River above Columbus. James wanted a more direct route and knew the railroads would provide just that. Damon said he had been taken to Andersonville by rail, southwestward from Macon, forty or fifty miles, so James planned to parallel the Macon & Western Railroad south until he found the Southwestern Railroad, which would lead him to the prison. Civilians and militia alike could make the route a dangerous one, but he would travel at night and conceal himself during the day. Rugged, pine-filled countryside, Damon had said, sparsely populated. James knew not what he would do once he reached Andersonville, but he had days in which to concoct a plan. His only solid idea embraced the tactic that Damon had used to get out of Andersonville—impersonating a Rebel guard. Thus disguised, he could hope to locate Nate and conjure some way to get him outside the prison.

"Any man deserts from my company, I'll hunt him down myself and shoot him."

Langdon's words returned so sharply from that long-ago night on Raccoon Mountain that James nearly fled the windfall. But he forced himself to relax, to breathe. No, he shook his head, Langdon would never put forth the effort to track him down, though the sergeant would be furious to learn he was out of reach. Once morning rollcall revealed his absence, Langdon would take great pleasure in crowing that James Keenan had deserted. James winced at the idea of being thought of as a deserter by the men of Company D, but there was no help for it, and he consoled himself with imagining their reactions when he returned with Nate. That is, if he returned before the boys were mustered out of the service toward the end of the month.

Well, he told himself, he would get nowhere fast unless he screwed on his courage and got moving. The rain had slackened slightly. He crouched even tighter against the fallen tree trunk when the picket stirred from his protection. The man softly cursed his pipe, then paced down the imaginary line of his beat until he passed James, probably headed for the next picket to procure a light for his tobacco. James hunched his shoulders, drew in his breath, and darted into the black Georgia night.

PART V

ANDERSONVILLE

"This beat anything I ever saw;
it is, indeed, a hell on earth."

-- Daniel T. Chandler, CSA

CHAPTER 26

Nate moved despondently along Market Street, listened to the familiar hail of sellers or those plying a trade, remembered the hucksters from his first day in this hell. Whatever had become of that fellow responsible for helping him find Ryan? Probably dead, just like the men who had previously set up their wares on this path, now gone, replaced by others. If he happened to ask about one of the men with whom he had bartered in the past, he was always told, "Dead." The word encompassed everything, chopped away at his will to live as an axe chips away at the base of a strong tree. Three thousand prisoners had died in July, including four boys from the Eleventh Michigan—Edwin Green, George Griffin, Napoleon Sprague, and James Ensign.

In June, before being taken outside to the hospital with bronchitis and diarrhea, twenty-three-year-old Ensign revealed a gold ring he had kept hidden in his waistband. Extracting it, he breathed on it and tried to polish it against his rag of a shirt. Then he palmed the ring to Nate, saying, "Keep this for me. If anyone gets out of here, it'll be you. Give it to my father, will you?"

"By God, Ensign, that could get you a mess of food. Why don't you—"

"No. I want him to have it. We never really saw eye-to-eye, but I meant to make things right once I got home." A rattling cough gripped him, passed. "Guess I won't have time for that now. So, you give it to him. Tell him I'm sorry."

With a frown, Nate had put the ring in his pocket with his tattered Bible. Ensign's trust moved him, for how could he be so certain that he would not use the ring for personal gain?

New prisoners arrived in the pen most every day, replacing the dead, swelling the ranks ever higher. Among them Nate searched for familiar faces, both disappointed and relieved when he found none. He thought of James whenever the prisoners originated from Sherman's ranks. With these men came news of the campaign's progress.

"They're at Atlanta," Nate kept reminding Ryan. "Won't be long and they'll get us all free." But, as he slowly moved down Market Street, he knew Sherman and James and the others would not arrive in time to save Ryan. Gangrene would win the ultimate race.

Along with yesterday's latest arrivals, disheartening news had raced through the stockade. General Grant had declared that no more prisoner exchanges would occur until the Confederacy agreed to recognize black troops as Union prisoners and exchange them along with white soldiers.

"A damned crime, that." Jared Taylor had raised the familiar complaint over a game of cribbage. "We didn't enlist to fight for no darkies, so why should we be made to suffer 'cause of them?"

Jared's voice now, calling his name amidst the hawkers' cries on Market Street. The scurvy-ridden young man gimped up to him, a humorless grin showing several gaps among sore gums. There was little left of the Burr Oaker, just skin and bones. Nate was little better, and he was glad none of them had a looking glass, for he wanted to avoid seeing the details of his own hideousness.

Jared asked, "Find anything?"

"No. I wanted onions or salt for soup for Ryan but…" He shook his head.

"Just as well. Scrapper won't eat the soup, and you can't afford to trade what's left of your hat. Get sunstroke in this desert of a place."

Nate looked beyond the stockade to the treetops. "Someday I'm gonna be yonder in them trees. Won't need a hat."

Jared chuckled. "Well, out of our boys, you're the only one left with any strength to escape." He leaned close. "Found a tunnel yet?"

"I think so. El Schreiber's Pennsylvania boys over near the north wall. They won't say as much, though; 'fraid I'm a spy. Said if they hear tell of a tunnel, they'd let me know. El's a friend of mine, so I'm hopin' he'll convince 'em to take me on."

"Good luck to you. Wish Sherman would hurry, especially with exchange gone up the spout."

Nate frowned. "Reckon I should get back. No use hangin' 'round here no more."

Jared led the way up the street, but when he turned off into the maze of shelters on the north side, Nate found he could not follow. His resolve had suddenly left him, and he lingered on the edge of the path. Jared hobbled back.

"What is it, Nate?"

He could not answer right away. Slowly he sat down, too tired to stand any longer in the hot afternoon. Puzzled, Jared sat next to him.

"What's the matter?"

Nate murmured, "Don't wanna go back just yet."

"Why not? You said no one had anything to sell you."

He hesitated, ashamed. He knew he should not say anything, that he should abide by Ryan's hard and fast rules but, truth be told, he lacked the strength to remain silent any longer. His fears had begun to erode his resolve over the past few days until now, when at last he admitted, "'Tis Ryan. Jared, I...I can't bear seein' him the way he is. Can't get up, all black and rottin' right in front of us. All them damned flies and maggots and mosquitoes; can't keep 'em off him. And when he's delirious—hell, most all the time—the stuff he says turns me inside out; thinks he's back home, talkin' to me parents or brothers, workin' in the fields. Truth is, he ain't never gonna be home again. I can't watch him die no more." Inside he wept, but his eyes offered no moisture.

Jared put a hand on his arm, both now oblivious to the weird commerce of Market Street and the scores of prisoners nearby, who were just as oblivious of them, just two more bodies taking up valuable space.

Nate babbled on, powerless to stop, no matter how hard he tried. "Hearin' Ryan talk of home... Best off if I don't think on that, but I can't help it when I hear him carry on so. Hardly nothin' left of me likeness of Katie. Can't even recollect what she looks like. How is that possible?"

Jared's tightened grip squeezed off Nate's flow of words. "I know it's hard with Ryan, but it's a comfort for him to see you, so as tough as it is, you need to be with him." With gentle determination, he continued. "Listen now. I'm not gonna talk stupid and say things'll work out. We know how it is. Hain't no miracles 'round these parts. But what I will say is this, Little Brother. Ryan's held on as long as he can. *He* didn't put hisself in them damned stocks. That's what's killing him. God damned Wirz..." He paused to compose himself and refocus. "What I'm a-saying is we need to do what we can for ourselves. We have to keep going, keep helping ourselves and others till we can't no more. You know—God helps he who helps hisself. Well, Ryan helped hisself and many others, you and me, but now this other thing has a hold of him. Only God can help him now. And maybe dying *is* God's way of helping." He frowned. "Scrapper's taken all he can. It's time for him to rest. But he's too worried about you to let go."

Nate stared at him in confusion, horrified by what Jared intimated.

"I can't…give him *permission* to die, Jared. I mean, I understand what you're sayin' but…" He pressed his burning eyes shut. Only then could he see Ryan as he had once been, laughing and joking with his brothers, healthy and powerful, tossing fifty-pound grain sacks like bags of fluff. When near Ryan now, such images would not come at all, not even to the darkness behind his eyes. "I'm afraid of him dyin', Jared. Don't know if I can take it. After seein' Brian dead, I…"

Jared put an arm around his shoulders, though Nate could barely feel the bird-like pressure. "There's still some of us left."

Nate opened his eyes, frowned. "Whit and Cowboy won't last long. Scurvy's in Whit's lower legs now. He jokes about it, says he looks like he's got two butter churns for legs. Cords all pulled up, so he can't walk. And Cowboy and me can't carry him and Ryan to the sinks no more, so our place is becomin' a right mess. Can't blame 'em, though."

"You have to keep goin' for your family if not yourself, Nate. Think of Katie and your folks, even if you can't picture 'em no more. They're there, waiting for you. You don't want your ma losing all of her sons."

Despairing of his options, Nate nodded.

"Come on now." Jared struggled to stand. "Let's get back to the others. They'll be wondering after us."

***

Nate sat near Ryan in the steamy darkness and listened to the distant rumble of thunder as a storm neared. He imagined it was the sound of Sherman's artillery, but this rolled from the southwest, not the north. He thought of his old company, of James and Elias and Abner, May and Hart, Colonel Stoughton, and he prayed they were safe, prayed none of them would suffer a fate like his. He had a difficult time remembering their faces, all except James's. For some reason, his messmate's image remained clear. Often he lamented his refusal to listen to James that night long ago when he had gone in search of Brian.

He stood and sniffed the air for rain, but no sweet scent penetrated the wall of deadly fumes. Seizing the opportunity to loosen some of the filth on their bodies, prisoners around his shebang stripped naked. He, too, carefully removed the rags that hung like crepe from his bony frame. He had a vague memory of being self-conscious of his nakedness even around his brothers when they swam in the Prairie River; how Brian used to tease him. Now he thought nothing of removing his clothes around others. Some in the pen lacked clothing altogether, having traded it away for more pressing essentials.

After arranging his mess's two tin cups and three canteen halves to collect the coming rainwater, he sat back down and hoped the storm would not bypass them. *God's somewhere out there, and He'll bring the rain.*

Distant mumbles escaped his brother's lips where he lay on the scooped-out ground, wrapped in Nate's stalwart sack coat, an ample blanket now for his diminished frame. A couple of inches on the other side of Ryan, Whitmore lay in a twisted heap, sometimes awake, sometimes asleep. Billy lay next to him, snoring, occasionally waking himself with horrible coughs from his drowning lungs. Neither lay as close to Ryan as they once had, for even in their weakened state, they avoided contact with the dying and dead flesh. The stench, like putrid cheese, was repulsive enough.

Nate yawned. Usually he slept during the heat of the day, then remained awake during the somewhat cooler night, but today he had spent too much time on the hunt for extra rations. Neither Ryan, who ate only a mouthful a day at best, nor Whitmore could eat the brick-like cornmeal rations they received from the Rebels, so Nate bartered for replacement items. Now the day's fatigue pressed his eyelids down. *I'll wait for the rain, then I'll sleep.*

When the storm arrived, the rain woke Ryan for a brief time. A flash of lightning allowed Nate to see his glazed stare reach upward. Perhaps the drops would ease the constant fever. Nate brushed the long, tangled hair from Ryan's face. His brother's tortured gaze turned to him. More than ever before, Nate admired his ability to suffer his agony in silence.

Through cracked lips, Ryan murmured, "Rain's good for the corn, aye?"

Nate's gut twisted. He nodded. "Aye."

***

Asleep, Nate was distantly aware of the storm's final growl as it marched away to the northeast. Only a few raindrops pattered against the now-slimy ground, heard somewhere in his dreams. He sat with Katie in the shade of Burr Oak's buckeye tree as a cooling summer rain sifted through the leaves. James stepped out of the mercantile and came toward them, a smile on his face…

Ryan's pained outcry jolted Nate awake. Someone cursing. A

presence nearby, sensed before seen. A dark shape in the night ripped frantically at the coat around Ryan, dragged him away.

Whitmore struggled in vain to get up, to reach Ryan. "Nate, stop him!" The assailant kicked away Whitmore's grasping hands.

A flash of lightning revealed Kevin Murphy just as Nate tackled him. They rolled across the ground, smashed into neighbors' shebangs, sending men scrambling with shouted protests. Nate grabbed a handful of Murphy's slippery hair, but the New Yorker snapped his head forward. The explosion of pain in his nose compromised Nate's grip. Murphy's hand spidered onto his face, ragged nails digging, but Nate clamped his teeth down. With an oath, Murphy pried his hand away. A blow to the temple stunned Nate, allowed Murphy to gain the advantage and roll on top of him. Hands closed like an iron belt around his throat. The New Yorker's labored, fetid breath overwhelmed him as he tried to reach Murphy's leering face with his free hand. Shouts from all around clouded his hearing. Billy's voice, his shape nearby, tugging uselessly at Murphy, his blows unheeded.

My knife, Nate tried to say, but Murphy's thumbs buried themselves painfully deeper. Sound tunneled away from Nate, fell to a loud buzz. Heat poured into him. Darkness draped over him. His own struggles tapered away.

A shriek pierced Nate's ears. The pressure on his throat, on his body, lifted, wrenched from him. He struggled to push clear. Another flash of lightning. Ryan clung to Murphy's left leg where the New Yorker writhed on the ground. Ryan's hand came away from the man's body again and plunged Nate's dagger into Murphy's thigh. With another scream, Murphy knocked Ryan away, ripped the dagger from his hand. Nate dived at him, but the Irishman sidestepped and kicked him in the ribs. Stunned, Nate tried to stand, to breathe, staggered to one knee.

Lightning again. Clean, white light.

Murphy drove the knife deep into Ryan's chest.

"No!" Nate howled, lurched forward, pushed Billy out of reach, fell into Murphy. They tumbled across Ryan. Fury provided strength where none existed. He saw nothing, heard nothing, only felt his fists strike flesh time and time again until a moist stickiness covered his hands, then someone dragged him away.

Jared's voice. "God almighty, Nate. You done kilt him. Holy hell—"

Nate turned in a confused circle. Dark shapes together on the ground. Whitmore whimpered Ryan's name over and over. Nate fell to his knees, shoved everyone away.

"Ryan," he sobbed, pulling him into his arms. His hand brushed down his brother's chest where the coat had fallen away. Hot wetness coated his hand. He shook uncontrollably, felt his brother shudder, heard the rattle in his throat.

"Nate," he rasped.

"I'm here, Ryan. I'm here." He clutched the paper-thin hand. "Don't go. Stay—stay with me."

"Nate." A flicker of lightning flashed in Ryan's hazel eyes. A moment of fear. "Oh…"

Nate's tears flowed as he rocked forward and back. He hoped the movement would keep his brother's attention, but Ryan's eyes slid shut, the fingers loosened.

"Ryan, don't go. Please don't go."

A whisper of words passed between Ryan's lips. Nate barely heard, "Go home…home."

The life drained from him; Nate sensed the passing energy of his spirit like a pheasant flushed from an autumn field, sent spiraling off in a beautiful flow. He squeezed Ryan's lifeless, decomposing body, tried to hold life inside of him, beseeched repeatedly, "Don't go. Don't leave me." But there was nothing left to hold.

He touched Ryan's cheeks, the cold already setting in. Nate's breath pulled deep inside his lungs, expanded his chest with pain until he voiced it all in one long wail.

CHAPTER 27

James awoke to the whistle of a distant train. Rain worked its way along the fallen tree beneath which he had taken shelter and dripped down on him until, before he knew it, his clothes were soggy. An apparent lightning strike had recently felled the tall pine tree, laying its upper half against an even larger oak so that its lower trunk provided a canopy of furry boughs close to the ground. James had crawled beneath them that morning to sleep away the day. But rest on this second day in the wild, wooded countryside had come no easier than on the first.

Looking upward through the limbs, he gauged the time of day— still another hour or so of daylight. He dared not move out before complete darkness, for if his calculations were right, he was close to the town of Macon. Any such populated area would mean a greater chance of someone seeing him. He had no idea the size of the town nor did he intend to find out. He would keep to the woods as he had the entire way thus far, mindful of the railroad off to the east, keeping him on the right path. If Henry Damon had been correct, this line would soon branch off into the Southwestern Railroad.

Being alone in the dark Georgia forests challenged his courage. Never in life had he been so isolated, so completely dependent upon himself. As he had before leaving the regiment, he battled constantly with his decision, but whenever he faltered, he thought of Henry Damon and all he had said. Would Nate look as gaunt and sickly as Damon? Nate had been alive when last seen, Damon said, but that was over a month ago. Even if he made it to Andersonville, what if he arrived too late? What then? To turn back now... What would he tell Lieutenant Hart? Without rescuing Nate, he would be viewed as nothing more than a deserter. Then what? The same fate as Frank Lane. Or worse since he was only an enlisted man.

The forest's songbirds lulled him back to sleep where he dreamed of home, forgot how tired and sore he was, how alone.

At twilight he awoke, senses instantly keen. Not a muscle did he move. For a long moment he lay there, listening, heartbeat increasing. The rain had slackened to sprinkles. Broken clouds in the sky beyond the tops of weeping pines and oaks. Something had disturbed him, but what? Slowly he rolled his head to one side, peered into the trees to the east, strained to see any slight movement amidst the underbrush. Nothing. Then the snap of a branch. He froze, waited. Fraction by fraction, he turned his face to the west. Evening shadows had already begun to eat up the dying sun. Movement, a dark shape gliding among the trees. James held his breath, squinted. A single man, moving southward. He would pass close to James's hiding place. A hunter perhaps? No doubt the Reb army had its share of deserters; perhaps this was one of them.

James's musket lay close beside him, but he dared not move to retrieve it. If the man discovered him, the quickest weapon at hand would be his bayonet. If only he had been able to acquire a pistol before leaving the regiment.

The man, dressed in dark clothing, halted three rods away. James risked not even a blink. He stilled his breath, prayed that the blue of his uniform blended seamlessly into the shadows of the boughs. The bearded stranger, short and stocky, wore a slouch hat, a musket slung over his shoulder. James's eyes widened. He knew that shape. The man turned his face from right to left, his narrow gaze reaching beyond James toward the unseen railroad.

Langdon!

A jolt of disbelief froze James. His first impulse was to reach for his musket, for if Langdon managed to see him, there would be little time to defend himself. Caution, however, forced him to remain motionless. Langdon had discarded his sack coat with its telltale blue sergeant's chevrons, wearing only his shirt and pants from which he had removed the blue infantry stripe down the outer seams. Any Rebel patrols or militia that might happen upon him would not immediately suspect he was a Union soldier.

At last the sergeant moved cautiously to the south. James closed his eyes in relief, ears still attuned. His hand drifted along the wet barrel of his musket. It was loaded. All he needed to do was cap and cock it. But there was a good chance the rain had spoiled the charge, so if he leveled his sights on Langdon and the hammer snapped down without firing, the man would detect him, and James had no doubt that Langdon's Springfield was loaded, his powder dry. Langdon would shoot to kill. James had no illusions that the man had abandoned the regiment simply to drag him back as a deserter. The accusations presented to the men of Company D after Elias's death had been the final insult. He had destroyed Preacher Langdon's reputation twice now, and the man was not going to allow it to happen again. So now the equation was simple—kill or be killed.

***

All night Nate sat with his brother's corpse to protect him from being robbed of his clothes, for even though the Regulators now policed the pen, lesser crimes by desperate men still took place under the cover of night. The next morning, Jared Taylor helped him carry the body to the dead-house outside the pen. Nate convinced the Rebel guard there to allow him to remain with Ryan until the wagon arrived to collect the bodies for burial.

"I'll stay with you, if you'd like," Jared offered. But the guard would hear none of that and threatened to send them both back to the stockade if Jared lingered.

Nate urged, "Go on back to the boys. I'll be all right."

Jared offered a solemn nod, touched his shoulder, worry in his eyes, not for his friend's safety as much as for Nate's grief and the toll it would take. No one wanted to be the last alive among their small community.

With Murphy dead, Nate's fears for his safety had vanished, though he warned himself against feeling too comfortable. Only now did he realize how much influence Murphy's existence had had upon him. He had feared for himself but more so for his sickly messmates. Last night had proven how vulnerable they were with only one healthy enough to put up a fight. Thank God the Raiders had been put down.

When other prisoners brought more corpses to the dead-house, the men regarded him strangely, but no one asked about his vigil, perhaps thinking him touched in the head to remain near the gruesome harvest of bodies, especially in the blistering heat. Some of the men cast covetous glances at Ryan's coat. Without hesitation, Nate growled at them, swore at them if needed, to discourage any rash thought of robbery.

His thoughts wandered. Would he be able to find where they had buried his brother if he survived and walked away from here? He had no idea where Brian had been laid to rest either. His parents had no body to keen over, no grassy place to visit, no headstone to adorn with flowers. Exhuming the bodies after the war, if they could ever be found, would be far too costly for the family to do.

As always, Nate's thoughts drifted homeward. He consoled himself that once free of this place, he would again be able to remember his family's faces.

He had to find a way to acquire a scrap of paper and a pencil to write home, to tell his parents of their most recent loss. Impossible to know if or when they would receive the letter, but the Rebels did empty the prisoners' mailbox regularly; he had seen it done many times. How he dreaded writing the letter. Perhaps he could delay a day or so. He felt too weak; surely the tears would come again. He did not want to subject his messmates to another display, determined to uphold Ryan's guidelines. But how would he explain to his parents that he had been unable to save his brother? To describe his debility and that of Ryan's messmates, to somehow relate the desperate violence of someone like Kevin Murphy... His parents back on their idyllic Michigan farm could never understand what it all truly meant. Even if he were able to stand face-to-face and explain, they could never grasp the reality, nor did he want them to. Yet neither did he want them to wonder about his failure to save Ryan. They would be proud to know Ryan had given his last to protect their younger son, and now that Ryan was no longer here to prevent the telling, Nate would write about everything Ryan had done for him, as well as for everyone around him. At least they would have that to sustain them.

Harness jangled nearby, and Nate got to his feet, rubbed his tired eyes. The dead-wagon with its slave crew halted in front of him, all regarding him as if he had arisen from among the dead.

To the closest slave, Nate said, "I want me brother put on last; don't want him underneath all these others."

The slave glanced at the bemused faces of his companions then laughed. One of them—the large young fellow Nate had met when Ryan had been a prisoner of the stocks—did not laugh. In fact, a small frown crossed his face, a slow rise of anger toward his callous companions.

"You boys hurry up, hear?" the Rebel guard, a mere slip of a youth, said from next to the near mule. "Don't pay no mind to that little Yank. Time for him to clear outta here."

Nate shoved the slave who reached for Ryan first, not strong enough to push him away but persistent enough to hinder him. "I said leave him for last, damn it."

The slave looked askance at the guard, but before the man intervened, the larger black man came around the tail of the wagon and thrust a thick arm between Ryan and the other slave. His size was more intimidating than his glower, but for whichever reason, the first slave backed down.

"We put this one on last," the big man rumbled.

"Don't make no matter," the guard insisted in his cracking voice. "They jest gonna be thrown together in a big ol' trench anyways."

Despair choked off Nate's response. He would have punched the boy if he had enough strength to muster. He considered his brother's decomposing form. If the darkies didn't pick him up proper, what was left of his leg might fall off. This he did not want to see.

A tentative hand touched his arm, and he looked through frustrated tears at the incongruously gentle face of the large slave.

"Don't fret," the man softly said. "I'll make sho' he ain't treated rough-like."

"The coat." Nate gestured, fought for his voice. "Please, don't let no one take it from him."

"I won't."

Touched by this unexpected charity, Nate rushed on. "His name's Ryan Calhoun, Eleventh Michigan Infantry. 'Tis written on that scrap there."

"Enough," the guard snapped. "Git this damned thing loaded. Ain't got all day. They'll just keep comin', too."

Nate clutched the slave's arm, marveled at the flesh and hard muscle. "You'll mark his grave?"

"Cain't write, Mister Yankee."

"Please...someone—"

"Someone will. There's a Yankee what do. I'll make sho'."

Cursing, the armed guard stepped toward them, leading with his bayonet.

"You best git along," the slave urged as he stepped back. "Cump will take care of your brother. Don't fret."

Nate sidestepped to avoid a poke from the militiaman, nearly tripped over a corpse. "Much obliged, Cump."

He did not, however, leave but instead simply remained out of reach of the guard. Not until Cump carefully lifted Ryan and placed him upon the grisly stack did the tension drift away. With it came silent tears, rolling untouched through the thick grime on his cheeks.

***

James knew he should have pressed forward before night could shield Langdon from view, but caution had slowed him, causing him to drop back in the forest. No crack shot, he would need to be close, very close to ensure his bullet found its mark. If he missed, he would not have time to reload before Langdon was upon him. The trees and underbrush had yet to yield a clear line of fire—a double-edged sword, of course, for the denseness also protected him from Langdon—and now night hovered a mere breath away. He wondered if fear governed his lagging pace more than anything else. Not fear of killing a man—after all, he had killed more than one man by now in this war—but fear of failure.

Should he continue onward with his usual night travels and risk confronting Langdon in the dark or lose valuable time by concealing himself and waiting until the light could reveal the sergeant as a clear target? What would Langdon do—wait for morning, perhaps just ahead of him? Or, thinking James still in the lead, would he press on, using the cover of night just as James did? James considered traveling west for a time, away from the railroad, before resuming a southward heading in hopes of shaking his would-be assassin. But so much time would be wasted, and his rations would dwindle. Deviating from his current course could also put him in even more danger of capture or losing his way. If he were not careful, he could end up *in* Andersonville. No, he needed to eliminate Langdon's impeding presence.

Moving smoothly from cover to cover, loaded musket always in hand, James began to lose sight of Langdon in the blurring gray of near night. Silently he berated his own vacillation as well as Langdon's insane drive to pursue him, to hamper him in his desire to help Nate. Was Burr Oak at the core of this compulsion? Or perhaps his defiance of the sergeant near Atlanta? Sometimes over the years, deep in the night when he lay abed back home and found doubt easily within reach, he had wondered if his accusations against Langdon lacked merit. What if his mother's state that long-ago day really had nothing to do with Langdon? But always the light of day would filter into his bedroom, and that old certainty, that sixth sense would overpower the reservations.

Now the memory of his mother's death gave him strength, provided him with the resolve to confront Langdon, to exact the revenge he had never dreamed would come. He had not considered murdering the man before, though he surely had wished death upon Langdon every day since his mother's passing. Now he would have his chance for vengeance, and this war had given him the tools.

What if Langdon killed him instead, though? Not only would Nate be lost, but no one would ever know what had become of him. He figured not many beyond the regiment would care, but just maybe his father would, or Heather Cabot. For them to hear of his death in battle…well, that at least would be honorable, but to be remembered as a deserter who had vanished into the Georgia countryside…

During these last few weeks, he often imagined returning home, especially when he thought of his comrades leaving him behind when their enlistments expired this month. Just as frequently, he thought of his father's letter mentioning their old house, and James clung to that hope of reclamation, a hope that made the idea of going home even more appealing, for it truly would be home, not simply that cold living space above the mercantile. But what would his father say about Uncle Pat's watch? He had yet to tell him. *Coward*, he berated himself whenever he considered his avoidance. Just maybe, if he explained more thoroughly the privation they had faced in Chattanooga—all of them, not just himself—his father would understand, would forgive the unforgiveable. Maybe.

James halted behind an old pine, ears attuned to every insect and frog, the trees still dripping from the recent rain. When he peered around the trunk to the middle distance where he had last seen Langdon, the sergeant's outline had vanished into the forest's ever deepening gloaming. He blinked, diverted his gaze slightly to try to locate the darker, moving shape, but…nothing. Damn it, where was he?

Longer he waited, his stomach pressing him now for food. He closed his eyes, tried to think clearly, to slow the troubled race of his heart. Then, frustrated, he stared up at the clearing sky, at the first wink of stars. Not at any time could he hazard striking a match to check his compass, yet he did not feel adept enough to navigate by the stars, especially here in this deep wood where so much of the sky remained hidden.

A flash in the night like a lantern suddenly uncovered then instantly doused again, a stab of yellow in the darkness off to his left just as he went to sit. The bullet's hiss, a hair's breadth above his head, reached his ears a fraction of a second before the gun's report. James dropped to the ground, musket half raised, wild eyes staring toward where the gun had flashed. Not far. His heart raced. How had Langdon doubled back so quickly? James cocked his musket, tried to keep his breathing quiet as he listened, waited. Should he flee or stay? Langdon would be reloading; this might be his only chance to put space between them, to get lost in the night. But then what? He worried that the shot had been heard beyond this immediate wood. Were there homes nearby? Citizens who would be curious about a shot fired?

Movement, just detected against the darker background of the forest. The noise of insects continued, mosquitoes piercing James's neck. He blinked to clear his vision, tried not to focus directly on any one thing. The crunch of feet on last year's dead leaves, darting from cover to cover, closer. James steadied himself on one knee, musket ready, waited for the shadow to reveal itself again. Langdon had come at him from the east, for that left any scrap of light from the sun's death offering contrast to James's form.

No shifting sound now. Silence beyond the shrill of insects. Surely Langdon could detect his breathing, his hammering heart, the rush of his blood. He strained to hear the sergeant reloading his musket but detected no such telltale rattle of rammer. No, Langdon had taken his one chance; he, too, would be concerned that someone might be drawn by further gunfire. Perhaps Langdon would think him wounded or even dead—he would want proof of his kill, and so James would let the sergeant draw closer.

Baiting remarks bounced around James's brain. He wanted Langdon to know he was not afraid, that he knew who was trying to kill him. But he refused such a catharsis and continued to wait. His muscles began to ache, urging him to shift his weight, the gun barrel wavering. Was Langdon slipping around behind him? Would it be possible for the man to move close without detection? Surely the ground cover would allow no such stealth.

Like the blur of a large owl in flight, Langdon flashed from one tree to another, alarmingly close. James's startled, wild shot came automatically, shattered the night. He cursed his foolishness, but there was no time to think of anything else—Langdon burst from cover and charged, musket gone, knife in hand. No time to reload. James clubbed his musket. Langdon ducked too late—the stock glanced off the sergeant's face, staggered his advance, but a rush of wind just past James's face warned of the striving knife. Something hot peppered his cheek—the smell of blood; his shot had not gone astray. With the empty musket, James deflected another blow, the blade of the knife vibrating against the barrel. Langdon's enraged roar filled James's ears as the knife came again. James collapsed his knees, pushed to the right as the blade gored the tree behind him. He realized then that Langdon carried the blade not in his dominant right hand but in the left.

James fumbled for his bayonet, pulled it from its scabbard, thrust the three-sided blade before him. Langdon restrained his headlong attack, took up a crouched position before him, blade felt more than seen in the darkness between them. The sergeant's breathing came in short, infuriated, pained rasps.

"Where are your protectors now, Keenan?" Langdon's quiet voice came dry and raspy. "No one here to stop me; no one here to know you're dead."

"I'm not dead yet."

"Soon enough, like that boy you think you can save, like Elias…like your mother."

James stabbed wildly with the bayonet, but Langdon jumped back. The knife sliced in; James snaked out of its way.

"A shame about your mother. A fine one, she was, coming around to see me all the time. She asked for it, you know."

James cut a swath with his longer reach, the smell of Langdon's sweat and blood filling his nose. He plunged the bayonet toward Langdon's stomach, then jumped back just in time, the knife tearing through his sleeve, the blade grazing his flesh. James's free hand latched upon Langdon's wrist before the sergeant could withdraw. Langdon swore and twisted to break free, to elude the bayonet. Weak blows from the man's right fist sledged against James's temple, but James hung tenaciously to Langdon's wrist, twisting to dislodge the knife, trying to drag the sergeant closer so he could drive the bayonet deep. Langdon let out a frustrated growl, whipping him against a tree, jarring the bayonet from his slippery hold. Desperate, James brought his other hand upon Langdon's wrist like a double vice, absorbed the weakening blows against head and shoulder. He braced one foot back against the tree trunk, used it as leverage to push forward into Langdon's writhing form. Langdon staggered back, lost his balance, and they tumbled to the forest floor together, still locked as one. They rolled, legs kicking, bodies squirming. Langdon's teeth sank into James's left hand, but he managed to yank it away. Blood from the sergeant's arm wound warmed James's cheek. Langdon roared when James's fingers sank into the wound. The sergeant's grip upon the knife loosened, and James twisted it free, took possession.

Desperate now, Langdon struggled beneath him, tried to squirm free. The knife fell repeatedly and drowned his words in blood. It flowed warm against James's fingers, its flecks flung upward to mingle with the sweat upon his cheek. He saw nothing, felt only rage, the frantic desire to kill this man quickly, to keep him from making further sounds, from speaking of his mother. He continued until he was certain, until all struggle had ceased, all breath gone, and he was left alone in the haunted wood.

CHAPTER 28

"Hain't nothin' shy of a miracle," the man in line ahead of Nate proclaimed to his companion.

"'God smote the side hill and gave them drink,'" another quoted, clutching a battered tin cup, as if his life depended upon it.

"God ain't forgot us," the boy behind Nate said.

"The rest of the world has," yet another grumbled.

"Buck up, Phil. At least we got us some *real* water. That'll save a lot of us. 'For the Lamb which is in the midst of the throne shall feed them and shall lead them unto living fountains of water.'"

"Enough of the damned preachin'."

In the late morning light, Nate glanced forward then back along the winding line of prisoners—over a thousand, he guessed—who somehow found space to queue among the thirty-two thousand inmates. Most had cups or canteens or half canteens or anything that could hold and transport water. Those who lacked such a vessel stood in line to drink their fill directly from the clear, bubbling spring that had burst forth from the ground near the Dead Line just northwest of Stockade Creek. At nearly ten gallons a minute, the spring spewed forth into a v-trough fashioned by Hill's police force and guarded by them as well. No one knew how finite the miraculous flow might prove, so everyone wanted to partake as often as possible. As part of Hill's contingent, Nate stood his own watch most every day, but this morning he waited merely as one amongst the eager throng.

Two days ago, the violent two-hour rainstorm that had revealed the spring had fallen so heavily that the rush of water down the pen's north and south slopes, as well as the swelling of Stockade Creek, had undermined the stockade walls. First to fall had been a section of the wall where the creek drained out of the prison to the east, first one log toppling outward, then another and another until a gaping hole nearly one hundred feet wide revealed the outer world to the inmates. Amidst the drowning roar of the tempest, few prisoners immediately knew about the breach, and those who did lacked the strength required for a bold escape attempt. Anyone with a scrap of protection had dived for cover when the skies had opened around noon, cowering from the sizzle of lightning as it struck all around. Nate could not see ten feet beyond his shebang, let alone the distance to where the fence had collapsed. Further discouraging anyone from venturing forth, the muffled thump of two cannon grumbled through the din, followed by the rattle of drums from the Rebel camps, summoning the militia from their dry quarters to protect the gap and keep any prisoners from making a break for the countryside. Shortly after the appearance of the militia, the stockade wall opposite the breach gave way as well, the timbers crashing inward and drifting down the creek before opportunistic inmates waded into the mess to claim whatever wood they could drag off. Just as word of these openings began to crawl up either slope, more militiamen filled the eastern gap, and the guards upon their perches doubled amidst the dark pall with its stabbing flashes of white. By the time Nate had rushed down the north slope along the eastern deadline, any hope for escape had vanished.

By the following morning, gangs of slaves had repaired the walls, much to the despair of those who had realized opportunity too late.

Perhaps one of the lightning bolts had split open the ground and freed the deep spring. No one knew for sure. Once the storm had passed and the worst of the rushing water eased, there had been the gushing spring, like liquid manna in the desert. Nate liked to believe that Ryan's spirit had influenced this miraculous flow, which the prisoners had dubbed Providence Spring, hoped that his brother could indeed somehow intervene for him, for all of them.

At the thought of his sibling, Nate closed his eyes, lifted his face to the warm sun. A pleasant day, not as broiling as the previous. Was it his brother's hand in the cooling breeze that tugged at his bedraggled hair? He remembered Ryan's last words. *Home.* Often since that day he had wondered exactly what Ryan had meant. Had Ryan been beseeching him to survive and return to their Burr Oak home? Or had he known that his younger brother, too, would eventually have to make the decision to struggle on or submit to the inevitable and follow him to his heavenly home? *If* he was allowed to go there after murdering Murphy.

"Nate!"

El Schreiber's call pulled him from his thoughts. The young Pennsylvanian hurried down the north slope toward him, his eyes black pools of guarded excitement. Schreiber, small like Nate but two years

284

older, wore his long brown hair tied back in a queue, which fell well past his shoulders. A scrap of colorless rag tied around his hatless head helped keep stray tendrils from his naturally thin face. It had been Schreiber who had lobbied for Nate's inclusion into his fellow Pennsylvanians' escape group, and when Nate had appeared, tear-streaked and desperate, the morning after leaving Ryan at the dead-wagon, Schreiber finally convinced his fellow Easterners. Nate had pushed aside his fears from his May tunnel work and spent as much time as possible underground.

Schreiber stopped next to him in line, breathless and grinning with a mouth still full of teeth, for El had been in the stockade only a month.

"Hey, bub," a man behind Nate said to Schreiber. "Don't fancy cuttin' into the line or I'll lam' you good."

"Hush your gab, old man. I ain't here for water." The anger left Schreiber's eyes when he turned back to Nate; Nate liked El's eyes, for although dark, they usually shone with friendliness and hope, something of which Nate was in desperate need. He leaned into Nate's ear and whispered, "Tonight."

Nate's heart leaped. "Are you sure?"

Schreiber nodded, then gave Nate's arm a quick slap. "See you later."

Tonight. Tonight! The word echoed in Nate's head, almost pulled him out of line to dance a jig, for after tonight he would no longer need to stand in line for water. How he wished he could share his news with Billy, Whitmore, and the Eleventh Michigan boys, but he had sworn an oath of secrecy to the miners. They mistrusted Westerners, even those Nate called friends.

After he filled two tin cups at Providence Spring and chatted with Sergeant Hill, who had come to check on the continued integrity of the new sluice, Nate hurried back to his shebang. There he found his comrades where he had left them under the mottled shade of a blanket. A lonely place without Ryan.

Whitmore cracked open his sunken eyes when he heard Nate's halloo. Since Ryan's death, Whitmore had all but given up. Seeping, purple ulcerations splotched his distorted, half-naked body, the rest of his flesh a muddy pallor. He had lost all his teeth, and often he spat out chunks of his sloughing gums. Eating proved impossible except for broths, and Nate currently had little with which to make one.

Next to Whitmore, Billy struggled to a sitting position, one of the tattered blankets wrapped around his shivering rack of bones. Silently he accepted one of the tin cups, and Nate helped Whitmore drink from the other. Billy closed his eyes and murmured a prayer of thanks for the nectar before breaking off into wrenching coughs, then spitting frothy blood.

Watching the two of them, Nate thought of the tunnel with a heavy wave of regret and guilt. How could he leave them, especially Whitmore, who was now totally helpless from the ravages of scurvy? Billy's meager strength would never allow him to stand in line for spring water. Without him, they could very well be dead in a short time. Yet, if he stayed, they would all be dead. Survival had been one of Ryan's rules.

With these responsibilities weighing on his mind, he sought out Jared Taylor and found the fellow Burr Oaker trying to mend his pants; he sat half naked upon the baked ground with a needle hewn from bone between his sore fingers.

"Howdy, Little Brother. Get some of that fine water?"

"Aye. Still can't believe it."

Jared shook his head and grinned as he worked. "Jacob is fetching me back some. Sure is a miracle how that spring appeared up out of the earth. Makes a fella feel a little bit hopeful, don't it?"

Nate sat next to him, watched him work for a time, unsure how to voice his reasons for stopping by.

"Something on your mind, Little Brother? That's a mighty big frown wearing a furrow into your head."

Nate hesitated. Jared had enough to worry about with his own dwindling mess without taking on more duties, yet who else could he turn to? "Jared, I need to ask you a favor."

"Shoot."

"Well…'tis Whit and Cowboy."

Jared's lips twisted. "Doing poorly."

"Aye." Nate picked at his ragged fingernails, glanced at the multitude of lice on and around him; old companions now. "If I wasn't here…you know…would you be able to help 'em?"

Jared looked up, his grin gone. "If you wasn't here?"

Nate bit his lower lip and stared at the distant treetops beyond the northeast wall. When he had rallied enough fortitude to look back at his childhood friend, he saw understanding in Jared's deepening frown. And he also saw with disarming clarity that Jared already missed him, just as he already missed Jared. To leave one another to such a great unknown, to perhaps never know what happened to each other once Nate reached beyond these walls… This was not supposed to be so difficult. If only they could all go.

Softly Jared promised, "You don't have to worry about Whit and Cowboy. They can move in here with me and the boys. There's room now."

"Much obliged." Nate gathered his resolve and shook the young man's bony hand. "See you back in Burr Oak under the buckeye tree."

Jared smiled. "We'll be home in time for harvest."

***

James's hungry gaze latched upon the smokehouse and only came away long enough to survey the empty yard around the adjacent ramshackle, single-story clapboard house. All was quiet in the first light of dawn except chickens scratching about in the dirt beyond the smokehouse. From his concealed position at the edge of the forest, he judged that the smokehouse itself would mask his approach from whomever might be awake in the house. The smokehouse door, however, could not be seen from this angle.

His gaze swept the scene again, from the crude dirt lane leading away from the isolated house, to the planted field beyond the house where cornstalks stood like tasseled green sentinels in the crisp morning. Pine forests surrounded the farmer's small plot of land, the same forests James had clung to these many days since he had left the regiment. A week perhaps; he had lost track of time, conscious of little except the railroad and the wilderness.

Surely he was almost to Andersonville. He had exhausted his rations two days ago and had stolen from what gardens he had come across close to the forest's edge, doing so always under the cover of darkness. But this morning, when he should be finding a safe place to get some rest, his nose had instead directed him to the smokehouse. He had not eaten meat since the day after leaving the Eleventh, and now the scent of smoked bacon drowned his mouth in saliva. Obviously he could not sleep near here, so he told himself that he would quickly grab something from the smokehouse, then be on his way before anyone could detect him.

Patched clothing hung limp upon a line that stretched from the corner of the house to an oak tree near the lane. James glanced down at his pants. He had tried to wash Langdon's blood from his uniform, but it had set into black, unyielding splotches. He had buried the sack coat, and a couple of days ago, he had stolen a shirt from another clothesline. The sleeves were too short, but at least a part of him had been freed of the reminder of that bloody struggle, an encounter he tried to avoid thinking about. He had done what needed to be done—for his sake, for Nate's sake, and for the memory of his mother and Elias—nothing more. He felt no victory in Langdon's death, only relief.

James knew to hesitate any longer could prove risky, so he darted from the shadow of the trees out to the stretch of open ground. When he reached the rear of the smokehouse, he paused in a tight crouch and listened for any movement from the house. Nothing. Taking his hat in his hand, he peered around the corner, waited. Then he smoothly swung to the front and slipped inside.

Pork, venison, turkey. The hickory scents made his eyes close in delight. He smiled and reached for a suspended slab of bacon.

The distant bang of a door froze him mid-reach. Dread sank throughout his body. The bark of a hound echoed, followed by the happy voices of children. Careful not to make a sound, he reached for his musket. He heard two children race past; from the sounds of it, each one tried to get to the nearby chicken coop first to retrieve eggs. James considered bolting for the forest once the voices became muffled, as if inside the coop, but the hound… It had stopped barking, and James, no friend of dogs, feared the canine more than he feared the children alerting any adults to his presence. He decided to wait, hoping the children would return to the house with the eggs and the dog.

Resting his musket on its butt, he used his right hand to pluck down some venison jerky. Without looking away from the door, he shoved the spicy meat into his mouth, chewed quickly so he could allow room for more. Then he carefully shrugged his haversack from his shoulder and filled it with anything small enough to squeeze inside. As he did so, he listened to the murmur of the children's rivalry in the coop, the abrupt protests of the hens. It reminded him of the children who would come into his father's store, sometimes with their parents, sometimes without, always begging for the peppermint sticks his father kept stocked on the counter, a place where no parent could miss them when they paid for their goods. Unwittingly, James smiled.

A bark from just outside the door startled him, and his musket nearly slipped away from him. A darting shadow along a tiny crack near the base of the door. The hound gave full voice, the rolling bay terrifying James as he slung the haversack over his shoulder and took the musket in both hands. The dog clawed at the door now, rattling it with its paws as if rearing up on its hindquarters. The nose snuffled madly, then claws began to tear at the earth. James stared at the ground in front of his toes, the musket barrel wavering there. Should he shoot through the door? No, too risky, for if he did not kill or seriously maim the cur, it would be on him before he could reload.

"Spider, you get away from that there smokehouse! Davy, I reckon that ol' coon's gotten in the smokehouse agin!"

Soon the boy's scolding voice drew near, one more mature than his sibling's but still with the squeak of a child. "Set yore basket down, Laurel. I'll hang onto Spider whilst you open the door and let it out. But you jump back soon's you open that there door, lest he bite you."

Horrified, James's grip tightened on the musket, his mind racing. The door swung open, and light poured in. The girl jumped back then gasped, wide eyes lifting from James's brogans to his face. No one moved or spoke; even the dog seemed taken aback by what it saw standing before them.

James wagged the gun barrel at the coonhound. "Don't let go of that dog or I'll shoot him, hear?"

The boy's shocked stare went from the gun to the blood on James's pants, and fear leaped into his eyes. The hound began to bark again, struggling against the child's grip on the scruff of its neck.

The girl, perhaps eight years old, freckled and wearing her strawberry hair in pigtails, recovered first. "What you doin' in our smokehouse, mister?" She spoke with more wonder than fear.

James had begun to edge himself outside of the shack, attention fixed upon the hound's flashing teeth. Fortunately, it appeared the boy loved his dog and believed James would indeed shoot if necessary, for he clung tenaciously to the cur.

The girl fixed James with a narrow stare and put her hands on her hips. "You best not be stealin' from us, mister."

"Laurel," the boy managed. "I reckon he's a sojer."

The girl scowled. "Not another one. Pa said we can't feed no more of you 'uns. Well? Is that what you is, mister?"

"No." James chanced a glance toward the house. He needed to get the hell out of here before their parents appeared, but he feared bolting would encourage the dog to break free. The girl's conversation seemed to confuse the dark canine, as if uncertain now whether this man was friend or foe.

"Our pa was a sojer," the girl continued, picking up her basket of eggs as though to protect them from being pilfered. "Got his arm took off by a cannon ball at Mission Ridge, so he ain't a sojer no more."

"Well, I'd stay and say howdy to him, but I have to be on my way now." James nodded to the boy and raised his musket slightly to show his resolve. "Remember, you hang onto that dog. Don't let him follow me."

289

"He won't bite you," the girl insisted. "He's used to sojers."

"I'm not a soldier."

The boy grew bold enough to say, "Look like one, but you don't sound like no one from 'round here."

The girl took a quick step backward, her mouth loosening again. "You ain't a Yankee, is you? From that there prison?"

Sweat poured from beneath James's hat. A sickly smile touched his lips. "Of course not. I wouldn't have a gun, would I?"

This seemed to appease her, and he suspected that she enjoyed strangers. No doubt she and her family lived quite isolated; during his sojourn, he had rarely seen two homes close together. A schoolhouse with playmates was probably even rarer.

"Now, I really must go."

"Pa might let you stop for breakfast," she said. "I'll go ask him."

The protest of door hinges snapped James's attention to the nearby house. A disheveled man stepped into view on the near edge of the front porch. One sleeve hung empty, but the right hand held a pistol. His sharp gaze leveled on James, eyes with the instant wisdom of a soldier who knew the enemy stood before him.

James hesitated no longer. He wheeled and ran for the forest, angling his path to put the smokehouse between himself and the Southerner. The man ordered the children into the house, yelled for the boy to release the hound, but the child argued against the demand. By the time James had gotten to the edge of the forest, he heard the pistol fire, though surely the man had little hope for reaching his quarry at that range. James tore his way through the trees, deeper into the thinning darkness. Never had he run so fast in his life.

***

A late afternoon storm over the prison pen had drained color from the heavens, making it difficult to discern where stockade wall met sky. Everything blurred to drab, humming gray. When Nate left the sinks, feeling weak and wobbly and cursing his afflictions, he cursed the weather even more, for its steamy heat pulled away what little strength he had mustered for that night's plans. How much did he weigh now? Eighty pounds?

Above the dull roar of the pen, the sharp noise of hammers and saws blended with a rhythmic work song chanted by slaves. After the great deluge had ripped away the stockade walls the other day, the Rebels had begun constructing a second stockade wall. This outer perimeter would not only dispel worries should nature demolish another inner section but would also make tunneling more difficult, for any miners would have several more precious feet to burrow—dangerous, precarious feet. These construction efforts had encouraged Nate to dig with even more determination and zeal when he had spent an hour underground that morning.

He wound through the now-familiar labyrinth of tangled shelters on the north slope, across Market Street, and to his shebang. Whitmore lay motionless on the filthy ground. Billy crouched next to the dying fire, hunched over a tin of beans for which Nate had traded that morning. They were wormy, but after boiling, the worms drifted to the surface.

Nate sat on his haunches between Billy and Whitmore, could say nothing for a time. He thought of the long, painful, hungry days they had shared, remembered the day they had met and how suspicious Jonas Whitmore had been of him. To think Whitmore and Billy had managed to survive imprisonment since Gettysburg, more than a year ago now, astonished Nate every time he considered it. He knew Ryan deserved much of the credit.

Billy gestured with the tin cup toward Whitmore. "Won't eat."

In frustrated disappointment, Nate sighed and silently bemoaned his inability to sustain these men as Ryan had. A foolish derision, he knew, for nothing short of a miracle could save Whitmore and Billy now. "C'mon, Whit," he said. "You can get down a couple beans, aye?"

The puffy gray eyes rolled up at him. Slowly he shook his head.

Nate chided, "A wee bit ungrateful, wouldn't you say? I traded me hat for them, after all."

A grotesque version of a smile twitched one corner of Whitmore's distorted lips. The sorry state of his mouth and swollen throat made speech a chore.

"You gotta keep your strength, Whit, 'cause Sherman's gonna be here soon. The Army of the Cumberland will save you Potomac lads. We always was worth more'n you paper-collar soldiers."

In the past, such baiting remarks had brought forth a heated war of words, but now Whitmore just smiled once more and closed his eyes.

Nate rested a hand on his friend's shoulder, gathered his strength, and quietly said, "'Tis time for me to leave, lads."

Billy sidled next to Nate, tipped his head in an effort to see his downturned face. "Leave?" He wheezed on the word, coughed.

Whitmore gradually opened his eyes. He reached up a withered hand to touch Nate's breast pocket.

Nate smiled unsteadily. "Aye. Your family's address is inside me Bible, Whit." He tried to laugh. "Ain't never been to Detroit. Farm boy like me will get lost. I'll need you with me, show me the big city. You and Cowboy both."

As if not hearing, Whitmore tapped the pocket again, then his hand fell back to the ground as lightly as a feather shed from a bird. Nate picked it up, held it in both of his. Whitmore nodded and closed his eyes.

Billy asked, "You've got my family's address, too, right?"

"Aye." With reluctance, he stood. "You can move in with Jared and the lads. I already talked to 'em about it. They'll help you out best they can."

Standing, Billy said, "Don't worry none about us. You just get back to God's Country."

Nate looked down at Whitmore, then back to Billy, who tried gamely to hold his composure. "Take care of each other, Cowboy."

"Always have, Little Brother." He produced a wan smile.

A lump strangled Nate, and he knew he could not say another word, so instead he embraced Billy, held onto him as he swallowed his tears. He knew he would never see them again.

CHAPTER 29

Night within, night without. The tight, suffocating tunnel filled Nate's nostrils with the dank smell of earth and the sour odor of filthy men, and nearly drove him mad for want of air. Impatient, he squirmed forward on his belly into El Schreiber's bare feet directly in front of him, hidden in the blackness. Schreiber could not move forward even if he wanted to, for his three fellow Pennsylvanians lay ahead of him; Nate had been relegated to last because the others had all labored upon the tunnel longer than he. Though he knew he should maintain silence, Nate softly called forward to urge the first man on, for surely he would be breaking through the surface any minute now. The others fearfully shushed him. Nate clawed at the dirt beneath him, terrified he would lose control if not free of this burrow soon. He fought against the voice inside his head that whispered doubts and warnings. *Go back. This is craziness. You'll get shot. You'll be buried alive. Go back to Jonas and Billy. You should never have left them, you selfish coward.*

A flow of wonderful fresh air burst down the tunnel, drew a gasp from all of them. Nate drank in the teasing waves that slipped past the men in front of him. Freedom…freedom! He had never realized freedom had a scent to it, a powerful, intoxicating scent. Unwittingly he shoved himself against his comrade again, lured by the night air.

"Hold on, Nate," El whispered. "Can't climb through me."

An eternity passed before they inched forward like earthworms. He held his breath, knowing the first Pennsylvanian had sprinted into the night. No gunshot to signify a guard's discovery. A torturous moment later they wriggled forward again. The second man must have gone now. Another halt. Nate knew he would surely lose his mind. Just up ahead. The blackness thinned, and the third man went. Nate thought he could feel the earth tremble ever so slightly as the Easterner bolted.

"Good luck, El," he whispered when his friend's turn arrived.

As Schreiber inched up the gentle grade, Nate could see beyond him. Night. Dark but not as dark as this snake's hole. Sweet, cool air. Though not free of the pen's stench, the gentle wafts were an improvement nonetheless, and surely the farther away he got…

A shout, the crack of a gun, a cry of pain from Schreiber. Dear God, no…no…he was so close!

Frantically Nate clawed his way upward. More shouts. He had little time before whomever had shot Schreiber could reload. Other guards on the fence line would be turned this way, drawn by the commotion. Only the darkness could save him now.

He hauled himself from the hole. Shadowy figures wavered several rods in front of him, one man on the ground. Calling on all his meager strength, he darted away from them, angling off to the right. More shots, wild this time; frightened guards blazing away at a mere ghost. More oaths and shouts, ordering him to halt, but he ran on, stumbled, kept going. He zig-zagged among hundreds of tree stumps north of the stockade, onward toward a black wall of forest ahead.

Slashing his way into the protective trees, underbrush scratched at him from top to bottom as he blindly crashed along. Were the others ahead of him? No time to pause and hazard calling out. Had to keep moving. Perhaps he had even run past them. Roots and fallen limbs tripped him up, pained his feet, but he kept going. On and on, deeper into the marshy forest, slowing only when exhaustion finally burned through his excitement. His lungs ached. His breath came in frighteningly loud rasps. His legs wobbled like rubber stilts, dragging him down to a jog until at last he slumped against a tree.

Gasping and trembling, he sank to the loamy ground, sick and lightheaded, retching up what little water he had drunk before entering the tunnel. He tried to hear beyond his breathing and pounding heartbeat, to detect pursuit or perhaps the Pennsylvanians. Closing his eyes, he took in one long breath, paused then slowly exhaled. He opened his eyes, listened again. Nothing but the creak of crickets and the faint breeze in the pine tops—a beautiful, lulling voice, so different from the constant noise of the pen.

He took in great gulps of air. No stench. Free. He was free! Nothing around him but trees, wonderful trees to hide him, trees that would provide merciful shade, trees that lived and breathed. Alive. He was alive here amidst these benevolent giants with their perfumed scent. They would protect him.

The sudden sharp bay of a hound catapulted him to his feet, chilled his blood. Turner and his pack—Turner who rode a mule and carried a pistol. The echoing voices of the dogs, still very distant, sent panic into his brain, and he fled deeper into the forest. Stars peeked through the clouds above, and he used their marks to turn eastward, in the direction of the Flint River some five miles distant, a waterway that he had been told would lead him northward. Water. How he longed for it, to drink, to lose his scent in it.

The weakness of his body overpowered his will, and after less than a mile, he slowed to a brisk walk. Strength drained out of him like blood from an open vein. The lightheadedness persisted, compromised his balance, sent him stumbling into trees and over logs. The loss of stamina gave way to despair. How would he ever make it to the river? True, he could not hear the dogs—perhaps they had picked up the scent of one of the others—but, hounds or no hounds, he needed to keep moving, to put as much distance between himself and the stockade as possible. He could not go back; he would rather die alone in this wilderness than endure another minute there.

On and on, a dragging trot the best he could manage, his feet cut and bleeding. He choked and coughed, tried to find more air for his searing lungs. He stumbled and fell. *Get up. Get up*! But he lay there, clung to the cool dirt and pine needles, wanted to stay there, wanted to sleep. *So damned thirsty. Have to make it to the river. Can't go back. Never see Katie again.* The thought of his fiancée rallied him to his feet and pushed him on.

The hot night air offered less and less oxygen, fought against his efforts to breathe. His vision waned, darkness crowding in like a curtain to shut out the world. He halted, leaned against a tree, waited, moved on, his gait now even slower. A tree. Maybe, if he could get high enough, Turner and the hounds would miss him. No, the dogs would know. Besides, he lacked the strength to climb. Trees…climbing trees. Lieutenant Marsh climbing that tree for General Negley near Davis's Crossroads. Davis's Crossroads, where James Ensign of Company A had been captured. Ensign…the ring for his father…

The ground rolled gently downward. Nate tripped and fell onto his face, one arm outstretched. The tips of his fingers felt…wet. Barely able to lift his head, he thought he detected a faint shine of pooled water at the base of a tree just beyond his reach. Groaning with the effort, he tried to rise to his hands and knees, but the curtain returned, made the night oily and thick, the buzz in his head now a roar. Water. His tongue touched his lips. A drink. A sip. He willed the puddle closer, but the blackness pushed him down into a deep, dry pit.

***

Nate floated on a cloud. One of those tall, billowy ones that skated across an August sky in Michigan, the ones he used to watch from atop a haystack, resting at noon with a sandwich and a bucket of cold water. It felt wonderful, that cloud. Light and airy, higher and higher, surrounded by rich azure sky. Cottony and feather soft. The wind played with his clean hair. He smiled, drifted onward, wondered where it would take him.

The harsh call of a crow intruded upon his dream, drew him back down to earth. Gradually he awoke. Was he back in the pen? No, trees above him, and beyond their towering reaches a blue sky stretching away. No clouds to sail upon. Morning. How long had he been unconscious?

Water. The pool was there in front of him; he had not simply dreamt it. Greedily he cupped his hands and scooped the water up to his lips. Stagnant and foul-tasting; he drank, nonetheless.

The faraway cry of a hound sent a lightning bolt of fear throughout his sore body. Without thinking, he hugged the tree next to the puddle for protection, listened to make sure his hearing had not played him false. There, another deep-throated bay, off to the west. How far was the river? Considering how short his headlong run from the tunnel, the river would still be a fair distance, indeed a great distance for someone in his condition. But what other choice did he have?

He lurched to his feet, using the tree for balance. Hunger made his head swim, but he pushed away from the tree and started out as fast as possible.

His bare, battered feet fell on soft, mossy ground still damp from the recent storms. Now the ringing howl of more than one dog echoed in the swampy forest. What meager strength had been gained from his rest quickly drained away. He stumbled again and again until finally he fell. With difficulty he raised himself on hands and knees, choked on dirt and coughed. Get up! *Get up!*

Somehow he managed to rise and scramble onward with staggering strides. The hounds gained ground, the forest seeming to shake with their cries. The blat of a cow horn wailed above the dogs' voices. He had been a fool to believe he could get far from the prison. He never should have left Jonas and Billy.

After a short distance, the ground turned even soggier. Cypress and tupelo trees—gnarled, moss-draped specters—rose out of shallow swamp water ahead. If he could squeeze out a little more energy, one last time… The hounds drew ever nearer. Their baying pitched upward in a frenzy, for now they could see their quarry quite plainly. Nate knew his folly was at an end, but at least he would not die in the pen; he had denied them that, had defied them as Ryan would have wanted. His gaze swung from tree to tree in search of a low branch; he wanted to get beyond the reach of the dogs, for he did not want to die that way. A bullet would be better.

Into the knee-deep water he splashed. He glanced back, saw Turner's mule crash through the underbrush, its rider cursing. The pack milled about, crying at the water's edge. Turner reined in the sweated mule and reached for his revolver.

"Here now, you damned Yankee! Halt or I'll shoot!"

Nate pressed on, Turner's oaths ringing through the air. A second warning. *Maybe*, he thought fuzzily, *I* can *get away. Maybe Turner won't shoot me in the back, won't come into the swamp.*

The pistol cracked. Its bullet slammed into his left shoulder, spun him around like a horse's kick. The trees, the sky...all whirled around him. Crows protested and flew upward, wings beating, flying away, away. Water swallowed him, bathed shredded flesh. The taste of blood in the water. He let go, went under.

***

James heard a noise from somewhere nearby, like the careful closing of a door or window, like the gentle touch his mother had used to shut his bedroom door after tucking him into bed at night. The memory made him dismiss the quiet sound, curled up and warm among the layers of musty old straw in the deserted stall. Rain beat on the sagging roof, leaked at the opposite end of the abandoned barn. It felt wonderful to be out of the weather; how many months had it been? Not since that tiny cabin he, Nate, and the others of his mess had constructed near Rossville last winter. His Missionary Ridge wound ached, his whole body battered and run down by his constant travel.

He had been on the move since yesterday morning's confrontation at the smokehouse. Although he had not detected any pursuers, he was not foolish enough to believe that the farmer had not alerted whatever authorities operated in this region. So he had pushed on all day yesterday and all of last night. He had to be within a few miles of the prison, just down the railroad tracks. When the rain began to fall, he had taken the chance of entering this rickety barn and burying himself in the straw to rest before moving on, to think further upon his plans, plans that he could no longer delay in forming. But before his thoughts had progressed far, blissful sleep claimed him. Sleep, where dreams came easily, pleasant dreams of home and friends; the war was not allowed in.

"Git up!"

Pain in James's ribs awakened him. He jerked to a sitting position, reached instinctively for his musket. Gone! A double-barreled shotgun and a pistol leveled on him from only a couple of feet away where two surly civilians glowered at him, one having shouldered James's musket. The taller and homelier man—young, with a patch over one eye—looked as afraid as he did cantankerous, a potentially lethal combination. The other, probably in his forties, appeared sturdy and determined, ready to shoot with the least provocation.

"Stand up," the latter snarled.

With his hands aloft, James got to his feet, desperately searching for some avenue of escape, but the men stood between him and the open stall door. The older man's attention took in the blood stains upon James's pants.

"Reckon we got our boy, Calvin."

James attempted to mirror the man's Georgian accent. "This is some kinda mistake."

"No mistake, Yank. Springfield rifle, blue-belly breeches, blood on 'em, just like Jake said."

"I took that rifle and these pants off a dead Yankee. I'm on a furlough; I'm headed home."

"Furlough?" the man laughed. "From what outfit?"

Mind racing, James stammered, "Cleburne's Division."

"Cleburne?" Now both men laughed. "Hain't no Georgia regiments in Cleburne's Division, Yank."

"If you're on leave," the one-eyed Calvin said, "show us your papers."

James pretended to search his pockets, face burning red with consternation, silently cursing himself.

"Mebbe he ain't a Yank," Calvin said. "Mebbe he's a deserter. I mean, why would a Yank be all the way down here? Musta deserted from one army or t'other. Reckon that gets him hanged or shot in either army."

"I—I'm not a deserter. I told you, I'm on furlough, but…my papers…they must have fallen out of my pocket."

The older man took a menacing step forward. "You ain't one of us, boy. But like Calvin reckoned, what's a Yank doin' way down here? Y'all still up by Atlanta, last we heard tell. Not from that prison neither, not carryin' that Springfield. Reckon we'll take you into town and lock you up. Let them militia boys get the truth outta you."

* * *

The town that the civilians had spoken of amounted to little more than a few shacks near a rail depot. A handful of ragtag citizens and militiamen stared at James in his blood-stained pants, most showing little more than dull curiosity as the two men prodded him along with their guns. Children ran alongside or circled him, throwing questions at both him and the two men while a nondescript dog barked excitedly at the youngsters, tail beating the air. Defeated and dejected, James kept silent, met no one's gaze, tried not to hear the derisive laughter. Unarmed, with his hands bound behind his back, he felt stripped and vulnerable.

They directed him to a shed not far from the railroad where a boy soldier—homegrown militia—stood guard. Calvin opened the door and shoved him inside. James staggered to keep his balance, stopped in the middle of the small space. The door slammed shut behind him.

A single window to his right—too small for a man to escape through—allowed weak sunlight to stream inward, its rays revealing a large black man sitting on the dirt floor in one corner, hands bound in front of him. They stared at one another for a long, silent moment, each wide-eyed and frightened. Unsure what he expected the man to do, James kept a cautious eye on him while backing away into the opposite corner of the same wall. He braced himself against the wall and slid down to sit. With the window closed, the shack stifled in the heat.

The black man furtively regarded him. His fingers moved nervously, his tongue trying to wet his full lips. James guessed him to be a runaway and realized he had nothing to fear from the slave.

"You from around these parts?" James asked.

The black man seemed surprised that James addressed him, and it took a moment for him to find his voice. "No, suh."

"Do you know where the prison is, the one they call Andersonville?"

"Why, yes, suh. I sho' do."

"Is it far from here?"

"No, suh. Not far; less than a day's walk. I he'ped build it. Lots o' slaves was taken from they massahs, like I was, and set to cuttin' trees and such. That was a long time ago. Now that place, it full o' Yankees. Stinks bad. They doin' poorly, them Yankee boys." He peered closer at James. "Is you one o' them Yankees? You got blue trousers like they wears."

299

James saw no advantage in deception, so he nodded.

"Did you run away from that prison, Mister Yankee?"

"No. I'm not from there."

Hope brightened the slave's expression. "Is the Yankees close? The ones come from up north?"

"Not close enough. Last I knew they're up by Atlanta."

"Where that?"

"A long ways away, I'm afraid." James figured the man had no idea what a mile was. Perhaps his knowledge of the entire world failed to reach beyond his master's lands. The idea that his own situation was now as dire as that of a slave gave James pause. He regarded the black man with a curious eye. "Why are you here?"

"I done runned away, but they catched me yesterday. Didn't get very far afore I got catched. Lots of folks always out a-lookin' for runaway niggers and boys what done runned away from the army." He stared mournfully at his big, calloused hands. "They's goin' to fetch me back when the next train come. Reckon they take you to that prison since you's a Yankee."

James frowned, nodded again. The slave had relaxed, and James realized he had, too. "What's your name?"

An unexpected smile appeared. "Cump. I's named the same as that Yankee general."

The slave's apparent pride amused James. "Cump Sherman, eh?"

"Yes, suh. He goin' to free the slaves when he come."

James struggled to his feet and moved to the window to survey his surroundings. The forest lay just beyond the railroad tracks. He glanced toward the door where the guard's shadow fell across the sunlight that crept beneath.

"When's the train due?"

"Cain't say. Never know no more, not since the war come."

James scowled. "So, it could be tomorrow, or it could be ten minutes from now?"

"Yes, suh."

He sighed in frustration. *Think, damn it. There has to be a way out of this. Damned if I'm going to end up in Andersonville.*

"Mister Yankee, if you ain't from that prison or them other Yankees up by Atlanta, why you here?"

James turned away from the window, drew back from the sun broiling through the glass. He studied the man, noticed a gentleness to his brown eyes, so incongruous to his hulking size. "I came here to find a friend of mine. He was captured and sent to that prison you helped build."

Cump's eyes widened. "He there?" He frowned and slowly shook his head. "Lot of them Yankees dead. I he'ped bury 'em. Dig big ditches, toss 'em in like wood. Lot of 'em didn't even have no clothes on." He curbed his words when he saw James's horrified expression, softened his tone when he continued. "You came all this way to he'p your friend?"

James sat back down, this time not far from Cump. "Yes, but now... Not sure how much help I can be to him."

"You a brave man, Mister Yankee."

James dismissed the compliment with a shake of his head. "My name's James." He stared toward the door. "I don't feel very brave, Cump. Truth be told, right now I wish I'd never left my regiment."

***

James dozed in the furnace-like heat of the shack. Sweat dripped from his hair and slipped from the end of his nose to mingle with the blood stains in his lap. He wished he could shrug out of his shirt, but his bindings prevented it. Flies buzzed and pestered, occasionally biting the back of his neck. Hunger and thirst poked at him. His canteen still held water, but it might as well be empty for the good it did him. He was vaguely aware of civilians beyond the shack. Sometimes he heard them close, no doubt staring in through the window, but he refused to open his eyes, refused to be a spectacle. Damn them all.

The rattle of the door shook him abruptly awake. A civilian entered, one he had not seen before, middle-aged and expressionless, carrying two tin plates. From the doorway the armed guard watched him set the plates on the floor, then move to untie the uncomfortable ropes from the prisoners' hands.

"No funny business, now," the man warned. "You try anything and that boy'll take your head off, hear?"

Once free of the bindings, James rubbed his sore wrists, watched the civilian back out into the sun's failing light. Before closing the door, the boyish guard grinned at James and said, "Best eat up, Yank. Won't get no victuals like that in prison."

Cump stirred and glanced from the plates to James. Stringy, undercooked beef and a small sweet potato sat upon one while the other held only bread. James scowled and proceeded to distribute the food evenly, then offered one of the plates to Cump. The slave stared at him.

"Go on, take it." The black man's astonishment made him

uncomfortable; he was no saint, for God's sake. With irritation, he added, "Don't you want it?"

"Well, I…I… Yes, suh, Mister James. I sho' do."

James sloshed the water around in his canteen to judge its quantity, then offered it to Cump. Again the slave stared, and again James did his best to ignore the reaction.

As he returned the canteen, Cump cleared his throat and wiped his lips with the back of his meaty hand. "Mister James, can you read?"

"Yes."

"You read the Bible?"

"Sometimes."

Cump reached inside his untucked shirt and produced a small book—battered, stained, and torn. "I cain't read, but mebbe you could read somethin' from this here Bible afore we eat, for a blessin'."

James took the small book, and when he opened it, three scraps of paper fluttered into his lap. He gathered them to tuck them back inside, but one of them—a battered daguerreotype—drew his attention. Why would a slave be carrying around the likeness of a young white woman? But then the familiarity of the woman's dress stopped his breathing, seemed to halt his heart in its beating. He peered closer, trying to make out facial details in the faded, crinkled image.

"Cump," he gasped. "Where did you get this picture?"

The slave remained silent, trepidation on his face once again.

James demanded, "Tell me."

"It—it was in that Bible when I—I found it."

James shuffled the pages back to the beginning, to the inside front cover. There! The small, halting hand of Mary Calhoun: *To my darling son, may Our Lord keep you always safe.* The words had all but faded. He scrambled for the scraps of paper.

"What is it, Mister James? You look like you done seen a ghost."

The first scrap had an address and a name—Jonas Whitmore. The other one had another name and Detroit address. Both written in a familiar hand.

"Where did you find this, Cump?"

"Well, suh, I…well, I…"

"Damn it, Cump, where?"

"Well, suh, truth be told, I found it on a Yankee, a li'l Yankee prisoner I tended in the hospital. Doctor say he not gonna make it, so I figgered that Yankee boy wouldn't miss that Bible."

"What was his name?"

"Don't know. Wasn't with him long."

"When? When were you with him?"

"Just t'other day. He done escaped."

"Escaped?"

"Yes, suh. But he got catched again. And shot, too. That's why he in the hospital."

"Shot?"

Cump nodded his frizzled head. "That Turner man with the dogs done shot him."

James's heart sank. "Did he die?"

"He was alive when I last saw him, before I run off."

"What did he look like?" He moved closer to Cump, and when the slave faltered, James clutched his arm, causing him to flinch. "You said he was little. How little? Show me!"

Cump stood and indicated the height.

"What color was his hair?"

"Hard sayin'. All them Yankees look the same—black hair from the pine fires."

James's frantic brain remembered Henry Damon's appearance. "What about his eyes? What color?"

"They's blue. I remember that. Had a brother, too, but he died in the prison; I loaded him on the wagon at the dead-house."

"Was his name Ryan? The dead man."

"Cain't recollect, Mister James. I's sorry."

James settled to think. Surely the wounded prisoner was Nate, for he would have no reason to give away both his Bible and Katie's picture to some other prisoner. Whose names were these, though, written on these pieces of paper? Had one of those men taken the Bible from Nate? Or perhaps Nate had sold it for food as he had sold Uncle Pat's watch. No, even if Nate had sold the Bible, he never would have forsaken his fiancée's likeness. And for Cump to mention a brother…

"Cump, you said you tended him at the hospital. Where's the hospital?"

"At the prison, outside the pen." Slowly he shook his head. "But they ain't gonna he'p him there. Folks die there."

James cursed.

A train whistle in the distance pricked their ears.

Low and foreboding, Cump said, "Here come that train for us."

With new determination, James stood close to Cump, his agitated voice near a whisper. "Listen, Cump, we have to get out of here, right now."

"But how, Mister James?"

303

James glanced at the door. He had no way of knowing if more than just the boy stood guard, and with the train's approach, the boy, if alone, would not be so for long.

He took hold of Cump's arm, said, "I have a plan."

CHAPTER 30

In trembling anticipation, Cump stood near the door, watching James. James, shaking just as much, gave him a nod of false confidence. Then, taking his canteen in hand, James used it to break one of the window's panes of glass. An instant later the guard came through the door to investigate, musket leveled. Cump's massive fist bashed the boy sideways into the far wall, senseless before he hit the floor. James confiscated the boy's cartridge and cap boxes.

"Run, Cump! For God's sake, run!"

James grabbed the musket and bolted after Cump. A woman and a child walking past the shack both screamed, drawing the attention of several men down the street. Shouts and threats charged after James as he ran. With the shriek of steel on steel, the train halted at the depot down to his left. Behind him, the woman kept bleating. He reached the tracks, leaped over them, Cump outdistancing him. Shouts from the depot now. A gunshot cracked from near the tired train. Its ball whirred past James's head, encouraging further speed from his legs, though it seemed he had already been running faster than the strongest wind. The pine forest loomed ahead of them. Once in its shadows, Cump waited for him.

"Run!" James panted. "Keep going. They'll be after us."

Cump readily obeyed, but he curbed his strides to match James's. James expected the slave to break off in another direction; instead, the black man stayed doggedly with him as they ran ever deeper into the trees.

"This way, Mister James. We go to the river. We be safe there. You'll see."

With little choice, James followed the slave eastward.

***

"Ain't far from here," Cump whispered in the darkness.

To north and south the broad, sluggish river stretched like a black ribbon before westward bends both upstream and down hid it from view. Moonlight glistened upon the surface, leaving silver marks where nature's debris had caught midstream and caused the water to swirl about it. A fine mist shrouded the shoreline and added to the heavy moisture in the warm air. The jump of a fish drew a growl of hunger from James's stomach. God only knew when he would next eat. The forests that rose on either side of the river echoed with the rhythmic chorus of night creatures, nothing more—no hounds or men's voices. They had managed to slip their pursuers some five miles back. Now it seemed as if they were the only humans alive in this vast wilderness.

After their escape, Cump had led the way to the river, and since then they had clung to the winding waterway, often taking to the river itself to mask their passing. Other times, to preserve quiet, they hurried along the marshy shoreline, speaking little. Indeed, they had only exchanged words once, shortly after reaching the river. At the time, James had expected Cump to leave him and strike northward to freedom, but to his shock the slave insisted on guiding him southward. When James had protested, Cump's reply had come with no hesitation: "You he'ped me get free from them folk. I'll he'p you find your friend, see if he alive still. Can always run away after." He had offered a brave grin.

The slave's charity had kept James's mind spinning for some time as they traveled. His experience with blacks had been limited to the servants in the Eleventh Michigan and to the contraband who found their way into Union lines during the campaigns. Henry Damon, he recalled, had talked about slaves who had helped him on his journey from Andersonville, and James wondered now if Cump had been one of them or perhaps one of his kin. What compelled them to assist their masters' enemy? Doing so earned them nothing more than thanks from those they helped, and it surely put them in great danger if discovered. James could imagine what would happen to Cump if he were found not only as a fugitive but as an accomplice to escaped Yankee prisoners. He watched the slave lumbering onward before him—seemingly tireless, his dark skin blending with the night—and felt immense gratitude and admiration. And immeasurable relief that he was no longer alone.

Cump halted and crouched at the edge of the river to cup his hands and drink. James did the same, refilling his canteen.

Softly Cump said, "You ain't gonna be safe since it gonna be daylight soon. I take you to a safe place. You can stop there while I go to the prison hospital."

"If Nate's still there, how will you get him out?"

Cump's white teeth glowed in the night. "You leave that to me, Mister James. I knows my way 'round."

"Won't they recognize you as a runaway?"

"We niggers all look the same to the white man. That's what they tell me. I can get in and out, and no one will know nothin'."

James frowned. "You don't have to do this, Cump. It's too dangerous. There must be a way that I can go instead."

"Oh, no, suh. You'd end up in prison yourself. Best this way." Cump's tone had taken on a stubborn quality. "I get that li'l Yankee boy out. Now, we best get along."

They left the river, travelling west for about a mile in the woods. James's nerves tightened even more, and Cump grew more cautious, stopping often to listen. Soon James saw the small, dark shape of a shack ahead. Vines crawled up its sides, and gray-green moss hunched in clumps on the sagging roof. Fire had blackened the structure and damaged the back wall but had not demolished it. James was unable to tell what the building had once been, but it had obviously been deserted for some time, which gave him some confidence in Cump's strategy.

"You hide here," Cump ordered as they hurried inside. "If somebody come, you go to the river and hide; I'll find you. I don't know how long it'll take me to get your friend, but I'll try to get him out afore mornin'. And that ain't far away."

"His name is Nate Calhoun."

Cump smiled. "Like Nathan in the Bible? Massuh's li'l girl, she used to read the Bible to us. Her pa didn't know. Used to read 'bout Nathan in the Book of Samuel."

James smiled at the slave's enthusiasm, hopeful that the black man would remember Nate's name. But he quickly sobered. "Cump, you don't have to do this. I can find another way."

"No, suh. No other way. Don't fret." He grinned wider. "I's the soul o' caution."

***

Nate knew he was dying, but he no longer cared. He drifted far away from the stench and moans and screams of the makeshift hospital—a small stockade built outside the southeast corner of the main prison, between Stockade Creek and the branch of another creek to the south. Dying would take days, he figured, just like with Ryan, but sooner or later he would have a place on the dead-wagon. Then he would be reunited with his brothers and all his friends who had died in this damned war. He should have listened to his parents; he should never have left Burr Oak. At least he had not married, so now Katie would not be a widow like Heather Cabot. James. James would be there for her when he returned to Burr Oak.

His wound burned with the power of a branding iron, but there was no medicine with which to adequately treat him. In fact, since he had been dumped here, no one had touched or spoken to him except a slave. Nate had asked for Father Whelan when he had first arrived, but if the priest had come, he had been unaware of the visit. The doctor was waiting for him to die and free up his meager space for some foolish wretch waiting at the south gate who thought the hospital held a cure. Hundreds lay around him, some under tent flies, some on pine straw, some with nothing at all for protection or comfort, all crowded together like cordwood. Some died in silence, others howled themselves voiceless. Others spoke in their own world of hallucination, as clear and dreamy as if well. He had heard them all yesterday, but tonight he traveled to distant places, far away from these horrors.

A gentle, whispery, deep voice drifted to him. "Nathan?"

Only his parents called him that and only when angry, but this time the voice lacked anger. *Did I sleep late? Did I forget to water the horses again? Did I forget the cow? Hell, 'tis Joseph's turn to milk the damned cow; I'm certain.*

"Nathan Calhoun."

"I'm here, Da'."

Arms worked beneath him. Something coarse covered him. He squirmed in discomfort.

"Too warm, Da'."

"Shh," breathed against his ear as he was lifted. His father must be afraid of waking his mother; she was abed with fever ever since hearing Matthew had been wounded at Gaines' Mill.

Nate wondered why his father carried him. He could walk just fine, had never been sick a day in his life. Well, not until Andersonville. But that was not life. So many other boys in the Eleventh Michigan had died, especially at the start of the war—died of disease, not bullets, died before ever seeing battle, for many had never been exposed to the illnesses that flourished in army camps. He remembered Ryan's letters from Kentucky where scores of Michigan boys died in camp and in the hospitals early on in their enlistments.

A gruff voice halted them. Nate tried to recognize the voice, did not try too hard, nestled deep inside the blanket, against his father's strong chest.

Another voice answered the first. Sounded like a black man. "Looky here. I has this beautiful gold ring. You let me pass, I give it to you."

A ring. A gold one. James Ensign had given him one...to take home. Wouldn't get there now. Where was it? They had removed his rag of a shirt when he came to the hospital, probably stole the ring, the Bible, Katie's picture.

"Katie!"

Again the soft voice hushed him. The blanket covered his head.

His father tripped, jarred his shoulder, drawing a weak moan. He wished his parent would stop. Maybe he was taking him home. Home, like Ryan had said. He could die there in his mother's arms, hear her voice, smell her clean skin, remember the music and dancing.

"Halt!"

Now whose voice? Sounded angry, shrill, like one of those damned Georgia Reserves.

"What're you doin' out here, boy? What you got there?"

Nate never wanted to hear another Southern voice, especially now because it tugged his father's image away from him. He hoped no one in heaven spoke with a Southern accent.

"My boy is bad sick," the thick voice replied. "Come to look for a doctor; cain't find one."

"Put him down. Lemme look at him."

Hard ground beneath Nate. No...he wanted to remain in his father's arms, to feel that protective embrace. What if he set him down and forgot him? Nate groaned, tried to protest, his tongue thick and uncooperative. The scratch of a match, the scent of sulfur. A presence hovered near, bent over him, a hand on the blanket.

"Blood! What in tarnation—"

A thud, a grunt. The presence evaporated. Something heavy struck the ground next to him.

"Da'!"

"It all right, Nathan. He won't be tellin' no one 'bout us."

The security of the strong arms, the hard feel of his father's chest. Nate smiled and sighed, relaxed deep into the blanket, drifted.

He smelled the sea, the breeze wafting over him from Lough Swilly, ruffling the blanket about his ears. A pony that belonged to one of the O'Neill boys had thrown him and broken his arm. With no doctor for miles around, his father had to carry him—the Calhoun family had no wagon or team—three hours to Letterkenny. The rough journey seemed endless to Nate, but he did not want to cry in front of his father.

"Tell me a story, Da'," he whispered. "A funny one. Tell me."

Darkness rolled in, fell over them, tore away the image of his father on the windswept emerald hills.

* * *

James jumped to his feet at the sound of Cump softly hallooing to him from outside the cabin. He hurried out into the pink and yellow veil of morning, the darkness cast back into the forest, revealing a day far less frightening than the night. Cump crossed the small clearing, his steps quick, carrying a blanketed bundle. James's heart wilted at the sight— this prisoner was too small, smaller even than Nate. Cump, his face etched with concern, brushed past him into the shack.

"He doin' poorly, Mister James. Talkin' crazy-like, too."

"But, Cump—"

"It's all right. I knows someone what can he'p."

Carefully Cump set the prisoner down in one corner, and when the tattered blanket fell away from the boy's face, James gasped. The prisoner's blackened hair stuck out in every direction, tangled and glued by pitch, filthy and long. A thin mustache and peach-fuzz beard shadowed his smudged face. His eyes were closed, lips cracked and swollen. A blood-encrusted bandage covered his left shoulder, and another bound his right side. The rest of his torso, like his face, was horribly thin, almost translucent, every rib countable. Cuts laced his bruised and bloody feet below shortened, ragged pants.

"Dear God," James breathed.

"He a sight, sho' 'nough, just like most o' them Yankees. But we fix him up."

James, frozen several feet from the unconscious waif, gestured woodenly. "But...this isn't Nate. You brought the wrong prisoner, Cump."

Dumbfounded, the slave looked between the two. "This the Yankee I done got the Bible from."

"Nate must have given it away...to this fellow."

"No, suh. In the hospital, I called, 'Nathan. Nathan Calhoun' and he done answered. Was a-carryin' on about his pa and someone named Katie."

James could not accept the slave's determined words, not while this stranger lay before him like something just exhumed from a grave.

310

"It him." Cump seemed insulted. "You stay here, Mister James. I's gonna get someone to tend this here poor boy."

James grabbed his arm before he could turn away. "You can't bring someone here; they could give us away."

"No, suh. Not this person. She won't tell. Mister James, you has to trust me."

At a loss, James frowned and looked down at the unconscious boy. Could this really be Nate? Was it truly the prisoner's appearance that deceived him? Or was he simply afraid to believe that Nate could have changed so much, so horribly, in such a short time? How was it possible? He turned back to Cump, saw the forbearance in his eyes, marveled again at what this man had risked for two strangers. That instinctive trust that he had felt in Cump back near the rail depot eased away some of his misgivings and natural suspicion, making him almost ashamed, especially considering the continued risks the slave was ready to assume.

"Cump, I told you, you don't have to do this."

The slave gave him an appreciative nod and said, "I be back soon's I can."

As James watched him hurry back into the western forest, he admired the black man's ability to still function after the arduous miles they had traveled. For his own part, James felt near collapse.

He shuffled over to where Nate lay crumpled in the corner. A part of him still did not believe Cump, did not *want* to believe this half-dead skeleton had once been the boy who had boarded that Burr Oak train thirteen months ago. For several minutes he stood over him, watching the slight rise and fall of his chest. Then he sank to his haunches. Lice; good God, more than he had ever seen. If he could get Nate to the river or if he had a razor or scissors…

"Nate," he said softly, touched his arm, then tried a little louder. "Nate."

The boy's breathing paused, then his chest rose as if in a great sigh. Evenly he exhaled, and his sunken eyes fluttered, slowly opened, blinked. In fear and wonder, he stared at the near wall, frowned, blinked again.

"Nate," James whispered, stunned by the dullness of his friend's blue eyes. They were Nate's, true enough, though. Something in their very depths flickered in confused disbelief.

"James?"

Unable to speak, James nodded and took Nate's limp hand, horrified by its bony quality.

311

"James?"

Again he nodded.

"Am I dead?"

"No…no. You're safe; you're free."

"Free?" His attention slid around the shack. "Sherman?"

James shook his head.

"Where are we?"

"We're holed up a ways from the prison. Cump went to fetch someone who can tend to your wound, someone he trusts."

"Cump?"

"He's the slave that tended you in the hospital before he escaped." James produced Nate's Bible. "He and I got caught by some Rebs north of here, but we escaped. He had your Bible."

Nate reached with trembling fingers, drew the Bible to his chest in a weak embrace. He closed his eyes for a moment, murmured, "How did you get here?"

"Found my way down from Atlanta; followed the railroad. Henry Damon told me about it. He made it all the way back to the regiment."

Nate's eyes widened. "Hank made it?"

"He did. Told us all about Andersonville. That's when I knew I had to get you out of there."

"You came…all this way…for me?"

Self-conscious, he shrugged. "Well, I'm the one who got you into this mess, aren't I?"

Nate tried to reply but choked and began to cough, the effort paling him and leaving him quietly gasping and spent. Still he clung to the Bible. The boy's utter helplessness left James deeply concerned and doubtful that they would ever be able to get away from this place alive.

***

Several hours passed and the sun rose high. The shack stayed relatively cool in the shade of the tall, thick trees, but soon the heat and humidity would penetrate even there. James briefly heard the distant baying of hounds and sat close to Nate's sleeping form with the musket across his lap, terrified, but the sounds faded, and he did not hear them again. He prayed that the dogs had not been tracking Cump.

Before Nate had drifted back into unconsciousness, James helped him drink from his canteen. When the cool liquid touched the boy's throat, Nate made a small, satisfied sound and reached to tip the canteen back even more, spilling some of the water in the process. James had to pry the canteen away from him before he could empty it. Then Nate had vomited some of the water before groaning in disappointment and falling back asleep.

James shredded the upper half of his underclothes to use as rags and bandages. He cleaned Nate's wounds the best he could, drawing soft, unconscious complaints from his patient. It appeared that the ball had entered below Nate's left shoulder and exited through his right side. There was no telling how much damage it had wrought during its travels, but perhaps Nate had been lucky. If he had been healthy at the time and received proper care, he might already be recovering, but his weakened condition had compromised such ability.

"Let's get you out of these lousy rags," he said, continuing a one-sided dialogue to settle his nerves. "I'll fix you up with my drawers. Better than nothing. They'll be too big, but they're in a sight better shape."

As carefully as possible, James removed Nate's pants, then he took the rags outside and buried them. Upon his return, he soaked some of the remaining strips of cloth and tried to clean the grime from Nate's skin.

In his unconscious haze, Nate murmured, "Leave me 'lone, Cowboy. I done washed already."

Afterward James gathered pine straw to use as bedding, but he knew Nate would need more than a soft bed and tended wounds to make the long trek north. Food and plenty of it would be required, but where would they find that? Using the musket to hunt would be too dangerous, for the noise of its discharge could very well compromise them. They could fish the river under the cover of night if only they had something to use.

Afternoon heat worked its way into the shack, wearing away James's resolve to stay awake. Even his hunger failed to convince his eyelids to remain open. He was unaware that he had drifted off until he awoke in near darkness with a start, Cump calling softly to him from across the shack.

James hurried over to where the slave stood just inside the doorway, an arm around a short, slightly overweight, wizened black woman holding a carpetbag. Age hunched her back beneath a frayed green shawl. Her hair, almost completely gray, was pulled away from her blunt features. Suspicious brown eyes flecked with gray regarded James from under a low brow.

Fatigue tempered Cump's smile. "Mister James, this be Lizzie. She raised me from a boy when they sold my mamma. Lizzie, this be

313

my Yankee friend Mister James."

Not sure how to properly greet a black woman, James bowed his head slightly. "Pleased to meet you, ma'am."

Lizzie cocked one wiry eyebrow, then gave a shallow curtsey.

Cump's gaze reached across the shack. "How's that li'l Nathan?"

"Asleep. I've done what I can for him."

"Don't fret, Mister James. Lizzie can make anything better—white folk, colored folk, horses, dogs."

The woman slipped from beneath Cump's protective arm and glided to Nate. She stood above him, expression softening with pity, then knelt and rummaged through the bag. James crouched next to her, reluctant to trust someone who appeared so discontented with her situation. She made a slight grunt deep in her throat, then said, "Go 'way from here, boy. I takes care of him."

James refused to move until her gaze revealed a crack in her stubborn wall, exposing genuine solicitude and assurance. He considered the risk she, like Cump, was taking to be here and knew he owed her respect at least. Perhaps she could, after all, help Nate. There certainly were no alternatives left him. So, at last, he slowly retreated across the room to where Cump sat just inside the doorway, his watchful eyes on the forest.

From a haversack brought with him, Cump offered James a roasted ear of corn. "We brung some truck with us, as much as I could fit in this here poke. Lizzie will bring us more tomorrow."

Eagerly James took the corn, glanced toward the woman bent over Nate. "She didn't want to come, did she?"

Cump rubbed his chin thoughtfully. "Well, it took some talkin' but she come; couldn't *make* her come. Few can *make* Lizzie do what she don't wanna do now that she old and Massuh not make her work no more, 'cept for tendin' the sick. She thinks I's a fool for comin' back here and he'pin' you Yankees. She say too many colored folk gettin' in trouble he'pin' Yankees. She ain't mad; just seems like it 'cause that's how she hides her frettin'."

James bit into the corn. "Did you run into trouble?"

"Just once. Some sojers. But I hunkered down and set a spell."

A weak outcry from Nate raised James's head, nearly brought him to his feet, but Cump rested a restraining hand on his arm.

"He tolerable, Mister James. Just stay outta Lizzie's way. She know what she's doin'."

James hesitated, then relaxed again. In silence he finished the corn before washing it down with cool, fresh water from a bladder Cump

314

handed him. He watched Lizzie as she worked over Nate.

"She's right, you know," James murmured.

"'Bout what?"

"You shouldn't be here. You should head out north on your own, find Sherman's men. The longer you stay here with us, the more dangerous it'll be for you. Even when we can leave, Nate won't be able to travel fast. We could still get caught. You should go."

"That wouldn't be right, me leavin' now. You saved me from that militia. I wanna he'p you. I'll go when you go."

"It'd be bad enough if you were caught on your own, but if they catch you helping an escaped prisoner, it'll be even worse for you. I don't want that on my conscience."

"I wants to he'p." Cump sighed in frustration. "All you boys fightin' to free us slaves. I figure I owe y'all a debt. That's why others have he'ped prisoners escape. We's in this together. I'll get my freedom, Mister James, and I'll do it gettin' you and Nathan back where you belong."

Now it was James's turn to sigh. He considered confessing that his motives for enlisting had nothing to do with slavery, but he decided for Nate's sake to allow Cump his illusions. Perhaps, considering all that Cump and this woman were risking for them, he should have thought about eradicating the evil of slavery as much as the preservation of the Union when he had enlisted. Maybe the abolitionists were justified in their cause.

"You get some sleep now, Mister James. I'll watch out for anyone comin'."

"No, I already slept a little, so I'll take the first watch."

Cump looked skeptical, as if afraid James would yet interfere with Lizzie's ministrations.

"You heard me," James said and reached for the musket at his side.

CHAPTER 31

Nate could hear her, sometimes near, sometimes far…his mother. He was certain of her presence, even though the voice lacked resemblance. No Donegal lilt; instead, thick Southern. He blamed the falseness of his ears on the war. Occasionally he heard his mother's true voice but only in dreams. The other times…not quite dreams, yet he could not say he was awake either, for he saw nothing more than fleeting blurs of dark colors. No matter how he tried to regain full consciousness he remained lost somewhere between the two worlds. One a world of pain and feverish heat, of burning thirst. He tried to talk to his mother, but his thick tongue got in the way, and he was unsure if anything intelligible ever made it beyond his lips. Her gentle touch soothed him, cleansing his wounds, wiping his face, helping him drink. Now and then he heard a man's voice in the background, deeper than his father's, but he was sure it truly was his father. Of course he would be there, silently worrying over him.

Often he heard James, and he wondered how James had gotten home from the war. After all, his enlistment still had two years left, or until the end of the war, whichever came first, if it ever ended. James had gone to Andersonville. Or had he dreamt that? Surely James had not left the regiment just to save him. That would be pure madness. James had expressed responsibility for his capture; well, that was plain foolishness, too. *After all, I was the one who insisted on going back to the field hospital for Brian.*

Brian. Sometimes Nate saw his face, heard his voice, or heard Ryan. But no matter how much he desired them to be real, he knew otherwise. He tried to tell his parents about their dead sons, but always his mother hushed him, her finger sometimes resting against his lips. Perhaps it was best if she did not know.

He heard James reading to him from the Bible, sometimes the Gospels, sometimes the Psalms. A puzzling prospect, for Nate could not remember James ever reading from the Bible. In fact, whenever he or one of the other boys in their squad read from scripture, James had often left the circle, gone away from the fire into the darkness. During the Atlanta campaign, however, Nate had noted how James usually remained to listen, though he feigned indifference, gazing off at one thing or another during the reading. But Nate knew he listened, and he hoped the words gave his friend comfort. How pleased he was to have his Bible returned. He had thought the Rebels had stolen it from him, but James had said a slave had it—Cump, the one who had taken care of Ryan.

It was the smell of fried fish that finally pulled him from drifting sleep, that ethereal, timeless world, pulled him away from the wavering visions of family, away from his home, back to the shack where he had last seen James hovering over him. A welcomed, miraculous sight Nate would never forget. In his unconscious state, he had often questioned the reality of James's appearance, of his own liberty, but now as his eyes slid open, he saw James settling next to him, the still-sizzling fish upon a small board in his hand.

A broad, relieved smile broke through James's thin growth of beard. "Cump," he called over his shoulder. "He's awake."

A large black man lumbered over from across the shack, a bright smile upon his face. As Nate began to take everything in, he recognized the kindly face of the slave whom he knew from the prison. But how had he ended up here with James?

"Well, looky here," Cump marveled, bending down on one knee near James. "I told you that fish would wake him. But recollect what Lizzie say—can't give him more'n a mouthful at a time else he get sick."

Nate became aware of his own cleanliness. It weighed upon him like a new suit of clothes. He wore a shirt now, also clean, one that hung like a curtain about his rail thin form and its bandages, his left arm immobilized in a makeshift sling. The pine straw beneath him smelled spicy and fresh. The folded quilt that served as his pillow also smelled as if it had just been taken from a clothesline where it had absorbed a wonderful breeze. The pain from the gunshot had diminished considerably; the sharpness came only when he tried to raise himself on his elbows.

"Lay still," James cautioned. "Don't want to set things bleeding again."

"I thought I was home."

"Afraid not."

Nate's attention shifted to the fish, his mouth watering. "How long have I been here?"

"Two days."

"By the prison?"

"For now, until you're stronger."

The terror he had felt the night he escaped crept back, urging him to get up, but James's hand restrained him, and his own weakness shocked him.

"You're not going anywhere, Nate. Now, just lie back and I'll mash up this fish for you. Might not agree with you, though, so we'll take it slow."

His solicitude distracted Nate's appetite. "You shouldn't be here. You and Cump should go."

"I didn't come all this way just to leave you behind. End of discussion. Eat this."

James set the makeshift plate in Nate's lap and helped him sit partway up. Nate felt lightheaded, but he was too intent on the fish to pay much heed. The bandage pulled on his right side when he lifted that hand to the plate. With shaking fingers, he scooped up some of the mashed catfish and shoved it into his mouth, barely chewing, knowing to do so would irritate his sore gums, but amazingly that discomfort was gone.

"Lizzie got some lemon juice in you. Said it'll stop the scurvy. And there's onion mixed in that fish."

Nate nodded, eyes closed in savoring delight. "Thank you, James. Dear God, thank you both." He considered Cump's pleased expression. "You shouldn't stay here. If James wants to stay, reckon I can't keep him from doin' anything else, but you—"

"He's coming with us," James said. "We've already talked it over. He can go home with you, back to Burr Oak. He can work for your father or mine, one way or another."

Nate saw by Cump's smile and eager nod that the slave could not be more satisfied with the arrangement. If getting Cump to Michigan proved difficult, perhaps he could join the black servants with the Eleventh Michigan. And though most of the men in the regiment did not subscribe to the fiery opinion of abolitionists in the East, they still treated the servants kindly. Nate shared his parents' viewpoint as a Christian that slavery was morally wrong, but that was as far as his concerns went. Yet here he sat with one, as much a fugitive, as much a man deprived of all rights and freedoms. The similarity of their situation and Cump's courage left him speechless and ashamed of his former apathy to the plight of slaves.

He returned his attention to the fish, which he quickly devoured, then looked for more.

"That's enough for now." James removed the board, and Cump hurried forward with a tin cup. Chicken broth. Nate nearly swooned at the wonderful scent. To his chagrin, James insisted on spooning it into him, explaining, "The less you move the better."

Cump supported him while James fed him. The lukewarm broth came in the same conservative portion as the fish, much to Nate's disappointment. And asking for more got him nowhere.

"Who's this Lizzie you keep mentionin'?"

"She done raised me from a boy, Mister Nathan. She powerful good when it come to mendin' folk. I brung her to he'p you."

"Where is she now? I'd like to thank her."

"She come back tomorrow to check on you and bring us more victuals. She'll be pleased to see you awake."

Nate hesitated, for he did not want to sound ungrateful, but the overpowering fear of recapture pushed him to ask, "You ain't afraid of her bein' followed?"

"She come at night now. Safer thataway."

Frowning, Nate lay back against the folded quilt.

"Don't worry," James said in an apologetic tone. "We'll get out of here as soon as we can, but you need your strength first. Hard telling what we'll run into on our way back to our lines."

Nate nodded, wished he felt confident and unafraid, wished these two men were not in this precarious position for his sake. "How far away do you think we are?"

"Hard telling. I probably came about a hundred miles. Maybe by now Sherman's taken Atlanta. Maybe they're closer to us now." James told him about Stoneman's failed raid and the fighting around Atlanta.

"How is it with the boys, before you left, I mean?"

The shadow that immediately commanded James's eyes, the way his friend avoided his gaze gave Nate a chill, and the explanation that followed was little more than fiction, he suspected. But he accepted James's vague answers, knowing his friend was concerned that bad news might further damage his precarious health. There would be time later to learn the truth. Besides, if the truth was indeed as painful as he figured, perhaps delaying the news would indeed be for the best. Since Ryan's death, his emotional endurance had all but failed him. And as James said, he would need every scrap of strength he could muster for their flight northward.

"Langdon's dead."

James spoke the words long after Nate had thought his narrative at an end, surprising him. There was no triumph in his statement, only tired relief. James stared between his drawn-up knees at the charred floor. His blond hair, long and dark with sweat, veiled his gray eyes. Absently James moved one foot, stirring a faint burned odor. Nate hesitated, curious but uncertain whether to ask for elaboration. Cump's broad brow furrowed, and his gaze sought Nate's as if for reassurance.

"He came after me," James said at last, softly. "After I left the regiment, I mean."

"What?"

"He said he would; remember? Last year at the start of the campaign. Said if one of us deserted... Well, he knew I hadn't just deserted; he knew I was coming down here for you. So it wasn't like he was just after me. He knew by killing me he'd be killing you, too. He was set against you the minute you came into that barn last winter near Rossville." He shook his head. "You boys should've let me kill him back then. But...it's done now."

Nate thought of the young man back in that Burr Oak store, refusing credit to a farmer's son. He could barely remember those two boys, but he mourned them, just as he mourned his brothers. Would he and James ever return to Burr Oak? And if they did, how could they ever pick up their lives where they had left them a mere thirteen months ago?

"James." When his friend at last met his gaze, Nate touched his leg. "I'm glad you killed him...you and not some Johnny. 'Tis justice and what he deserved. Now maybe you can find some peace...and your father, too."

"Peace," James mused. He glanced all around them as if others stood near. "After all this, how will any of us ever find peace again?"

***

James listened to the trees dripping on the shack's roof, the leaves still shedding last night's rain. The forest steamed before his eyes where he hunkered near the doorless threshold, musket in hand. Birdsong filled the air, musical and lulling. The morning had broken without sunshine, only weak light that filtered through high gray clouds beyond the thick canopy. His eyelids drooped. Soon Cump would spell him on watch, and he could finally sleep. Even his growing anxiety could no longer keep fatigue at bay.

From the opposite side of the shack came Nate's troubled, mumbling voice. Another bad dream. The boy had too many, every time he slept. He had shared some of his prison experiences, enough to turn James's stomach and make him curse in helplessness to think of the thousands still suffering just a few miles away. When the breeze was just right, he could smell that place. At first, he had thought the stench that of a dead animal rotting somewhere near in the forest, but Cump and Nate informed him of its true origin.

Lizzie had come and gone in the night. James found himself worrying about her traveling back and forth. God only knew how many poisonous snakes and perhaps even alligators were out there amidst the swampy landscape. She was a tough old bird, though; he certainly gave her that. Thinking of her now brought a wry smile. She still would not speak to him much, but he could tell she was warming to him; she had even brought him a worn pair of pants and a battered hat. He knew her aloofness stemmed not from any personal dislike for him but instead from her adopted son's insistence on helping the two Yankees, her way of coping with a potentially lethal situation for one, if not all, of them. On the other hand, she treated Nate with something close to tenderness, like a hen with its chick, fussing over him, scolding him gruffly if he refused to eat what she prescribed and what she prescribed only. When she heard Nate had hobbled around yesterday in the moccasins she had brought, she set their ears ringing with admonishments, threatening never to come again.

An outcry from Nate awoke Cump. The boy suddenly thrashed about, and they rushed to his side.

"Nate. Nate, wake up." James shook his arm, afraid he might start yelling in his confused sleep.

Nate bolted upright, eyes wide, face dripping sweat. He gasped, "Dogs!"

"It's all right. You were dreaming."

"Mister James," Cump whispered loudly. "Listen!"

Over Nate's ragged breathing, the distant cries of dogs contrasted with the forest's serenity. They seemed to be to the west, toward the river. James had never heard them from that direction. Had they detected his scent from days ago down by the river?

Nate had a hold of his arm in a painful grip. "We have to get outta here," he desperately whispered, as if the dogs were already within sight. James had never seen such terror on his friend's face, not even during their first skirmish. Cump's eyes were as wide and wild as Nate's.

"You're not strong enough to travel," James insisted. "We have to lay low, like we have been."

"No, James. We have to go…now."

Cump wrung his hands and anxiously watched James for a decision.

Fighting his own fear, James said, "We stay here and we stay quiet."

"Mister James, sounds like they's a-comin' this way."

Nate started to use James as leverage to gain his feet, but James restrained his trembling efforts. "Cump, carry Nate over to the barrels. No more talking, hear?"

As Cump took Nate's protesting form to the northwest corner of the shack where they had previously created a barricade with four upright barrels, James scattered the pine straw bedding and shoved their rations under a loose floorboard. Nate was small enough to fit inside one of the barrels, but he would not submit.

"Damn it, Nate, get in there," James said as he rushed over, musket in hand.

"Please, Mister Nathan."

The barking drew closer, no longer faint but clear and ringing.

Nate grabbed the front of James's shirt, pulled him close. "By God, James, shoot me if you have to. I can't go back there. I won't. Promise me—"

"Damn it, Nate." James pried frantically at his fingers. "Let go and get down in there. I won't let them take you. Do you hear? Let go."

Finally, Nate acquiesced and melted down inside the barrel so Cump could secure the lid. Then James and Cump huddled in the small space between the barrels and the corner, James armed with the musket and Cump with a stout length of oak wood he had procured from the forest their first day here. Nate's fear threatened James's courage, a fear that had its own smell, its own temperature, like a winter blast. He must not let it infect him; he needed a clear head for all of them.

Focusing now on the dogs' voices, he deduced it to be a small pack. Close, very close. He could hear a man's voice now, yelling some unintelligible profanity at the canines. *We're gone up*, he thought.

"Oh, Lordy," Cump breathed before James's glare pushed him back into silence.

A moment later a mule brayed just outside the west wall. Inch by inch James slid the barrel of the musket along the top of the nearest barrel, sighted it on the doorway. To his dismay, his shaking hands made the gun waver, so he took a stronger grip, rested his cheek against the stock, closed one eye, drew in a long, sustaining breath.

An explosion of howls shook the cabin as the hounds charged

inside—a motley trio. Noses to the floor, they raced about, snuffling, whip-like tails furiously beating the air. One barked and scratched at the floorboard beneath which James had hidden the rations. The other two quickly joined him, whining and clawing.

A bearded man wearing a calico hat and shabby clothes stepped through the door, a cocked pistol in hand. His narrow eyes swept the one-room shack.

The roar and smoke from James's musket filled the room. The man cried out, reeled, dropped the gun as he fell. The dogs yipped and cowered in momentary confusion. James feverishly reloaded as the smoke cleared, revealing the man's still form. Two of the hounds trailed over to their dead master while the third headed for the barrels, black eyes homing in on James. With no time to finish reloading, James dropped his ramrod and clubbed the musket as the dog lunged at the top of the barrel. The stock fractured the cur's head. The other two abandoned their master and charged back across the shack, hackles raised, teeth bared.

"Stay behind the barrels, Cump," James shouted as he grappled for a percussion cap in the box at his waist. "Keep 'em off me."

Cump used the long stick like a sword, jabbing and swinging at the hounds, who danced out of reach then back, flashing white fangs, teeth snapping.

"Hurry, Mister James!"

Somehow his shaking fingers seated the cap. He steadied the gun on one of the barrels and blasted the foremost cur across the room. The buck-and-ball sprayed the second dog as well, and it yelped and streaked out of the cabin, tail between its legs.

Panting, Cump leaned against the barrels and dragged a forearm across his wet brow as James quickly reloaded.

"He'll run home," Cump said. "Someone bound to come a-lookin' for that man."

James shouldered the gun as Cump lifted Nate's pale, shaking form from the barrel. "Go fetch that mule, Cump. I'll get our rations and see what that fellow has on him. Grab his pistol and ammunition on your way. No choice now; we have to get out of here."

"But Mister Nathan…he can't—"

"I'll be all right," said Nate leaning heavily against one of the barrels, sweat streaming in rivulets from his shorn head. "Hurry…"

James asked, "Do you think you can ride?"

"Right now, I could ride a wild hog if it means gettin' the hell outta here." Nate's wan grin reminded James of the farm boy from Burr

Oak and gave his confidence a much-needed boost.

CHAPTER 32

Free of his makeshift sling, Nate clung to the mule's bristly mane, for he had little strength in his legs to steady himself any other way. He had never been an enthusiast when it came to mules, especially after the ordeal on Raccoon Mountain, but this creature seemed far more compliant than its stubborn army cousins, perhaps because so little was required of it, simply to walk at a relatively brisk pace, carrying nothing more than a bird-like passenger. Or perhaps the animal knew its rider lacked the strength to participate in any mulish games and thus decided upon leniency for lack of a challenge.

During the four days they had thus far traveled, Nate constantly thought of his family. Being quit of Andersonville had somehow freed up an endless flow of memories, things that had seemed lost forever, beaten down and drowned by that hellish place but now bursting forth like Providence Spring. As he rode, he often rested his hand against the Bible in his pocket or withdrew Katie's mangled picture to remember.

"Who that lady, Mister Nathan?" Cump had asked him on the first day.

"You can call me Nate, and James just James."

Cump considered this with a serious expression. "It wouldn't seem fittin' if I did."

"Well, you do as you please, but there's no need." Nate handed the picture to Cump, who walked beside the mule while James led it. "That's my fiancée, Katie Moylan. Ain't she a beauty? We're goin' to be married when I get home, once I don't look such a fright, that is. Don't want to scare her off." He grinned, feeling stronger every time he spoke of his betrothed.

Cump admired the photo, turned it over. "What this writin' say on the back?"

Nate's face reddened, and he reclaimed the daguerreotype. "Reckon that's just for me to know."

When James chuckled, Cump grinned. "You got a lady waitin' for you, Mister...um, James?"

"Not that I know of, Cump."

"Don't let him fool you," Nate countered. "There's more than one girl in Burr Oak who would walk down the aisle with James, if he'd ever ask 'em."

James quickly deflected the conversation. "What about you, Cump? You have a girl back on that plantation?"

"Reckon I did. Well, I say I did; mebbe she say somethin' else."

Their conversations never ran on for long, for they were too concerned with travelling as quietly as possible through the dark woods. Using a compass James carried, they avoided the railroad that James had used to guide him on his journey southward and decided against the river because of its twisting nature. Instead, they traveled northward on as direct a course as the topography would allow. They moved mainly at night, but in their anxiety to reach the Union lines, they often journeyed into the mornings before halting to rest, picketing the mule a distance away as a safeguard, for completely concealing the animal was impossible. Twice they had spotted civilians—hunters, perhaps—but had been fortunate enough to avoid detection.

They had exhausted their rations just yesterday. Nate knew he had received the lion's share, though both James and Cump denied any such collusion. Since then, they had eaten a few peaches and pears that James had stolen from a farm. Nate had savored the fruit with every single bite, afterwards sucking the last bit of flavor from his fingers and rolling the peach pits around in his mouth until he nearly choked on them.

The first hint of dawn faded the forest's shroud to the east. Frowning, Nate wished the light would not appear so fast, for he wanted nothing to impede their flight.

Through sleepy eyes, he watched James's shoulders moving back and forth with his steady, long-legged gait. Thinking of all James had risked to rescue him, Nate took great satisfaction in knowing the depth of his comrade's affection, an affection Nate returned in a measure greater than he had ever considered possible with another man. While Nate had endured Andersonville, James had suffered his own hell after Nate's capture. A terrible bond that Nate knew could never be equaled, could never even be fully explained, if either of them cared to try. But they would not, for to speak of it meant to relive what had forged it, and those trials were best forgotten, at least for now while all was still raw.

Nate's attention shifted to Cump's silent, lumbering form, the man's eyes always scanning the forest around them. Thinking back on their chance encounters at the prison, Nate shook his head. Surely it had been the hand of Providence, a hand guided by his brothers that had directed Cump to him and that kept him near now.

"There's something I don't understand, Cump," he said, startling the slave in the quiet of the forest. "Why'd you help me and James? I mean, takin' James to that cabin and bringin' Lizzie there and all. Why not just keep runnin' when James got you free?"

For some time Cump remained silent. His gaze fell to the ground, as if he were being careful where he stepped, but then vigilance returned his attention to their surroundings. His usual benign demeanor changed slightly, darkened like clouds before rain. James glanced over his shoulder, but Cump met no one's eyes as he finally spoke.

"I had me a brother once, just like you, Nathan. I was jus' a boy, less than you is. Jacob was older than me. He got sick with the swamp fever, and even Lizzie couldn't make him better." One of Cump's big hands drifted absently to stroke the mule's sweated shoulder. "I thought of him and me when I saw you with your brother after he died. And when I met Mister James and found out he your friend—well, more like a brother, I reckon, comin' all this way and puttin' hisself in some powerful danger—I couldn't he'p but think I was meant to he'p you, that the good Lord want me to. Why else would he put me in them places he put me?"

The similarities between his own thoughts on the matter and Cump's gave Nate pause, made him feel more assured in his beliefs, more protected in his hopes for their escape.

"I'm sorry about your brother, Cump."

The black man nodded, and some of his good nature pierced his sorrow. "That's all right, Nathan. In some way, he better off now."

Nate frowned. "Well, *he* may have died a slave, but if James and me have anything to say about it, you'll be a free man the rest of your days."

***

Nate relished the sunlight that filtered down through the trees. The golden shafts teased a smile from him where he lay in hiding beneath a windfall with his companions. He could enjoy the brightness now, for he had the benefit of shade, protected from the constant glare that had so oppressed him at Andersonville. He would never again take shade for granted. A mockingbird called from the tree above him, then flew off, its speed drawing his envy. A slight breeze sent the long green pine needles above into whispering conversation. Another lost memory drifted to him—sitting in the shade of the buckeye tree near James's store, Katie next to him, her hand in his, the song of a robin from above.

Next to Nate in the small swale, Cump and James slept soundly. It had taken some heated debate, but finally James had agreed to let him stand watch while they rested. Nate considered his friend in the peacefulness of sleep. Only now, with the constant concern washed away by slumber, could he remember James as he had been when they first joined the Eleventh Michigan. Immature, cynical, selfish. All that was gone now, ground away by these many months of hardship shared with brothers in arms. Before his capture, Nate had thought he knew James well, but now he realized he had lacked a complete grasp of his friend's qualities. Yet he did know James well enough to know that simple guilt would not have been enough to merit such a rescue scheme. Something had triggered James's desertion of the regiment, something still unspoken, something beyond the chilling narrative of Henry Damon. He feared the revelation, though in truth he wanted to know. But he would wait for James to reveal it.

From a shallow ravine below their hiding place, the mule brayed once, not loud enough to wake his companions but loud enough to turn Nate. Instinctively he sank closer to the ground when he caught sight of a man approaching the mule, an armed man. Nate shook James by the shoulder, and as he came instantly awake and alert, Nate put a silencing finger to his own lips and gestured toward the mule. Cump stirred, remained silent when he saw their expressions.

James took the musket from Nate. In its place he handed over the pistol, whispering, "You two head out north of here. If he starts this way, I'll get rid of him."

"No," Nate protested. "We should stay together."

"We need that mule. Now go on before it's too late."

"James—"

"Cump." James jerked his head to the north, and before Nate could speak another word, Cump pulled him backward out from beneath the windfall.

"C'mon, Nathan. We gots to go."

"Cump—"

The slave scooped him up and started off through the underbrush in a half-crouch. The time for further protest was gone lest he draw attention to them. Instead, he looked over Cump's shoulder, back toward the windfall, but he could not see James through the tangle of timber and brush. After a short distance, Cump stretched out of his hunched position and took longer strides, his breath coming hard from exertion as well as from fear. He, too, often glanced behind, and Nate knew the same conflicting desires swirled in Cump's heart as in his own.

"Cump, we should stop. We should go back."

"Mister James…he say to run, so we run."

"We don't need that damned mule. I can walk on me own."

Cump refused to listen. The forest undergrowth had thickened, and he needed concentration to forge his way through. Low branches swiped at them as Cump tried his best to duck and dive beneath them, nearly falling twice.

"Put me down. I can run. We'll go faster."

"No, suh. Faster this way."

The crash of a musket echoed far behind them, drew Cump to a halt, mouth wide, eyes flashing white back in James's direction. A second musket answered. Their gazes met in a brief instant of dread. Nate struggled to free himself.

"Damn it, Cump. We have to go back."

Cump wavered but maintained his grip. At last, with a pained expression, he started out once again to the north, ignoring Nate's oaths.

They had gone no more than a dozen yards when a man's voice called out from the forest, harsh and demanding, close on their right flank: "Hold it right there, you God damned nigger!"

The dark shape of a man separated from behind a stout pine, a man much larger than the one who had approached the mule. The black hole of an aimed musket, the yellow splash of a sunbeam against the man's face. Nate cried out a warning just as Cump ducked to the left. He crashed through the underbrush, his movements awkward and unbalanced as he tried to keep his hold on Nate while plunging onward. Nate fumbled with the pistol, prying it from between his body and Cump's. The Southerner shouted again for them to halt. Cocking the pistol, Nate tried to steady it above Cump's right shoulder, to find his mark on the man sprinting after them. The Southerner's eyes widened when he saw the pistol, and he brought his musket up. Simultaneously Nate discharged the pistol, the reports of both weapons deafening. The world between them vanished in smoke and flame. With a sharp grunt, Cump jerked forward, lost his balance, tumbled, nearly crushing Nate as they fell.

Clawing blindly in search of the pistol, Nate heard Cump's gasps, knew… His fingers closed around the pistol, raised the shaking weapon, pointed back into the cloud of powder smoke. But no target emerged. Dazed and breathless, Nate dragged himself behind a tree, the pistol still glaring backward, waited. The distant report of another musket from James's direction. Cump slowly writhed onto his back, a bloody patch low on his right side growing large and dark. Nate peered again through the smoke, listened. No movement, no voice. The smoke twisted and rose, revealed the dead man beneath it, half his face torn, crimson and gory.

Nate scrambled over to Cump, ripped at his shirt to locate the wound.

"Cump. Cump, can you hear me?"

The slave's stare was distant, lost among the treetops. Frothy blood smeared his lips, darkened his teeth. He blinked hard, tried to focus on Nate, who wadded a shred of his shirt and pressed it against the flowing wound. Fighting to speak, he instead coughed up black blood. Helpless, Nate clutched Cump's hand, received a weak, unknowing response.

"Go help...Mister...J—James."

"Cump, hang on."

"Nate!" James's voice broke the quiet of the forest.

Through a blur of tears, Nate spied James running toward them, musket in hand. James leaped over the dead Southerner and slid to his knees beside Cump. He pushed Nate's hand away from the wound and paled.

"Hang on. I'll get the mule. We'll get you up on him, and we'll find help."

Cump's hand searched for James, who grasped it tightly, as if doing so would somehow stop the flow of blood. Slowly Cump shook his head, breathed, "No use."

James tried to stand, to start back toward where they had left the mule, but Cump held fast to him, managed to draw him and Nate closer. He stiffened in pain, shuddered, fought his way back, forcing life into his gaze if only momentarily.

"Don't tell...don't tell Lizzie. She think I's free."

James pleaded, "Let me go, Cump. I'll fetch the mule."

Cump shook his head, the light dimming in his eyes. A small smile touched his lips as he looked from James to Nate. "Don't tell... I's free..."

His eyelids slipped downward, his grip gradually loosened, but the smile remained.

CHAPTER 33

The mule grew increasingly tired and slow, but James was determined to put as many miles as possible between themselves and the two dead civilians, even risking the daylight hours in which to travel. He constantly listened for the baying of hounds, but no such harbinger disturbed the forest. He rode the mule now, too, mounted behind Nate, a leafy branch in one hand as a crop to urge the mule onward.

They said little for the first few hours, too dismayed by Cump's death to speak. James feared that if he tried to express his emotions he might very well break down, for the strain of the past weeks swelled like a towering wave above him, and it was only a matter of time before it crashed down. While Nate's health improved each day, James knew he needed to stay strong in the event of another confrontation with civilians.

How he mourned Cump and missed his strong presence. What a relief it had been to have someone upon whom to lean, to know that he was not left only to his own devices. The magnitude of his grief surprised him, considering how he had only known Cump a short time. He had seemed less of a slave and more of a fellow soldier. Looking upon Cump's lifeless face, he had experienced a new understanding, saw a man worth fighting for as much as he had fought for his comrades in the Eleventh. They all had a common enemy. Perhaps by helping them Cump had felt that he had been striking a blow against his oppressors.

"Do you think the folks in Burr Oak would've accepted Cump?" James asked.

Nate made a thoughtful sound, hesitated. "Hard tellin'."

James considered this. "Before the war, would we have accepted him?"

Softer still, Nate replied, "Truth be told, probably not. But things sure have changed, ain't they? I know I'll never look at a black man the same way I did afore Andersonville."

A few minutes on, James noticed a thinning to the trees east of them. A road. Just as he started to guide the mule northwest into heavier foliage, the distant clatter of hooves and the noise of men and accouterments sent them spilling off the mule's back and slipping into hiding. The blur of horses and dust from a platoon of Confederate cavalry at full gallop took but a moment to pass, men moving too quickly to take notice of the distant mule blending with the shadows of the trees. Were they running from something or to something? James held his breath in fear of the mule braying, but the animal paid little heed to his fleet-footed cousins and instead searched the ground for whatever forage it could find. Lying flat, close to each other, James felt Nate tremble, and he remembered the boy's request to be shot rather than risk recapture. No, by God, it would not come to that.

Once the horsemen could no longer be seen or heard, Nate asked, "Can we rest? Just for a wee bit?"

James hid his disappointment at the delay. "Let's get away from the road, then you can sleep. Reckon the mule needs it as bad as we do."

Storm clouds gathered as they bedded down near a fallen log. Pistol in hand, eyes on the surrounding forest, James tucked himself close to where Nate lay.

"I'll just sleep a little while, James. Don't let me sleep long, then I'll spell you."

Somehow James remained awake for an hour. He watched the clouds build above the tall pines and sail past on the hot wind. *So damned tired. Leg hurts. How much farther? Don't know if I can make it. Can't let Nate know I'm done in. Have to get him back to the regiment. Must be getting close to our lines.*

Nate slept soundly, now and then murmuring unintelligibly. As time slipped by, James lacked the heart to wake him, and soon he lost the battle to stay awake.

***

Nate awoke to the rumble of thunder and found himself drenched to the skin. The rain fell straight down, rattling amidst the forest growth. The faded light of late afternoon barely penetrated the gloom. James had put their blanket over him as weak protection against the dampness while James himself huddled next to him, unprotected, sound asleep, the rain trailing down through his thin beard. Nate was reluctant to disturb him. How many miles had his friend walked in the past three weeks for his sake?

332

At last, he gently shook him, the nagging fear stirring once more.

When they started out again, Nate rode with his head bowed, watching the rivulets trail down the neck and shoulders of the mule. "Wonder what day it is."

"Don't know."

"The regiment's three years must be up. Wonder if they've gone home." Nate frowned. "Bet not many re-enlisted. I wonder if Ryan would have."

"Would you?"

Nate looked over his shoulder to see if James were joking, but his friend's expression showed no hint of jest. Softly he admitted, "I dunno." They traveled a bit farther before he spoke again. "I bet Elias and Abner won't re-enlist. Elias has those little ones, and I wager Abner's folks want him back more'n ever 'cause of Jeremy."

James tensed and drew in his breath, barely discernible. Again Nate looked over his shoulder, but this time James avoided his eyes. The cold realization struck him that James had said little about Abner and Elias since their reunion. He tried to twist himself around in the saddle, to force James to meet his eye.

"Are they all right...Elias and Abner?"

He could tell it took a monumental effort for James to finally look at him. The sorrow over Cump's loss had suddenly compounded. A weakness that no longer allowed him to conceal the truth. Nate's hands on the reins grew cold.

"Just before I left the regiment, Abner was wounded and sent to the hospital."

Nate tried to swallow in a throat suddenly dry. "And Elias?"

The rain's patter eased up.

"Langdon murdered him."

"What?"

The startled jerk of Nate's hands halted the mule, but James brushed its flank with the crop to send it forward again. As James related the events surrounding their friend's death, Elias's image returned to Nate with painful clarity, not simply the memory of when he had last seen the man but the recollection of when he had first met Elias and his family. Not all of Burr Oak's citizens had instantly warmed to Nate's immigrant family with their foreign voices, but the Coopers had displayed no such prejudice and had been the first family to truly welcome the Calhouns. Elias had displayed no fear of being ostracized for his hospitality, just as he had shown no hesitation to befriend James when most of Company D had offered the young man nothing but blunt hostility at the start of his enlistment.

By the time James fell silent, a sheeting of tears blurred the forest. Nate blinked to fight back the onslaught.

"I should have known," James murmured. "After Elias stood up for me at Kennesaw. I should have known Langdon wouldn't let it be, especially the way the campaign just kept grinding on. It was getting to everyone. I should have watched Langdon closer."

"There's no way you could have known he would do somethin' like that." Nate fingered the soggy leather reins. "You can't keep blamin' yourself for everything that's gone wrong. 'Tis no more your fault that Elias is dead than it was that I stumbled like a fool into them Rebs and got captured. I never thought no different about you. Same with Cump. 'Twas his decision to come with us."

He swiped away the renegade tears, sniffed, and looked back at his friend with hard insistence. James's mustache twitched into a small half smile. He gave a slight nod, a mix of gratitude and compliance. Then he took the reins from Nate to guide the mule back in the direction of the road.

"We have to be close to our lines by now." James returned the reins, then produced his compass, consulted it. "We'll parallel that road for a bit, as long as it keeps going in this direction." He showed the compass to Nate. "This was Elias's. His son sent it to him. So you could say Elias helped bring you back as much as me and Cump."

Nate took the silver object. The lump returned to his throat as he turned it over and over, remembered Elias's quiet, strong presence beside him that night before Chickamauga. "He was like a father to me."

"To all of us."

"Aye."

Their conversation dropped away as they drew closer to the road to the east. For the next hour, they paralleled its path, careful to remain far enough away to avoid immediate detection should riders appear again. Nate fought against fatigue but kept drifting off, his head bobbing with the mule's rhythm. James's arms slipped around him as he took over the reins, his embrace offering a comforting, stable balance, and before long Nate surrendered to sleep.

He knew not how long he slept, but when he awoke with a start, he saw that the weather had cleared, and the sun piercing the forest had fallen far to the west.

"Riders coming," James whispered, making Nate realize what had awakened him. James pulled him from the mule, then led him away from the animal.

Nate's ears picked up the distant rumble of hooves coming down the road from the northwest. The forest here was more open, the trees spaced wider apart, the ground less swampy. It seemed that the earlier rain had not fallen this far north; he smelled no dampness. In a crouch, James ran for a particularly large tree, face turned toward the road and the approaching thunder of mounted men. But before they could reach their sanctuary, he yanked Nate down to the ground beside him, flattened himself amidst the forest debris. Their attention remained upon the road, their breath coming in shallow gasps. A dark knot of riders appeared through a veil of dust as they eased their mounts from a canter to a walk. Nate pressed his face to the ground, prayed.

"Dear God," James whispered.

Nate tensed even more. He held his breath.

"Dear God," James repeated, this time in a clear, ringing voice, rising to his knees. "The flag! *Our* flag!"

The flash of colors caught Nate's eye—red through the green and brown of the forest, white amidst the dying billow of dust, blue like the uniforms beneath the guidon. Even at this distance Nate swore he could hear the small pennant's snap in the patrol's breeze, calling to him, assuring him. Never had he seen anything so beautiful.

PART VI

GOD'S COUNTRY

"We owe it alike to the living and
the dead, that a proper knowledge
and a realization of the miseries
which they endured be entertained
by all."

-- Clara Barton

CHAPTER 34

A grin slipped through James's fatigue, for he had never seen Sergeant Benjamin Bordner speechless. Beyond Bordner's shocked face and those of his equally disbelieving guard detail, the campfires of the Eleventh Michigan beckoned. Old comrades reclined around them in the hot August night. Music drifted in the breezeless air, tired yet joyous voices accompanying banjo and fiddle in a rollicking tune called "The Irish Volunteer," a song Nate had taught the boys of Company D. Even from this distance, James sensed the mood of the camp—contentment, the profound contentment of men pulled back from the battle lines in front of Atlanta where Sherman's armies still besieged the city. A mood heightened by the near prospect of so many returning home.

"What's the matter, Sarge?" James asked. "I can't tell who you're more surprised to see—me or Nate."

The guards behind the Fawn River noncom murmured among themselves in almost distrustful tones, their faces in shadow.

Bordner at last stammered, "We—we thought you was dead or captured or—or…" He scowled. "And you expect me to believe that's Nate Calhoun…or what's left of him?"

"The genuine article." James draped his arm around Nate's shoulders. The boy had done little but grin like a happy hound since the cavalry patrol had welcomed them back into the arms of Federal forces.

Nate shook the sergeant's limp hand. "I ain't never looked better, have I, Sarge? I know *you* ain't."

"Holy Christ," Bordner breathed.

"Come now, Sarge," James cajoled. "Be a good fellow and take us to the lieutenant. We're played out and starved. Had a hell of a time finding you boys. They said you were just pulled back a few hours ago."

When they stood before Lieutenant Benjamin Hart, the officer suffered the same debilitating surprise as the Sergeant of the Guard. He sat upon the shattered remains of an old oak, the tree a victim of artillery fire from whose army God only knew. Since their rescue, every mile James had traveled back to the Eleventh had shown scars from the endless siege and the subsequent battles fought since he had left the Army of the Cumberland. Abandoned, ransacked homes, a shredded landscape with no signs of life other than that of the military and the mournful spectacle of refugees heading south, Southerners with hollow, hate-filled eyes and oaths upon their lips, even the children. James felt little sympathy for them, not when he looked at his frail comrade or thought of Abner, Colonel Stoughton, Cump or the countless other casualties of the regiment.

First Sergeant David Burleson stood behind Hart, who had his troublesome right leg stretched in front of him, his hand absently rubbing it. The two men watched in respectful silence as James and Nate devoured the food that had been hastily gathered for them. Between mouthfuls, James told the story of his journey south and of Nate's rescue and their return trek. Just beyond the circle of light thrown by Hart's campfire, men had gathered, the black wall of uniforms growing every minute, but Burleson had warned them all back. Their quiet, excited murmurs, however, carried to James, and he was eager to be reunited with David May and the others of his company.

"You know, James," Hart said when the story finally concluded, "if Nate wasn't sitting right here in front of me, I wouldn't believe a lick of your tale. But here he is, and what a sight you are, lad."

Nate finished lapping up the last morsel of food from his plate and fork and broke into a broad smile for all those within sight.

"This isn't the first time you've been absent without leave, James," Hart said. "A damned noble cause, true enough, but absent all the same."

"Both times on my account," Nate said. "Blame me, Ben, not James."

Hart offered a tired smile. "I'm afraid the army won't look at it that way, Nate."

James saw no anger or resentment in Hart's blue eyes, only admiration. How worn the man looked. *Dear God, he's only twenty-five—younger than me—but he looks at least ten years older, maybe fifteen. Do I look that way? No, I haven't been fighting in the trenches for the past three weeks like the regiment.*

Hart scuffed the toe of his boot against the red soil, his gaze now downward in thought. James held his breath, prayed that Hart would find a way to allow leniency.

When the lieutenant looked at them again, he smiled uncomfortably, briefly, then his attention wandered to the shadowy men beyond the firelight, then farther across the Eleventh's bivouac, as if in search of men who no longer existed. "Truth be told, Nate, James wasn't the only one who felt guilty about losing you. Back in May when we heard about your brother—about Brian—I should have let you go. I should've known what you would do if I didn't. Just like Ryan going back after Henry Platt at Elk River. Maybe Brian would be alive; maybe you never would have been captured."

Subdued now, Nate said, "You was just doin' your duty, sir. I never held it against you."

His words failed to ease the bitter regret on Hart's face or the sorrow there from learning of Ryan's death.

"I wanted to go after Ryan at Elk River, but...but I didn't. I've regretted that every day of my life, especially now. So I understand why you left, James, believe me."

Silence stretched between them, and Burleson stepped forward to place another log on the sputtering fire.

Hart continued. "I expect us to get orders soon, relieving the regiment; some of the boys are past their three years as it is, myself and Burleson included. Unfortunately, the damned army won't let a regiment muster out until the last company reaches its three years. Three of the companies didn't muster in until September of '61." Irritation creased his brow. "Hell, yesterday the boys mutinied when the damned fools ordered us to the front lines. Couldn't blame the lads for not wanting to go; I felt the same way. By God, we've done our share." Abruptly he halted, remembered himself. "The others, like you, who enlisted later than the rest of us will no doubt be on detached duty until the regiment is properly reorganized. But you, Nate, I'll request that you accompany the regiment to Chattanooga tomorrow. You'll need some time in the hospital, then I think a furlough home is in order." A remnant of his old humor resurfaced. "I reckon that girl of yours would dearly love to have her fiancé back in Burr Oak, even if it's only temporary."

"But what about James, sir?"

Hart considered them, glanced up at Burleson's curious countenance, set aside his coffee cup, and stood with a wince. James exchanged a timorous glance with Nate. They watched the lieutenant move around behind the log, his gait slow and thoughtful, hands behind his back, fingers moving restlessly. Again the officer's attention drifted to the restless gathering of the company's men, a group that had fallen silent, as if understanding the gravity of the moment. James wondered how many of Company D remained. Bordner had told them that in Company A only thirteen privates had answered rollcall that morning. At least Abner was still alive; Burleson had informed them of his recuperation in Chattanooga.

Hart came halfway around the fire circle, almost to where James sat on the ground next to Nate, but then the lieutenant paused, stroked his mustache a moment, looking deep into the fire. At last he retraced his steps until he stood before the log where he again hesitated in deliberation. James thought he would go mad waiting. Hart eased himself back to the log. He wagged a finger at Burleson to draw him closer.

"Sergeant, I believe there's been a clerical error." His gaze shifted to James. "As we know, Private Keenan was reported absent without leave about the same time as Sergeant Langdon."

"Yes, sir."

"Well, we must rectify that error and have the record show that *Corporal* Keenan was *not* absent without leave but, rather, captured by the enemy. He recently escaped from Andersonville with Private Calhoun."

Burleson smiled. "Yes, sir. I'll make sure that mistake is corrected immediately; I'll inform Colonel Mudge myself."

***

Nate watched the Michigan countryside slip past the windows after the train pulled away from the Bronson station. The summer green of the trees had begun to fade in preparation for the coming glory of autumn. Harvest time. Thank God he would be home for it. Exactly how much physical help he could offer his father remained to be seen, but he knew any assistance, no matter how small, would be greatly appreciated. He looked forward to the work, to the sweat and strain of muscles, activity for his hands to keep his mind occupied, to heal in all ways, to remember, to forget, to come home in the evening from the fields to his mother's cooking, to sleep in a bed and rest in quiet safety. His only reservations lay in seeing his dead brothers' rooms, to know they would never sleep there again; they would never come home. Hopefully his parents had news about Joseph and Matthew, good news. Their enlistments would be up; perhaps they were home.

Next to him, James sat in silence, his gaze also on the scenes sliding by. Unlike Nate, he sat without fidgeting, seemingly unexcited, adorned in a new uniform whose sleeves bore the double stripes of a corporal. Though James closed his eyes for a time, Nate knew he was awake, just as he knew, regardless of outer appearance, that James was anxious about his return home, so anxious in fact that he had told no one in Burr Oak about his furlough.

They had made it to Michigan before the rest of the Eleventh, though now, in mid-September, the regiment's three years were officially up. The Eleventh had left White Pigeon in '61 with one thousand men but would return with only three hundred and forty, many of that number being men who had been detailed from the regiment and those picked up from the hospitals on the way home. The Eleventh's return had been delayed when the regiment received orders to quell the trouble caused by Confederate cavalry under General Joe Wheeler in Tennessee. Nate felt almost guilty returning home while the boys of the Eleventh toiled beyond their time. The injustice of it left him bitter toward the army.

Before the regiment had embarked on its new mission, Lieutenant Colonel Mudge, encouraged by Lieutenant Hart, offered James the furlough, but James had initially turned it down.

"You have to come back home with me," Nate had insisted. "I'll need a best man for me weddin'."

"Best man? Me?"

"Who else am I gonna get at such short notice?" Nate teased. "Abner's home, but he won't be fit enough this soon. Besides, 'tis either come home with me or be bored here in Chattanooga. They'll attach you to some strange outfit, then where will you be till I report back for duty? Besides, the Lieutenant 'strongly' recommends it. He knows you're beat, and he fancies you deserve *somethin'* for savin' me."

"Nate Calhoun, is that you?"

He turned at the sound of the familiar voice and found Elias Cooper's wife, Beatrice, making her way up the aisle, a smile of wonderment on her round face. James stirred, drawing her attention.

"And James Keenan!" she cried.

Both men got to their feet, and Beatrice surprised Nate with an embrace. If there had been room, he suspected she would have pulled James into her arms as well, but she simply reached to press his hand. Tears swam in her shadowed brown eyes, matching the melancholy of her black mourning weeds.

"I just got on board in Bronson and was in the next car when I heard that two soldiers bound for Burr Oak were aboard. How good it is to see you both. Oh, but Nate, you're so thin! You poor boy."

"Nothin' me mother's cookin' can't fix, ma'am."

"Your mother... Such a dear woman. She comes to town to see me and the children a couple of times a week since we got the news about Elias." Beatrice had no knowledge of the truth of Elias's death, nor would she ever; Nate and the others of Company D had vowed to keep the circumstances a secret.

"Please, ma'am," Nate gestured to the empty seat across the aisle from his, "won't you sit down? This road never was too smooth, was it?"

When they had settled into their seats, Nate asked, "How are your children?"

Beatrice smiled away the sadness in her eyes. "We're just coming back from visiting my sister in Bronson; Zack stayed home to work. I think it did them some good to be away from home and distracted. My sister spoils them, of course, and that cheered them a bit."

Haltingly, James produced Elias's small compass from his pocket and stretched across Nate to present it to her. "I brought this back for you, ma'am. It's the compass Zack sent to his father this summer."

With wonder and reverence, Beatrice received the instrument, the tears threatening to return but held back with self-conscious blinks.

"Zack wondered what had become of it," she said. "It wasn't among his pa's effects the army sent back to us."

"You might say that compass saved me life, Mrs. Cooper. James used it to find me and get us back to our lines."

James made a small, discouraging sound, but Nate ignored him.

"He did?" Beatrice closed her hand around the compass, drew it close to her heart.

"'Tis true. James and me have Elias to thank for gettin' back to the regiment."

"What you did for Nate...why, it's all over town, James. You're a hero. Folks was still talking about you carrying that flag up Mission Ridge, but now they're talking about this, too."

Nate chanced a glance at his reddening friend. James seemed about to cuss but somehow held his temper in check.

"How did you know I had anything to do with Nate coming back?"

"Why, I heard it from Mrs. Calhoun, of course. She read Nate's letter to me. She's so excited about you coming home, Nate. It's so good to see her happy again. She's been terribly broken up about Ryan and Brian. Poor boys. I'm so sorry. And Joseph and Matthew still off, fighting the war."

Nate had no desire to suffer James's wrath for his mother's revelation to everyone in Burr Oak. James had asked him not to share what had happened with anyone outside his family and to caution his family against it as well. Nate had agreed, though he thought James's modesty and desire for anonymity unwarranted. Surely the news would reach the village from some other source within the Eleventh. But he understood James's desire to return without fanfare, for so many families had lost loved ones to the war. Those men, James declared, were the true heroes, but they would never receive the reward here on earth that they so justly deserved.

"I must return to my children. Won't you come sit with us in the next car? They will be so excited to see you both and hear about their father from those who served with him."

Nate agreed, eager to avoid being alone with James now that his mother's indiscretion was known.

***

When the train chuffed into the Burr Oak station within the hour, Nate's parents and Katie waited on the platform. Disbelieving his sight, Nate stared through the window as the car slipped past them and squealed to a halt. Many times he had imagined this reunion, but seeing them now flooded his very soul with emotion so deep that he feared he would never be able to move from his seat or utter a single word to anyone. To see his mother's mourning attire and the black crepe upon his father's hat brought a jolt of grief for his brothers, especially for Ryan. The emotion nearly drowned his elation at seeing them there with Katie, Katie whose face was already streaked with tears.

Beatrice Cooper gave his hand one last squeeze before she followed the handful of other passengers down the aisle, her children in her wake.

"Are you getting out?" James asked.

"We're really here."

"We are. But if you wait too long, we might end up in White Pigeon."

Nate's family moved closer to the door, anxious glances searching the windows. He wished James's father were there, but James had asked him to keep the news of their return strictly limited to the Calhouns.

With forceful resolve, Nate contained his strange mixture of uncertainty and jubilation as he reached the platform. His parents stared at him, as if fearful that touching him would reveal him as nothing more than a wish. Tears filled his mother's eyes, tears that he could tell had been present long before now, perhaps never absent since hearing about Brian. His mother choked upon a small sob and tried to speak but could not. He sensed a disturbing, uncharacteristic weakness in her, as if she was on the verge of collapse, so he reached for her first, drew her into his arms. His father waited nearby, smelling wonderfully of soil and animals. Moisture in his eyes, too, the same disquieting fragility, so unlike his father. Nate fully realized the strain that had lain upon them since he had left last year, a strain that had never lessened, only increased. How he wished he had never caused such suffering.

Nate's outstretched arm included Katie in his embrace. Her quiet sobs mingled with his mother's. He buried his face in Katie's hair, the scent of her filling him like that of a bouquet, that sweetness he had feared the prison pen had banished forever. He breathed it in until his lungs could draw no further, and then he kissed her.

At last they freed one another, and his father offered a brief, strong embrace and patted his arm while the two women wiped their eyes.

Katie's hand brushed his cheek. "You're so thin. Didn't they feed you in the hospital?"

Nate grinned. "The hospital wasn't the problem." He did not want to talk or think of all the things he had omitted from his letters to her since being in the hospital.

Katie's gaze went beyond him, widened. "You didn't tell me James Keenan was coming home. And as a corporal, no less."

Embarrassed for having forgotten his friend, Nate stepped over to where James stood awkwardly near the edge of the platform, their bags next to him. He put his arm around his friend's shoulders, drew him closer to his parents.

"James didn't want a big fuss made."

His parents' expressions transitioned from joy to deep, inexpressible gratitude. His father shook James's hand, his voice husky. "We're forever indebted to ye, lad. We cannot tell ye how much it means to us to have one of our sons back. God bless ye."

James cleared his throat, tried to find another place to look besides the tearful couple but found no escape. He stammered, "Thank you, sir."

Nate laughed and gave him a shake before he stepped to Katie's side and took her hand. "James ain't never been one for speeches, so let's not embarrass him no more."

Undeterred, his mother stood on her toes to kiss James's cheek, whispered, "Thank you."

"Now, Ma, you've gone and turned the corporal red as a cherry. Why don't the three of you go back to the wagon, and I'll be there directly?"

His mother wiped at the remainder of her tears, smiled at his chiding and touched his arm as if still disbelieving his presence. "You must come to dinner this Sunday, James. You and your father."

"Yes, ma'am. I'll tell him."

Nate's father smiled at James and retrieved his son's bag. Katie squeezed Nate's hand, then kissed James's other cheek before following the Calhouns off the platform.

"Well, Corporal, I reckon 'tis been quite a spell since you was kissed by so many women, especially ones so fair."

"True enough." James wistfully watched them go.

"You ain't goin' to stand out here all day, are you?"

"Maybe." Sudden defiance deepened James's tone. "Maybe I'll get back on the train. This was your idea, remember. You said no one would know what happened but your folks."

"Ma wasn't supposed to tell no one, but can you blame her? Besides, everyone would find out soon enough when the rest of the boys come back. 'Tis nothin' to be ashamed of; you should be proud. I'm sure your pa is."

James scoffed and looked in the direction of the village. "Just because we've changed doesn't mean my father has."

"Come now, James. You've read his letters to me. Sounds to me like he's changed. And what about Heather Cabot? She'll want to see you. You're a bloody hero, damn you."

"A hero. What do people here know about real heroes?"

Nate took hold of his shoulder. "I'll tell you what they know. They know I came back 'cause of you, came back when so many others haven't. Jeremy, Major Bennet, Elias Cooper, Jared Taylor—for God's sake—all of 'em. Ain't nothin' they can do for them; but you and me, us bein' here gives 'em reason to believe the others really will come back someday, too."

James frowned.

Gently Nate urged, "Go home. Let your father be proud. Let him show you he's changed."

At last James allowed a small smile, afraid yet hopeful. "See you later, farm boy."

347

***

The streets of Burr Oak lay quiet in the early evening, a relief to James, for he wanted no one to delay him from finding his father while he had a certain level of determination to know the truth. The couple of villagers who saw him on Front Street and then Third Street pumped his hand and welcomed him back, congratulating him on his brave deeds. Their enthusiasm surprised him. Before going off to fight, his appearance had not stopped citizens on the street and opened their expressions into smiles and well-wishes. While the attention embarrassed him, it also stirred a surprising amount of pride, adding to his confidence.

When he drew abreast of the young buckeye tree, he paused to reverently rest a hand against its trunk, a smile forming. Then he moved on to the mercantile where he paused before the front window where the Keenan name caught the failing sun's glint. How marvelously unchanged the place was. Had he really been gone over a year? With a touch of shame, he remembered thinking the store would fail without him, that his father would abandon it. But here it was, the glass clean and shining, the walkway swept.

Through the window, he saw Elias Cooper's son, Zack, behind the counter. The sight of the boy, so changed in physical stature, paralyzed James, for the image of Elias as he was laid to rest in the red Georgia clay flashed before him like a passing freight train.

Curiosity brought him back to his senses, and he entered the store. It was quiet; closing time soon. No customers, just Zack with his head down, counting money, his lips silently mouthing the numbers. The scuff of James's feet raised the boy's head, and when their eyes met, James saw Elias in that rifle pit, his brown eyes empty and pleading.

"Mr. Keenan!" Zack rushed around the counter to shake his hand. "I didn't know you was coming home today. The regiment ain't back, is it?"

"No, not yet." James pushed away the ghosts and forced a smile. "I didn't realize you were working here until your mother told me on the train just now."

"Your pa hired me last month. The store's been real busy."

James pictured his father in one of the village's two taverns while Zack struggled to run the store. "Isn't my father working?"

"Not right now. Was earlier." Zack smiled with a startling brightness, such a sharp contrast to the tears James had just witnessed at the train station, and a welcomed sight indeed. "Your pa was just

348

talkin' about you, about how you saved Nate from that there Reb prison." Admiration sparkled in the youngster's eyes.

James recalled Elias's fear that Zack would run off to fight, a fear James had shared in a letter to his father. Was that why his father had hired Zack, to keep him safe in Burr Oak? No, his father was not that charitable.

Zack rushed on. "Your pa's real proud of you. He's been tellin' everyone who comes in the store how you helped Nate Calhoun, just like he did when you carried the flag up that ridge in Tennessee. Just loves to talk about it. Why, he said just t'other day how he wisht you'd get to come home for a spell." He paused to catch his breath, and some of the energy fled like a gray cloud darting across the sun. "Your pa's been real good to me, lettin' me work here so's I can help Ma. She's much obliged to him; invites him over for supper as often as he'll come, being all alone here an' all."

James frowned. "I'm sorry about your father, Zack."

"Yeah," Zack murmured. "Lotsa folks lost someone, not just us." He looked up. "We heard that they can't find Preacher Langdon nowheres. He just up and disappeared from the regiment. Mr. Thornton came in here and told us. Your pa acted kinda funny when he heard."

"How so?"

"Well, he smiled, right pleasant. I recollect 'cause I was surprised by him a-smilin' and all. Thought it odd after hearin' such puzzlin' news."

James grunted, drawn away in thought.

"Well, I reckon you wanna see your pa, and I need to finish up here and get home."

James brought his attention back to the boy. "We'll talk some more about your pa later, all right?"

"Yes, sir. I'd like that." His smile came as a reflection of his father's mild expression. "I'm so glad you made it back, Mr. Keenan."

James thanked him and started for the stairs, but Zack's voice halted him.

"Where you headed, Mr. Keenan?"

Puzzled by the odd question, James turned. "Upstairs to see my father."

"Oh, but he ain't upstairs."

"Then where is he?" Thoughts of the tavern returned.

"He went home."

"Home?"

"He didn't tell you?"

"Tell me what?"

"He's living over on Main Street. In your old house."

HISTORICAL NOTE

While large cities in the North provided thousands of volunteers for the Union cause during the American Civil War, small towns and rural villages across the United States also sacrificed thousands of their sons and fathers, populations that could little afford the devastation wrought by the war. When I set out to write this novel, I wanted to focus on men from one of those small towns, and thus James Keenan and Nate Calhoun were created. While not actual people, their characters represent the real men whose diaries and letters and newspaper accounts I used to understand the world in which the men of the Civil War era lived.

Burr Oak, in southwest Michigan, sacrificed so many of its villagers to the war, and I am a better person for having studied its history. Even these decades later, it has retained its charming rural setting amidst the farmland of St. Joseph County. When I visited there on a research trip, its streets had been reduced to the dirt streets of old due to a construction project, so I was easily able to envision its 19th century look.

I used many sources in writing this novel, primary as well as secondary, but one in particular was invaluable and that was *When Gallantry Was Commonplace: The History of the Michigan Eleventh Volunteer Infantry, 1861-1864* by Leland W. Thornton. In keeping with my desire for small-town boys, I looked for one of the lesser-known Michigan regiments, one that was comprised mainly of men from the farmlands of Michigan, not the larger cities like Detroit or Flint. Mr. Thornton's book made that possible. I also wanted a regiment in one of the western armies, for so much has already been written about the Army of the Potomac.

Many of the secondary characters in this novel were real people, men such as Benjamin Franklin Hart and David May, as well as all the officers and non-commissioned officers (except Robert Langdon) of the Eleventh Michigan who appear in these pages. Frank Lane was court-martialed as presented in the story, a tragedy that attests more to the devastation of war upon the psyche than to any lack of character on Frank's part. The men of the Eleventh Michigan who were prisoners at Andersonville in this story were also factual people. Henry Damon did escape as described in the novel. Jared Taylor died in the prison and was buried there. I had the honor of visiting his grave.

351

AUTHOR'S NOTE

Years before writing this manuscript, I had the seed of a story. Beyond that, nothing. In 1993, the seed grew and blossomed after several inspirational experiences related to visits to Gettysburg, Antietam, and Washington, DC.

I have never written anything which came so easily or gave me so much satisfaction. After several instances that I will describe only as wonderfully disturbing, I am convinced the ease with which this story was written came from those about whom this book was written—the men who gave "the last full measure" to reunite this country and thus make it the symbol of freedom it is today.

Most people have lost that focus, that acknowledgement of what the men of the Civil War did. This book's purpose is to remind us of their sacrifice, especially that of those who died in the human tragedy known as Andersonville.

ACKNOWLEDGEMENTS

There are many people I need to thank for making this book possible. Please forgive me if I leave anyone out.

First and foremost, Wayne C. Mann, former Director of Archives and Regional History Collections, Western Michigan University, and great-grandson of Melvin Lyon, Company D, Eleventh Michigan Infantry. Not only did Wayne provide a wealth of information on the Eleventh Michigan, but he also read portions of the manuscript for the sake of accuracy.

James Ogden, III, historian at Chickamauga and Chattanooga National Military Park.

Alan Marsh, Cultural Resources Specialist, Andersonville National Historic Site.

Kerry Chartkoff, former Archives Specialist, Michigan State Capitol. Not only was Kerry helpful with information regarding the Eleventh Michigan's battle flags, but she is devoted to the preservation of all of Michigan's Civil War flags.

Leland Thornton, whose wonderful book on the Eleventh convinced me to use the regiment in telling this story, and William Scaife, who has provided the public with extensively researched maps on the Atlanta Campaign.

Kay Lancaster of Burr Oak for her support, knowledge, and friendliness. Meeting her convinced me that I had chosen the perfect hometown for my main characters. Thanks also to Burr Oak's wonderful Carol Ankney.

I would like to send out a special thanks to the hard-working men and women who strive to maintain the national parks and historic sites. Of those, Andersonville and Pickett's Mill are two of the most powerful and unforgettable.

And last, but not least, to Tinney Sue Heath, Kim Rendfeld, Sue Ann Connolly, and Joseph Mishler for their valuable input.